THE HAUNTING
OF
WILLOWWYNN

THIS IS AN IRRESISTIBLE BOOK; DEFINITELY NEW ORLEANS.

—Lily G. Graves
New Orleans

Norma Hubbard continues with her new book with her contagious vibrating language, a joy to read. Her real experience in New Orleans comes through in present day skillful verbiage. This book is a charming presentation of middle class living in the 50s.

—Ann Cook Humphreys,
Ageless Book Shopp

Also by Norma Hubbard

Novel: The Archbishop's Daughter

Short Story: The Game-of-Tug-of-War

i

Published by
Wimberley Books
P.O. Box 4736
Panama City FL 32401-8736

Cover Illustration and Author Portrait:
Betty Tenhundfeld-Johnson

ISBN: 0-9631969-1-X

Wimberley Book Company

Printed in the United States of America

Manufactured in the United States of America

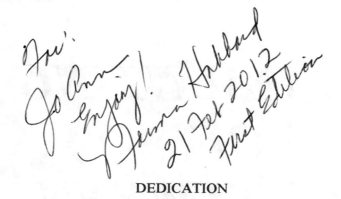

For:
Jo Ann —
Enjoy!
Norma Hubbard
21 Feb 2012
First Edition

DEDICATION

To Harriett and Jimmy Hentz,

This book is dedicated to my beloved friends and neighbors, who are so special and so close to my heart.

Lovingly,

N.H.

APPRECIATION

To my husband, Rob,

For caring so much; for never making demands; for being so supportive; for being kind and considerate and understanding; for making it all possible—and so beautiful.

With all my love, forever and always,

N.H.

THE HAUNTING OF WILLOWWYNN

NORMA HUBBARD

Kendra sat across from CR; the coffee table between them. "W-w-what do you want to talk about?"

"Me.—Do you know who I am?"

"You look like Carol Rogers, but she's dead."

"How do you know what Carol Rogers looks like?"

"You look like the photograph of the young woman in the silver frame and, since this is Carol Rogers' room, I assumed that's who you are; except an older version."

"Yes, I am Carol Rogers; and yes, I am dead."

Kendra sucked in her breath. "W-w-what do you want with me? W-w-what does the dead want with me?—I'm alive."

"To function in a solid state, I need one of your lungs and half your body."

"I knew it! When I first saw you take solid form, I became breathless and had trouble breathing. That's when you started syphoning off my air. Wasn't it?"

CR nodded. "You panicked and became breathless. You're breathing fine now."

"It seems so, but I don't want to share my lungs or my body with you, or anyone.—Living or dead."

"It's too late. I've already chosen you. My soul will join your soul. Two souls, one body.

Chapter One

It was one of those honeysuckle mornings filled with sweet smelling scents, gentle soft breezes and lemon-yellow sunshine. On this blossomy April Fools' day, 1950, spring had surprised New Orleans. It was abloom every where. Slender-stalked daffodils, decked out in their bright yellow bonnets, stood swaying beneath tall trees, whose bare branches were leafing out with tiny unfolding leaves.

Tender green shoots were poking through the earth's warming womb; grass was turning velvety jade; buds on bushes were swelling and bursting open; bashful crocuses were shyly showing their blooms; and baby birds were learning to sing, as nature quietly went about the explosive business of being born again.

On this sweet and dreamy day, Miss Molly Primrose Applegate and her niece, Kendra Louise Applegate, seated at their cherry gatelegged table, had a certain conversation while sipping their coffee in the golden glow of the morning sunshine, that came pouring through the kitchen's wide window, streaking over them and the table.

"Kendra Lou," cautiously began Aunt Molly Primrose, putting down her coffee cup and looking across the table at her niece, "I know you said you never wanted to hear the name of *you-know-who* mentioned in this house—"

"And I meant it," replied Kendra in a low tone, holding her voice steady. "Let's not spoil our breakfast discussing *him.*"

"Well, it's been a year since *you-know-who* married Allison Edwards, and *you-know-who's* been livin' happily ever after while you've been livin' like a cloistered nun. All you do is go to work, come home and read. Every time I look at you your nose is buried in one of them ol' murder mysteries. That ain't no life for no pretty young girl, like yourself. You shouldn't keep everythin' pent up inside. That ain't no good, either. You got to talk about it.—"

Kendra made no reply. She glanced out the tall, wide window, beside the table, into the vacant lot and saw fat and fluffy, ginger-colored Sholar Picarara preening his fur contentedly while sleek and slim gray Motel was pouncing on dead leaves.

"For a change, Sholar Picarara and Motel aren't fighting."

"Never mind about them nasty ol' Tom cats. Let's get back to you. Ever since you was little, I told you there was good times and bad times in life. You had one of them bad times—life dealt you a heavy blow, knocked you off your feet. But it's time for you to stand up tall and walk straight toward them good times. You got to start datin' again, and quit actin' like you're waitin' for *you-know-who* to come back, because *you-know-who* ain't comin' back. You got to face facts."

Kendra looked wearily at her aunt. "If we're going to discuss *him*, we might as well use his name. First of all, it's been ten months since Jack jilted me, not a year. Secondly, Jack would like to come back."

"How do you know that?" demanded her aunt, her white eyebrows mounting high on her forehead, her button-bright blue eyes questioning and wide. "Have you talked to Jack since his weddin'?"

"Yes. He came to see me right after his honeymoon—you were at work—and he told me Judge Edwards paid him big bucks to marry his daughter—Allison is dying of a rare blood disease. She's got about two more months."

"How awful.— And after she dies?"

"Jack said he'd be free to marry me. He said he did this horrible thing so we'd have lots of money when we married."

"Gawd save us! Who ever heard the like of such doin's? Not me. And to think Judge Edwards concocted such a sordid scheme; and your Jack jumped at it." Aunt Molly Primrose was thoughtful for a few seconds, and then: "You ain't been mopin' round, all these months, waitin' for Allison to die so Jack can be free to marry you?" she asked, looking suspiciously at her niece.

"N-no, indeed. I told him to get lost. I've been hurting because I was left at the altar. Jilted because Jack wanted money more than he wanted me. I've just been going through a mean time, but it's coming to an end. I think I'm myself again, and can control my own destiny."

"Thank you, Lord! I'm so glad the healin' is started to take ahold. Ten months is a long time to suffer-'n'-hurt."

"I guess many a girl's been left at the altar, and many a more will be left. I can't speak for those girls but, for me, it was like dying and nobody bothered to bury me. Just recently I've been able to stop thinking of that horrible day. I'm past pleasuring myself imagining various tortures for Jack. Like guilloting him.— I'm trying hard to put it behind me."

"Good." Aunt Molly Primrose poured her niece a fresh cup of coffee. "You know, spring's here, a time when young people start dreamin' of love and marriage. It's time for you to start datin'."

Kendra took a short sip of her scalding Creole coffee that had been made pale with yellow cream. "I'm not going to date again."

"But *why-y-y?* Nobody knows you and Jack was plannin' to marry. Everybody thinks you was engaged to Kenny Joe and, when he got killed in Ko-reah, you went into mournin' for him. Nobody knows you was—er, jilted. At first I was upset that you had planned a secret weddin' but, now the way things turned out, it was for the best."

"I can't see having the man you love marry another girl on the exact same day and time he was suppose to be marrying you—secret wedding or not—turn out for the best."

"Maybe not in that sense.— Kendra Lou, you know the stigma a jilted girl carries. Men, for some crazy reason, don't want nothin' to do with no jilted girl. You've escaped bein' eyed with embarrassment and pity—you've escaped them fumblin' remarks about slighted girls who were about to be married and the groom didn't show up. You've escaped all that blight and blot—no trace of any of it stains you."

"I'm grateful for that; but I'm not going back into circulation."

"You don't wanna end up like me, an ol' maid. You're too pretty and too young to spend all your spare time in seclusion, readin' them ol' detective stories for fun. That ain't no fun. And it ain't natural, nor healthy to shut yourself up for the rest of your life over the likes of Jack Trenchard. You gotta get out and be with young people."

Kendra made no reply. In silence, both women sipped their coffee and ate their breakfast: Creole cream cheese and Lost Bread—"nectar of the gods." Then Aunt Molly Primrose started up again: "I'm glad you're shut of him. He's an orphan who don't know who is momma and daddy is; and that's dangerous. What's bred in the bone comes out in the flesh. Goodness is free, but it ain't cheap. Bad blood tells. Remember that, Kendra *Louise.*"

"Let's not rake all this up again."

"I'm finished talkin' about Jack Trenchard.—You know, the other day, Elmyra Foughtenberry said to me that her son was dyin' to take you to the picture show, as soon as you wanted to go out again. She said Junior's makin' real good money at the post office. He's now supervisor of the night shift.

"She said he makes enough to support *her*, a *wife and a family*. She ought to know cause she manages his money and monitors his movies. That Elmyra's a born boss.— What do you think of Junior?"

"Not much. He's a sniffer and a spitter and a draft dodger. Junior joined the guard to beat the draft. I have no respect for a draft dodger."

"Well, there's Giross Hartman. Ruthie says her son would give you his head, if you'd have it."

"I think Giross better keep his head. I can't imagine a headless floor walker."

"Maison Blanche has just promoted him to head floor walker, and pays him good. Giross is nice-lookin', and dresses fine. Every day he wears a fresh boutonniere in his lapel. Don't frown, Kendra Lou, you'll hurt your good looks. What you got against fine-lookin' Giross?"

"Nothing except he's also a draft dodger—*and* a floor walker."

"A girl lookin' for a fine husband and a good provider can't be too picky or too worried about whether the man joined the Gawd to beat the draft. Well, there's only one bachelor left on Starlight Street and that's that good-lookin' Eyetalian, Sonny Ganucci, who's fightin' on the front lines in Ko-reah. I don't think Sonny would make you a good husband. He's too much like yourself, a dreamer."

Kendra glanced out the window in time to see Sholar Picarara and Motel hissing and spitting at each other. "A bloody battle's brewing."

"I told you to forget them Toms. —When we all waved good-bye to Sonny, at Union Station, juggling that big duffle bag, he said he was gunna save his money so when he came home he could open a pizza parlor. Said he could make a mint whippin' up pizza pies. Nobody on Starlight Street ever heard of or tasted no pizza pie. If that boy thinks folks is gunna buy a pie smeared and smothered in red sauce, he's a dreamer, for sure."

"Sometimes dreaming is all a guy or a girl's got. If Sonny comes home alive and not in a pine box, like poor Kenny Joe, I'd like to help him get his pizza parlor. Don't look so excited, Tante, I'm not thinking of marrying Sonny. We're just good friends."

Molly Primrose closely studied her niece's pretty face.

Kendra Louise—age twenty-two—was a luscious looking young woman. She was tall and lissome and graceful, with honey olive skin that was soft and creamy. Her mop of sugar-brown hair was like spun silk, with gold strands shimmering through her wavy locks. These long locks, when the humidity was high, turned into a mass of gypsy ringlets, soft and round.

Sometimes she wore her brown-gold hair on top her head, with curls breaking into misty tendrils around her face; sometimes, parted on the side with a deep wave dipping down over her left eye, a la Veronica Lake. Her big dreamy brown eyes, heavily fringed, glinted with gold, making them look amber colored. Nature had painted her cheeks a blush rose. Her wide mouth was interesting and inviting.

She had a beautiful face and body, with long legs, high breasts and narrow hips. She glowed with health and energy. Most of her good looks she got from her momma, Gen Rose, who died giving her birth. From her handsome daddy, Tom Applegate, she inherited her fine bones, her height, her stubbornness; though when she was a stubborn little goose, her aunt always said,"Your momma's comin' out of you." When she was a good little goose, her aunt said: "My brother Tom will never be dead as long as you're alive, Kendra Lou."

Tom Applegate died in a sanitarium of T.B. when Kendra was two, and his pretty petite sister, Molly Primrose, a spinster and seamstress, who worked for D. H. Holmes Department Store when women didn't work, raised her brother's child. Everybody said it was her duty. Molly Primrose said it wasn't a duty, because no body liked a duty. It was all love.

When the tragedy struck, Molly Primrose, a born-in-the-bone Catholic, who, up until the tragedy, believed the sin of sins was to find fault with God, told friends and neighbors that "Gawd" had cheated her handsome brother and his pretty bride.

Friends and neighbors said, "You can't boss Gawd," but agreed they couldn't figure out what "Gawd" had been thinking to take such a young couple from the face of the earth when there were so many mean old fogies hobbling around Canal Street. If He had to do some snatching,"Gawd" should've grabbed Himself a couple bums, not the momma and daddy of a pretty angel-child.

That pretty angel-child was now a private secretary whose brain always worked at top speed. She was educated; and seldom slipped into the slang language of New Orleans. Up until being jilted, craved adventure and excitement; but had not money to indulge her cravings. So her longings manifested themselves in reading novels and dreaming about going some where and having a good time.

Of late, Kendra had gotten the "nutty notion" in her pretty brown-gold head to quit being a secretary and become a private eye. This didn't, at all, go over big with Aunt Molly Primrose. Up until this point, the two women got along beautifully, except for Kendra's "nutty notion," and her extravagance.

Whenever Kendra bought something that her aunt thought unnecessary she'd say: "I'm sixty-two and ain't never charged a thing in my livin' life, and never will. If you can't pay cash for it, you don't need it. Chargin' is the devil's doin's."

None of this fazed Kendra. She continued to charge things, read and dream. She often imagined herself a famous female detective able to crack any case. The more detective stories she read the more convinced she was that she could easily tackle any murder case, and boasted that supposed fact to her aunt, who always said: "I don't think the New Orleans Po-leece Department will be cawlin' you, no day soon, to solve no murders, especially since there ain't been none."

Kendra's standard reply was: "I'll probably stumble on a murder that has passed right under the big noses of the whole New Orleans Police Department; and I'll solve it. Just wait and see."

"Kendra Lou," gently said Aunt Molly Primrose, finishing her breakfast, "I love you. You may be my brother's child, but you're really mine. Everythin' I have is yours. This here double, that my dear parents left me, will be yours when I die."

"*Please*, Tante, don't speak of dying," mumbled Kendra.

"No. Let me finish. I'm at the tail-end of my life. Some might say the useless part; but I don't feel useless. I intend to keep on working until the call comes. And when that call comes, you won't have to worry, cause I have a small insurance policy, enough to bury me—"

"I'm not worried about *that*—"

"I won't be no burden."

"You wouldn't know how to be a burden if your name were burden." Kendra stretched her pretty hand across the table and patted her aunt's spidery fingers. "You precious old thing, you've already worked forty years. It's time to be thinking of retiring."

"I told you I intend to keep on workin', if Holmes'll have me."

"Holmes will gladly have you. Holmes and your boss, Mr. Straveinia, could never replace their head seamstress."

Her aunt beamed.

Molly Primrose was a spry sixty-two, and was both quick-minded in her thoughts as well as her body movements. She was still slender and straight, no hint of a dowager hump, a disfigurement that plagued women her age. She had apple cheeks, fair skin, few wrinkles and a coronet of white silky plaits that crowned her nicely shaped head.

Molly Primrose was a product of her upbringing, which included the Great Depression, and that dreadful experience had taught her to save, not to take chances, to be humble; to fear God and to love God; to keep before her mind the bliss of heaven and the pains of hell; not to day dream in too big a way; and to gear herself for disappointments.

"Tante, Mr. Straveinia, knows you're dependable and the best seamstress," tacked on Kendra. "He'll keep you forty more years."

"When you flatter me this way, Kendra Lou, I feel almost young and shiny again."

"To me, you'll always be young and shiny."

"I'm afraid, now, all my shinin' comes from within."

"I don't care what you say, Tante, you're a beautiful little lady."

"Oh, stop it, Kendra Lou, you're just teasin' me. Let's get back to this other business—your findin' a good husband. Before that call comes, I want to see you married, settled and havin' Gawd's-givin'-gifts—babies."

"Stop worrying about that call coming. I'll be getting married sooner than you think. I've made up my mind to marry an older man who's already established. A man who has his education behind him, owns a mansion, has a fat bank account and a new automobile, all paid for."

"You forgot to say *April Fool*."

"Today is *April Fool*, but I'm not joking. Tante, if Jack Trenchard can marry a rich girl, I can marry a rich man."

"Sounds like you're playin' tit-for-tat. Don't talk nonsense."

"I'm-not-talking-nonsense. *I-mean-it.*"

"Kendra Lou, you're so nice to look at: you're so clean and fresh. To me, you're sunshine and springtime all rolled into one. A girl like you could have a fine husband, so please don't go lookin' for the wrong kind, for the wrong reason—money. And another thing, since you don't date, how are you gunna find your rich catch?"

"In the obituary notices."

Aunt Molly Primrose had just poured herself a fresh cup of coffee and brought the cup to her lips. She didn't take a sip. She just stared over the rim at her beautiful niece, pop-eyed. Slowly she put the cup down. "Are you tellin' me you're gunna marry a dead man?"

Kendra laughed a throaty laugh. "No. A live one. A living breathing widower. I'm going husband hunting via the obituary notices. I'll pick out only names of widowers who list exclusive addresses. I'll be looking for a fairly young widower, without children because, when he dies, I want to inherit all."

"Gawd save us! Who ever heard the like of that? Not me. You know, Kendra *Louise*"—when Molly Primrose was dead serious with her niece she called her Kendra *Louise*—"it's harmless for a woman to day dream, but when that woman starts to act out her day dreams the situation is serious. Could even be dangerous. Very dangerous."

"Good. I need a little danger in my safe and sound mousey life."

"Shame on you! Don't you ever let me hear you say that again," flared her aunt, angry and upset. "Wantin' danger in your life is wicked, and

Gawd is lissenin' to you. He could punish you for that. You've been taught that men and women are put on earth to prepare their immortal souls for eternity. You should be thinkin' of the bliss of heaven and the pains of hell, not hopin' for somethin' dangerous to happen to you. You better say a good Act of Contrition tonight."

For a few moments neither spoke, and then Kendra, in a flash of irritation, said: "You know, Tante, my life, for the past ten months, has been rather dull, and if God wants to punish me for wishing some excitement into it— *why you've just been hounding me to get out, date, circulate*—"

"I *want* you to do that. But I *don't* want you to go lookin' for *danger* and *trouble*, lookin' for no rich widerwar. You know, it's one thing to spot a widerwar's name in the obituary column, but quite another to meet and marry him. How do you propose to do that? Or have you thought that out?"

"From *A* to Z. I'm simply going to send him a note of condolence, a well-written carefully worded letter of sympathy. Pretend I knew his wife. Get my foot in his door, and then just say all the things he wants to hear. You know what I mean."

"Gawd save us! *Yes, I know.* Catch him off gawd while he's grievin' and weak. While he's lonesome and hurtin' and susceptible to the charms of a beautiful young woman. Why not waylay him at the graveyard's gate. Have a spare marriage license in your pocket and a handy priest to perform the weddin'. Instead of the widerwar havin' to go home for a funeral feast, make it a weddin' spread."

"When you put it *that* way, you make it sound like—"

"What it is—settin' a trap to catch a rich, grievin' widerwar, who's in a daze."

"I have to have an *excuse*—"

"You mean a *lie*—"

"An *excuse* to get my foot in the door, so our relationship can begin.—Why are you frowning?"

"Because I never heard the like of it.—I think you're bored and lookin' for the wrong kind of excitement."

"A little excitement wouldn't hurt. My life and job are humdrum."

"Now you sound like you're tired of workin'. You gotta work, Kendra *Louise*, until you're married."

"I'm not tired of working. I just wish my job was more exciting, more glamorous, and paid more. I'm sick of typing dull threatening letters to poor people, 'Dear Homeowner, we have placed a lien on your home. If you don't pay up, we'll take your property.' I'd like to be off some where having a good time chasing spies or climbing mountains, or, better yet, working on a murder case. Anything would be better than taking dictation from Mr. Prosper. *Ugh!* I can't stand the sound of that pipsqueak's nasal twang. And the way he drops his g's: ' Good mornin'..."

"Lissen to me, *Kendra Louise Applegate*, forget about all that day dreamin' stuff. None of that's gunna happen, especially doin' detective work. There ain't no female detectives, and never will be. Now as far as Mr. Prosper is concerned, he pays you $160 a month to type and take dictation, twang or no twang. And believe me that's a fine salary for a young woman. I've been workin' forty years and all I make is $100 a month—Forty years to get where I am—to get that $100.00."

"You're worth more. I'd like to be paid what I'm worth— $3-400 a month," sighed Kendra. "If ever I get a chance to make big bucks, I'll fly from Mr. Prosper's office."

"No workin' woman is worth *that* kind of money, so get *that* monkey foolishness out of your head. And you might as well forget about flyin' from Mr. Prosper's office, because women never will make big money...women ain't the bread winners.... Why, I don't know what's come over you covetin' the salary of bigshot exec'tive men."

"I'm not coveting any bigshot's salary. I'm as smart as any man, can perform my job as good or as better than any man, and should be paid accordingly."

"Women have always known they were smart as men, but they used to have enough sense not to tell it. Nowadays they tell everything they know, and some of what they don't."

"All I want to do is marry a bigshot so I can share in his bigshot salary. I wouldn't need to find a rich husband if I could earn what I'm worth."

"What's all this money talk? You broke?"

"No. Just deep in debt. I was a fool to help put Jack Trenchard through law school."

"You'd think now that he's a high falutin' attorney in his father-in-law's law firm, he'd pay you back."

"He considers his having Judge Edwards help Miss Stella Dora get out the crazy house payment.— I owe everybody, even the painter who painted our kitchen last month."

The two women looked at the freshly painted kitchen. It was wide and white with a high ceiling, from which hung a shaded light bulb. The walls were tongue and groove; the floor was covered with black-and-white checkered linoleum. A white wooden kitchen cabinet, with glass doors, stood against the right wall, and next to it was a "new-fangled" electric icebox. At the left of the icebox stood a footed, white porcelain stove, with black stenciling. It had four gas burners and a warming oven.

On the back wall, above the single sink, was a "new-fangled" cylinder shaped electric hot water heater, recently installed. Across the room, in the center of the wall, the window, which wore a gauzy yellow cotton curtain, trimmed in red rick-rack, over-looked a small jade lawn, the footage borrowed from the adjacent lot. Between the window and the lawn was a narrow alleyway. Bordering the alleyway, next to the house's foundation, were clumps of mint. On the opposite side of the alleyway was a flowerbed fringed with fern and filled with yellow daylilies and plumes of purple and pink phlox.

In front of the open window, stood the gatelegged table, a century old and satin-smooth. Not a scratch on it. Before their treasured china—all blue-and-white castles, bridges and willows—could be placed on this prized-table, which had belonged to Kendra's great-grandmother, it was padded and spread with a stiffly starched and ironed linen cloth, that, because of all the starch, could stand by itself.

"The kitchen looks pretty," mumbled Kendra, her elbow on the table, her face resting in her hand. "It's worth being in debt for."

"Nothin's worth bein' in debt over. I begged you not to charge that new-fangled 'lectric icebox, but you wouldn't lissen...Our ol' icebox was good enough. It hadn't given way on us...It kept our food nice-'n'-cold...Faithful Dennis Boy delivered ice twice a week...We always had plenny ice...When you bought that 'lectric icebox, you helped to put Faithful Dennis Boy out of work and close down the icehouse."

"I'm sorry about Faithful Dennis Boy and the icehouse, but I'm not sorry about us having a nice new icebox, with no drip pan. I hated emptying the drip pan on that ol' icebox."

"I didn't mind a bit. I also didn't mind washin' our clothes on the scrubboard. That's how I washed clothes all my life— You didn't need to run off to Sears and Roebuck and charge that new-fangled washin' machine, with its finger-catchin' wringer. I didn't need no washin' machine."

"But I did."

"Like you needed a hot water heater, too. I didn't see nothin' wrong with fillin' the kettle and heatin' water on the stove. Applegates for fifty years used that kettle to heat their bath water. Now you're saddled with a new payment."

"It's worth it. I was sick of heating water in that old kettle."

"Then you shoulda bought a new kettle, not a hot water heater. And another thing, credit's never worth it. I told you, when you first got your job, not to let them fast-talkin' salesmen slick you into takin' out charge accounts, buyin' on time. You got not one charge account but three. You charge at Holmes, Maison Blanche and Sears and Roebuck. I don't approve of puttin' a little bit down, and then makin' payment after payment. You ignored my free advice, and now you're in debt. There's only one way out of this mess, and that's for me to start makin' some of your payments."

"No you won't. I did the charging. I'll do the paying."

"I'd feel better if you let me pay on the washin' machine and the 'lectric icebox. You can pay on the hot water heater and your nice automobile. Thank Gawd you didn't try to charge no new automobile."

"I wish I had a brand-new Dodge."

"There ain't nothin' wrong with your second-third or fourth-hand Dodge. It has a good twelve years or so to its credit. Of course, the day after you bought it, you had to buy a new battree and one, two, three, four new tires. Anyways, it starts up every time you crank it, and you don't even have to choke it."

"Yeah, the ol' rattletrap starts every time, and takes off up-the-street coughing and jerking."

"Well, at least it takes off. Nell Miller tells me her son-in-law, Chowlee, has to choke his new, two-door, flashy red Ford every single mornin', summer-'n'-winter. His Ford don't cough-'n'-jerk, but it don't take off all the time either. I'm glad your Dodge is black and has four doors. All the chirren on Starlight Street like it."

"That's because I let them ride on the running board." Kendra sighed.

"Are you on your period?"

"No."

"Well, you're sure actin' like it. I think you need a dose of castor oil."

"I don't need a physic. Having all these debts makes me want to go somewhere and have a good time. Forget my troubles."

"You can't go no where. You got to work. Pay off them debts."

"I know. But as soon as I get one of these debts paid off, I'm going to buy us a TV. We're the only ones without TV in the neighborhood."

The neighborhood consisted of neat, white-painted gingerbread doubles, built on brick foundations and roofed with slate. These houses had been built seventy or so years before, by the same builder who used the same set of plans for each house. All had five rooms; all had front and back galleries, which ran the width of the house. Some had been trimmed in hunter green, some in gray. The lawns and back yards were regularly cut, and full of flowerbeds.

The residence of Starlight Street lived simple clean lives: they married, had babies, raised their babies and died. Their chief entertainment was visiting. After supper, everybody sat on his gallery, rocked, fanned and gossiped. They had a lot to chat about—shame and bitterness being low on their list—a lot to laugh about—and a lot to cry about

The Applegate double was trimmed in dark green, and its front gallery was furnished with white wooden chairs, a settee, a swing and a couple rockers. Their back gallery was used mainly for storage. The washing machine was there, along with the old icebox.

Their back yard looked like a pretty park. It was always noisy with chirping birds, either perched on branches in the sweet olive tree, that was so full of snowy blossoms you couldn't see the leaves; or in the oak, that was hung with stringy strands of gauzy gray moss and honeysuckle, coming together in a tangle; or in the wide-spread fig, its dark green leaves, thick and dense. Beneath these trees, the black soil was feathered over with delicate maidenhair fern and green moss.

Tater Beelack, an old colored yardman, kept the grass cut and the flowerbeds spaded up. Molly Primrose and Kendra Louise kept the beds weeded, watered and planted full of sweet-smelling flowers.

A fence of pink-and-white heavy-headed roses separated the left side of the yard from the vacant lot; a brick walkway, starting at the back steps, led to the clotheslines, which were strung in front of tall spikes of slender green bamboo that fenced in the back of the lot. In front of the bamboo stood a bright flaming bed of scarlet cannas.

On the right side of the house, a row of blue purple hydrangea, broken by a stone birdbath, divided the Applegates' yard from the Wheelerhands', their tenants. Beneath the birdbath grew pink periwinkle.

The inside of the Applegate double was bright and friendly and full of personality. Welcoming. One room followed another: the parlor; Aunt Molly Primrose's bedroom; a hallway, where the telephone was; a bathroom off the hall; Kendra's bedroom; and the kitchen, all opened into each other through French doors which wore white sheer curtains.

The rooms, all painted white, were large with high ceilings; the floors were shiny pine; the furniture, handcrafted cherry wood, had first belonged to Great-Grandmother Mary Kate Applegate; then to Grandmother Fanny Applegate; now to Aunt Molly Primrose Applegate. All was in cream-puff condition; and Molly Primrose was making sure it would be that way when she left it to Kendra Louise.

The tall windows in each room wore white lace curtains. The sofa and parlor chairs were slip-covered with bright flowery chintz; there was always a big bunch of pink-and-white roses on the center parlor table, along with the family album, covered in faded maroon velvet.

The shabby album contained pictures of good-looking kinfolk, long gone to glory, who Kendra didn't know but, because of her aunt regularly chatting about them, as if they were alive, felt she knew them better than a lot of the living. Her aunt said they were all "Gawd-fearin' and hard-workin'. They were right-headed and none simple-minded or mindless.

Kendra could identify even distant cousins, their husbands, their children, their children's children; and those dead cousins, who had baked the best coconut cakes and pecan pies; who made the best fried chicken and potato salad; and who had made the best fig preserves.

Aunt Molly Primrose, using her kinfolk's recipes, never made a coconut cake without saying, "Kendra Lou, have a slice of your Cousin Catherine Celeste's cake; have some of your Cousin Ida Mae's fig preserves; try some of Cousin Julia's fried chicken."

In this same album was a picture of Kendra's beautiful parents on their wedding day. A tiny facsimile of that picture her aunt had enclosed in a gold locket, with a chain, and gave it to Kendra the day she made her First Holy Communion. From that day to this, that locket hung about Kendra's neck, and banged her breast and hurt her heart.

There was also an old envelope, stashed in the back of the album, which held a few snapshots, which her aunt had found in her dead brother's wallet. She didn't know the people in the pictures but, because the snapshots had belonged to her brother, she kept them.

Above the mantel hung handsome pictures, in mahogany oval frames, of Grandfather and Grandmother Applegate; bookshelves flanked the mantel; a radio stood in one corner; a victrola in the other. Kendra kept a stack of slithering records next to the victrola. The Applegate double was enjoyed.

"Even the Wheelerhands have TV," muttered Kendra, "and you know how conservative they are."

Aunt Molly Primrose's tenants, the Wheelerhands: Big Joe, his pretty wife, Stella Dora, and their handsome son, Kenny Joe, and Big Joe's plain old-maid school teacher sisters, sparrowlike, Miss Lettie Lou and Miss Effie Vi'let, lived happily together.

The Wheelerhand family took as much pride in their home as their landlady. They had been renting and living next door to Molly Primrose for twenty-five years. They paid $20 a month rent, plus utilities. Kendra

Louise and Kenny Joe grew up together. The Wheelerhands were family.

"Even the Wheelerhands have TV," repeated Kendra.

"Good for the Wheelerhands. I don't want no television in this house.Why, Nell Miller, ever since her son-in-law, Chowlee, bought that seventeen inch Philco, comes to work so sleepy-eyed and tired out she can't see to thread a needle. From the minute she gets home from work until that noise box goes off the air, Nell watches it.

"She even watches violent rasslin', tellin' me, with tears in her tired eyes, how some big brute beat up on a little brute. The things Nell tells me about how those big mean rasslers pound one another, pull hair, bite and kick, makes me sick to my stomach. When she's not watchin' rasslin', she's watchin' wild westerns. Every two minutes the sheriff shoots or hangs somebody, right before Nell's tired eyes

"It would serve Nell right if the liberry revoked her card. I hope they do. That'll teach her when she gets her fill of her Philco. And another thing, TV's got Nell and her sister-in-law, Lulu DuPree, at auds, over Liberace. They're both in love with Liberace. Lulu swears Liberace is flirtin' with her. Winkin' at her, leering' at her, actin' like he wants her. Nell swears he's doin' the same to her. If Nell's husband, Amacee Miller, Gawd rest his soul, was alive, Nell wouldn't be lustin' after no Liberace. Not for a minute.

"Anyway, as soon as Lulu's husband, Ray Roy DuPree, leaves to go bowl, she paints her mouth blood red, makes a gin and tonic, tunes in on Liberace, pulls down the shades, strips, and sits in front of the TV buck necked, sippin' her gin-'n'-tonic and apuffin' on one Camel after another, exhalin' smoke both from her wide nostrils and her red slit mouth, together, while her half-shut long black eyes are glued to Liberace. Nell caught her in the act.

"Lulu swears Liberace's *after her,* pantin' to seduce her. She claims he can hardly strike the sharp keys on that grand pianer, from starin' straight at her nipples. Nell's furious with Lulu because she can't sit necked herself and watch Liberace. Her daughter's always around."

"Nell and Lulu are nuts. Liberace goes for men. He's a big fruit."

Aunt Molly Primrose's apple cheeks turned a deeper red. She didn't want to discuss *sissies,* so she abruptly switched the subject. "Kendra Lou, are you really gunna go lookin' for a rich widerwar, or are you just jokin'?"

"Really and truly I mean to marry a well-fixed widower, and I'm going to find him in the obituary notices. Don't look so upset...you're always saying you want me to be happy."

"Kendra Lou, your happiness is everything to me."

"Then help me with my plan. Don't hinder me."

"My sense of right and wrong won't let me help you destroy yourself. Help you run to ruin."

"I'm not going to destroy myself."

"Yes you will. This scheme of yours could lead to bad trouble."

Two weeks later the bad trouble began. "Tante, I think one of your clients is dead," cried Kendra, seated at the gatelegged table, the *Picayune* opened to the obituary notices.

Her aunt responded with a little start of surprise. "Who is it?" she demanded, pouring coffee, and then seating herself.

"It says here in black and white:

Mrs. Carol Sloan Rogers, 47, of Willowwynn, died at home unexpectedly of an apparent heart attack on Friday, April 13, 1950. She had been a resident of New Orleans, since 1948, moving here from San Francisco, California. She is survived by her husband C.C. Rogers.

Visitation and viewing will be Sunday, April 15, 1-5 p.m., at Gilliard's Funeral Parlor. On Monday, Mrs. Rogers' body will be shipped to San Francisco, to rest in the family vault.

"Isn't that the Carol Rogers who buys a store of clothes from Holmes', and every single stitch has to be altered by you, only you?"

"Yes. I'm afraid that's her," confirmed Aunt Molly Primrose, her blue eyes pained. "She always looked so good-'n'-healthy."

"H'm—"

"She looked real good, a couple days ago, when she bought a beautiful black silk suit. Almost like she was buying her funeral outfit. I hemmed the suit. She was supposed to pick it up yesterday afternoon. I thought it unusual when she didn't show or send her secatary, Icelynn Farnsworth. That's the first time Mrs. Rogers missed pickin' up an altered article of clothin', and that's because she was dead. Poor, sweet dear. After-while I better call Nell to see if she's heard the bad news."

"Forty-seven isn't really old," remarked Kendra, race-reading each word of the obit notice.

"No, it ain't. Mrs. Rogers never looked her age. She looked like a woman in her late thirties—still pretty. She had sea green eyes and a mass of short, silky chestnut hair, naturally curly it was. She was about your height, Kendra Lou. Built a lot like you. Come to think of it, she reminded me a lot of you."—Her aunt was thoughtful.— "She had buttermilk skin, and a fine figure."

"And she was rich. Willowwynn's in the Garden District."

"Yes, she was rich all right. Willowwynn Mansion is on Prytania, right next door to Greenwood Manor—Judge Edwards' mansion."

"Y-e-s—"

"Mrs. Rogers," went on Aunt Molly Primrose in a sad voice, "told me she was an only child, and when her mother was killed in an automobile crash she couldn't stand livin' in the family's San Francisco mansion; so she and her husband moved to New Orleans. They bought a mansion on Prytania, and called their new home Willowwynn, after the one in San Francisco, and made it as like the San Francisco one as possible."

"That's interesting. The obituary notice doesn't list any children. Did she have any?" Kendra quickly scanned the printed notice again.

"No chirren. All she had was her husband; her secatary, Icelynn Farnsworth; and a protege, accordin' to Nell Miller."

"How old is Icelynn Farnsworth? Is she good-looking?"

Her aunt shrugged."She must be in her forties. She's attractive. Dresses nice; has a good figure. She's of medium height, has short blonde hair. Wears it in a pageboy, parted in the middle, with a full bang across her forehead. Her eyes are ice blue. Like her name, she's cold. Never seen her thaw." Molly Primrose shivered.

"Do you think Mr. Rogers might fall in love with Icelynn?"

"For heavensakes, Kendra *Louise*, how should I know that?"

"How old is Mr. Rogers?"

"I dunno. Nell Miller said she saw the Rogerses together—I never did—and she thought he looked the younger. Of course, you can't go by sleepy-eyed Nell—that Philco's causin' her to go blind."

"Do you know who was the rich one? Or were they both rich?"

"I believe Nell said Mrs. Rogers had the money."

"Well, what does Mr. Rogers do? Live off Mrs. Rogers?"

"I dunno.—I just sewed for Mrs. Rogers I didn't check her income tax return, or take down her family history. Somebody said Mr. Rogers has an office in the Maison Blanche Building, so I suppose he's a businessman of some sorts."

"A bigshot executive, eh?"

"Possibly." For a second or so Aunt Molly Primrose was silent. "You know, Mrs. Rogers' new black suit is paid for and, dead or not, it's due her. I suppose I could call her secatary and have her pick it—"

"Don't do that...I'll personally deliver it."

For half a second Aunt Molly Primrose stared blankly at her niece, and then a light bulb went on in her head. "Gawd save us! You don't mean to say you're goin' after Mr. Rogers, do you?" she stiffly asked.

"Yes, I am. This is a perfect opportunity. No children, no relatives—and Willowwynn is bigger and better than Greenwood Manor. Mrs. Rogers' passing is almost like divine intervention."

Molly Primrose gave her niece a withering look. "Leave Gawd out of this."

"Why should I? I think He's helping me. Tante, we'll go to the wake together."

"No, we won't. I sewed for Mrs. Rogers...I liked her...but I wouldn't want to give the impression I was a close friend. That would be like I was tryin' to get in on a good thing, and I won't cheapen myself like that. If you go to that wake, you go by yourself."

On Sunday afternoon, Kendra went to Carol Rogers' wake only to learn it had been cancelled. She returned home.

"You certainly paid your respects in a hurry."

"I didn't pay any respects. There was no body, no grieving husband on hand, so I signed your name in the register."

"*Kendra Louise Applegate,* you had no right to sign my name!" cried Aunt Molly Primrose. Her apple cheeks, redder than ever. "Oh, well, I guess, since the wake was cancelled, it don't matter. I'm glad your little adventure is over."

"It's not over. I'm going after Mr. Rogers, and you, Tante, are going to help me get him. Tomorrow, after work, bring Mrs. Rogers suit with you."

"Kendra *Louise*, you know I can't do that."

"Tante, I need your help. *So help me!*"

"*All right, all right,* I'll bring the suit if I can remember it. But if it's already on the delivery truck, you're out of luck."

"I don't think it's on the truck. That suit's going to open Willowwynn's door, for me"

"So you can thumb your nose at—"

"Jack Trenchard."

Chapter Two

The next morning, Kendra, on an errand for Mr. Prosper, fearing her aunt would either forget Mrs. Rogers' suit or, worse yet, say it had already been taken to delivery, hurried to Holmes. She found her aunt on her knees pinning up a circular hem on a pink taffeta gown.

"Kendra Lou, what brings you here so early?"—She looked at her watch—"You just dropped me to work an hour ago. Anything wrong?"

"No. Nothing's wrong. Mr. Prosper sent me on an errand to Maison Blanche and, being so close by, I thought I'd drop in and say hay; and, at the same time, pick up Mrs. Rogers' suit."

Molly Primrose's blue eyes met her nieces' brown-gold ones, and she said very matter-of-factly: "The suit ain't here" She put the last pin in and stood up. "Every time I kneel I get stiff as a stick." Again, she looked at her watch. "The suit's on the truck, and the truck's gone. I'm sorry."

Kendra was annoyed, but tried to keep her annoyance from sounding in her voice. "M'm...I was afraid of that...I guess I'll have to find another way."

"I suppose so," said her aunt, now biting a strand of thread held at arm's length from the spool. She threaded her needle. "You better hurry back to the office. I'm sure Mr. Prosper's waitin' for you."

"I'm sure he is. See you later, Tante."

On her way to the elevator, Kendra met sleepy-eyed Nell Miller—tall, skinny, sallow-skinned, gray haired—carrying a box.

"Hello, Mrs. Miller, nice to see you."

"Nice to see you, Kendra honey. You been visitin' your aunt?"

"Just to say hay."

"That's so sweet of you, sugar. Your aunt's some lucky to have such a nice niece.—Oh, Kendra honey, ain't it a *shame* about poor Miz Rogers?"

"It sure is."

"You know, Miz Rogers bought a suit just this pas' Wednesday, your aunt altered it, and then before poor Miz Rogers could pick it up, she up-'n'-died."

"That's too bad."

"That suit, Kendra honey, is right here in this box," whispered Nell, nodding significantly. She held the box out and shook it. "I'm takin' it to delivery," she added in a confidential tone.

"Hasn't the delivery truck left?"

"In ten minutes." Again Nell shook the box. "This suit would've been beautiful on Miz Rogers. Perfect for a burial outfit, but the paper said she was cremated today—burnt up. A big hot fire for poor pretty Miz Rogers." Nell quivered. "They even cancelled her wake, and nobody knows why."

Kendra nodded.

"I don't know what gets in people's heads, at death, to make them think of fire. I can't stand the thought of pretty Miz Rogers being burnt up. Such lovely hair she had, and those big green eyes, and that buttermilk skin, all going up in flames—*poof*!"

"Don't think about it like that, Mrs. Miller. After all, Mrs. Rogers was *dead*. She wasn't Joan of Arc being burned *alive* at the stake."

"True, true," sniffed Nell, sighing deeply. "By the way, *Joan of Arc's comin' to the Lois State* real soon.— Kendra honey, d'ya know if they burn up people buck necked, or in their clothes? I'd think buck necked would be better. Don't ya?"

"I never thought about it one way or the other. Isn't it about time for your break?"

"As soon as I drop this here package to delivery, I'm headin' for the cafeteria. I need a cuppa coffee somethin' awful. I didn't go to bed until the TV went off the air."

"I'm going right past delivery. I'll drop it for you."

"How sweet of you, Kendra honey. This won't put you out, huh honey?"

"*Not at all.*"

Mrs. Miller handed over the box, and walked toward the right; Kendra to the left, to a waiting elevator.

"Main floor, Sam."

"Yaz, Miz Applegates— Heah we is."

The elevator stopped with a jolt, and Kendra's stomach stayed on the floor above, as it always did when she rode an elevator.

"See you, Sam."

Holmes' main floor was already jammed with shoppers, as Kendra picked her way through the crowd, her heart racing with excitement. Since she didn't want to appear in a hurry—she imagined all the shoppers knew the box she was clutching held the late Mrs. Rogers' black silk suit—she took her sweet time. She sauntered toward the side door, hoping to give the impression she was just another shopper and not a wicked woman turned thief. As she passed clerks and customers, she heard snatches of sentences from them. She saw and heard men, women and small children talking and smiling. Some were even laughing out loud.

Gripped in an upsurge of excitement, she went along, tightly clasping the box to her bosom when, suddenly realizing the enormity of what she had done, half of her wanted to return the box, while the other half cried out for adventure. Her face felt feverish; her feet sluggish, as if the soles of her shoes had been smeared with glue.

Slowly she threaded her way around counters, aisle displays, gorgeous gowns on mannequins, every invention of fashion, from pocketbooks to hats, and somehow or other she knew taking the suit away from Nell Miller had already added salt and savor to her flat and tasteless life.

At last she wound up at the side exit. For a moment she hesitated and, then, without qualm, passed through double glass doors.

Five days later on a Saturday morning—her aunt at work— Kendra, armed with Mrs. Rogers' suit and a sympathy note in her pocket,was ready to make that special delivery to Willowwynn. She looked in the mirror and pirouetted several times, carefully checking her overall appearance.

She was pleased with the white grosgrain ribbon in her shiny hair that hung to her shoulders in a shower of brown-gold gypsy ringlets, round and soft, and was glad she had chosen her daffodil yellow voile dress, with its fitted, pin-tucked bodice, side pockets and cuffed elbow-sleeves. She looked lovely for her adventure.

Ten months before, also on a Saturday morning, Kendra had looked in the same mirror and liked what she saw. A bride. For her secret wedding, she had chosen a beautiful creamed colored Crepe de Chine dress that had a cowl neckline, a circular skirt attached to a fitted hip yoke, and full sleeves gathered into French cuffs.

Coral jewelry, creamed colored calf pumps, matching pocketbook and a broad-brimmed straw hat had completed her outfit. She looked just like one of those picture-book brides.

Her groom, Jack Trenchard, was suppose to pick her up at ten o'clock, and then they'd drive to St. Bernard Parish to tie the knot. Afterwards, they'd call her aunt and tell her the secret, happy news.

At ten-fifteen, the phone rang and Kendra lunged for it. Wrong number. By ten-thirty, when Jack still hadn't shown up or phoned, she called his rooming house and learned that earlier Judge Edwards' driver had picked him up.

"Of all the luck," muttered Kendra to herself. "I bet the Judge is making Jack take care of some trifling legal matter. He should've called to let me know he'd be late."

Since Judge Edwards' law firm hired only single young attorneys, who agreed to remain single for two years, Jack kept Kendra a secret. She had never been to his office, or to Greenwood Manor, the Judge's mansion, where Jack worked half days on Saturday.

"I'll drive over to Greenwood Manor, park and wait for Jack. I don't care if the Judge sees me."

Kendra found Greenwood Manor surrounded with automobiles, and so was the house next door. "It looks like the Edwardses are having a party," she said to herself, as she searched for a parking space.

Finally she spotted one and squeezed into it, leaving a fourth of the front of her Dodge hanging over into the driveway of *Willowwynn, No. 10 Prytania,* so posted a sign on one of the black lamp posts, flanking the drive.

She glanced across the side street at Greenwood Manor and saw the high iron gates were flung open wide. They were wreathed with white roses and pink-and-white satin streamers.

Kendra got out the Dodge, crossed the cobblestone street and passed through the massive iron gates. To the left of the gates was a thick hedge of giant, red-blossoming oleanders. Quickly she stepped behind the hedge. No one could see her, but she could see the general outline of things. The Patio was packed with people.

There were rows of white wooden chairs set up on either side of an aisle. Every where were white wicker baskets spilling over with big bunches of pink-and-white roses and lilies of the valley. Round tables were covered with damask cloths that touched the ground.

There was a wedding canopy adorned with white roses and long, pink satin streamers. Beneath it stood a black-robed Judge Edwards; Kendra recognized him from seeing his picture in *The Picayune.* The Judge nodded to the pianist, and she started softly playing; the guests took their seats; the bride and groom, their backs to Kendra, came down the aisle, to the wedding march.

If Kendra hadn't known better, she'd have sworn the groom's back belonged to her handsome Jack Trenchard. Jack was over six foot, lean, with black curly hair, blue eyes, that were so blue they looked purple, olive skin, rosy high cheekbones, hollow cheeks, a cleft in his chin, and warm red lips. Every time her aunt saw Jack, she said he reminded her of an Applegate. "Could pass for your kin, Kendra Lou."

Staring hard at the groom's back, Kendra vaguely heard Judge Edwards in an ultrarefined voice say: "Do you, Jack, promise to love, honor and cherish Allison..."

The Judge had said *Jack, but that couldn't be her Jack. Her Jack was marrying her that day, not another girl. Yet, the groom, Jack, was wearing the same suit her Jack had bought for their wedding. Her Jack had made only one payment, and she had made the rest—$250 worth.*

"I do," said Jack Trenchard's voice.

That was her Jack's voice, but it couldn't be. Kendra shivered with misery while her mind raced and tumbled in mad confusion. Sick and numb, she stood behind the oleander hedge and watched and listened, breathless and trembling.

"Do you, Allison, promise to love, honor and obey?"

"I do," promised Allison.

The earth moved beneath Kendra's feet. The courtyard spun with dizzying speed. Waves of nausea and faintness washed over her.

A short while ago she had been so happy, so well; and now it seemed as if she were going to fall over dead. To steady herself, she snatched at the sturdy branches of the oleander hedge, holding on tightly, waiting for the wave of sickness to subside.

Only half conscious of what the Judge was saying, his next words, however, rang loudly and clearly. "Does anyone know why Allison and Jack shouldn't be married?"

Inwardly she screamed through sealed lips, *"I do—I do—He's suppose to be marrying ME right now!—"*

The heat had grown suffocating, and the Judge's voice now seemed a long way off; it rose and fell. A frenzy gripped Kendra, and she knew she had to leave her hiding place, get to her automobile, go home, go "pine black crazy" and die.

As she turned to leave, the hem of her beautiful wedding dress, the first and only boughten dress she had ever owned, for her aunt had made all her clothes, caught on a thorny vine and ripped out.

She didn't care. She hated the dress. She hated everything and everybody. All she wanted to do was get home—get away from Jack Trenchard and his bride.

She stumbled to the street, caught her heel in one of the loose cobblestones and fell face first, spread-eagle. Her beautiful broad-brimmed hat flew off her head and blew clean across the street. Her chin hit the rough bricks, forcing her bottom teeth into her top lip. She tasted blood. She tried to get up. She couldn't. For a few minutes she just laid in the street, crying, choking and gulping for air. A pair of strong masculine hands lifted her.

"Well-ell, I can see both your knees are badly skinned, your stockings are ruined, your beautiful dress is quite dirty, your pretty face is tear-stained and streaked with dirt; other than that how are you?" asked the stranger in a soft but powerful voice.

"I'm—I'm all right."

"Good. I'll get your hat, and then take you home."

"T-thank you; but—that won't be necessary," answered Kendra in a choky voice. Her eyes were too blurry with tears to get a good look at the kind, caring man.

"You sure you can get home by yourself?"

"Y-yes. Just help me to my automobile."

Behind the wheel of the Dodge, Kendra, as soon as the stranger was out of sight, rested her throbbing head on the steering wheel, and her whole body shook with sobs. After a while she straightened up, blew her nose, wiped her eyes, swallowed hard and cranked the Dodge.

She drove in a daze, the old rattletrap coughing, sputtering and jerking up the street. Flashbacks of Jack and Allison constantly popping up before her amber eyes. She had to get home in a hurry—rip off her dress—cry some more and no doubt die for sure.

As she turned into Starlight Street—only four blocks to go and she'd be home—colored Mozis, driving his horse and wagon down the middle of the street, was calling out: "*Water—melloooons. Ah'sgots water—mellooooons fresh fum de vine, end raid to the rin'. Ya-Ya! Ah's gots water—mellooons sweet as wine. Ya-Ya! Water—mellooons!*

As the Dodge crawled behind the wagon, she was vaguely aware of voices echoing up and down the street. Some raised in dispute, some in noisy merriment; doors and windows, as usual, were wide open; screen doors were slamming; children were out in full force: some were riding bikes, some skating, some pushing blue scooters, others pulling red wagons, some racing about, their puppy dogs either bounding and barking at their sides, or treeing cats; some kids were playing tag, laughing and shrieking when captured. Their voices howling with glee, while their mommas, who either stood in their doorways or sat on their steps, screeched: "Don't do that...Mind me...If you don't mind me, you're gunna get it...."

Mozis, finally realizing someone was behind him, veered to the right, and Kendra passed him. Just as she reached her block, she saw, to her horror, Charity Hospital's big red ambulance, pull from in front of her double, its red rotating light flashing, its siren screaming. The sparrowlike Wheelerhand sisters, Miss Lettie Lou and Miss Effie Vi'let, were standing on the banquette, wringing their hands, watching the red streak speed away.

As always their little sharp faces were heavily powdered with cornstarch, two round rouge dots circled each thin cheek, a thread of matching lipstick brought attention to their thin lips, gold-framed spectacles hid their slightly bulging gray eyes, and their feathery white hair was piled on top of their heads like a puff of meringue.

Across the street a fringe of neighbors had gathered: Lizzie Slap Springmeyer; Mooching Mamie TuJax; Elmyra Foughtenberry; Rosa Ganucci; Lolotte DuPuy; Ruby Faye Pujowl and Levinia Gervaise.

Kendra, still weak and in shock, brought the Dodge to a stop. Stiffly she got out the automobile and limped toward the Wheelerhands: "What was Charity doing here?" she asked, alarm in her voice, fear in her eyes. "Is anyone hurt?"

"Oh, Kendra Louise," wailed the Wheelerhand sisters, not even noticing her limp, or how pale and disheveled she was, "Kenny Joe's been killed in action, in Ko-reah."

"Oh, my God—*No!*"

"Yes. Big Joe got the telegram, turned white as lard, and cried 'My Kenny Joe's dead.' Then he clutched his chest...his eyes rolled back in his head and he fell at Stella Dora's feet. It was awful.—Here's the telegram.—Stella Dora's gone in the amberlance with him."

Kendra read and reread the big blurry black letters printed on that yellow piece of paper, shaking her head in disbelief and thinking how short life was. Thinking how much Kenny Joe's momma loved him and her husband, Big Joe; and how she must be hurting. "If only I could take some of Miss Stella Dora's hurt," she said to herself.

When Kendra was little, Stella Dora Wheelerhand minded her while her aunt worked. Kendra loved pretty, blonde Stella Dora, who painted her lips red and wore $2 Grant's housedresses. Her fine figure did wonders for those cheap dresses.

Stella Dora was the best babysitter ever. She read and told stories to Kendra and Kenny Joe; looked at picture books with them; helped them color in their coloring books; let them dip their butter-smeared French bread into their cafe au lait; and didn't make them eat their spinach. She did, however, make them return five of the six weak-legged kittens that Lizzie Slap Springmeyer's cat, Preggie, had.

Kenny Joe named the kitten they kept Tommy Apple, out of core.

Tommy Apple turned out to be Annie Apple. She also let them keep Sponge, out of water, the stray puppy dog that Kendra had found and named. There was a succession of Tommy and Annie Apples and Sponges.

Stella Dora never punished or whipped them. When Kendra and Kenny Joe wielded the hose through the kitchen window, Stella Dora got it all dried out, and never told a soul.

Every day she gave them each a nickel for the ice-cream man; she often made custard pies for them; however, the crust always wound up on top of the custard. And when she gave the house a good going over, to keep them busy, she gave them flour and water, and they sprawled on the kitchen floor and made cement pies.

The only time Stella Dora threatened to "wear out" Kendra was when she got in a fight with Sonny Ganucci, the Eyetalian kid across the street. It seemed Sonny kicked Kenny Joe in the shin, and Kendra lit into Sonny. In her rage, she accidentally punched Kenny Joe in the eye, blackening it.

"In the name of glory, I can't believe my beloved nephew's dead," murmured Kenny Joe's aunts. "He just graduated from college."

Kenny Joe had just gotten his degree in business—it took the financial help of the entire Wheelerhand family to put him through Tulane—and, upon graduation, the Army drafted him. Sent him to Korea, a short three months ago, and now he was dead. Killed in action so said the yellow piece of paper with the black printed words.

Handsome Kenny Joe was a superb young man. He was of medium height, with a thatch of sunburst hair, chocolate eyes, fair skin, beautiful features and a sculpted body.

Since Kendra and Kenny Joe had been two peas in a pod, from little, family and friends knew the "chirren" would grow up and marry.

Just before Kenny Joe shipped over, Kendra told him she loved Jack Trenchard; and he asked her if she were really and truly sure of Jack. If not, he wanted to be in the running.

That's when Kendra told him she could never marry him because she loved him like a brother; and that she'd be secretly marrying Jack on the first Saturday in June. Tears had filled Kenny Joe's chocolate eyes, but he still insisted if things didn't work out, he'd be there for her. Things didn't work out for Kendra, and Kenny Joe was dead. Killed in action. Killed in the flush of his youth, so said that yellow piece of paper with the big black letters.

Weak from the trauma and shock of stumbling onto Jack Trenchard marrying Allison Edwards, and still shaky and sore from her fall, Kendra didn't need this new piece of bad news. She needed her bed. She needed to close her eyes, sleep, block out the nightmare.

However, some where in her benumbed brain, along the farthest edge of her thoughts system, a voice whispered: *You can't walk away from the Wheelerhands for the peace and quiet of your room...You can't put your feelings first...Think of Kenny Joe...He was your friend, your comrade...You loved him like a beloved brother...Now his family needs your support..your comfort...your courage....*

"Miss Lettie Lou, Miss Effie Vi'let, I'll take you to Charity so we can check on how Mr. Big Joe's doing, and be with Miss Stella Dora."

At Charity Hospital, the three women, too upset to notice signs, passed through the emergency room entrance marked *Colored Only*. The place was littered with stretchers, bearing cut up colored, though it was quite early in the day for this regular knifing or razor carnage. These helpless victims were moaning, crying, screaming. Pain and pity filled the air—and stench.

A nurse directed them to the *White* section. There were only a few whites in the waiting room. Instantly Kendra spotted Stella Dora, ran up to her and threw her arms around her. They clung to each other.

"My Kenny Joe loved you with all his heart," choked Stella Dora, her kind blue eyes filled with pain and sorrow.

"And I loved him," she answered, and quickly changed the subject. "How's your husband?"

"I don't know. They wouldn't let me go in with him." Stella Dora started crying, and so did the Misses Wheelerhands. Falling tears cut roads into their cornstrached faces. By the time the doctor appeared, their eyes were drowned in tears; their faces road ruts.

"Mrs. Wheelerhand, I'm Dr. Godchaux." Doc was short and swarthy, with dark hair and eyes, and a handlebar mustache. "I did everything I could for your husband— I-I'm so very sorry—"

For a moment or so Stella Dora looked blank. "Doctor, a-a-are you —s-s-saying—my Big Joe's—d-d-dead?"

"Yes. I'm so sorry."

"Doctor those dirty rat Ko-reans not only killed my Kenny Joe, but my Big Joe, too. I hate the whole damn rotten lot of 'em. *I hate 'em.*"

"So do I, Mrs. Wheelerhand."

"My Kenny Joe's last letter said he was chasin' them Chinamen commonest from South Ko-reah back to the 38th parallel. I say to hell with them Chinamen commonest. To hell with that 38th parallel. I don't know what no 38th parallel looks like, let alone means. It ain't right-'n'-

reasonable that my only chil' should die for somethin' I don't know nothin' about. And now my big Joe, the man who gave me my Kenny Joe, is dead."

Kendra kissed Stella Dora's cheek.

"Oh, Kendra Lou, I forgot to introduce you to Dr. Godchaux. Doctor, this is Kendra Louise Applegate, my Kenny Joe's girlfriend. Ain't she beautiful? My Kenny Joe was beautiful, too. My Kenny Joe loved her to pieces, and she loved my Kenny Joe to pieces."

Hearing this, Kendra felt a slight sense of guilt, and made no reply.

Doc looked her up and down, his dark eyes briefly resting on her shiny mop of tangled curls, her dirty face, swollen lip, and ripped hem. "I'm so sorry, Miss Applegate.— Have you been in an accident?"

"I fell. But I'm all right."

"Excuse me a moment. I've got some pills for all of you ladies."

In a few minutes Doc returned and handed each woman a packet of pills. "Take two and go to bed."

"Before we can go home and go to bed, I got to see my Big Joe, and then we got to go see the undertaker," moaned Stella Dora, looking like she needed four of those pills instead of two.

Several hours later, Kendra parked the Dodge in front of her double. Aunt Molly Primrose, who was seated on the swing when the automobile pulled up, sprang to her feet and flew to meet her niece and the Wheelerhands.

"The neighbors told me all about it!" cried Molly Primrose, her arms outstretched. "I can't believe it!" She kissed the Wheelerhands and, when she got to Kendra, she stopped cold; and examined her as if she hadn't seen her before. "W-h-what happened to you?"

"I fell."

"A-a-are you all right?"

"Yes."

"Everybody come on in. I've got coffee and some sandwiches."

Kendra to herself: "I need to be alone for a while." Aloud:"Dr. Godchaux said Miss Stella Dora and the Misses Wheelerhands are to take two of these tablets and go to bed."—She turned to the Wheelerhands—"When you all wake up come have some supper with us."

"He told you to take two tablets, also," reminded Stella Dora.

Kendra nodded.

The Wheelerhands went to their double; the Applegates to theirs. Inside, the sunlight was streaming through the parlor windows. It streaked the floor, glinted across the furniture and up the walls. Kendra collapsed on the brightly slip-covered sofa, where big peonies, bathed in sunlight, were blooming on the chintz. Molly Primrose sat close by.

"Kendra Lou, I know Kenny Joe gettin' killed in Ko-reah and Big Joe droppin' dead, after readin' that terrible telegram, are two tragedies. But, by the look in your sad eyes, somethin' else *bad* had to happen; though for the life of me I can't imagine anythin' worse than the deaths of our best friends and neighbors."

Kendra lay limp and exhausted. She made no reply.

Molly Primrose patted her niece's hand. "Kendra Lou, you might can fool the Wheelerhands into thinking you're hurtin' for just Kenny Joe and Big Joe, but you can't fool me. Nor Gawd."

Still no reply. "Well, that's a beautiful dress you're wearin', but it's all dirty and the hem's torn. Where did you get it? I didn't make it."

"I bought the whole outfit at Holmes: my hat—it's in the Dodge—pocketbook, shoes. All for $100."

"A hundred dollars!" gasped her aunt. "Where did you get that kind of money? Rob your savings?"

"No. I put it all in the layaway. It took me six months to get it out."

'Well, why didn't you tell me—show it to me?"

"Because it was a secret. This morning I was suppose to marry Jack Trenchard, in this outfit. We were going to tie the knot in St. Bernard Parish, because marriages aren't listed in the paper in that Parish. Afterwards we were going to call you, pledge you to secrecy, and then go across the lake for our honeymoon."

"Who ever heard the like of my niece plannin' a secret weddin'? Not me."

"It was a secret because the Judge has a rule that young attorneys, entering his law firm, must be single; and remain so for two years. I was going to continue to live at home; Jack, at his rooming house."

"Live a lie, eh?—What about Kenny Joe?—Gawd rest his soul! I thought when you married it would be in a church, and Kenny Joe would be the groom."

"Kenny Joe was too much like a brother, to marry. Besides, I'm *in love* with Jack. Obviously he doesn't love me, because this morning he married Allison Edwards."

"Oh, my dahlin' Kendra Lou, how terrible."

Kendra shook her head in agreement, and then told her aunt the whole unbelievable tale. "There's more. Since Jack couldn't afford to buy me a wedding ring, I told him I would wear my mother's, and he could have my father's. Yesterday evening, when he was here, I gave him my parents' beautiful gold wedding bands. I guess he put my mother's ring on Allison's finger; my father's on his finger."

"Then they'll just have to take them off. Of all the cheap nerve. I can't believe my dahlin' dead sister-in-law's and my dear brother's weddin' bands are bein' worn by this Allison Edwards and Jack Trenchard. Your parents, this very minute, must be spinnin' in their graves."

"I suppose so."

"Kendra *Louise,* we got to go get your parents' weddin' bands back, *right now!"*

"We can't go get it now because they're probably already left on their honeymoon. We'll have to wait until they come back."

"I think we should call Judge Edwards *right now!"*

"I'd rather wait and see if Jack'll return the rings on his own. If not, we can call Judge Edwards. I don't want to go near Greenwood Manor. You'll have to go get it."

"Gladly. I'll gladly go after Tom's and Gen Rose's rings."

"There's something else, Tante. Jack had $200 of his own saved up, and wanted me to put my $200 savings with his. I did."

"Gawd save us!" groaned Aunt Molly Primrose.

"I also paid for his wedding suit, the suit I thought he'd wear when he married me. He never owned a tailor-made suit, and wanted one for *our* wedding. He made one payment, couldn't afford another, so I made the rest. His suit cost me $250, and he *wore it for Allison Edwards, not for me,"* cried and choked Kendra.

"Oh, Kendra Lou, I never heard the like of it. I'm sick for you. Come, let me put you to bed."

"I can't go to bed dirty like this."

"I'll clean you up, and then tend to those bo bos on your knees. I think your lip needs an ice bag. Have you eaten anythin'?"

"Nothing all day. I feel too sick to eat."

"You need some food in your stomach and a good night's sleep."

In Kendra's bedroom, Molly Primrose undressed her niece, got a pail of warm water, several washrags and went to work.

"Tante, burn this dress. Burn everything that's connected with this horrible day."

"I won't squander money like that," sharply replied her aunt. Still more sharply: "I'm gunna hem the dress and clean it. This is a perfect Sunday dress. You can wear it to church.— I know you told me why you was gunna let a JP marry you and not a priest, but I still can't believe it. None of this would've happened if your mind had been on your immortal soul. If you'd been thinkin' of the bliss of heaven and the pains of hell."

"Tante, when I'm around Jack I never think about my immortal soul.— The JP was a must, because of Judge Edwards' rule"

"Humph! Jack married the Judge's daughter. What happened to *that* rule?"

"Rules never apply to the people who make them."

"Who ever heard the like of that? Not me," muttered Molly Primrose as she tended her niece.

Kendra, washed, fed and tucked in bed, as if a little girl, slept.

On Sunday morning, Molly Primrose brought a breakfast tray to her weary niece. "Kendra Lou, good news. Jack didn't give your momma's weddin' band to Allison Edwards."

"How do you know?"

"Allison Edwards' weddin' picture's in the paper. She's seated in a chair, her right leg crossed, with her left hand restin' in her lap. She's got a diamond on her left finger."

"God, how could Jack afford a diamond when he was always borrowing lunch money?"

"The Ol' Judge must've paid for the ring.— Don't you worry about what Jack could afford or couldn't afford. Forget Jack Trenchard. He ain't worth a single thought."

"I know it. But I can't get him out of my mind. I hate him and I love him all at the same time. And I'm so jealous of Allison."

"Once you get over the first rage of jealousy you'll be all right."

"I hope so. I never dreamed anyone could hurt like this."

"We still gotta get your parents' rings back.—Now eat," urged her aunt.

Kendra ate a couple bites of her grits and egg, drank some creamy coffee, and then asked about Stella Dora, Lettie Lou and Effie Vi'let.

"Last night I fed them a good supper, and early this mornin' brought them breakfast.They told everybody on Starlight Street that you're prostrate with grief for Kenny Joe—and we gotta leave it that way. We don't want *no* body to know you been slighted. Men don't marry slighted girls. —Er, poor Stella Dora can't stop cryin'," said her aunt, shifting subjects."I think if she had the whole blasted Ko-rean Army and that fiend, Sung, in front of her, she'd wipe 'em out."

"I'd help her."

"Me, too."

Kendra didn't ask to see Allison's bridal picture; Molly Primrose burned that sheet of the Sunday paper, and then gave her niece a pill. She slept.

OnMonday morning, Kendra struggled awake and dragged herself out of bed. Depressed, listless and grieving, she went to work. Her boss, nasal twang, pig-eyed, Henri Prosper, a short, fat, bald man, with a fringe of hair at the back of his head, a snub nose, and stubby fingers, wasn't very understanding or sympathetic.

Seated at his desk—his feet barely touched the floor—Mr. Prosper looked at Kendra, over his horn-rimmed glasses, and said through his nose: "Good mornin', Miss Applegate. I read in this mornin's *Picayune* about your neighbor, *Lou*tenant Wheelerhand, bein' killed in Ko-reah, and his poor papa droppin' dead when he got the news. I'm so very sorry. —Er, I've also heard that you were engaged to *Lou*tenant Wheelerhand. I'm sorry for your loss but, since you weren't married, I can't give you paid time off to attend the funeral. You can, however, go to the funeral, but you-will-be-docked."

"The Wheelerhands are family. I'm going to the funeral."

"I see. I suppose you'll also want to go to Mr. Wheelerhand's funeral."

"Both Kenny Joe and his father will be buried on the same day."

"That's good.— But remember, no pay."

On Friday morning, Kenny Joe and Big Joe were laid to rest. Continually during the wake and funerals, the sparrowlike Wheelerhand sisters took turns chirping mournfully how Big Joe had dropped dead after he read *that awful telegram.* Kendra dreaded and hated that recital for the obvious pain it had caused Miss Stella Dora.

On Friday evening, kind, good, Miss Stella Dora lost her mind. Two weeks later, the Wheelerhand sisters asked the Applegates to drive Stella Dora to the State Insane Asylum, at Jackson, Louisiana. Neither the Applegates, the Wheelerhands or anybody else on Starlight Street had ever been past the New Orleans' city limits.They never went about, because all thought, except Kendra, New Orleans was the world.

Ever since Kendra had gotten her Dodge, she had been talking about going some where and having a good time. Any where, as long as it was past the city limits. And now, seated behind the wheel, wearing a pale yellow batiste blouse and a dark brown broadcloth circular skirt, at long last she was going some where. She was making a dreaded trip to the crazy house.

Her aunt, all in gray, hatted and gloved, sat beside her in the passenger seat; Stella Dora, an overnight redhead in a blue gingham housedress, sat in the back seat, squeezed in between the prim and proper Misses Wheelerhands, who were dressed in puce voile.

The five women were traveling on the winding river road, silently snaking their way to Jackson. The first to speak was Miss Effie Vi'let; she tried to go into her mournful recital of how Big Joe had dropped dead, but Molly Primrose interrupted with: "This road is so crooked it could brake a snake's back."

They all agreed; then Effie Vi'let tried again, but Stella Dora interjected: "Kendra Lou honey, don'tja wanna know how I got to be a red head?"

"I sure do. Tell me."

"I took a tube of Million Dollar red lipstick and colored the left side of my hair; I used Cherries in the Snow, to color my right side. I just had to be a red head for my first ride past the city limits. "

"You did a good job."

"I think so, too. Kendra Lou honey, *I'm a million dollar baby from the five-'n'-dime—*"

"S-s-shhhh," cried the Misses Wheelerhands.

"You know, I've never been out of New Orleans," went on Stella Dora, ignoring her sisters-in-law, "and now I'm goin' on a trip. Thank you, Kendra Lou honey, for takin' me."

Silence. Pitiful Stella Dora had no idea her first ride past the city limits would take her to the crazy house, for electric shock treatments.

As the Dodge rolled along, the scenery slipping by—the levy on the left; on the right, shrubbery, tall trees and scattered plantations—Stella Dora was constantly interrupting her sisters-in-law's morbid recital. Laughingly explaining, over and over, how easy it was to be a red head; and singing, "*I'm a million dollar baby from the five-'n'-dime.*"

After she had thoroughly gone over how easy it was to be a redhead, she moved on to "how them sneaky-eyed, yeller bellied Ko-reans, them gooks," had killed her Kenny Joe and her Big Joe. Every time she'd mention Kenny Joe and Big Joe's name, she'd sob a little.

When they got to the crazy house the Wheelerhands finally told Stella Dora what was going to happen to her, and she refused to get out the automobile.

Attendants had to be fetched; and two burly guys came to the Dodge, roughly grabbed Stella Dora, pinned her down, tied her up and forcibly dragged her off crying, kicking, and screaming: "Gawd help me! If my Big Joe and my Kenny Joe was alive, you'd never get away with this...Let go of me, you two brutes...You're hurtin' me...I'm Kenny Joe's mother...He gave his life for you, for everybody...He died for the 38th parallel— What does the 38th paralle look like. Some body tell me."—Silence—"Kendra Lou honey, you loved my Kenny Joe...Don't let Lettie Lou and Effie Vi'let put me away...I'm not crazy...I'm just hurtin' and I can't heal yet...Let go of me-e-e!...I'm Kenny Joe's mother...If you love me, Kendra Lou honey, help me...Please-e-e-e help me!...."

Kendra closed her brown-gold eyes, but the tears still trickled through her thick lashes, down onto her chalky-pale cheeks.

"Kendra Lou honey, if you won't help me, your aunt will...*Molleeee, Molleeee Primrose,* I been your neighbor for twenty-five years, and while you worked I helped raise your Kendra Lou...I helped you then, won't you please help me now?..."

Where soft-spoken and tiny Stella Dora got her lung capacity and strength was beyond Kendra. The burly attendants had a time with her.

While they wrestled with Stella Dora, dark storm clouds came boiling across the sky. A flash of lightning, a threatening clap of thunder and the heavens exploded with rain.

The Applegates, teary-eyed and choking, the Wheelerhands, stony-eyed, turned their backs on poor, struggling Stella Dora, and darted for the Dodge, clambering into their seats.

Fumbling, Kendra put the key in the ignition, pushed in the clutch, pressed the starter, yanked the gear stick into gear, popped the clutch and tore out the parking lot; Stella Dora's pregnant pleas and looks exploding before her brown-gold eyes and in her ears.

The Dodge clattered away from the crazy house as fast as its coughing, sputtering and jerking self would let it. As they fled, it rained a sopping rain.

Chapter Three

How many miles Kendra had put between her and the crazy house she didn't know. All she knew was she was trundling down a wet highway, heading for home, leaving behind Miss Stella Dora and that horrible shocking scene.

Silence reigned supreme, except for the rackety sounds of the old Dodge, the clunk and squeak of the wipers, moving slowly and noisily across the windshield, barely clearing off the splattering gray rain, and the whir of the tires rolling over swishing puddles, filled her ears.

Aunt Molly Primrose, her button blue eyes sad, her apple cheeks pale, was first to speak:"I ain't never seen the like of such a downpour. When I woke up this mornin' my rheumatism was givin' me the fits; so I shoulda known it was gunna rain cats and dogs."

She paused, her eyes straining to see the road. "Kendra Lou, this storm's gettin' worse. The puddles in the road are big as pools, and the wipers can't keep up with the rain," she said; and, using a Kleenex, wiped the windshield in front of her, and some of Kendra's. "You better pull off the road."

"I can't. We'll sink on those soft shoulders. I need to find an off road.—Give me your Kleenex so I can wipe the rest of my side," said Kendra, her left hand holding tightly to the steering wheel, her gold-brown eyes glued to the road.

"Here's the Kleenex," said her aunt. "M'm—M'm—M'm—my side's foggin' up again," she added, disgusted. "I guess I'll have to keep wipin' it all the way to New Orleans,"

"I'll wipe the back winder; it's fogged up, too," observed Miss Effie Vi'let, using her hankie.

"Good," replied Kendra. "I can't see a thing out the back window. My side's like yours, Tante, it keeps fogging up."

"I wish you could pull off this big highway. Drivin' in all this pourin' down rain makes me nervous."

"As soon as an off road comes up, I'll take it."

A few minutes later, Kendra left the main highway and, after driving a short distance, cried: "Oh, no I'm in a private driveway!...Look...Straight ahead there's a big building, and here comes an automobile." She veered to the right, giving the automobile plenty room to pass.

The on-coming old blue Studebaker, pulled alongside Kendra's Dodge and stopped.The rain, slanting in the opposite direction, allowed the young driver, who had a cheerful good-looking face, to roll down his window. He wore a black leather glove on his left hand.

"Hello...I'm Dr. Reed...Are you here to visit someone?"

Kendra cracked her window enough to talk. To her amazement, Dr. Reed resembled Kenny Joe. After her first wide incredulous stare, she stammered: "I'm, I'm Kendra Applegate, and er, n-no, we're not here to visit any one. My wipers aren't working too good and, since it's raining so hard, I thought I better get off the main highway. If this road is private property, I didn't mean to intrude."

"You're not intruding. Just ahead is the leper colony. The only one in the U.S. for lepers; however, you're welcome to sit in the waiting room or park adjacent to the hospital, under the shed."

Kendra hoped her horror hadn't broadcast itself in her eyes. "My God," she said to herself, "I've just left the crazy house and landed at the leper colony in Carville, Louisiana." Aloud: "Er, thank you—I think we'll take shelter under that shed."

Doc drove off; Kendra parked under the narrow open shed, which had a tin roof that leaked-leaked-leaked. The women, goggled eyed, stared in shocked silence at the leper hospital, which loomed large before them. Every weatherboard looked as if it were infested with leprosy germs and seeping sores. No one spoke. They just stared, hypnotized.

The storm's intensity soon worsened. Sheets of rain, driven in by the wind, whipped the front, sides and back of the Dodge, with a fiendish force; lightning lit up the sky; thunder crashed; and the wind howled furiously, compounding the women's fear. Their eyes, drawn like a magnate, remained on the hospital.

"Lawsey, I can't believe we're sittin' out here, a few feet from dirty lepers, in a ragin' storm," softly remarked Miss Lettie Lou, her voile dress damp and wrinkled, her piled up hair, looking like meringue gone flat, broke the silence. "For all we know we might be in a hurricane, and the wind carryin' all them leprosy germs to this here automoébile. I got the willies," she added shivering.

The Applegates, also damp and disheveled, shifted in their seats to face the white-faced Wheelerhand sisters more directly. The lines in the Wheelerhands' faces were caked with cornstarch.

"Of all the places to stop for shelter—Gawd save us!—" replied Molly Primrose, sighing and shivering. "Oh, well I guess any port in a storm'll do. Let's hope we ain't in no hurricane."

"We're not," assured Kendra, coming out of her daze. "If sitting outside is bothering you all, we can go inside. I've got a big umbrella in the trunk. I'll get it and walk one of you, at a time, to the waiting room—"

"Kendra Lou, that old black cotton umberrella's got broken ribs and is full of holes," discouraged her aunt.

"It'll help keep some of the rain off you, and you'll feel safer inside."

"No-o-o-o, we won't! It's bad enough settin' one foot on the premises of a leper hospital, let alone sittin' amongst them lepers in their waitin' room, their germs crawlin' all over us."

"*We're with you, Molly Primrose!*" joined in the Wheelerhands, their wet dresses clinging to them.

"Just being here makes my flesh crawl," tacked on Molly Primrose.

"Speaking of flesh, mine feels itchy all over," complained Miss Effie Vi'let, just above a whisper, and then started scratching. "I'm sure under this here shed must be full of leprosy germs."

"Sitting under this shed or in the lepers' waiting room, won't cause you to catch leprosy," muttered Kendra, out of patience. "You feel itchy because it's hot in here. Just crack your window a little, and you'll feel better."

"We-ell, maybe you're right," agreed Miss Effie Vi'let, cracking her window. "That's a lit'le better."

"Did you all notice how much Dr. Reed resembled Kenny Joe," remarked Kendra, shifting the subject.

They all did. —"I also noticed," added Miss Lettie Lou, "that he wore a black leather glove on his left hand. I bet he's got *it.*"

"I bet he does, too," put in Miss Effie Vi'let. "They say the fingers go first," she added, her white sharp face, all knowing.

"And he talked face to face to you, Kendra Louise," pointed out Miss Lettie Lou. "I wish we had some of that Dr. Tichenor's antiseptic so you could gargle your throat good—kill them leper germs."

"I got a bit of sherry with me," offered Miss Effie Vi'let. "You wanna swoller a drop or two, Kendra Louise?"

"No, thanks. I don't have any leper germs in me.—Tante, where's that old dilapidated string bag of yours with the coffee thermos?"

"Right here at my feet. You ain't thinkin' of drinkin' no coffee with all them leprosy germs flyin' around, are you?"

"It's safe to have a cuppa coffee.— Let's have one."

"Lawsey, if you two are gunna drink coffee a few feet away from lepers, Lettie Lou and me might as well eat a banana-'n'-a-ham sandwich. My string bag's full of food. Plenny food for us all."

"No thanks," said the Applegates.— "Here's your coffee, Kendra Lou."

"Hold it a minute, Tante, while I wipe away some of this fog."

"Lawsey, don't wipe off that fog," softly cried Miss Effie Vi'let."That fog's a curtain. It's keepin' them lepers from spyin' on us, from those long winders, like we was a bunch of monkeys in a cage at Audubon Park. I don't wanna sit out here and let lepers watch y'all drinkin' coffee and us sippin' sherry-'n'-eatin'-bananas-'n'-ham sandwiches."

Kendra quit wiping. She took a deep breath and let it out slowly. Molly Primrose, anticipating a come back from her niece, laid her left hand on Kendra's right thigh, as if she were anchoring a small child about to stray. She followed up with a pinch.

"Ouch!" cried Kendra, rubbing her thigh.

Bang! Bang! The older women jumped.

"Good glory! them lepers are shootin' at us!" gasped Miss Effie Vi'let. "This is too much excitement for my heart. My palpitations!"

"That was a pine cone banging the roof. It'll happen again, so don't palpitate any more," was Kendra's unsympathetic reply.

"For a pine cone, it sure sounded like cannon fire," remarked Molly Primrose.

"A tin roof always magnifies sounds," added Miss Lettie Lou, all knowing.

Silence.

Kendra drank her coffee, and what she said next ended all talk concerning lepers. "When the rain slacks up some, let's go back and get Miss Stella Dora. Take her home where she belongs."

Bang! Bang!

"There goes my heart again—them palpitations."

"Molly Primrose, did you hear what Kendra Louise just said?"

"I sure did. I think it's a good idea."

"*Stella Dora stays* where she is," flatly and firmly stated Miss Lettie Lou, with a hardness and coldness of stone in her face.

"Exactly where she is," softly repeated Miss Effie Vi'let.

"Stella Dora's pine black crazy," quietly went on Miss Lettie Lou. "A right-minded, educated woman never woulda made such a show of herself, back there. Our trip shoulda been pleasant and peaceful, but Stella Dora made it tough. She displayed no sense of shame. Her only hope is shock treatments. We can't have a crazy woman around the house."

"Why not?" asked Kendra."Southern folks seldom put their people away. If they did, the streets of New Orleans would be empty. Most every family is either got a kooky cousin; a crazy nephew; or an eccentric aunt. No body seems to mind.They hide them in the attic; and let them out at night, to catch the breeze. Take our neighbor, old lady Pujowl, her family lets her roam at will, and she's pine black crazy."

"She can't help it," put in Aunt Molly Primrose."She gets it from her momma. Lisette Gaudet, Gawd rest her soul, was pine black crazy."

"Well, nobody can even walk on old lady Pujowl's banquette without her charging after them with her heavy headed cane, cursing and hollering her head off. Threatening everybody she comes in contact with. She carries that cane, not for walking but for hitting.

"If she's sitting on her gallery, that heavy headed black cane, resting againt her knee, and sees a poor little sparrow land on her lawn, she flies down the steps swinging her cane and cursing at the tiny creature. And when she walks to the streetcar stop, you better pray you're not going in the same direction. She curses all the way."

"Funny thing though," interjected Molly Primrose, "once Bea-actress Pujowl's on the streetcar she stops all that whoopin'-'n'-a hollerin'-'n'-a cursin'. When she gets off at Canal and St. Charles, she starts up again."

"If anybody deserves to be pinned down, tied up and dragged into the crazy house, it's old lady Pujowl," observed Kendra.

"I'm sure if Bea-actress' son, Poochie Pujowl, and his nice wife, Ruby Faye, had her examined, the doctor would declare Bea-actress mindless, and put her away," said Miss Lettie Lou, in a calm voice.

Bang! Bang!

"Of course they would," tacked on Miss Effie Vi'let, grabbing her chest. "I wish those pine cones would have pity on my poor heart"

"My point is, up until you all sprung the crazy house on Miss Stella Dora, she was never wild and violent. All she's doing is grieving her heart out, and the kind of pain she's got isn't easy to handle"

"Nevertheless, she's still out of her mind," softly insisted Miss Lettie Lou.— "Who in their right mind would color her hair with lipstick?"

"A lot of women color their hair red. Instead of using dye, Miss Stella Dora used lipstick. That's not so bad. Let's go get her."

"*No,*" softly and emphatically replied Miss Lettie Lou.

While this to-do was going on, Molly Primrose had used all manner of sign language, to silence her niece, but had failed. Not knowing what to say to end the argument, said something stupid: "Gladys Gooseneck, the mid-wife who delivered Kendra Lou, Gawd rest her soul, said if Kendra Lou hadn't come feet first, Gen Rose might've lived."

Kendra grimaced; her hand went to the gold locket around her neck, and she pressed it to her heart.

"Lawsey, I wouldn't believe a thing that Goose, Gladys Gooseneck, ever said," murmured Miss Effie Vi'let. "She attended Stella Dora, and Lettie Lou and me was suppose to help, but never got the chance."

"What happened?" asked Molly Primrose, surprised.

"That Goose took out a rag and a bottle of ether and soaked the rag with the ether. Then had Lettie Lou sniff that old rag to see if it was potent enough, when the time came, to knock out Stella Dora."

"That Goose made me sniff it three times," interjected Miss Lettie Lou, an inflection in her soft flat voice.

"On the third sniff, Lettie Lou fell out. Seeing my sister out cold, brought on my palpitations, and that's when the Goose tricked me into sniffing that ether rag. When we both woke up, Kenny Joe was a couple hours old."

Kendra smothered a laugh; Molly Primrose, still surprised, said: "Well, who ever heard the like of that? Not me."

"Let's get back to Miss Stella Dora," said Kendra, frowning.

"Don't frown like that, Kendra *Louise*, you'll hurt your good looks," cautioned her aunt.

"In-the-first-place," went on Kendra, "why can't Miss Stella Dora be treated at Charity for her depression and grief?"

"Because Charridy isn't equipped to give shock treatments," replied Miss Lettie Lou. "Dr. Rondaux said Stella Dora would never be right again without 'lectric shock treatments. He said if the shocks work, she should be better, if she's ever gunna get better, in, say, six months. He gave us no hope. She may have to stay locked up—forever."

Bang! Bang!

"Oh, my poor heart," moaned Miss Effie Vi'let.

"You know," said Molly Primrose, again changing the subject, like a popgun,"have you all noticed how Lizzie Slapp Springmeyer, of late, hasn't been showin' off her operation scar?"

"Yes; and I'm so glad," replied Miss Effie Vi'let. "Poor Lizzie Slapp Springmeyer is really and truly maimed. When Dr. Belcher cut off her left breast he made a crater in her chest; he even gouged under her arm, all the way to her elbow. It's horrible. I never saw anythin' like it in my livin' life. Have you, Lettie Lou?"

"No; and I don't wanna see anythin' like it again. It looks like her flesh was scalded raw. She shouldn't have let that Dr. Butcher, oops, I mean Belcher, cut off her breast."

"She said she had no choice. She said she caught a disease called cancer. I've never heard of it. As far as I know, no body else on Starlight Street has cancer, or has heard of it, either. I wonder who she caught that cancer from?"

"Why can't Miss Stella Dora stay home and be taken care of at Charity's mental ward, without shock treatment?" persisted Kendra.

"I do believe Lizzie Slapp caught cancer from that old cat of hers—Preggie," said Miss Effie Vi'let, ignoring Kendra. "As you all know, cats carry seven deadly diseases in their tiny moufs, and never ever should be allowed in the house. Lizzie Slapp was bad about lettin' that old cat in her house."

"Preggie's been dead for years," put in Kendra, disgusted, "and couldn't give Mrs. Springmeyer cancer."

"Dead or not don't make no never mind. Preggie, when she was alive and in *that* house, gaped and let out them seven deadly diseases, and—"

"Name them seven deadly diseases," demanded Kendra, eyes flashing.

"Diphtheria, for one," replied Miss Lettie Lou.

"Cancer, for another," answered Miss Effie Vi'let.

"Scarlet fever," contributed Aunt Molly Primrose.

"Enough," muttered Kendra, gesturing.

"As I was sayin'," went on Miss Effie Vi'let, "that old Preggie gaped on Lizzie Slapp, and let out that cancer germ, and it landed on her left breast."

"You know," submitted Molly Primrose, "one good thing come of Lizzie Slapp's cancer, and that is she got out the habit of liftin' her dress above her knees, showin' off her long pink drawers. She was all the time daintily tip-toein' around the neighborhood, her drawers showin'."

"I know," breathed Miss Lettie Lou. "Lizzie Slapp—she's a reg'lar Mardi Gras, that one, with her spiky pink hair, that reminds you of a pokiepine; her red painted mouth; her dresses every color of the rainbow—always held up her dress, as if she was walkin' in a flood of water, and didn't wanna get her hem wet."

"One things for sure she not only dresses to please herself, but gives color and life to the dullest of days," joined in Miss Effie Vi'let. "I used to be so embarrassed seein' Lizzie Slapp sashayin' down the middle of Starlight Street, headin' for the streetcar stop, her dress hiked high above her knobby knees, her drawers showin'. I'm glad that's out of her system. Of course there's that forgetful side of her we've got to contend with. One minute you tell her somethin', and in the next, she straight off forgets it. You gotta tell it again."

"Besides her forgetfulness she's deaf as a post, plus she's turned man crazy," observed Miss Lettie Lou. "She's after Lolotte DuPuy's nice-lookin' quiet bachelor brother, Antlee Theaud and his guv'ment pension."

"Moochin' Mamie TuJax's also after him and his check," added Miss Effie Vi'let. "And both of them are old enough to be his mother. I guess which ever one can out live the other will get him."

"You know, those two forgot about dignified and distinguished Otis Peckinpaw and his social security check," submitted Miss Lettie Lou. "Of course, Otis is just livin' to escape dyin'. If anybody should get Otis, I sup'ose it ought to be his neighbor, Miss Lavinia Gervaise."

"Miss Lavinia Gervaise is a spinster and will never marry. Besides, Otis Peckinpaw's a born bachelor, who's so tight he squeezes a penny till is screams. A wife of his would never see the color of cash. In a few years Otis'll need to be taken care of; and no older woman in her right mind wants that," concluded Miss Effie Vi'let.

"Forget about Otis Peckinpaw," said Miss Lettie Lou. "Let's get back to Lizzie Slapp. She's not only man crazy, but she's nervy as well. She's always pesterin' Kendra Louise to drive her all the way to Airline Highway, to Swaggerman's, so she can make groceries."

"And her moochin' a ride, with poor dead Lester Erwin's old green Hudson sittin' in the garage these past ten years," offered Miss Effie Vi'let.

"Poor Lester Erwin, if he hadn't had that dead liver, he'd be alive today," lamented Miss Lettie Lou. "That dead liver turned him yeller and then took him."

"And if he hadn't had that awful port wine birthmark on his fair face and neck, he'd have been a handsome man," observed Miss Effie Vi'let. "That birthmark ruined him," she added, wrinkling her nose in distaste.

"I don't know why Gawd lets babies be born with them nasty-lookin' birthmarks on their pretty faces and not on their lit'le ugly behinds. Gawd treats some folks dirty," offered Miss Lettie Lou.

A terrible crash of thunder exploded overhead, shaking the shed. The women blessed themselves; and, for a second or so, they were quiet. Then Miss Lettie Lou started up again: "Maybe we better not be findin' fault with Gawd, cause that's the wickedest thing we can do. His ways are mysterious, and we can't boss Him. He could send us a judgment. Anyway, Lizzie Slapp hasn't moved that green Hudson since Lester Erwin died. I bet those tires are rotten to the rims."

"They are," verified Molly Primrose. "But Lizzie Slapp says she starts up the Hudson every mornin', and lets it run a good while to build up the battree."

"Too bad some doctor couldn't have rubbed off Lester Erwin's ugly birthmark."

"Some things can't be rubbed off. Can't be changed," softly murmured Molly Primrose. "One of 'em is bein' born with a port wine birthmark on your face."

Bang! Bang!

"Lawsey, my heart! You know, Lizzie Slapp was a produstunt before she married Lester Erwin, who, up until his marriage, danced and played poker. He quit the dancin' because Lizzie Slapp told him the sure fire way to open the gates of hell was to dance up to 'em. But he didn't quit the Saturday night poker playin'. Now Lizzie Slapp says when she goes to meet Lester Erwin on the other side she's worried that he won't be standin' at the bottom of the golden stairs to help her walk up them steps into heaven, because he just might be playin' poker with the devil.

"Lizzie Slapp says if Lester Erwin ain't there, waitin' for her, she's gunna try not to go straight off to the judgment bar. She's gunn try to look around. Try to find our first parents. Adam and Eve. Mainly Adam, because she wants to tell him he didn't act gentlemanly when he was confronted about that apple business. He kept a-hollerin' 'Eve made me do it...Eve made me do it.' She thinks Adam shoulda taken his licks without draggin' Eve into it. Of course, if Lester Erwin's waitin' for her, not playin' poker, she won't have a chance at Adam."

"If Lester Erwin's playin' poker, I guarantee it'll be with his good buddy, Oscar TuJax," put in Molly Primrose. "Oscar died a week after Lester Erwin; and Moochin' Mamie claimed Lester Erwin called him to the other side just so he'd have somebody to play poker with. And lazy loungin' Oscar, who always had a pain handy, jumped at the chance to die. I don't think Moochin' Mamie was mad at Lester Erwin for callin' Oscar, because he was a bad husband. He never beat Moochin' Mamie, but every day he hurt her."

"Why did you all hustle off Miss Stella Dora, without getting a second opinion?" persisted Kendra, like a cat waiting at a mousehole.

"Kendra Louise, you're old enough to know it's not nice to ask personal questions," calmly answered Miss Lettie Lou. "I know you was engaged to marry Kenny Joe, my dear departed nephew, but fate fixed that. So our affairs are none of your business. Some time fate intercedes for the best. I'll just pretend I didn't hear that question."

Hearing Miss Lettie Lou say she'd rather see Kenny Joe dead than married to her, was only a pinprick, but it still felt like a stab. Kendra, however, ignored it. "I know it wasn't because of money. She's got Kenny Joe's insurance—$10,000 from the government; plus Mr. Big Joe's insurance."

Miss Lettie Lou removed her gold-rimmed spectacles—her eyes stuck out more than usual—and, with a palsied hand, wiped her glasses. "I'd like to know who-told-you-that? Who told you our personal business?" she asked, staring stony-faced at Kendra, before replacing her glasses. Her eyes nearly bulging out of her head.

"Miss Stella Dora...the day before the funerals."

"It's true the guv'ment gave her $10,000 for Kenny Joe's death; but Big Joe's insurance barely covered his burial—"

"Miss Stella Dora told me Mr. Big Joe left her a $5,000 life insurance policy, plus he had a burial policy. She showed them to me."

"*Oh-o-o-o*— Stella Dora had no right to do that. Just goes to show you she's nuts."

Kendra looked hard at both the Wheelerhand sisters, and saw their faces had undergone an altered change from fragile sparrows to two tough old birds—chicken hawks, ready to devour Miss Stella Dora.

"Why?"

"I repeat that's none of your business. Besides, Stella Dora in her condition and lack of education, couldn't handle that kind of money."

"Well, who's handling her money?"

"Lawsey," interrupted Miss Effie Vi'let, "it woulda been so much better for all concerned if Stella Dora had dropped dead instead of our dear Joe. I wish we'd buried Stella Dora and not Big Joe."

"Gawd made a terrible mistake takin' Big Joe and not Stella Dora," though His ways are mysterious, and we can't boss Him, cause he might send us a judgment," softly wailed Miss Lettie Lou.

"Maybe when she goes dodo tonight she won't wake up tomorrow. That would be for the best," said Miss Effie Vi'let.

Kendra and her aunt stiffened. "Well, who's handling Miss Stella Dora's money?" repeated Kendra, through tight lips.

"I am," quietly replied Miss Lettie Lou. "Stella Dora signed over her money to me. At first I had a lot of trouble convincin' her she didn't need that kind of money now that the two people she loved most in the world were dead. I had to hammer that fact into her head."

Kendra groaned.

"I also had a hard time persuading her that she was unworthy of so much money, because of her lack of education."

"But you and Miss Effie Vi'let *are* worthy?"

"Y-e-s. We *deserve* the money."

"So you got her, while in the midst of grief, to sign over both Kenny Joe's and Mr. Big Joe's policy?"

"I did. We did."

"Then I guess she's pine black crazy after all."

Aunt Molly Primrose's pale cheeks went back being apple red. She gave Kendra a killer pinch.

"If you're after my thigh, you got it that time."

"I'm after your tongue," answered her aunt, just above a whisper, and then changed the subject. "Can you all believe Ruthie Hartman let her floor walker son, Giross, move her off Starlight Street all the way to Met-tree, of all places? The only time any one moves from Starlight Street is when the undertaker comes and gets 'em.—Why, Met-tree is a godforsaken place. Nothing's there. Just wilderness, wild animals and a few scattered houses. I tell you it's the back of beyond.

"At Kenny Joe's and Big Joe's funerals, Ruthie told me she misses her neighbors and Starlight Street somethin' awful. She ain't got no neighbors, no body, in Met-tree. That floor walker, Giross Junior, with that boutonniere in his lapel, needs to have his mind examined."

"If you ask me, he needs to be hoss whipped, like the no-count son he is," softly put in Miss Effie Vi'let. "If ol' Giross Senior was alive, that floor walker, Giross Junior, with that wooden expression on his face and that boutonniere in his lap-pel, woulda never got away with movin' his mother to Met-tree. Thank Gawd he didn't move her clear away from New Orleans. She'd gone and died dead by now."

"I'm glad Ruthie's gone from Starlight Street," said Miss Lettie Lou. "She was a reg'lar borrower. Every day, for twenty-five years, she borrowed our broom so she could sweep her steps and banquette. Years ago when she first asked to borrow our broom, I asked if she didn't have a broom of her own. She said she did, but she didn't want to use it on her dirty steps and banquette."

"That's Ruthie for you; crazy as a June bug," laughed Molly Primrose. "Every Saturday afternoon, for twenty-five years, Ruthie's come over to my house with a big Mason jar for me to fill up with roses."

"Why, Ruthie had more flowers than you, Molly Primrose," said Miss Effie Vi'let.

"I told Ruthie that, and she said 'If I cut my flowers, I won't be able to enjoy them on the bushes. This way, if you cut yours and give me a bouquet, I can enjoy flowers both inside my house and outside.'"

"I'm glad that cheeky Ruthie's moved," quietly said Miss Lettie Lou.

"I bet nobody in Met-tree's loanin' her a broom or givin' her cut flowers," put in Miss Effie Vi'let.

"I wish Ruthie hadn't rented her double to that old man crazy moocher, Mamie TuJax," mumbled Miss Lettie Lou.

"You know," offered Molly Primrose, "our good Eyetalian neighbor, Tony Ganucci, hinted to Rosa about movin' to Gentilly. Now *Gentilly* is the back, back of beyond. Rosa got that notion out of Tony's Latin head mighty fast. She threatened him with the rollin' pin."

"Those Eyetalians are so emotional and so prolific," softly mumbled Miss Lettie Lou. "Rosa's *that way* again."

The three older women nodded.

"Ol' Ganucci sneaks her out at night for a walk," tacked on Miss Lettie Lou, winking significantly.

"Rosa's havin' a late-in-life baby," explained Miss Effie Vi'let, no doubt for Kendra's benefit. "It'll be a relief to the folk of Starlight Street, I can tell you, when Rosa's periods are finished and done with. I wonder if that good-lookin' Sonny, way over in Ko-reah, knows his momma's *that way*. I hope not. It might affect how he shoots."

"Speaking of Sonny," put in Miss Lettie Lou, "Tony Ganucci better poison Sonny's o'l Tom cat, Sholar Picarara, now that a baby's on the way. Cats are known to take a baby's breath. Smother 'em to death. Y'all know Sholar Picarara eats spaghetti and meatballs. I never knew an Eyetalian Tom cat before. He needs to be poisoned."

"Mr. Ganucci would never poison his son's cat," cried Kendra.

Molly Primrose could see a terrible row coming on, so she quickly cut in, trying to direct the conversation into another channel. "That good-lookin' Sonny didn't wait to be drafted. He joined the Army. Let's hope the dear boy gets out of Ko-reah alive."

This harmless remark fanned the fire further, for Miss Lettie Lou replied: "Sonny had to join the Army. He needed a job. Sonny's not too smart. Now take Junior Foughtenberry, he's the supervisor of the night shift at the Post Office. He's smart. Real smart. He didn't join the Army, thanks to his momma, Elmyra, who's a born boss and knows how to manage men, got him to join the Gawd. Now all Junior has to do is go to Camp Poke Loosieanna, two weeks out the year, for maneuvers.

"If only Kenny Joe had been smart, he'd have joined the Gawd, and never allowed himself to be drafted into the reg'lar army. I never dreamed Junior Foughtenberry was smarter than our Kenny Joe."

"Joining the Guard is an easy out for *draft dodgers and slackers*," responded Kendra, hot as a hornet. "I hope Junior's Unit gets shipped over, so I can *laugh* my head off. Junior could *never* be smarter than Kenny Joe—Junior is just a plain old *Fought*—enberry."

Molly Primrose, red-cheeked and short of breath, delivered another killer pinch to Kendra's thigh, and then for the umpteenth time changed the subject: "Do you all remember the day Lizzie Slapp was carryin' on about that old fallin' down picket fence that separated her property from the Ganucci's?

"She said it was an eye-sore, and demanded that Tony Ganucci tear it down and put up a new one. She also wanted it whitewashed. At the time, Tony was waterin' the daylilies along that fallin' down fenceline, and aimed the hose right for Lizzie Slapp's big mouth. He nearly drowned her before she could scream for help. Somebody cawled the po-leece, but, by the time they got there, Lizzie Slapp was as dry as a bone. No evidence."

"I say we go get Miss Stella Dora and let her use some of her insurance money to pay for her treatment, right at home."

"I already told you, Kendra Louise, an uneducated woman, such as Stella Dora, don't deserve no $15,000," replied Lettie Lou, nettled. "She'd just fritter it away on lipstick and fingernail polish."

"And maybe spend a good $5,000 on cornstarch," muttered Kendra beneath her breath.

"She better be grateful the State is giving her free medical, because I'm not about to furnish funds for her treatment."

"But *that's* her funds!"

"I already told you she can't manage *that* kind of money."

Kendra and her aunt briefly cut their eyes toward each other, exchanging knowing looks, and then transferred them to the back seat.

"I didn't know if you weren't educated you didn't deserve a little money. No education, no inheritance. Is that it? I suppose you'll dole out a dollar a day to Miss Stella Dora when she comes home."

"If she comes home," tersely replied Miss Lettie Lou, staring hard at Kendra. Through the lens of her glasses, her bulging eyes said as plain as speech: "We understand each other now."

Kendra knew that God watched over birds, and said to herself: "I wonder if He's watching these two white-faced chicken hawks." Aloud: "Miss Lettie Lou, I can't let you get away with this. As Kenny Joe, who's in heaven, is my witness, I'm bound and determined to see that Miss Stella Dora comes home and gets her money back."

"Kendra Louise, if you felt that way, why did you drive Stella Dora to the lunatic asylum? If you hadn't driven her, we'd have had no choice but to have her treated at Charridy. It's all your doin's. It's your fault."

Kendra looked stricken. The truth lay before her, hideous and bare. To herself: "Those two crazy chicken hawks—should be locked up, not Stella Dora—they've tricked me into being Judas. If only I hadn't been so torn up over Jack jilting me, so busy having a pity party for myself, I would've seen through this terrible scheme."

"Who ever heard the like of that?" marveled Molly Primrose. "Not me. Been knowing you two all these years, and never dreamed you was tricksters."

"Face the facts, Tante, they're two conniving female Judases."

"Gawd save us, Kendra Lou, don't bring Judas in on this!" She quickly changed the subject again. "The Ganucci family is also goin' to Swaggerman's to make groceries. It looks like everybody on Starlight Street is runnin' off to make groceries at Swaggerman's. I'm not...and never will. Everybody's abandoning' poor Mr. Pizzla, and his bike boy, Benny Luigi— This Swaggerman's place is a big barn. You go there and they give you a big buggy, and you gotta fill it up yourself. Walk up and down aisles lookin' for your groceries.

"That's silly and tirin' when all you have to do is either call up Mr. Pizla, tell him what you want and he sends the items over with Benny Luigi. Or you can go to Mr. Pizla's store, give him your list and he walks all around his store and finds those items for you."

"Tante, Pizla's a chiseler. He cheats. I caught him with his hand on the scale. And his grocery store's funky dirty."

"I still like my corner grocery store. If this keeps up, all the Mom and Pop groceries stores are gunna go out of business. We gunna progress outselves out of existence. You saw what happened when the 'lectric icebox came out—no more Faithful Dennis Boy—no more icehouse."

"Molly Primrose, you better put your niece on notice about mindin' her own business," muttered Miss Lettie Lou, through tight thin lips, a deep splash of red fighting its way through all that cornstarch.

Before Molly Primrose could answer, Effie Vi'let said: "You know, Kendra Louise, we really love Stella Dora. At first, we was shocked when our brother, a math teacher, married a girl who worked at the five-'n'-dime—"

"Shush—don't tell her that!" admonished Lettie Lou.

"She's guessed it by now, with Stella Dora singin', all the way from New Olreans to the crazy house, *I'm a Million Dollar Baby from the Five-'n'-Dime.*' She let the cat out the bag herself, and after pledgin' she'd never tell.— Kendra Louise, our brother married an uneducated clerk, from the dime store. He disgraced us. We tried to discourage Big Joe in his choice—"

"But he wouldn't lissen to us," cut in Miss Lettie Lou. "The poor man was infatuated."

"It was dreadful, our only brother marryin' a mere clerk, though nice-'n'-pretty-'n'-kind," submitted Miss Effie Vi'let. "Had she only gone to Normal School and become a teacher—"

"She could've talked like you: 'chirren; he don't,'" mumbled Kendra,

"W-w-what's that? What did you say, Kendra Louise?"

"I only said chirren," repeated Kendra in a mumble. "Nothing."

"Well, you know what people think of dime store clerks," said Miss Effie Vi'let, shaking her meringue head and throwing up her hands.

"No, I don't. I think the dime store would be a natural for Miss Stella Dora. It's a cheerful place, full of personality—with clerks at every counter, ready, willing and able to serve you.

"A candy counter—all the yummy chocolate you can imagine; a mouthwaterng bakery; a delicious-smelling lunch counter, full of the clutter and clatter of plates and glasses; music; parakeets and canaries in brass cages, chirping; a jewelry counter, with an engraver who can put your name, right then and there, on a bracelet or a locket; and the toy counter, with some mechanical toy or another performing, can entertain kids and adults all day long. I bet she worked at the toy counter."

"She did," answered both Wheelerhand sisters.

"I couldn't think of a better place for Miss Stella Dora to work. Did Kenny Joe die not knowing his dear mother, before she married, had worked at the dime store, as a toy counter clerk?"

"Yes. We're grateful for that," replied both Wheelerhand sisters, in hushed voices.

Kendra's eyes misted. She wiped them, and then addressed Miss Effie Vi'let. "You went to school to learn to teach kindergarten. Miss Stella Dora didn't need schooling to teach, she was a natural born teacher."

"Are you saying Stella Dora could do *my* job?"

"Yes; and then some. When she told Kenny Joe and me stories and read to us, she used my name for the little girl and Kenny Joe's for the little boy. She played and laughed with us. And when we were bad she never made us feel as if we were really bad. No kindergarten teacher ever did that for me.

"Miss Stella Dora made us say our morning prayers; Grace before meals; taught us manners; the Pledge to the Flag; and to sing *God Bless America*. She taught us our ABCs, to count to ten, to share, to have fun.

"When the ice-cream man came by and she only had one nickel, she dug down deep in the sofa until she found another; so both Kenny Joe and me could have an ice-cream.— To me there wasn't a better kindergarten teacher around," ended Kendra, breathless.

"Stella Dora was wonderful with my Kendra Lou," added Molly Primrose, blinking back tears. "I don't know what I'd have done without her."

"You paid for her services, Molly Primrose. We're not faultin' Stella Dora's babysittin' abilities," explained Miss Lettie Lou. "She's just uneducated, that's all Effie Vi'let and me are sayin'. It's not her fault. I guess you could blame Big Joe for marryin' beneath himself. Stella Dora married up."

"And when a *man* marries beneath himself, he hurts himself," tacked on Miss Effie Vi'let. "Not like when a woman marries beneath herself; the husband can't hurt her."

"Lawsey, Kendra Louise, I don't know what's come over you. You're makin' this out to be tragic when it's trivial," added Miss Lettie Lou.

"It's trivial to *you* because you're not in the crazy house. You've got Miss Stella Dora's home and her money. To me that's tragic."

Two disgruntled "humphs" came from the chicken hawks.

"And another thing, you two sound as if living, all these years, with your brother's wife was a penance."

A look of martyred endurance crossed their white faces. "It was."

"Lucky you performed that penance because, since Mr. Big Joe paid the rent, if you had found fault with Miss Stella Dora, I bet you'd have been out in the street in no time flat," brazenly said Kendra.

"Oh, I don't think Big Joe was *that* crazy about Stella Dora, to go against *us*, his sisters," put in Miss Effie Vi'let. "It was her good looks that captured him, not her mind. I thought, as soon as she faded, Big Joe would rue the day he married her. But she didn't fade. She's well preserved."

"That's enough," said Miss Lettie Lou in a repressive tone. "Where are my good gloves. I've lost my new good white cotton gloves. I just bought them for the funerals. Are you sittin' on my gloves, Effie Vi'let?"

"I don't think so."

The Wheelerhand sisters, now agitated and upset, searched the backseat for the lost gloves.

"I bet you dropped them when we ran away from Stella Dora," suggested Miss Effie Vi'let. "Do you think that's when she lost them, Molly Primrose?"

"Probably."

"Buy a new pair," suggested Kendra. "You've got $15,000 bucks at your fingertips, you can afford a new pair of gloves. Shoes, too."

"Gawd save us! For shame!" whispered Molly Primrose, her button blue eyes stern.This time she didn't pinch Kendra, she just shook her head, for she knew her niece was past the point of being civil.

Under any other circumstances, Molly Primrose would've never added the next piece of information; but, being cooped up in the Dodge, with those two chicken hawks; the leper hospital looming large before her; the raging storm inside the automobile and out; Kendra raising merry hell; and the reckless turn the conversation had taken, drove her to say: "Did I ever tell you how my fiancé, William Kavanaugh, caught cold and died within a week's time of gallopin' pneumonia?"

"N-no," gasped Miss Effie Vi'let. "I'm *so* sorry to hear it."

"No need to get so upset. It happened a long time ago."

"Well, did you know, Molly Primrose, that I'm not an old maid?" volunteered Miss Effie Vi'let, nodding. "I was married for six months, and am proud of it. I bet you didn't know that."

"Right now I don't know bee from bumble. I always thought you was an old-maid, like myself."

"Well, I'm not. Lettie Lou and you are old maids, but not me. For six months I was married to Trey Calhoun. Dear Trey took care of his ailin' mother until she died. He promised Mother Calhoun he wouldn't marry until she died."

Kendra to herself: "I bet you ol' chicken hawk you were saying one flying novena after another for Mother Calhoun to die."

"We waited a year after Mother Calhoun's death to marry. On our honeymoon poor Trey took sick and died six months later, leaving me a young wider."

"Did he have insurance?" slyly asked Kendra.

"Not a penny."

"Why didn't you ever tell us you had been married?" asked Molly Primrose, stunned by the news.

"I guess," put in Kendra, "because Mr. Trey Calhoun probably worked at the dime store."

"*No, indeed!* Trey worked at the bank. The reason I didn't tell was Lettie Lou thought, since it was such a short marriage, I should keep it a secret —"

"Dark secrets," interjected Kendra.

"And another reason," went on Effie Vi'let, ignoring Kendra, "and really the main one, was you couldn't teach if you was married, or had been married. So I could keep teaching and support myself, I let everybody think I was an old maid. I had no choice but to lie."

"Effie Vi'let, you're *really and truly* an old maid," mumbled Miss Lettie Lou. "You can't count a six month marriage to a bedridden man a real marriage. I doubt if it was *consummated.*"

"*It was!*" cried Effie Vi'let, blushing through the cornstarch. "You just can't reconcile yourself that I got a husband and you didn't. I'm a married woman, and when I retire from teachin' I'm gunna call myself Mrs. Trey Calhoun. *You'll see!*"

"And everybody'll laugh at you. You just wait and see yourself," sneered her sister.

"I don't think they will," rejoined Kendra, "since Mr. Calhoun wasn't a dime store clerk"; then turning to her aunt: "Tante, you've never mentioned any one but William Kavanaugh. Was there no one else?"

"No one. William spoiled me for anybody else. However, lanky, Lincoln like, Giross Hartman, Senior, Gawd rest his soul, had asked me to marry him. I turned him down. He married Ruthie."

"*Giross Hartman!*" gasped Kendra, wrinkling her nose in distaste. "Gosh, if you had married Giross Senior, Giross Junior, Maison Blanche's head floorwalker, with the boutonniere in his lapel, would've been your son."

"Then aren't you glad I didn't?"

"I surely am."

"Look!" cried Miss Effie Vi'let. "The rain's stopped!"

"We've been carryin' on so much we didn't even notice the sun's out," said Molly Primrose. "It's a wonder Gawd didn't send us an instant judgment, or let the lightnin' strike us dead."

"If God was going to send us an instant judgment, or let the lightning strike us dead, He'd done it back at the crazy house when we run off and left poor Miss Stella Dora, pleading for mercy."

"Lawsey, there's a rainbow over the leper hospital!" pointed out Miss Effie Vi'let. "I wonder what Gawd could be thinkin' of to let a pretty rainbow hover over such a nasty place?—Do you all see the rainbow?"

"We see it." Then Lettie Lou, added: "Effie Vi'let, don't try to boss Gawd. Gawd knows where he wants that rainbow."

"If I were a rainbow, I'd much rather hover over the leper hospital than over this automobile."

"Kendra Lou, don't start that if game," admonished Aunt Molly

Primrose."You ain't never gunna be no rainbow." Then she changed the
subject: "This is my first trip away from New Orleans, and my last.
Kendra Lou, no matter how much you beg me to take a trip, to go some
where and have a good time, I ain't goin'."

"Neither are we," tacked on the Wheelerhand sisters.

Without another word, Kendra turned the key in the ignition, pressed
the starter button, pumped the gas pedal, wrapped her fingers around the
knob on the gear stick, put the Dodge in gear, let out the clutch and took
off for home.

Chapter Four

Kendra, when she woke up on the morning after driving Stella Dora to the crazy house, had a tiny cold. A couple days later, her slight cold, because she was at a low ebb and ripe for any kind of catastrophe that might come along, turned into pneumonia. She missed three weeks work without pay.

During the last couple days of her convalescence, she spent a good deal of time outdoors soaking up sunshine. She sat in the back yard on the stone bench beneath the old oak, with its low sprawling branches, covering her like a tent, breathing in the fragrances of roses and honeysuckle; while cat, Sholar Picarara, soft and fat and fluffy, lay curled at her feet, sleeping; dancing sunshine casting golden shadows over them and the yard and the wash on the clothesline.

One of the shadows landed on the birdbath, where several sparrows were chirping and splashing; another settled on the rose fence, where a drowsy hum of honey bees mingled with the noisy sparrows and the twitter of other tiny birds. It seemed half of the bees walked across the roses, scattering and shattering their soft petals, while the other half crawled into the blooms and tumbled back out, drunk on a load of nectar. Because of all this scattering and shattering, the earth beneath the rose bushes was sprinkled with a sweep of soft petals, pink and white.

The old clothes poll was also awash in sunshine. This old poll, Kenny Joe and she had taken turns riding, he at a wild full gallop, she at a pony trot. Now a velvety black caterpillar was pumping his way to the top of the poll; a green lizard was zig zagging toward the bottom. They were on a collision course. A crow cawed; a mockingbird mocked it.

Out of the blue a hummingbird appeared, its scarlet iridescent head glinting like a diamond. Its tiny body was painted turquoise. This fragile creature, God's perfection, was hanging suspended in a worldwind of tiny wings. It stuck its needle-thin bill again and again into the slender throat of a yellow day lily before it flew off to pillage the sweet olive tree.

Kendra, sensitive to nature and beauty, leaned her brown-gold head against the gray/green tree trunk, and enjoyed her surroundings. She sat thinking a million or more thoughts—all a jumble. One minute on Jack Trenchard, imagining how sweet it would be to send him to the guillotine; in another on the tragedy of Stella Dora being dragged into the crazy house; on the bickering, at the leper colony, while they waited for the storm to pass; then on the strange and recurring dream she had while in the clutches of pneumonia; then on Kenny Joe's and Mr. Big Joe's tragic deaths.

Thinking of Kenny Joe brought whisperings of the past, and images and memories jostled in her. She closed her eyes and saw herself in pigtails and pinafores, and Kenny Joe in short pants. She recalled the day they had made a pact always to live on Starlight Street, to be friends forever and to die on the same day—going straight to heaven, by-passing purgatory.

"Maybe we ought to go to purgatory for a while, Kenny Joe, cause all you do in heaven is drink milk, eat honey and sing. I like milk, but I hate honey and I can't sing."

"Well, let's hope you don't take a dislike to milk."

She sat there laughing until she thought of something even funnier. "Kenny Joe, what if God up and dies on us? No body on earth could go to His wake."

"Unless a few of us volunteered to die."

"But what if those who volunteered couldn't get in heaven. God's wake would have to be in heaven."

"Heaven might be a problem all right. Let's just hope and pray God don't up and die on us."

Then there was the day she asked Kenny Joe: "Help me pick a nice nickname for God. If God had a softer sounding name, I wouldn't be so afraid of him."

"That name God does sound harsh and fearful.—If we only knew God, we could ask Him what nickname He'd like."

Aunt Molly Primrose overheard them, and said it was the wickedest of notions to try to rename "Gawd." She punished Kendra, and sent Kenny Joe home to tell on himself.

Kendra laughed again, though it would've been easier to cry. Childhood memories and events crowded her mind, even the day she and Kenny Joe got their first pair of skates now seemed a great occasion. Soon after they got their skates, Sonny Ganucci had a Halloween party. Kenny Joe went as a candle and she as a pumpkin. They got the prize.

"I've got to quit thinking of bygone days or, for that matter, quit thinking altogether, if I want to keep my sanity," she said to herself.

No sooner had she said this, her mind jumped to the day Dr. Herbert said she had pneumonia. That night, burning with fever, she dreamed of a beautiful mansion, that was filled with the finest of furniture: carved armoires, inlaid tables, hand-painted China, gold-bordered mirrors, tapestries, crystal chandeliers, four-poster beds.

A spiral staircase led to the second level, where the mistress' bedroom and sitting room were. A female voice said: "This is the Powder-Blue Bedroom. All the answers can be found in this room."

"But I'm not looking for answers," replied Kendra, to the voice.

"You will be," said the voice.

Then the dream, the vision, the hallucination, ended. The next morning, Kendra told her aunt all about her dream. She even sketched the floor plan of the mansion.

"What did it look like on the outside? The grounds?"

"I don't know, Tante. I was only inside."

"Well, you had quite a night. What a vivid dream, and what remarkable recall you have. Your fever must've gone up, or the chicken broth was too rich. In any case, Kendra Lou, it was just a dream. Forget it."

That night, Kendra dreamed again of the Powder-Blue Bedroom. Thereafter, every night, for a week, she looked forward to the dream. She may have even willed herself to dream about the Powder-Blue Bedroom.

"I wonder if there's such a room," mused Kendra, still seated beneath the old oak tree, opening her eyes, but still slouched against the tree trunk.

Before she had chance to think further about the dream, a visitor strolled into the yard. She sat up straight, smoothed her mop of breeze-blown gypsy ringlets, and cleared her mind with an effort.

She wished she hadn't been caught wearing her old faded and frayed blue-and-white gingham dress, with the square neckline and short puff sleeves. She knew she looked plain and pale; and to make matters worse she hadn't bothered to put on any lipstick.

To herself: "I know I look a fright." Aloud: "W-w-what are you doing here?" she asked in a wooden voice, keeping her seat, only because she was too shaken to stand.

"Now is that any way to greet a man just home from his honeymoon?" asked Jack Trenchard, beaming broadly. He was wearing a blue shirt, white slacks and white bucks. "Aren't you going to ask me to sit down?"

As usual, Jack's good looks disturbed Kendra. His black curly hair glistened and gleamed, his rare, dark blue/purple eyes, more vivid and penetrating then ever, in a glance, took her all in.

She felt like kicking herself for being caught in an old faded cotton dress while Allison no doubt, at that moment, was decked out in summer silk. "N-no, you can't sit down."

He sat down any way, right next to her. She slid toward the opposite end of the bench. All this commotion woke up Sholar Picarara. He gaped and stretched himself into an upside down U. Then he looked at Jack, with those green insolent eyes of his, that had black exclamation points for pupils, and trotted off on his little padded feet, his plumy tail held high, waving like a banner.

"I said you couldn't sit down? What do you want?"

"To see you. Why are you so pale?"

"I'm just getting over pneumonia. I'm fine."

"I'm sorry. You look pale but pretty. Fresh and natural. Is it any wonder I want to see you?"

"Well, I don't wanna see you."

"Yes, you do. If not for me, then to know about your parents' wedding bands. I bet you've been worried sick about their rings?

"I have. Where are they?"

Jack stood up and removed a ring box from his pants' pocket. "Right here in the little box you gave them to me in." He opened the box, and the rings lay on a bed of white velvet. He handed her the box. "I'm glad you trusted me enough not to come after them." Next he removed a check from his shirt pocket. "This should cover your savings and the money you put out for my wedding suit." He handed her the check.

Kendra glanced at it—$450—and nodded.

"I know what you're thinking: 'Where's my money for all the law books, for the tuition I put up?' Well, I'm not going to pay that back. That was an investment."

"For who?"

"For you. Let's go in the house. This is Saturday, so I know your aunt's working half a day. We can be more private in the house."

"No."

Jack sat down. "Don't you want to know why I married Allison?"

"And left me waiting at the altar—"

"I left you in the lurch, not in the church."

"Same difference. I can't believe you're acting so cool about the way you treated me. Yes, I want to know."

"Kendra darling, after I explain things, you'll understand. But before I tell you anything, I need your word that what I say will always be confidential."

Kendra nodded her brown head, the gold in it shimmering and shining in the soft sunlight.

"A nod won't do. Swear you'll never tell another soul."

She raised her right hand: "Cross my heart and hope to die. I swear never to tell. Satisfied? Or do you want me to get the Bible?"

Jack took a deep breath and let it out slowly. "No— You know how much I love beautiful things, and how much I wanted to be rich."

"Yes, I know."

"If I had married you, I'd have never been rich. We'd have put a small down payment on a little house in a neat subdivision, and the balance we'd have paid like rent, every month for thirty years."

"That small down payment would've given us a deed to the house."

"And that deed would've entitled us to pay property taxes and utility bills. And when the house was finally paid off, we'd have all kinds of major house repairs: plumbing bills, roofing bills. You name it. In the end we'd have a dump on our hands. I didn't want that for me or for you."

"Most people in love don't mind house payments. Love is synonymous with sacrifice."

"Love doesn't enter into it. If I had married you, we'd have wound up living on Starlight Street, in your aunt's double. Heaven forbid."

"There's nothing wrong with Starlight Street or my aunt's double. I like it. You came here often enough, and ate so many free meals I lost count. The way you came around here, I assumed you liked it."

"You were the attraction. All my orphanage life I dreamed of living in a big house, and now I do. Greenwood Manor is absolutely magnificent. Beyond my dreams. I wish you could see it, Kendra."

"It all boils down to your wanting the big house more than me. I don't wanna see your *big* house."

"Kendra, I know you're amiable and adaptable, so don't be hateful. It doesn't become you.— Let's sit on the back gallery."

"No. Those two snoops, the Wheelerhand sisters are home."

"I thought the Wheelerhands were like family. Don't tell me...let me guess...you're mad at Kenny Joe, so you're mad at his family."

"Kenny Joe's dead and buried. Killed in Korea. The telegram came the same day you married Allison Edwards. When Kenny Joe's father got the bad news, he dropped dead. We buried him and Kenny Joe the same day. Kenny Joe's momma lost her mind. Miss Stella Dora's in Jackson."

"Oh, I'm sorry...I'm *really* sorry, Kendra. I know how much you liked Kenny Joe and his parents. That's a damn shame.— Why did they put her in Jackson, and not the mental ward at Charity?"

Kendra told the whole sordid story, and all Jack did was shake his head and say: "It's a damn shame about Kenny Joe and his parents. It's too bad the draft got him. You know, there are such things as deferments."

"Yes, I know. I suppose you got one of them *deferments.*"

. "Yes, I got a deferment. I'm needed to run Judge Edwards' law firm." He chuckled.

"The Judge fixed it for you, eh?"

He laughed out loud. "That's what I like about you, Kendra, you're right up front. You call a spade a spade. Judge Edwards is a *very* powerful man."

"Powerful enough to get Miss Stella Dora out of Jackson?"

Jack shrugged. "Probably. But I'd have to know more about it."

"Later, I'll tell you what I have in mind. Let's get back to the main subject—your *jilting* me."

Jack slowly nodded. "Er, at the time Judge Edwards took me in his law firm, he had an ulterior motive, which I never suspected. He knew I had been raised in an orphanage and didn't know who my parents were, and didn't hold that against me. He said being unencumbered with family would give me more freedom.

"Of course, he knew I had worked my way through law school, and I lived in a rooming house. He knew everything about me except you. He still knows nothing of you, and never will— Even if the Judge had known of your existence, I don't think it would've made a difference in what eventually happened." He sighed deeply.

"Go on," prompted Kendra.

"Well, six months after I had asked you to marry me, the Judge, impressed with my mental capacity, my good looks and my excellent health, made me a proposition. At first, I found what he had proposed appalling, but as time went by, it appealed to me."

"What appealed to you?"

"A partnership in the Edwards' Law Firm, $300,000 cash up front, $20,000 a year salary, a brand new Buick convertible, an expense account, a mansion to live in, all the refinements of life; and all I had to do was marry his only child."

"Is Allison an ugly duckling?"

"A beautiful swan."

"Well, what's wrong with her that she needed a boughten husband?"

"She's got a rare blood disease. She needs frequent blood transfusions. The family doctor, Dr. Lopez, seems to think she's got about a year. Maybe a little less. He also says she's sterile."

Kendra's hardness crumpled. "I can understand the Judge wanting his only child to have some happiness before her young life's cut off."

"Exactly. Before this illness had been discovered, Allison had been engaged to Cameron Claremont, *the Claremonts* of New Orleans. The banns of marriage announced at the St. Louis Cathedral. Since Cameron is an only child and needs to produce an heir to take over all those Claremont millions, he had to break his engagement to Allison.

"Naturally, her broken engagement left her miserable, which made the Judge miserable. That's when the Judge got the idea of finding a husband for his daughter. And when the Judge gets an idea, that appeals to him, he moves fast. I had just come along. He sized me up, investigated me, and decided I was to be his son-in-law."

"I thought the Judge had a rule about single lawyers entering his law firm, couldn't marry for two years."

Jack laughed. "The Judge made the rule; the Judge broke the rule."

"Does Allison know you were picked to be her source of solace?"

"No. No one in the family knows. That was part of the deal."

"Then the Judge just simply introduced you to Allison, you wooed her and she fell for you. Is that how it was?"

"Basically. The Judge invited me to dinner at Greenwood Manor. The food, the sterling, the crystal and the china overwhelmed me. Of course, his daughter was *de*-lightful."

"*Of course.* So you went to dinner on the nights you told me you had to work late, didn't you?"

"Yes. After I went to dinner, that first time, I said I'd never go back; but when the next invitation came, I was ready. The Judge didn't want me to move too fast, so it took me about three months to make Allison fall in love with me."

"While you were seeing me and making plans for *our secret wedding,* you were busy making Allison fall in love with you".— She felt a sense of soreness and outrage. To herself: "He betrayed my faith and trust in him. My love for him should be dead. But it isn't." Aloud: "Why did you put me through so much hell? You borrowed my savings, you got my parents' wedding bands, you let me pay for your wedding suit. Month after month I made payments on that suit, those payments you object to. Why didn't you come clean with me, Jack?"

"I wasn't thinking of those things. I was trying to decide whether to marry you and be poor, or marry Allison and be rich; which would ultimately make you rich. If I hadn't come here the night before our planned wedding, I would've married you.

"But seeing all these doubles jammed up against one another, and then eating stew for supper, off your aunt's only set of china, I knew I had to marry Allison. I knew I had to live at Greenwood Manor."

"Where every dinner was a gourmet meal served on a new set of Spode. And, of course, the meal was free. You were good at zooming in on anything free. Didn't you take Allison any where?"

"I took her to the opera and to the theater. The Judge paid for it."

"You took me window shopping in the French Quarter; for walks in Audubon Park; to KB's fountain to eat eggsalad sandwiches and drink malted milks; and now and then to a picture show. I always paid for the food and the picture show, and you seemed to enjoy all those free outings. You never had any money, even lunch money."

"I know. I had a wonderful time doing all those things with you. It's just that I didn't want to do those kinds of things for the rest of my life."

"Maybe we wouldn't have had to do just free things all our married life. A lawyer makes good."

"Not good enough for my taste. Kendra, your being Catholic—"

"You were raised in a Catholic orphanage, remember?"

"I know. You found your Catholic God. I'm still looking. Anyway, your being Catholic, you'd have wanted a half dozen kids."

"Yes, I want children. Half dozen sounds fine."

"I want *one* child."

"Then you must be delighted that Allison can't have *any* children."

"Yes and no. I wish she could've had one child. That would've locked in Greenwood Manor and all the Edwards' money."

"Without children, you don't come in for a share of the property."

"No. Allison has money from her grandmother, and I'll get that. But I'd love to own Greenwood Manor—now."

"Allison may be dying soon, but her parents aren't. You'll have to wait."

"I know. But, when they *do* die, Greenwood Manor has to go to somebody. Why not me? there beloved son-in-law."

"I knew you loved money and high living, but not so much as to sell your soul."

"Cut the crap about selling my soul. Whenever money's involved, people always say dumb things like sell your soul, or money can't buy happiness."

"Dumb or not, the truth will get you every time."

"I had to take advantage of the great opportunity Judge Edwards was offering me, a nobody orphan. I'd never get another crack at *that kind of money,* a debutante wife, a mansion and an enviable social standing. I had to take it, Kendra. *I had to.*"

Silence. Then in a rush of words:"I'd never be anybody with you, because you're a nobody, Kendra, from Starlight Street, a hard-working nobody secretary who brings home a lousy $160 bucks a month. And to get that piddling amount of money, you have to put up with a louse like Henri Prosper. So when I *do marry you* in a year or so, I'm going to make you a somebody."

That remark had been a piercing stab, for Kendra never had thought of herself as nobody. She was somebody, because God had made her. Pained, she closed her brown-gold eyes as tightly as she could, but stinging tears still streamed down her face.

"Don't cry. For God's sake please don't cry." He reached for her hand. She shook him off. "*Don't* touch me."

"Kendra, I love you...I'm going to marry you when Allison dies. I'm going to make your life secure and serene. We're going to be rich."

"No, we're not. I'm never going to marry you. What you have in mind comes under the heading of you can't have it both ways."

"If I were planning on having it both ways, I'd have asked you to let me set you up in a swanky apartment in the Quarter, make you my mistress—never marry you."

"You better not ever suggest that to me, *Jack Trenchard.*"

"You don't have to worry about that. I'm going to be completely faithful to Allison—make her life, what's left of it, happy as possible."

"And there's the Judge to make sure you do."

"I don't need the Judge to make me walk the line. Being faithful to Allison won't be a hardship. She's lovely, educated, witty and charming. She's everything desirable and wonderful, but I don't love her. I love you. Now are you going to wait for me or not?"

"Not."

"Don't be foolish. A year or so isn't so long to wait. You'll only be twenty-three, or four, at the most. —I'm glad Kenny Joe's dead, because if he were alive, you might marry him on the rebound."

"How awful of you, Jack. I don't know how I could've ever thought I loved you."

"I'm just being realistic."

"I think you better be more realistic about Allison. You might fall in love with her; and, when she dies, you'll feel so miserable and guilt-ridden.You'll want to kill yourself."

"I don't think so. I'm in love with you. When Allison dies, I'll be even richer, and then I'll marry you—the woman I love."

"No, you won't. Allison just might fool you and not die. I hope she outlives you.There's something very dirty about a man like you."

"There was something very clean about Kenny Joe, and you wouldn't have him. Dirt, then, must appeal to you."

"Kenny Joe was *clean*, and he wanted to marry me, but I couldn't marry him because I loved him like a brother, not a lover. He deserved love, not just kindness on my part."

"I love you, Kendra. What I did I did because I love you."

"You-did-it-all-for-yourself. Don't drag me into this piece of dirt. I want no part of it, you or your money, when you come into it."

"I'm already in it. The Judge gave me $300,000. It's in the bank."

"Good for you and the bank."

"Kendra, I came here with a purpose, to erase any grievance you may have regarding us. So let's not fight, because when I leave I won't be coming back until after Allison dies."

"You're never coming back; I'm about to throw you out right now. But before I do, I want to know if the great Judge Edwards can get Miss Stella Dora out of Jackson; and get her money back from the Wheelerhand sisters?"

"I'll ask him."

"Also ask him how much it's going to cost me?"

"Why not let Stella Dora pay for it out of her 15 Grand?"

"I can't do that. I drove her to Jackson, watched those two bozos tie her up and didn't lift a finger to save her. If I hadn't been in a stupor of sorts, this wouldn't have happened.— I'm paying for it."

"A guilt trip, eh?"

Kendra shrugged. "Call it what you like. I'm paying."

"In that case, consider all those law books you bought me as payment for my part in getting the Judge to help you."

"Do you want me to throw in the tuition, also?"

"No. Just remember, if the Judge pulls this off, you owe him."

"How much?"

Jack shrugged. "I don't know. It might not be money...It might be a favor some day...Who knows?...But I *do* know that Judge Exum Edwards does nothing for nothing."

Unable to imagine her ever doing a favor for Judge Edwards, Kendra shrugged. "So I owe the Judge a favor."

"Also, Kendra, all transactions will be made in your aunt's name. I don't want the Judge to know of you, because when Allison dies and six months down the road, when I spring you on my in-laws, I don't want them to suspect I knew you while their daughter lived. Deal?"

"Nothing's too fantastic to be true. I think you should know on the day you were suppose to marry me, I went to Greenwood Manor, looking for you. I found you there marrying Allison."

"Did anyone see you?" asked Jack, upset.

"I don't know. I hid behind that tall row of Oleander bushes."

Jack laughed."No one saw you.Then it's a deal."

"A lot can happen in a year."

"Then let's wait and see.— My notebook's in the automobile...I'll get it...Come with me and see my canary yellow convertible."

Seeing the convertible over with, Kendra and Jack returned to the back yard, and sat on the bench. Jack, pen and pad perched on his knees, said: "Now tell me everything there is to know about Mrs. Wheelerhand's plight."

As soon as the tale was told, he left. Ten days later, Stella Dora had been transferred to the mental ward at Charity; her $15,000 back in her name, in the bank, and under the care of a bank trustee. Six weeks later Stella Dora came home to Starlight Street.

"How do you think she looks, Tante?"

"Lost. There's a lost look in her sad blue eyes. I think those 'lectric shocks did that to her. She's a broken woman."

"She'll come out of it. Thank God she only had a few shock treatments. If she'd have been left there to rot, as those two chicken hawks had planned, I think Miss Stella Dora would've either went completely nuts or died."

"I wish she'd make Lettie Lou and Effie Vi'let move."

"Those chicken hawks'll never move. They have too good a roosting place. However, I'm tickled pink that Miss Stella Dora's making them share in the rent and household expenses."

"So am I, Kendra Lou. And how are you doing, my dear niece?"

"I'm healing, Tante. I'm healing."

Back to the present. One more time, Kendra peered in the looking glass, readjusted the white ribbon in her hair, patted the front of her daffodil yellow voile dress and checked the seams of her stockings. She was pleased with her overall reflection; however, there were signs of strain in her sparkling eyes, as she grabbed up the big pasteboard box with Mrs. Rogers black silk suit and said: "Here I come, Willowwynn...."

Chapter Five

Kendra parked the Dodge in front of Willowwynn, glanced toward Greenwood Manor and thumbed her nose, saying: "That's for you, Jack Trenchard." She snatched up the big pasteboard box, that sat on the passenger seat, got out, walked around the front of the Dodge and jumped across the gutter.

The mansion she sought stood just ahead of her. No one was in sight save a mockingbird hopping across the green grass, making his day's marketing, while a couple blue/ black butterflies flitted to and fro.

Willowwynn was a big white two-story stucco house, Spanish styled. It was square shaped, and roofed in red tile. Six French doors opened onto the second-story balcony, that was supported by black iron balusters, and enclosed by an iron bannister and railing. It reminded Kendra of fine black lace laid over white silk taffeta.

On the first floor, imposing carved mahogany double doors were hung high, and each had a big brass knocker. The doors were flanked by six graceful French windows, long and narrow. They were all open.

Large white pedestaled flowerpots, filled with green asparagus fern, flanked the stone steps, which led to a wide, white tiled gallery, that was also supported by lacy black iron balusters, and enclosed by an iron bannister and railing.

The gallery was furnished with groupings of golden wicker: rocking chairs, arm chairs and settees, which wore thick, blue polished cotton cushions; bouquets of cut red roses, in crystal vases, graced the tea and side tables; and plant stands sported white pots of pink geraniums.

Old oaks, strung in gauzy gray moss, stood majestically in the front yard; while tall, slim, straight pines, their fan-like branches draped with cones of smokey purple wisteria, were swaying in the breeze. Silence, beauty and pride reigned.

Kendra mounted the steps, crossed the gallery to the double entrance doors, lifted one of the heavy knockers, and knocked. No one answered her summons. "Some body's got to be home, the windows are wide open," she said to herself. Again she knocked. Still no answer. She knocked some more and called out at the same time. No answer. "Somebody's got to be here. I'll go around back."

She went around back and found a high red brick wall surrounded the property. The wall was broken by an ornate black iron gate. She passed through the gate, and looked around. Red, yellow, purple and pink colors burst upon her gold-brown eyes, as she stood spellbound, staring at a breath-takingly beautiful brick paved patio, laid out in a Herringbone pattern, and filled with potted plants of every size and description.

Bordering the wall, to her right, were flowerbeds, lined with drifts of purple and red alyssum. Behind the alyssum was a sweep of white caladiums; past the caladiums were clumps of black-green cast iron plants and butter-yellow daylilies. Above this section of flowerbeds, mounted on the wall, was a white lion's head, sparkling water spewing from his roaring mouth, into a lily pond.

Farther along were groupings of palms, banana trees and bamboo. In front of this tall lush green foliage was a big black crane fountain, splashing water; and beneath it were white pots filled with flaming geraniums. Black and white tulip urns, on pedestals, were filled with rich red bougainvillea; a Victorian urn sprouted Swedish ivy, dusty-miller, multi-colored coleus, white alyssum and purple periwinkle.

Large terra cotta pots were spilling over with a mixture of green foliage, yellow mums, purple petunias, pink geraniums, purple heart, blue jew, yellow marigolds, and red and white caladiums.

Aside from the flowers, there were groupings of patio furniture: white iron tables, chairs, benches, settees and coffee tables. All the chairs, benches and settees wore thick polished cotton cushions in a floral pattern of pink-and-white roses with jade green leaves on a light beige background.

One of the white tables was littered with an assortment of garden tools, a rag and an open bag of potting soil. Some soil had spilled onto the table, down onto one of the chairs, ending in a black pool on the red bricks. Next to this table stood a balloon tire wheelbarrel, loaded with a bale of peatmoss, open and bursting forth.

Kendra's roving, brown-gold eyes next caught sight of a blue-and-white tiled gold fish pond, with a gushing fountain. Its airy spray, glistening in the sunshine, held her attention for a few minutes, and then her eyes moved onto a long curving driveway, thickly lined with red rose trees.

The massive black iron gates that led into the drive were closed. At the end of the drive, there was a white stuccoed three-car garage, and on top it an apartment, roofed in red tile. There was a turnaround in front of the garage. A red awning covered a brick walkway, which led from the garage to the back gallery.

Kendra advanced forward, turned around and gazed at the back of the house. Like the front, the back upstairs level had a balcony enclosed with a black iron bannister and railing; on the ground floor gray stone steps led to the gallery, also enclosed with a black iron bannister and railing, and supported by balusters. Flanking the gray steps were large white pots of pink geraniums.

The gallery had a gray tiled floor, and in the far left corner there were two pink-cushioned white wicker armchairs placed at a round table which wore a white eyelet skirt. A small white flowerpot of pink geraniums sat in the center of the table. Lush green ferns in white urns, on tall pedestals, were placed to advantage in front of each baluster.

"Hello," called out a man's voice.

Kendra spun around in time to see the man step from behind one of the rose trees that lined the drive. Clippers were in his canvas-gloved hands. He walked toward her, took off his gloves, tossed them on the table, with the potting soil, and snatched up the rag and wiped his hands.

She noticed his hands were not earth-grimed; his fingers were long and tapering—beautiful hands he had. He also wasn't wearing a wedding ring. "Hello," returned Kendra, in a daze of color and beauty, looking the man up and down. He had a smudge of black dirt on his fair, friendly face.

"What can I do for you?"

"Well, I've been at the front door, yelling *anybody home*, and knocking the knocker almost off. I knew somebody had to be home because all the windows are open. When nobody answered, I ventured back here.— I have a package for No. 10 Prytania."

He eyed the box. "The housekeeper's off today, so I guess I'll have to take that package."

"Who are you? The yardman?"

The minute those ridiculous words slipped from her mouth, she couldn't catch them back. The man, before her, couldn't be a yardman, despite his rough clothes, faded, navy cloth pants, old white cotton shirt, opened at the throat, and his mud-caked sneakers, still spelled quality. And then there were those hands. They belonged to a professional, not a man who earned his living by digging in the dirt.

He smiled, showing off very white teeth. He was handsome for an older man of, say, thirty five or forty. He was of medium height, slenderly built, had fair skin, brown-gold hair, like her own, loose and tumbling on his wide forehead. His cheekbones were high and hollow, his chin square, and his friendly looking eyes were so blue they looked almost navy. His voice was pleasant and cultured.

"Yes, I'm the yardman. Who are you?"

Expecting to be told he was not the yardman, Kendra was caught off guard and stammered: "Er—well—I'm—I'm the delivery man."

He looked her up and down. "You don't look anything like a man. Too many curves. Do you have a name, Delivery Man?"

Color blazed in her cheeks. "I'm Kendra Louise Applegate, and I've come to deliver this package." She held it out.

He didn't take it.

Puzzled by the yardman's reluctance to accept the package, she stammered again: "It's, it's a suit that the late Mrs. Rogers bought, from D. H. Holmes. My Aunt Molly Primrose, who works for Holmes, as a seamstress, altered it; and nobody has bothered to pick it up."

Still no comment from the yardman. His navy blue eyes kept staring in Kendra's pretty face, pinning her.

"Er—this is the Rogers' residence, isn't it?"

He nodded.

The yardman's silence and close scrutiny made Kendra say something she hadn't planned. "My aunt asked me to deliver this package to the housekeeper, so she could put it with the rest of Mrs. Rogers' things. In that way, Mr. Rogers wouldn't see it, and wouldn't be troubled by any more painful reminders."

"That was kind and thoughtful of your aunt, and you." He looked at the box. "Is there really a suit in that box?" He raised his eyebrows, questioningly.

"Of course. Why would you think otherwise?"

"I just figured, since you're not wearing a wedding ring, you were one of the steady stream of single women coming here, ever since Mrs. Rogers died. Using every excuse under the sun, to get their feet in Mr. Rogers' front or back door. You know, rope in a rich widower. I suppose you've got a well-written sympathy note with you, for me to give to Mr. Rogers."

Kendra, stunned with surprise, tried hard not to let it show. To herself: "Why, it's as if this yardman was a fly on the kitchen wall and listened in on my conversation with Tante. I don't like him at all." Her right hand slipped into her dress pocket where the sympathy note was.

"You got that note in your pocket, eh?"

"No, I don't," icily denied Kendra, removing her empty hand.

"Turn your pocket inside out."

"You turn your pocket inside out."

"You look familiar."

"You don't."

"I've seen you some where. It'll come to me."

"No, it won't, because I've never seen you before in my life. Let's get back to this package. I'm here to deliver it, not rope in Mr. Rogers. I'm sorry to disappoint you."

"Open the box, then, and we'll see if I'm disappointed."

Kendra slapped down the box on the same table where this obnoxious yardman's canvas gloves lay. She roughly 'ripped it open and, to her horror, found it filled with sheets of white tissue paper.

"Well, where's the suit?" asked the yardman, his navy blue eyes twinkling. "I'm disappointed, for all I see are sheets of paper."

Kendra gulped."There must be some mistake. I'm—I'm sure my aunt put the suit in *this* box, gave it to Nell Miller, a co-worker, who handed it over to me."

"Did you see all these transactions?"

"N-no. But Nell said—"

"Ah-ha. It's obvious you can't trust Nell, nor your aunt. Can you? For your information, the suit you said nobody bothered to pick up was delivered a number of days ago. Last Monday to be exact."

Kendra stood stricken, staring into the yardman's smiling navy blue eyes. Suddenly her brown-gold eyes were snapping mad. "If you knew the suit had been delivered, why didn't you tell me? Why did you ask me to open the box?"

"I wanted to catch your act."

What could she say? The yardman had said it all; so she gathered up the sheets of paper and the torn bits of box and started to leave.

"Don't rush off. I must say, of all the ladies who came here, hoping to get their feet in Mr. Rogers' door, you were the only one who got her whole body, not in the door, but on the patio. And another thing in your favor, you're the prettiest; however, your scheme was the cheapest.

"The other ladies brought gifts: fried chicken and potato salad, chocolate cake, lemon pie, fudge, flowers and sympathy cards—but all you brought was a box full of tissue paper, and a card that you won't take out your pocket. No manners at all."

"*What's-your-name?*"

"What do you want to know my name for?"

"Because I'm going to report your rudeness to Mr. Rogers."

The yardman laughed out loud. "My name is Mr. C.C. Bennett."

"Well, C.C. Bennett, you're going to be reported."

"No, no. That's *Mr.* C.C. Bennett."

"All the yardmen I know I call either by their first or last names."

"How many yardmen do you know?"

"Actually only one. Ol' Tater Beelack, a fine colored man—"

"What color is colored?"

"Why—black."

"Then why don't you say black man."

"Because everybody from New Orleans calls colored people *colored.*"

"I'm from California. All those wrongs don't make it right. I guess I'm the only *white* yardman you know."

"And the last, I hope. I knew you were away from here by the sound of your voice.— As I was saying ol' Tater Beelack is a fine colored man who can't read or write and signs his name with a big X. Can you read and write, C.C. Bennett? And how do you sign your name? With a little x?"

He laughed out loud. "I can read a little and scribble my name some. Actually, I print. So I guess that puts me a cut above ol' Tater Beelack."

"Below."

"You're just mad because your scheme backfired."

"For the record, though I don't know why I bother to explain to the likes of a rude yardman, I honestly and truly believed the box had a suit in it. I didn't come here to rope in Mr. Rogers," easily lied Kendra. "I'm not on the lookout for *any* man, rich or poor."

"You're the first woman I've met who's not on the lookout for a rich husband."

"You sound like you've met a lot of women. How many men have you met who aren't on the lookout for rich wives?"

He laughed again. "How old are you? Twenty?"

"Twenty-two. How old are you? Forty?"

"Thirty-seven. Do you have a boyfriend?"

"I—I did. My boyfriend was killed in Korea. Lieutenant Kenny Joe Wheelerhand was killed chasing communist Chinese back to the 38th Parallel. When he came home we were going to be married." As soon as this lie rolled off her tongue, she felt small and cheap for using Kenny Joe this way. This smart aleck, rude, awful yardman had forced her—in order to save face—to say such a lying thing.

"I'm very sorry. Did Kenny Joe give you an engagement ring? I don't see one on your finger. You know, you could wear it on your right ring finger, in his memory."

She shrugged. "It's put away." To herself: "This ol' yardman is too shrewd for words. I better not tell him any more lies." Aloud: "Well, I really must go."

"Did you have a definite wedding date set?"

"Er—n—no. Are you married?"

"No."

"Where do you live?"

"Uptown. On Starlight Street—four blocks off South Claiborne. I live with my maiden aunt, Miss Molly Primrose Applegate."

"And where are your parents?"

"My mother died when I was born; my father when I was two."

"I'm sorry." He cleared his throat. "I know where Starlight Street is. All row houses standing side by side and flush to the sidewalk. Step out your front door and stand on your sidewalk; spit out the side door and your spittle hits your next door neighbor in the eye. Right?"

"Wrong. A lot of doubles in New Orleans are as you describe; but not the doubles on Starlight Street. My aunt's is set back a good fifty feet from the banquette, and there's a vacant lot next to our side of the double, so we borrowed twenty-five feet of that lot for a side lawn."

"But your aunt's tenants—I assume she owns the double—"

"She does."

"Your aunt's tenants aren't so lucky, are they? They don't have a vacant lot to turn into a side lawn."

"No, they don't; but they've never complained." To herself: "Don't talk anymore to this insulting thing. Just get the hell out of here."

"Oh, I'm not knocking row living—"

"Well, you sure had me fooled."

"I just can't picture a beautiful woman, like yourself, living in a double. Correct me if I'm wrong, but the minute you enter the front door of your double you're standing in the parlor; you then pass through French doors into a bedroom; next you go to a small hall, off the hall is a bathroom; then comes another bedroom; and, lastly, the kitchen. To complete your home, there's a big back gallery, a small back yard, with fig, pecan, oak and magnolia trees."

"Something like that except the pecan and magnolia trees are on the vacant lot; and our back yard isn't small. It's big and pretty. Nothing like this, of course." She spread her hands. "This is contrived. Our yard is natural. We have lots of flowers and shrubs and birds. It's an enchanting yard."

"Is Tater Beelack your yardman?"

"Yes. He cuts our grass every week that he's not down in his back, and spades up our flowerbeds when they need spading. My aunt and me do all the weeding."

"And you love living on Starlight Street so much, that when you do marry, you're going to ask your husband to live with your aunt. Aren't you?"

"Maybe."

"Where do you work? D. H. Holmes?"

"No. I work for the New Orleans Homestead on Barrone Street. I'm a private secretary."

"You don't by chance work for ol' Henry Prosper, the poop with the nasal twang? He pays peanuts."

"Yes, Mr. Prosper is my boss, so don't go calling him a poop. He pays me very well."

"You're loyal. That's a good trait. How much does Henri Prosper, the poop, pay you?"

"I can't believe you asked me, a total stranger, how much I make."

"Didn't Tater Beelack ever ask you? Yardmen are notorious for asking personal questions. Didn't you know that?"

"C.C. Bennett, I've got to go. Good-bye."

"No, no, no, you don't. I'm not just plain C.C. Bennett. I'm *Mr. C.C. Bennett.* This yardman insists upon being called *Mister.* Now say *Mister* C.C. Bennett."

"You're crazy as a June bug, *Mister* C. C. Bennett."

He laughed. "Have a cup of coffee with me. It's past Noon."

"Where are you going to get a cuppa coffee?"

"I'm going to make it."

"In Mr. Rogers' *kitchen*?" asked Kendra, incredulous.

"Where else? Come help me."

"No, indeed. I'm not about to go in Mr. Rogers' house."

"For a young woman who invented a suit to be delivered to Mr. Rogers, and who's carrying a sympathy note in her pocket, though you won't own up to it, you're suddenly shy concerning Mr. Rogers."

Kendra gave him a dirty look. "I'll have a cuppa coffee, but I'm *not* going in the house. I'll wait here while you make the coffee."

"Good. Since you won't come in the house, we'll sit on the gallery." He nodded to the table in the corner with the white eyelet skirt and potted pink geranium. "I suppose you drink coffee with chicory. That thick mud."

"I do; and I love it," replied Kendra, climbing the back steps; C.C. Bennett following her.

He seated her. "Well, today you learn to love pure coffee. Good coffee, for a change—Maxwell House. A good rich brew."

"Yuck! Does Mr. Rogers allow you to sit on his gallery and serve strangers pure coffee?"

"Mr. Rogers isn't here, so what he doesn't know won't hurt him."

"I see. What if Mr. Rogers shows up while you and me are drinking pure coffee? You could be sacked, you know.— Don't say I didn't warn you."

"You warned me. I'll be back in a few minutes."

As he walked away, Kendra rolled her brown-gold eyes to the ceiling. — A few minutes later, Mr. C.C. Bennett, yardman, returned pushing a white wicker cart laden with a china luncheon service. He wheeled the cart next to where she sat, and passed her a cup and saucer.

She turned the cup over, and cried: "*Spode!* God save us! as my Aunt Molly Primrose would say—and you're using linen napkins and sterling silver! You've got some nerve."

"Well, I see you have an eye for good china and linens."

"Yes. We have a very old, beautiful and complete set of china—all castles, bridges and willows. We eat off it every day. It's a miracle we haven't broken a piece yet. We're *very* careful with it.

"And rightly so. Pour the coffee," he ordered, seating himself. "I raided the icebox and found this plate of egg and olive finger.sandwiches and some petitfours, to go with our coffee."

Kendra stared at the yardman in disbelief. "You mean to tell me you just helped yourself to all this food—"

"Why not? Don't you like egg and olive sandwiches and petitfours?"

"I love egg and olive sandwiches and petitfours—*but—*"

"I'm glad you *love* egg and olive sandwiches and petitfours. So do I. Now pass the sandwiches and pour the *pure* coffee."

"I'm only taking *one* sandwich; one petitfour." She held up one finger.

The two ate in silence. Kendra sparingly; Mr. C.C. Bennett heartily. He was the first to finish. "I'll have another cup of coffee and a cigarette." —He lit up. "Care for one," he offered through a cloud of smoke.

"No. I don't smoke or drink."

"Miss Goody Two-Shoes sits before me." He blew out a puff of smoke and watched it curl upward.

Kendra poured more coffee. "I know I said I'd only eat one petitfour, but it was so good, I think I'll have another—the one with the pink icing." As she nibbled away, her eyes, for the tenth time, roved round the gallery. "You know, this is an irresistible place to have lunch. I could really be enjoying myself if I weren't so nervous about Mr. Rogers showing up."

"Then enjoy it and quit worrying about Mr. Rogers, and start worrying about your lack of manners. You haven't complimented me on my expertise as a yardman. All you said was the patio was contrived."

"That got to you, eh? I'm glad." Again, Kendra looked around, admiration in her eyes. "It's contrived, but breathtakingly so. Beautiful. I've never seen anything like it in my life except in magazines. I think I could stay right here on this patio forever. It makes me feel so good I could hug myself."

"Remember it rains a lot here and it gets cold in the winter, so you couldn't live on the patio forever," said Mr. C.C. Bennett, his navy eyes looking into Kendra's brown-gold ones. He stubbed out his cigarette and studied her face for a few fixed seconds, and then smilingly added: "Rather than see you hug yourself, I can do that for you."

"No, you can't," laughed Kendra.

"Since you won't let me hug you, I've got a proposition for you."

She shook her brown-gold head. "I'm not interested in any hugs or propositions."

"You haven't felt my hugs or heard my propositions, so how can you say you're not interested?"

"What's the proposition?" asked Kendra, amused.

"Mr. Rogers needs a secretary, for about six months, until he can get all the paperwork cleared up regarding his wife's death. How would you like to be his private secretary?"

"Do you, the *yardman*, hire and fire for Mr. Rogers?"

"I do."

Again, Kendra shook her head. "I have a job. Besides, my aunt told me Mrs. Rogers has a secretary, so let her take care of all the paperwork. There, your problem's solved."

"No, it's not. Miss Farnsworth's on vacation. She doesn't even know Mrs. Rogers is dead."

"You're kidding! You mean nobody's got in touch with Mrs. Rogers' secretary to tell her the boss is dead?"

"No one knows where she is. Icelynn Farnsworth is not due back until the middle of May. The paperwork can't wait that long. There are hundreds of thank you notes to be written, not to mention acknowledging all those well-worded sympathy cards written by women, like yourself, who tried to meet the rich widower."

Kendra stuck out her tongue at Mr. C. C. Bennett. "My aunt also told me Mrs. Rogers has a protege. Let him help."

"He's out of town, and not expected back for another six weeks."

"Death takes priority. Call this, what's-his-name?—"

"Kyle Osborne."

"Call this Kyle Osborne back to town."

"Like Iceylnn Farnsworth, Osborne can't be reached."

"What about Mrs. Rogers' personal maid? Can't she help out?"

"Josie Sato is Japanese, and she and her family are now back in California."

"You know, this all sounds very odd. Do you have any idea why they cancelled Mrs. Rogers' wake?"

"The morgue accidentally cremated her. So there was no body for a wake.— The deputy medical examiner, instead of performing an autopsy on her, shipped her body off to be cremated."

Kendra held her nose. "That stinks like rotten catfish. No autopsy, no body! How convenient. I'm surprised I haven't seen anything in the *Picayune* about Hippolyte Delacroix investigating Mrs. Rogers' death."

"Do you know Hippo Delacroix?"

"Heck no. I know him because he's the state attorney, and I've seen him on TV a time or two. I've been told the handsome Creole is rich, and considered a catch."

"True. Would you like an introduction?"

"No—He's not my type."

"I'm sure *you're* his type; however, I'm certain his ma mère, Bell Delacroix, would find you too modern for her baby boy. Bell's a domineering Creole woman, who's hunting a wife for her forty-year-old son. She wants grandchildren—soon."

Kendra wrinkled her nose in distaste. "I'm not interested.—Do you know if Mrs. Rogers was alone when she died? Her death unattended? If so an autopsy should've been performed. That's automatic."

"You sound more like an investigator than a secretary. Are you an authority on automatic autopsies?"

"I'd rather be in investigative work than typing. No, I'm not an authority on autopsies; but I know unattended deaths call for one."

"Brilliant deduction, Holmes."

"You needn't act smart. I think I would make a good investigator; and don't tell me there're no female investigators. I already know that.— The obit notice said Mrs. Rogers died of a heart attack. My aunt says she never heard Mrs. Rogers ever complain of having heart trouble. Did you?"

"No. But that doesn't mean she didn't have heart trouble. Her doctor said, about six months ago, he told her of her heart condition. Evidently she just ignored her problem." He shrugged. "She didn't tell anybody."

"I don't believe that. Her death should be investigated."

"You're a suspicious person. Give me one good reason why there should be an investigation?"

"I could give you a lot more than one, but for starters I've heard Mrs. Rogers was rich, and that Mr. Rogers wasn't. He probably married her for her money, and maybe even killed her for it. I bet Rogers got all her dough and property."

"He did."

"I think he should be investigated. He might've done her in to get her money. To get all this." Kendra spread her hands to encompass the mansion and the patio.

"Why don't you call Delacroix and suggest that possibility to him?"

"I might just do that."

"Good. While you're deciding how to stir up Delacroix to investigate Mr. Rogers, how about telling me what your salary is?"

"I guess the only way to get you off the subject of my salary is to say my weekly envelope—take home pay—is $38 bucks," replied Kendra, reproachfully. "I work Monday through Friday, 9—5. No Saturday work," she added roundly.

"Mr. Rogers will pay you $350 a month, 9 till however long it takes to get the day's work done. And maybe some Saturday work."

Kendra whistled. "That's a lot of money. What are the duties, aside from writing thank you notes and answering all those well-written sympathy notes from women trying to meet up with Mr. Rogers?"

Mr. C.C. Bennett chuckled. "That's basically what the job entails. Just think, you'd have to write a thank you to yourself."

She stuck out her tongue at him.

He smiled broadly. "You'd also have to get Mrs. Rogers' papers and desk in order. And maybe pack some of her personal effects."

"You know, since there was no formal funeral, and Mrs. Rogers was *accidentally* cremated, I don't think Mr. Rogers should worry with thank you notes. I think in the circumstances, the less said the better."

"Mr. Rogers goes by the rules. Every courtesy—phone call, note, flowers—must be acknowledged, and he's not up to doing it."

"Then the man must be devastated by his wife's death, or pretending to be."

"He's not devastated. He's sorry and sad and not in the mood to follow up on the many little wearying details that involve death. He needs a secretary, at Willowwynn, to see to these added responsibilities."

"Mr. C.C. Bennett, the $350 salary is *very* tempting, but I'm not about to give up my *permanent*, but boring job, for a *temporary* boring job. I'd be bored silly writing thank you notes."

"You only make $160 a month. You'd earn twice that."

"As I said, the salary is *ve-ry* tempting, but I need long-term job security. I've got a lot of debts to pay off."

"You've been making bills, eh? No doubt charging clothes, left and right—that pretty yellow dress you're wearing looks expensive."

"My aunt made this dress. She makes all my clothes. I charged things for the house: a washing machine, a hot water heater, an electric icebox. The necessities."

"Well, that's commendable."

"Listen, those thank you notes you speak of can be dashed off in a couple hours. I'll be happy to write them for Mr. Rogers. No charge. Just give me the names and addresses and, of course, what Mr. Rogers basically wants to say. I'll write them tomorrow afternoon. I never have anything to do on Sunday except go to Mass, and afterwards read or listen to records."

"With a name like Applegate, I figured you were Catholic."

"With a name like Bennett, I figured you were protestant."

He laughed. "Mr. Rogers never accepts free services. Your job, as his secretary, would also include paying household bills, here at No. 10 Prytania. If Mr. Rogers saw that he couldn't do without your services, you could become permanent. In that case, you would also take over the paperwork for the Bay St. Louis cottage and the mansion in San Francisco."

Kendra whistled low.

"Being Mr. Rogers' secretary will be totally different from being Mr. Prosper's."

"Well, when Miss Farnsworth returns and finds another secretary here will she raise the roof?"

"No."

"When would Mr. Rogers want me to start?"

"Immediately."

"That's impossible. I'd have to give Mr. Prosper two weeks' notice. Besides, how do you know Mr. Rogers, who hasn't even seen me, would hire me sight unseen and without testing my secretarial skills. Wouldn't he want, at least, to interview me? Read my resume? See some references? Talk to Mr. Prosper about me?"

"He relies on my good judgment."

"Oh, spare me."

"How long have you worked for Henri Prosper, that old poop, who talks through his nose?"

"Three years."

"You're more than qualified. No resume needed."

Kendra looked at her watch. "Goodness it's 4:15! I've got to get to Confession and then home. My aunt, on Saturdays, serves supper at 5:30 on the dot."

"You confess *every* Saturday?"

"Certainly."

"I can see, in your case, that would be very necessary. Don't forget to tell your confessor about your little escapade today. Coming here under false pretenses. Lying about that sympathy note you got in your pocket."

"I can't believe I've been sitting here talking all afternoon to such a rude man."

"I guess when you're having fun time flies.— Want the job?"

"No, thank you," sweetly replied Kendra, rising and scraping back her chair. "Oh, Mr. C.C. Bennett, I hate to leave you with the dishes, but in the circumstances"—she laughed a bubbly laugh, walked down the steps, over to the table where the empty Holmes' box was, and picked it up.

Mr. C.C. Bennett joined her. "I'll walk you to your automobile." A few moments later he opened the driver's door of the Dodge, took the box from her and tossed it on the passenger's seat. He studied the automobile for a second or so, and said: "I've seen this Dodge."

"*Oh, brother, here we go again.* You haven't seen my Dodge. Unless you're one of the owners. I'm the fourth or fifth owner"

"I'm not one of the owners; but I think I've seen *you* and *your* Dodge. Anyway, I've enjoyed our lengthy clash."

"So have I," laughed Kendra, as she climbed into the Dodge. "Good-bye, Mr. C.C. Bennett, and thank you for lunch, the awful coffee and the unusual conversation."

"You want the job," he asked again.

"No." They shook hands, laughed together, and then Kendra drove off.

Chapter Six

When Kendra arrived home, her aunt was putting the pad on the gatelegged table."Everything'll be done in a few minutes," she announced, moving from table, to sink, to stove. She stirred a big simmering pot, and then moved back to the sink. "You been to Confession?"she asked— "I went to the Jesuits before I came home."

"Y—yes. I barely made it"—She sniffed the air.—"What you cooking?" she asked, peeking over her aunt's shoulder into the simmering black iron pot, that was giving off delicious-smelling flavors. "What ever it is, it's making my mouth water."

"It's just a pot of feu of pickle poke, Creole tomatoes, snap beans, new potatoes and some cajun seasonings; and I made a side dish of fried sweet potatoes just for you. I hope you got a good appetite."

"Mmmmm—that sounds delicious—I had a finger sandwich and two petitfours for lunch.You didn't mention dessert—We're not having any?"

"You know we always have dessert, except durin' Lent. I stopped at Katz and Bestoff and got a coconut custard pie—your favorite."

"Mmmmm—that *is* my favorite. I'll finish setting the table."

Molly Primrose moved to the stove again, stirred the pots and pans and tasted their contents while Kendra ballooned a white, Irish linen cloth. It landed a little off center; she corrected the miss. Then she set the table with their blue-and-white china, casually remarking: "I've been to Willowwynn today; been there all afternoon."

Molly Primrose's white eyebrows mounted high, and her button blue eyes grew dark and serious looking, as she gaped at her niece in total disbelief. "What was you doin' at Willowwynn?"

"Delivering a pasteboard box of tissue paper, of which I had no choice. You better lower the fire on the rice; it's starting to boil over."

Automatically her aunt lowered the gas jet, stirred the rice and then tasted a few grains. "It's done," she said, and strained it. "Everything's ready. Let's eat. Why didn't you have no choice?"

Both sat down and said Grace before Kendra answered."Last Monday when I tried to pick up Mrs. Rogers' suit, you said it was at Delivery."

"I thought it was. I thought Nell had taken it there. After you left, I found it on the workbench, and took it myself. Evidently, Nell, later on, spotted our big box of tissue paper, thought it was Mrs. Rogers' suit, and remembered she was suppose to take it to Delivery."

"Nell didn't get a chance to take it to Delivery. I met her in the hall, and she said she was taking Mrs. Rogers' suit to Delivery, and—"

"And you offered to do that little chore for her."

Kendra nodded. "All week long I've been toting that taped up box of tissue paper in the trunk of my Dodge, believing I had the suit."

"And all week long me and Nell, not wantin' to ask Mr. Straveinia for another box of tissue paper—he counts every piece of paper we use and every pin we lose—we've been goin' crazy lookin' for our big box of tissue paper, never dreamin' you had it. Nell didn't mention a thing about lettin' you take a package to Delivery, nor even seein' you."

"I guess she's getting forgetful."

"No, she's not. It's that seventeen inch Philco's fault. Because of that ol' Philco, she's not gettin' her proper rest, and she can't do her job right. I'm gunna have *another* talk with her. Wasn't the suit delivered? How did you find out the box you had was full of tissue paper?"

"No one was home at Willowwynn except Mr. C.C. Bennett, the *yardman,* and he insisted that I tear open the box. You can guess the rest. He then accused me of deliberately coming to Willowwynn, using the suit as an excuse to get my foot in Mr. Rogers' door, to rope in a rich husband."

"How terrible of him to say such a thing, even if it was true."

"He also said my scheme was the cheapest. All the other women who beat me there brought gifts of fruit and food. I brought paper."

"Why-y-y-y, the *nerve* of *that* yardman. Who ever heard the like of him? Not me. I'm surprised you didn't give that yardman cards and spades."

Kendra shrugged. "He also said I was the only woman to get not only my foot but my whole body on Mr. Rogers' patio."

"Of all the insultin' things to say. Kendra Lou, I don't like him at all. He sounds like a commonest. I still don't understand why it took you all afternoon to explain the tissue paper."

"Mmmmm—this pickle pork's so tender it melts in my mouth.— It only took a few minutes to explain away the paper. I was caught, and furious at myself for getting caught."

"I hope your little scheme learned you a lesson."

"It did." She took a bite of food. "I spent the rest of the time on Mr.

Rogers' beautiful back gallery, overlooking an exquisite patio, with my host, Mr. C.C. Bennett."

"You spent the *whole afternoon visitin' with a yardman?* Where was Mr. Rogers?"

Kendra looked around the table."Where's the bread?"

"We're having corn muffins for a change—oh, no-o-o-o, they're still in the oven," she cried, leaping up."My memory's short as my nose."

"Your nose is long enough. Are they burnt?"

"N—no. Just a little brown."

"Good. I like them brown and burning hot.—The butter melts faster that way—I told you Mr. Rogers wasn't home. No body was there but the yardman. He fixed us *pure* coffee and a light lunch. The coffee was as weak as monkey pee, and tasted the same."—Kendra made a face—"We sat in white wicker armchairs, at a round table with a white eyelet table skirt, and pink geraniums for a centerpiece. It was heavenly. We ate on Mr. Rogers' Spode china; used his Tole flatware; and wiped our mouths on his best Irish linen napkins."

"Kendra *Louise*, how could you? What if Mr. Rogers had come home and caught you and *that* yardman? I can't imagine you eatin' with a *yardman*, not to mention wastin' your time and *his*, no doubt talkin' monkey foolishness. What could you possibly gab about, for hours, with a *yardman?* Here, have a muffin. Watch it, it's *hot."*

"O-o-o-o-o, it is!—Phew!—" She spread the top of the muffin with a lump of butter, bit it and talked thickly. "To understand, you'd have to meet Mr. C.C. Bennett. He's the most fascinating yardman I've ever met. He's thirty-seven, extremely handsome and *ve-ry* unique."

"I never met a fascinatin'-'n'-unique yardman in all my born days," confessed Aunt Molly Primrose, pop-eyed, her apple cheeks redder than ever. "Nor have I ever heard one called *Mister*, either. The only yardman I know is our Tater Beelack, a fine nigra man, who can't read or write, and who signs his name with a big X.

"My sainted mother, your beloved grandmother, Gawd rest her soul, said when she was a girl her family had a yardman by the name of Beaver Brown. My mother said Beaver Brown didn't have sense enough to pour pee out a boot, with the directions written on the sole."

"Stands to reason if Beaver Brown couldn't read, he couldn't pour the pee. Could he?"

"Can your fascinatin'-'n'-unique Mr. C.C. Bennett read-'n'-write? And how does he sign his name? With a little x?"

Kendra laughed a quiet laugh with a low gurgle in her throat. She took a sip of her iced tea. "This tea's delicious. Nobody can make iced tea like you can, Tante. Mr. C.C. Bennett says he prints. Of course, he's joking. You'd have to meet this yardman to appreciate him. He acts like he owns Willowwynn. He also acts like he's Mr. Rogers' right-hand man."

"Kendra *Louise*, please don't talk like you're muddled-minded. Mr. Rogers would never give a *yardman* any authority."

"We-ell, this yardman almost convinced me to quit my job and go to work for Mr. Rogers, for about six months. Maybe permanently, if Mr. Rogers found me to be indispensable."

Dead silence. "Kendra *Louise*, you wouldn't dare even think of quittin' your fine job just on the say-so of a *colored yardman?* You know he can't be right in his head."

"What color is colored, Tante?"

"Why *black*, of course. Why did you ask such a silly question?"

"Mr. C.C. Bennett asked me that question, and I answered just like you did. *Black.*"

"That's the right answer."

"I know. Anyway, Mr. C.C. Bennett is a white yardman."

"Who ever heard of a *white* yardman? Not me. Lawnin'-'n'-weedin' jobs go to *colored* men. This C.C. Bennett is takin' away a job from some poor colored man."

Kendra shrugged. "I came this close"—using her right thumb and forefinger, she made the space of half an inch. "I came this close to wanting to give Mr. Prosper, that ol' poop, two weeks' notice."

"*That ol' poop!*" repeated Aunt Molly Primrose, incredulous. "What in the world's come over you? I've never heard you speak so disrespectfully of your boss."

"Mr. C.C. Bennett knows Mr. Prosper, and he calls him an ol' poop; I agree," said Kendra, her mouth full of food. She swallowed, and then added: "Mr. Prosper is an ol' poop with a nasal twang."

"Kendra *Louise*, in my presence, don't call Mr. Prosper an ol' poop. You sound like you're sidin' with *that* crazy, counterfeit, *white yardman*, who might be a commonest. You sound like you *like* him."

"I do. Being with him was fun. I had a good time." To herself: "And I never thought of Jack *once*." Aloud: "No harm in it—we'll never see each other again." She looked dreamy-eyed. "I can't explain it, but we clicked. There was chemistry between us. No sense denying it."

"Don't talk to me of that chemistry stuff. You know I don't put no store in such things. I don't believe in love at first sight, either."

"I didn't say I'm in love with him; but I think I could fall for him."

"Gawd save us! Fall for a *yardman.*"

"If there hadn't been something between us, I'd have walked away, but I stayed on for more and more of his insults. Actually, they weren't insults. He spoke the truth, and the truth can get to you." Kendra looked thoughtful. "You know, the truth is never popular. Sometimes it's downright dangerous."

"Humph.— Kendra *Louise,* you know I want you to make a suitable marriage. You know, I didn't raise and educate you to marry no *yardman.* A *yardman* can't support himself let alone a wife and family. You know what we pay Tater Beelack—$2.50 a week. And we give him 50 cents more than the rest of the folk around here."

"Chicken feed. —I'm not going to *marry* a *yardman.*"

"I'm glad to hear it."

"You know, if only I had the courage to quit my *permanent* job and take that temporary one, I could make some big bucks. But I want long-term security. Do you know what I could make working for Mr. Rogers? Listen to this"—she gestured with her fork—$350 bucks a month. I'd be able to pay off most of my debts, put some money by and then go some where and have a good time. But I don't have the guts to do it." She threw up both hands, fork and all.

"I already told you, Kendra *Louise,* women don't make *that* kind of money. Every time you get a ten cent raise, you spend it in your mind twenty different ways. The Lord only knows if you got a $175 dollar raise, how you'd spend it. And as far as goin' some where and havin' a good time goes, I think that trip to Jackson and the stop off at the leper colony should last you the rest of your life. I know it will me.—

"Not me. I still want to go some where and have a good time."

Aunt Molly Primrose shook her head. "Anyways, Mr. Rogers don't need no secatary. He has his wife's secatary."

"Miss Farnsworth is on vacation, and won't be back until the middle of May. She doesn't even know Mrs. Rogers is dead. They don't know where Miss Farnsworth is, so they can't call and tell her."

"Why-y-y-y, that's very strange indeed."

"I thought so. Mr. Rogers wants thank you notes to go out *now*, to all those people who sent flowers to Mrs. Rogers' funeral, the funeral she didn't have." She took a bite of muffin and a sip of tea. "If you think not being able to locate Miss Farnsworth is strange, wait to you hear this. They can't find Mrs. Rogers' protege, Kyle Osborne, either."

"My-y-y-y, that *is* aud."

"There's more. Mrs. Rogers died unattended, and her body was sent to the morgue for an autopsy, which it didn't get. Instead she was accidentally cremated. *That* stinks as bad as rotten catfish."

Her aunt frowned. "I don't like it, Kendra *Louise;* and I don't want you mixed up with either Mr. C.C. Bennett or Mr. Rogers. Just from what you told me the whole thing sounds very strange and suspicious. I think the state attorney—I can't think of that big Creole's name—"

"Hippolyte Delacroix. Mr. C.C. Bennett calls him Hippo—Says he could introduce me to him—I said I wasn't interested."

"The yardman doesn't know the state attorney?— I think that Mr. Delacroix should investigate Mrs. Rogers' death , *and that* yardman."

"Evidently, Mr. Delacroix thinks everything's OK."

"Then it must be," shrugged Aunt Molly Primrose. "Anyways, if Mr. Bennett was investigated, I think you'd find him to be an impostor, a commonest and a mugglehead. Also, if you resign your job, you'll find out you don't have no job with Mr. Rogers."

"Mr. C.C. Bennett is not a communist, or an impostor. So get that out of your head right now; and, since he's not colored he doesn't smoke muggles. You told me only colored people were dope heads."

"That's true. But there are some low-down whites who do it, too. Stop frownin', Kendra Lou, you'll hurt your good looks.— I don't trust that Mr. C.C. Bennett whether he be a white, colored or a pink yardman.— Are you ready for your pie and coffee?"

"Yes."

The two ate their dessert in silence, except for an occasional: "M'm...this pie is good"; and when they finished Kendra announced: "I'll wash the dishes."

"I'll dry," offered her aunt. "Afterwards we can sit on the front gallery for a little while, before we go to bed. Remember, we can't stay up late cause we got to get up early for Mass."

"I wish just once I could get up late on Sunday, drink coffee and read the funnies. Laze around and just play hooky from church."

Aunt Molly Primrose gasped. "Kendra *Louise*, you're talkin' wickedness. I've told you over and over that men and women are put on this earth to prepare their immortal souls for eternity. If you deliberately miss Mass, you're committin' a mortal sin; and you can go to hell for that. Never see heaven? Remember, to save your soul, think of the bliss of heaven and the pains of hell. *Never miss mass!*

The next morning, Kendra and her aunt attended, as usual, the 6:00 o'clock Mass, at Ursuline Convent Chapel. Kendra's mind was on Mr. C.C. Bennett and, all through Mass she had been mechanically getting off her knees, standing up, crossing herself, and saying *Amen*. Mass flew by. They were home by 7:15 and, instead of, as usual, having their breakfast and reading the paper, they both went back to bed for forty winks.

At a little after 11:00, Molly Primrose woke up groggy and in a startled state of disbelief. Never had she slept so late; she woke Kendra, who was also groggy and not believing she had slept the whole morning away."

"The mornin's gone," moaned Aunt Molly Primrose, "and I haven't even fixed breakfast."

"Tante, let's just have coffee, French bread and some Creole cream cheese," suggested Kendra, yawning.

"That's not much for Sunday breakfast, but I guess it'll have to do. I can't believe I slept like that. I don't think I've got enough time even to make us a good main meal, either. I was going to fix us baked chicken-'n-'stuffin', but I promised Rosa Ganucci I'd go to her house around 3:00 and mind the twins, so she and Tony could go some where and relax. I promised her I'd stay till 5:00."

"Tante, Rosa has two married daughters. Let them help her."

"I know; but they got babies of their own. Besides, I'm crazy about those two beautiful baby boys. Rosa has had nothin' but beautiful chirren. I can hardly wait for you, Kendra Lou, to get married, and have beautiful babies."

"Some day," mumbled Kendra, still sounding sleepy and somewhat cranky. "Tante, it's almost lunch time, so forget the main meal. The coffee and Creole cream cheese will hold us till supper. Go on and mind the twins, and when you come home I'll fix us waffles, ham and scrambled eggs for our supper. How does that sound?"

"Delicious."

At 2:45, Molly Primrose left for Rosa's house; Kendra, wearing her faded and frayed gingham dress, with the square neckline and the short puff-sleeves, was sprawled on the parlor floor, her white ballerinas free of her feet, was drinking coffee and reading the funny papers—*Blondie*.

The front door and windows were wide open, letting the breeze billow the curtains in and out. She heard a creaking sound coming from the floor boards on the gallery, and looked up. To her complete surprise there stood good-looking Mr. C.C. Bennett, staring at her through the screen door.

He was wearing khaki pants, a short-sleeved blue oxford shirt, open at the throat, and brown loafers. His brown-gold hair was loose and tumbling onto his forehead; his navy blue eyes, twinkling.

Kendra, staring, sat speechless and motionless.

"Are you going to remain seated on the floor, staring up at me, or are you going to get up, open the door and invite me in?"

Rising in slow motion, she slipped her right foot into her shoe; her left shoe had some how got shoved under the sofa, so she snatched it up and limped to the door. Before opening the door, she dropped the ballerina to the floor and proceeded to work her foot into the shoe. The back caved in and she had to balance herself on one leg and, using both hands, tugged on her other shoe."Er—come in. W-w-what do you want? Are you here because Mr. Rogers wants me to write those thank you notes?"

"I told you Mr. Rogers pays for services rendered. I'm here because I wanted to see the doubles of Starlight Street, particularly this one. You bragged on it so much I had to see it for myself."

"H-how did you get here? Ride the streetcar?"

"I drove. I parked a few blocks away so I could walk and inspect doubles before I got to this one."

"We-ell, what do you think, not that it matters to me?"

"I think this room is charming and fine—too bad you made such a big mess with the funnies spread all over the floor—"

"Er—won't you sit down." Kendra tried to tidy the disorder. She snatched up her coffee cup and set it on the parlor table, next to a letter from Sonny Ganucci, and a stack of Sherlock Holmes' novels.

"You can't make it neat now. And I don't want to sit down. I want to see the house." His navy blue eyes scanned the parlor, resting on three pink-and-cream cabbage roses in a milk-glass dimestore vase, sitting on the parlor table. He noted Sonny's letter."I thought Willowwynn had the most beautiful roses in all New Orleans, but I see I was wrong. Where did you get those roses?" He nodded to the vase.

"In the back yard. We have a whole fence of them."

"Later show me *that* rose fence. Now I'd like to meet your aunt."

"She's at a neighbor's house—Rosa Ganucci. She's minding *and* worshiping Rosa's baby twins; so Rosa and her husband can have an afternoon alone."

"How nice. I assume, that letter from PFC Sonny Ganucci"—he nodded to the letter—"is a relative of Mrs. Ganucci's."

"Her son. Sonny's in Korea.—"

"She's got a *son* fighting in Korea, and *baby twins?*"

"The twins are what the folk of Starlight Street call late in life babies. A mistake. A slip.— Sonny and I grew up together. We write to each other. He just asked me in that letter if I remembered the day he kicked Kenny Joe in the shins, and how I lit into him? While pounding Sonny, I accidentally punched Kenny Joe in the eye. Gave him a shiner."

Mr. C.C. Bennett chuckled softly. "So is Sonny your new beau?"

"Of all the people I know, you ask the most personal questions. Sonny is my *good* friend, not my boyfriend."

Mr. C.C. Bennett smiled, stooped down and picked up two of the books, from the stack on the table, and looked them over. "H'm...*The Adventures of Sherlock Homes* and *The Memoirs of Sherlock Holmes*. "Both dilapidated. That tells me you've read and reread these books."

"True."

He replaced the books, and then walked over to the bookshelves. "Your shelves are filled with worthwhile literature," he said, taking them in with a glance. "Most of the classics; and even a few books on travel and adventure." He turned his back to the bookshelves, looked over the furniture, and remarked: "Solid cherry. I'd say handcrafted."

"I'd say you were right. It was made by Applegates."

He stepped back a pace and looked her over critically with those navy-eyes of his. Her honey-olive skin was soft and clear, her cheeks were tinged a rosy pink, and her mop of golden-brown hair was a mass of gypsy ringlets. "You look absolutely beautiful—but never wear that childish dress again. It makes you look about seventeen."

"I like this dress. It's comfortable, for around the house."

"And well-worn. No doubt you resurrected it from the rag bag."

"I don't recall asking your advice about my wardrobe."

"I assume that album contains kin and kith" observed Mr. C.C. Bennett, changing the subject."Show me *only* your parents' pictures."

Kendra showed him the pictures.

"I think you favor your handsome father. Your mother is lovely. You may close the album now." He looked around the room. "I see you haven't got a television set."

"That's right. I'd like one, but my aunt doesn't want one. She thinks TV's a waste of time."

"She's right."

"Do you have a TV?"

"I do."

"And you waste your time watching it, don't you?"

"I do. Now I'd like for you to show me the rest of the house."

"The house is upset because my aunt and I got off track today."

Kendra told him the bare bones of how they had gotten off track. "I can't ever remember us sleeping a whole morning away."

He laughed."*Show me the house.*"

"Right this way, for the grand tour," sang out Kendra, sounding like a guide. She opened the French doors which led to her aunt's bedroom.

Mr. C.C. Bennett passed through, carefully looked over the room and said: "Ve-ry nice. Neat, airy and attractive. Dignified. That cherry sleigh bed is beautiful," he added.

"Yes, it is. All our furniture is cherry and in perfect condition."

"Don't brag. It doesn't become you."

"I'm not bragging. I'm stating facts."

They entered the hallway. "The bathroom's right there." She pointed. "I know you don't want to see it."

"Yes, I do."

His navy eyes zeroed in on a handful of bobbie pins scattered on the back of the commode. "I know that mess of pins isn't your aunt's."

"I think you've seen enough of the bathroom."

They proceeded to Kendra's bedroom. After Mass, she had flung her white cotton gloves and Mother of Pearl prayerbook on the bedside rocker; her bandanna she had carelessly tossed over the back of the rocker; she hadn't bothered to make her bed. Any old slapdash sort of way she had thrown back the bedspread just to make the bed look half way decent.

"Don't tell me. Let me guess who this unmade bed belongs to—"

"*I-told-you* I was off track today."

"No excuse. H'm, nice hemstitched sheets. Custom made."

"My aunt made them. She's suspicious of ready-made sheets—and also has her doubts about some labor-saving devices. She thinks we're going to progress ourselves right out of existence."

He chuckled. For a moment he looked around the room, and then walked over to her dresser table and picked up a small colored photo of Kenny Joe in uniform. "This must be the young man you were going to marry. A good-looking kid."

"Kenny Joe Wheelerhand was beautiful."

That morning when she was rummaging through her dresser drawers for a bandanna, she had come across a small snapshot of Jack Trenchard, looked at it, and left it on her dresser, face down. Mr. C.C. Bennett sat down Kenny Joe's picture, and then picked up Jack's.

His navy blue eyes narrowed. "What are you doing with a picture of Trenchard, Judge Edwards' son-in-law, in your bedroom?"

"That's a-none-of-your-business-question, and I'm going to pretend you didn't ask it. Come, I'll show you the kitchen."

He turned Jack Trenchard's picture face down, and frowned.

"Stop frowning. You'll hurt your good looks."

"Show me the kitchen."

In the kitchen. "The patina on this gatelegged table is exquisite," remarked Mr. C. C. Bennett, running his hand across the table. "From the looks and feel of it, I can tell it gets museum care."

"My aunt makes sure *that* table and all the furniture in this house get museum care."

He chuckled. "I see you've got another bouquet of those beautiful roses." He picked up the vase, from the center of the table, and his eyes narrowed. "Miss Applegate, *this* vase is a *Sevres.*"

"I know. It belonged to my mother. We only put it out on Sundays. The rest of the time I keep it in my hope chest. After Sunday breakfast, I usually take the Sevres' vase, with the roses, and put it on the parlor table. Later, when we eat our main meal, I put the bouquet back on the gatelegged table. That way we get more enjoyment out of the vase and the roses."

"Well, why isn't this rare and lovely vase now on the parlor table?"

"I told you I've been off track all day. I'm not myself."

"Why aren't you yourself?"

"If I knew, I'd be myself and not myself. Do you want to see the back gallery?"

"Of course, I do."

On the back gallery. "When I was a little girl," said Kendra, dreamy-eyed, "I knew summer had officially arrived by the first night my Aunt Molly Primrose and I slept out here."

"Do you still sleep on the gallery?"

"Yes—when it's real hot—that's the only way to beat the heat, and, at the same time, put yourself in touch with the stars, watch a misty moon light up a blue black sky, and, at the same time, listen to all those mysterious night noises.

"One summer, while sleeping out here, I got the childish notion that I'd like to visit the man-in-the-moon. My aunt laughed and said the man-in-the-moon lived too far up in the sky; and would never have a visitor. I guess after TV being invented, impossible things now seem possible. Who knows, some day someone just might visit the man-in-the-moon."

He laughed; then they both looked at the back gallery.

"You know, I guess if nobody on Starlight Street had a back gallery, I suppose they wouldn't know where to store things, shell peas or string snap beans."

He laughed again. "What are front galleries for?"

"For grown-ups to rock and make talk about other people; for young folks, to loiter; to swing; to share secrets; to hold hands; and to linger over good nights."

"Your eyes look dreamy with memories."

"I was remembering the first time I helped my aunt move the gatelegged table to the back yard. We sat it under the oak tree, next to the stone bench, so we could eat our lunch in the shade and our supper in a breeze."

"You mean you brought *that* beautiful table outdoors?"

"We never left it out all night. We used it until my aunt found that small dropleaf for a buck, at a second-hand store on Magazine Street."—She pointed at the table over in the corner—"It was black, but we sanded it down and painted it white enamel. It stayed out all night."

"I see it's survived nicely"; then, "you share this back gallery with your tenants. Does that low-lattice partition provide enough privacy?"

"It used to before Kenny Joe and his father died. I've had a falling out with Kenny Joe's aunts: Miss Lettie Lou and Miss Effie Vi'let."

"Can't patch it up?"

"No. Come on, I'll show you the back yard."

They stood in the sparkling sunshine on the walkway where tiny cushions of cool green mold nestled between the old red bricks, and looked—and looked—and looked at a fairyland of glory. Sunbeams danced about and birds sang. The Bridal Wreath, that hemmed the foundation, was laced over with airy white flowers; a sweep of yellow daylilies banked the bridal wreath; and working these lilies was a tiny hummingbird. His plumage was brilliant turquoise, with conspicuous patches of iridescent pinky mauve around his eyes, at the bridge of his beak and on his light gray underneath.

They watched breathlessly as this little creature hung suspended in a whirlwind of tiny wings, sticking its black needle bill again and again into the slender throats of the daylilies. Then, like magic, he disappeared.

"Hummingbirds are enchanting," softly said Clark

"Only God could make so much beauty, so much perfection in such a tiny, enchanting creature. A perfect purity," murmured Kendra.

He looked deeply into her eyes, and in that exquisite moment their minds met and they shared a mental bond. The bonding was so exquisite it hurt her; and to cover her pain and ecstasy, she reached out her hand and snapped off a spray of the bridal wreath and stripped it of its leaves. Then impulsively tossed the twig away.

They turned toward the rose fence and saw a myriad of humming honeybees, preparing to plunder the roses of their sweet nectar. The ground beneath the rose bushes was scattered with a sweep of soft petals, pink and white.

Above them the sapphire sky was slashed with rifts of rosy-pearl and splotched with fluffs of cottony clouds. "If I were a bird," mused Kendra, "I'd never build a nest in a fig tree. I'd soar up to one of those soft clouds and make my nest."

"I'm glad you're not a bird," laughed Clark.

"So am I, really."

"You said the grounds around Willowwynn were contrived, and your back yard was natural. It's naturally beautiful. It reminds me of a back yard that's been illustrated in a fairytale book."

"Now that you mention it, I think so, too.—Look! the bird bath has"—and she counted aloud—"six sparrows, splashing," she said, blinking in the sunlight.

Just then a baby mockingbird fell from its nest in the fig tree, flapping its wings desperately and squawking loudly. Instantly, its alarmed momma swooped down to its side, protecting it. The baby bird ran a few feet, its wings flapping wildly, got off the ground a foot and then belly landed. After three or four failures, he took flight, his momma at his wing, and both made it back to the nest.

A blackbird perched on a twig in the sweet olive cawed in applause; and every mockingbird in the fig tree mocked it. Just then a pair of pigeons, with iridescent necks and pink feet, swooped down close to the bird bath. They strutted about, cooing while Mr. C.C. Bennett examined the roses, whose petals gleamed and glistened with tiny moisture pearls.

"Beautiful. Absolutely beautiful. What do you do to keep them so healthy; and their leaves so clean and free from black spots and spider?"

"All my aunt does is throw our coffee grinds and tea leaves around the roots. As for the leaves, when they start turning a little yellow or white or get those tiny black spots, she makes up a bucket of soapy water and throws it on the bushes. It works wonders."

"Never heard of it; but I'll try it. The sun's in your eyes. Let's sit on the bench, in the shade."

They sat on the stone bench beneath the old oak, its branches sheltering them from the sun; its knotty roots covered with maidenhair fern as green as a new leaf. Sunshafts sifted through the branches, splashing over them, gilding them almost golden.They sat enfolded in a dream-like serenity while tiny breezes, as soft as silk and honeysuckle-scented, caressed their faces. He looked at her and touched her with his eyes only. She felt her cheeks burning, her heart racing with excitement.

He reached forward and lifted a silky strand of her hair, and it twined itself around his tapering finger. His eyes still on her face, he soon released her hair, and then lifted her hand gently until it was against his lips. He didn't take his eyes off her flushed face.

Suddenly the pigeons took wing in a flutter, as fat and fluffy Sholar Picarara and tiger-striped Motel, sleek and glossy, emerged from under the house, making a loud commotion. They went tearing round and round the yard like two possessed cats. They frisked and frolicked about; pounced on each other; wrestled and rolled around the ground. Then suddenly they stopped. Their ears went flat, their backs raised, they spit and smacked at each other, until Motel beat his retreat no doubt for home.

Ordinarily, Kendra enjoyed a visit from Sholar and Motel, but not at that moment. At that moment she was waiting to be kissed by the yardman, who almost looked disconcerted, by the fighting Toms.

"Sholar thinks he owns Starlight Street," laughed Kendra. "He's a fearless fighter. He vanquishes strange cats and routs dogs."

Spotting Kendra, Sholar trotted over, his plumy tail held high, as if he were waving a banner; and, with his fat sides, stropped her ankles, making little mewing sounds, as if in conversation. His motor running full throttle.

Without warning, he leaped into her lap. She cuddled and stroked him before turning him toward Mr. C.C.Bennett, for inspection. "Meet Sholar Picarara. The other cat is called Motel, Sholar's buddy. They both possess multifarious lineage."

"Your alley cat?" asked the astonished-looking yardman.

"I wish he were. Sholar belongs to the Ganucci family; Motel belongs to our neighbor, Antley Theodd DuPuy. Sholar's really Sonny's cat. Look at those green eyes of his, glowing like two jewels slashed with black exclamation points for pupils."

"Insolent."

"Exactly. Sholar is an insolent cat who loves spaghetti and meatballs. Did you ever hear of a cat eating spaghetti and meatballs?"

A small smile tugged at the corners of his mouth. "Never did. I also never heard a cat called Sholar Picarara. Perhaps the Ganucci family should've named him Spaghetini or Vermicelli—"

"Or Linguine—"

"Or Fettucine—"

They both laughed. "I think he visits over here because they're lots of birds he can stalk.— Sholar Picarara, are you dreaming of mockingbird pie for your supper?" asked Kendra nuzzling his nose with hers, forgetting about those seven deadly diseases he carried around in his tiny mouth. "Or would you prefer a nice lizard stew?"

Sholar Picarara squirmed in her arms, and she sat him down. He gaped and gave a humped-back stretch, and then trotted off to lay in the fern fronds. One eye opened, the other half closed.

"Loot at him. He looks like a one-eyed cat peeping in a seafood store."

Mr. C.C. Bennett laughed.

"My aunt said right before Sholar's face that every time a cat gaps he lets out two or more of the seven deadly diseases he carries around in his mouth. That being the case, a cat can't come in the house. Ever since my aunt made that ugly remark, Sholar won't give her the time of day. I've tried, when she's not home, to entice and lure him inside, with tempting morsels of food. He won't come. Evidently he wants an apology, which he won't get from my aunt."

Mr. C.C. Bennett laughed. "You said there was a vacant lot next to you. It looks to me as if there are at least three. Who owns them?"

"I meant we only borrowed footage from the lot next to us. I don't know who owns the property. Those lots have just always been there."

"I see."

"Well, Mr. C.C. Bennett, you must be thirsty by now. How about a glass of iced tea or lemonade? We don't have any pure coffee."

"Can you make a cup of *hot* tea?"

"Sure. I drink hot tea when I'm sick. It tastes like medicine." Kendra screwed up her eyes, nose and mouth.

"I can't help it if you haven't got good taste in liquids."

They went in the house and sat at the gatelegged table. Mr. C.C. Bennett sipped his hot tea from a blue-and-white china cup, and Kendra drank her cold lemonade from a jelly glass. Over their drinks, they chatted comfortably. She learned they had interests and ideas alike. Her aunt would've said they were sealed of the same tribe.

"You know, I could go on chatting like this till midnight, but I promised my aunt I'd fix supper. We usually have a real nice Sunday dinner, around 2:00, but, since we slept the morning away and my aunt had to mind the Ganucci twins, we're going to have breakfast food for supper. You wanna stay?"

"Yes. I'll help you. But first I'd like to wash up."

While Mr. C. C. Bennett was washing, Aunt Molly Primrose, wearing a simple floral cotton dress, her white silky hair in a coronet of plaits, entered the kitchen through the back gallery. "Kendra Lou, have I got somethin' to tell you. It's about that Moochin' MamieTuJax. You know

I've always been a little suspicious of her bein' allergic to milk, eggs, cream, sugar, butter—"

"Tante, Mr. C.C. Bennett—"

"For heaven's sake, Kendra *Louise*, don't mention *that* yardman's name to me. Because of Mr. C.C. Bennett, we got off track today."

By this time Mr. C.C. Bennett had washed up and was returning to the kitchen when he heard his name being bantered about.

"If you hadn't talked my ear off, half the night, about how abrasive, autocratic, and dictatorial he is, I'd have never had to go back to bed this morning," loudly and clearly complained her aunt.

"Shhhh—."

"Don't you Shhhh me, Kendra *Louise*. I don't ever again wanna hear about how handsome, how special and how different Mr. C. C. Bennett is. I also don't wanna hear about the right chemistry at the right time business, or this love at first sight business, either."

"Tante, I never said a word about love at first sight," contradicted Kendra, just above a whisper. Barely audible. "*You* said that."

"Well, it was *you* who mentioned there was chemistry between the two of you. Like I told you last night, Kendra *Louise*, I didn't raise and educate and feed and fend for you to fall in love with and marry no poor penniless *yardman*," was Molly Primrose's very audible reply.

"And I told you I wasn't in love with Mr. C.C. Bennett," whispered Kendra.

"A *yardman* can't support himself let alone a wife and family. So forget this Mr. C.C. Bennett, fascinatin'-'n'-unique *white* yardman. I think he's a crazy commonest. An impostor. A dope fiend— Now let me tell you all about Moochin' Mamie TuJax's fake allergies."

"I'd love to hear about Mooching Mamie TuJax's fake allergies," said Mr. C.C. Bennett, coming into the kitchen, his navy eyes twinkling.

Molly Primrose's button blue eyes popped; her apple cheeks paled. "Gawd save us! Who are you? What are you doin' in my house?"

Kendra groaned, closed her eyes and just shook her heard. To herself: "I wonder how much he heard."

"Since your niece has no manners, permit me to introduce myself. I'm Mr. C.C. Bennett, your servant." He bowed deeply. "Your niece has invited me to supper. Is that all right with you, Madam?"

"Er—er—of course, Mr. C.C. Bennett. *Oh, Mr. Bennett, I'm so—*"

"Shhhh—not another word, Miss Applegate. I was going to help your niece prepare supper, but I'd much rather have you tell me about *that* Mooching Mamie TuJax's allergies. Let's sit in the parlor, and talk."

Molly Primrose gulped.

"Go on, Tante, you can't get around him.—"

A good thirty minutes later Kendra announced supper, and Aunt Molly Primrose, on the arm of Mr. C.C. Bennett, was led to the gatelegged table, all smiles and blushes. After she said: "Bless us O Lord for these thy gifts which we are about to receive," Kendra passed a platter piled high with golden waffles smothered in soft sweet butter and bubbly hot syrup; accompanied by a side dish of fried sweet ham and fluffy scrambled eggs. Hot creamy coffee for them; steaming black tea, for Mr. C.C. Bennett, *the yardman,* were served.

Throughout the meal, Mr. C.C. Bennett courted Aunt Molly Primrose, and Kendra knew by the time supper was over, her aunt had been completely charmed and captivated by the *yardman.*

"Well, Kendra, your aunt and I hate to leave you with the dishes, but I'm now dying to hear about the eccentricities of Lizzie Slapp and the tragedy of Stella Dora. Come, Miss Molly Primrose, let's go to the parlor, your niece can handle these few dishes." He gave Kendra his most charming smile. His navy eyes twinkling.

She stuck out her tongue in turn.

The crashing, scraping, washing and drying of the dishes didn't take long. Soon the dishpan sat inverted on the drainboard, and the dishtowel spread on top it, was left to dry. Kendra then joined her aunt and Mr. C.C. Bennett, who stood as she entered the parlor.

"Your Aunt Molly Primrose has just finished telling me all about Miss Lettie Lou and Miss Effie Vi'let, the two chicken hawks."

Kendra rolled her eyes; her aunt rose and excused herself. "I'm delighted, Miss Kendra Louise Applegate," began Mr. C.C. Bennett, still standing, "that such a pretty girl finds me fascinating and unique." He traced his right forefinger slowly down the curve of her cheek.

"Don't forget abrasive, autocratic and dictatorial."

"I believe your aunt said something about chemistry, love at first sight— Come sit with me on the swing. I want to hold your hand."

"Well, I don't wanna hold yours."

"In that case I must go." He pulled her to him and gave her a hard hug and left.

For the second time Kendra was disappointed. She wanted him to kiss her. While she stood in the middle of the parlor, thinking of the kiss she didn't get, her aunt joined her.

"Oh, Kendra Lou, I see he's gone. What a perfectly lovely *yardman.* Who would've ever thought a *yardman* could be so delightful? So handsome? So charming? So understanding? Not me."

"Nor me."

"He told me he wasn't a crazy commonest or a dope fiend."

"And you believed him?"

"Oh, yes. Kendra Lou, I do believe he's much more than a *yardman*. He's probably one of those fancy Dan landscape men, and just too modest to admit it. Don't' you think so?"

"I think you got him pegged."

"And Kendra Lou, if he's not a landscape designer, maybe he could be persuaded to go to Delgado Trade School and become one. Or learn some trade. I'm sure he'd succeed at whatever he put his mind to. Of course, if he prefers being a *yardman*, I'm sure things could be worked out."

"*What* things?"

"Well, once you're married you two could live here, rent free."

"*Married!* Tante, I'm not going to marry Mr. C.C. Bennett. I've only seen him twice, and you've got us married. Besides, I thought you said a yardman couldn't support himself let alone a wife and family. Now you've changed your tune. I tell you *that* Mr. C.C. Bennett could sell ice to an Eskimo."

"Well, Kendra Lou, you could work until the babies started comin', and then I could help you two young people."

"Last night you said he was too old for me. You said his being fifteen years my senior was too great a span."

"Oh, don't be silly, Kendra Lou. Your beloved father was ten years your mother's senior. What's an extra five years. I think things can be worked out, my dahlin' niece," said Molly Primrose, her button blue eyes, dreamy and dreaming of her niece and the yardman.

"Tante, do you want to tell me about Mooching MamieTuJax and her fake allergies."

"Oh, I do. You know how she never has eggs, milk, cream, sugar or real butter in her house because she says she has too much respect for her insides. So when she invites you over to her house for coffee, you get it black and without sugar. But when she comes to your house, she loses all respect for her insides, and claims she can tolerate cream and sugar in her coffee just fine in other people's houses."

"In other words she's suffering from cheapitis."

"Exactly. Whenever her relatives come from up the country, she borries, from Rosa, real butter, pure cream, sugar. She returns oleomargarine; canned milk; no sugar. Rosa can never get any sugar back from Moochin' Mamie TuJax. Just saccharine tablets. Another aud thing about Moochin' Mamie is every time she invites a neighbor to lunch she only serves boiled turnips, black bread and black coffee. Any more no body wants to eat at her house."

"And what did Mr. C.C. Bennett have to say about all those turnip lunches?"

"He took it very seriously, but offered a simple solution. He said all the neighbors should take turns inviting Moochin' Mamie TuJax to lunch, and feed her a rutabaga instead of a turnip."

Kendra laughed out loud.

"He was also very interested in the crazy actions of Lizzie Slapp Springmeyer, and the meanness and hard-heartedness of Lettie Lou and Effie Vi'let. I told him about our trip to Jackson, and he was especially interested in the part about you accidentally findin' shelter at the leper colony."

"I bet he was. Well, Tante, it's getting late and I've got to take a bath and go to bed. Tomorrow starts another work week."

Chapter Seven

Kendra's office duties were: At 8:30 sharp, put the coffee on; dust Mr. Prosper's desk and telephone; fill his fountain pen; sharpen his pencils; and then do similar chores for herself.

Mr. Prosper's routine was: Arrive at 8:45, via a private entrance, and buzz Kendra on the intercom. Immediately she'd serve him his first cup of coffee; at 8:55 she'd warm his coffee, empty his ashtray; and at 9:00 was seated in his office, taking dictation.

On Monday morning, when Kendra walked into her office, wearing a saffron linen suit, a cream silk blouse and cream accessories, her brown-gold hair in a neat thick chignon, Mr. Prosper, in a dark pin-strip suit, was standing at her desk, waiting for her. To herself: "What's he doing here so early?"

"Good mornin', Miss Applegate—come into my office—you don't need your steno pad."

In Mr. Prosper's office. He sat at his desk; Kendra stood in front of his desk, wondering what the bad news was. For a minute or so, Mr. Prosper said nothing. He just looked over his horn rimmed glasses, his blue pig eyes closely studying her, as if seeing her for the first time. Appraising her narrowly, his fat, stubby, fingers drumming the desk.

"What is it, Mr. Prosper? Anything wrong?"

"Miss Applegate, my boss, Mr. Clark Rogers, contacted me over the weekend and said he wanted you transferred to his residence, to act as his secretary. He said you were in full agreement, with the transfer. I believe he needs your services for six months.

"If he hadn't just lost his wife, I'd have somehow or other refused; however, in such sad circumstances I agreed to let you go on a temporary basis. To take your place, I called up, from the steno pool, Miss Calliope—"

Clio Calliope was a gum-chewing, good-looking big busted blonde, who couldn't type or spell; but that didn't matter. For she had the biggest bust in the building and, to the bosses, *that* mattered.

Kendra opened her mouth to interrupt her boss, to tell him she hadn't agreed to any transfer, and to remind him of Clio's limited skills, thought better of it, and said to herself: "He knows all Clio can do is deep breathe, expand her chest and talk breathlessly."

"You will remain on our rolls," twanged out Mr. Prosper, " but Mr. Rogers will pay you. I told Mr. Rogers I paid you $160 a month; however, I suggested, since you'll just be a temporary employee, that he pay you $125."

To herself: "This is how the ol' poop's getting even for my agreeing, which I didn't, to work for Mr. Rogers."

"Now when Mr. Rogers no longer needs your services and you return to your present position, you'll have to work your way back up the pay ladder. You will not come back here and make $160 a month."

All this was said through Mr. Prosper's snub nose, and had left Kendra breathless and with a sense of outrage. All she could think of was getting her hands on Mr. C.C. Bennett. This was his fault. He deliberately lied to Mr. Rogers about her wanting to work for him.

To herself: "Yesterday, when he was making up to Tante, he didn't say a word about this. I'll strangle the so-'n'-so with my bare hands; he'll rue the day he railroaded me into working for Mr. Rogers, and causing me to lose my seniority here. Oh, just you wait and see, Mr. C.C. Bennett."

"Well, Miss Applegate, don't you have anything to say?"

"Yes, I have a lot to say. First, Mr. Prosper, I didn't agree to work for Mr. Rogers; and, if I had, you didn't have the right to suggest to Mr. Rogers that he pay me $125. I can't live on that. I have bills."

"Mr. Rogers is not in the habit of tellin' falsehoods," muttered the ol' poop. "Now regardin' your salary, I am your boss and I have every right to suggest to Mr. Rogers what I think your salary should be. As for your bills and obligations they are not my concern. Those are personal problems. You made those bills. I didn't."

"That's not the point, Mr. Prosper," replied Kendra through tight lips. "I'd be a fool, and my aunt didn't raise a fool, to leave this $160 a month *permanent* job for a $125 a month *temporary* job. Only to return, in six months, and have to work my way back up the pay ladder. I refuse to work for anybody for $125 a month." To herself: "You hateful ol' poop."

"Miss Applegate, you brought this on yourself. Also, Mr. Rogers *didn't* say he was going to pay you $125 a month. I only suggested that amount to him, and he said he'd think about it."

"I'm not leaving my office, Mr. Prosper, until I know what Mr. Rogers will pay me. Call him up, right now, and find out."

"How dare you talk to me in that tone. Do you realize who you speaking to. *I'm-your-boss. I-can-fire-you.* What *do* you think of that?"

"If you fire me, I'll have a job, for six months, with Mr. Rogers, and then I'll have to look for another job. Of course, if Mr. Rogers, who is your boss and who owns this establishment, likes my work, I could wind up right back here, or stay on permanently with him." Kendra stopped breathlessly, shocked by her behavior.

Mr. Prosper picked up the phone, gave the operator a number. "Hello—Mr. Rogers—this is Henri Prosper—Er—about that $125 a month salary I suggested that you pay Miss Applegate, I'm afraid she won't work for that—Oh, I see—Oh, Mr. Rogers, that's far too much to pay a secretary—Well, that's up to you, sir—Yes, sir, I'll tell her—Goodbye, sir." He turned to Kendra: "You will be paid $350 a month," spit out Mr. Prosper, his pig eyes narrowed to snake slits.

"I'll earn it, I'm sure."

"And when you return, I'll continue to pay you $160 a month, but you'll never get $350 out of me. No woman's worth that money."

Kendra changed the subject: "Mr. Prosper, when did Mr. Rogers become your boss?"

"He's always been my boss. Everybody knows Clark Rogers owns this Homestead," replied Mr. Prosper, closely studying Kendra's face.

"It's news to me."

"Tell me, Miss Applegate, how do you come to know Mr. Rogers, and not know he owns this establishment?" suspiciously asked Henri Prosper, in his nasal twang. "He's never been here; and *socially* you'd never ever know him," sneeringly added Mr. Prosper, a very class conscious poop.

Kendra wasn't about to mention Mr. C.C. Bennett, the yardman, recommending her to Mr. Rogers. "I don't know him. I wouldn't know Mr. Rogers if he walked in here right now. The only possible explanation is my aunt, who sewed for Mrs. Rogers, must've bragged to that lady about my secretarial skills." She shrugged. "I suppose at one time or another Mrs. Rogers mentioned my name to Mr. Rogers, and now that he needs secretarial help he thought of me."

"Possibly. Well, your aunt was right about your skills. You are an excellent secretary. You are a responsible and dependable young woman who, until now, I didn't think made up wholesale falsehoods." He shrugged. "I suppose if you can hold your sassy tongue, you'll do a fine job for Mr. Rogers."

"I have told you no lies."

Mr. Prosper waved Kendra's retort away with a stony gaze, and sneeringly said: "Mr. Rogers is waiting for you, so gather any personal items you may have in your desk—remember don't take anythin' away from this office to supplement the one at Willowwynn—and hurry to your new job, at No. 10 Prytania, as if you didn't know the address. Go on. You don't want to keep Mr. Rogers waitin'."

"N—no, I don't." To herself: "Nor do I want to keep Mr. C.C. Bennett waiting for his just desserts." Kendra turned to go.

"Er—Miss Applegate, there-is-one-more-thing. Er—I've never heard any gossip about you and—er—men. I hope I never shall; but to be on the safe side I have some good advice for you. Don't let workin' at a mansion go to your head.

"Life at Willowwynn will be like nothin' like you've ever known, or will ever know. I'm sure, workin' at Willowwynn will afford you many opportunities for mischief. Remember your place. Remember who you are—only a paid employee. An attractive secretary, that's all.— Er—Mr. Rogers is not yet forty, and a handsome widower, a wealthy, eligible man." He hesitated.

"Yes, Mr. Prosper," clearly and coldly replied Kendra, looking directly into her boss' pig eyes, "do go on."

"Er—I don't want you to delude yourself with the possibility that when Mr. Rogers marries again he'll pick his wife from the likes of the steno pool. He won't. She'll come from the debutante ranks. Do you take my meanin'?"

"Clearly, sir." To herself: "You ol' poop."

Half hour later, Kendra stood on the back gallery of Willowwynn, facing a middle-aged, smiling, short, shinola black woman who wore a white cotton dress and a stiff, red, bib apron.

The maid was stout, double-chinned, flat-nosed and liver-lipped. Her underlip was thrust out. She had a mouthful of white teeth, except for two gold front ones, set in blue gums. She wore elastic stockings. Her hips, the eighth wonder, were an ax handle across, and her buttocks, the ninth wonder, formed a shelf which could easily accommodate a silver tea service. Her hair was tucked beneath a red tignon, tied in a bow on her forehead, some gray, brillo-like hair escaping. She had full, expressive brown eyes, lively with interest and curiosity. The whites of her eyes pierced the blackness of her face.

"Miz Applegates?" she asked, smiling brightly.

"Yes," answered Kendra. "And you?"

"Ah's Gussie Rae Booker, Mistah Rogers' housekeeper."

The two shook hands. "I believe Mr. Rogers is expecting me."

"Him wuz 'spectin' yo, but him gots ah foam cawl end had to leaves on bizzness. Him sez yo is to use de rent table, en de liberry, foah yo desk. Ah'll shows yo to de liberry. Rites dis way, Miz."

Kendra followed Gussie Rae's bouncy wake and, when they reached the kitchen, she saw another stout maid, dressed exactly like Gussie Rae. She was talking on a wall phone, next to an open pantry.

"Dats Xariffa Diamond, tawkin' to her no-count gamblin' brudder, Black Diamond. Him's ah huckleberry pas' ma persimmon, efen Ah evah saws one.Him's tryin' to borrie fifty cents. He cain't gets it fum him's frien', Bubba, cause Bubba's en jail. Bubba be black, black as midnites. Ah said dat to Bubba's black face, end him jes laughs end sez: 'Gussie Rae Booker yo ain't gots no rooms to tawks. Why, yo is hal'f pas' leben, yose'f.'"

A smile played hide and seek around Kendra's lips.

"When Xariffa's tru tawkin' wit her brudder, she's gunna cawls Mistah Pasafuma, de grocery man, end makes our groceries foah de dey. En ah lit'le while, Mistah Pasafuma's bike boy, Blucher Dawdle, dat ol' slo' poke, will deliver dem groceries."

As Gussie Rae Booker talked and walked, Kendra glanced around at the kitchen. It was a stark, large white room, with only a utility table, stove, icebox, and, of course, a pantry.

To herself: "So this is where Mr. C.C. Bennett made our coffee."

Gussie Rae stumped off on her stout legs; Kendra close behind her. They passed through a swinging door into a small hall. "Tru dat doah is ha'f ah baf," said Gussie Rae Booker; and then proceeded into a large white marble-floored rotunda, where the sweep of a freestanding spiral staircase, with a black iron railing, led Kendra's amber eyes from the white marble floor to a magnificent Waterford chandelier.

Returning her eyes to ground level, she noticed on the left wall a carved console with a Louis XVI ormolu. Flanking the console were Queen Anne gilt chairs with cabriole legs and upholstered in blue silk, woven with gold and silver threads.

The two women left the rotunda and entered a wide bright entrance hallway, also with a white marble floor and parchment colored walls. Toward the middle of the hallway, fixed to the wall, was a French gilt mirror, and beneath it a black iron console, with a white marble top. In the center of the console, purple peonies, red roses, yellow lilies and white dogwood blooms were spilling over the edge of a crystal urn.

Flanking the console were benches covered in pale gold linen damask and appliqued with claret colored flowers. To the left and right of the benches were French doors that led to twin parlors. Kendra peeped through the panes and saw both rooms were decorated in pale gold and white. A rosewood Steinway stood in the far right corner of the first parlor. To herself: "I'll explore these rooms a little later."

Eyes back in the hallway, she noticed, across from the iron console, an ebony caned-bottomed settee, whose claret cushion was of linen damask. It almost begged to be sat on. She pressed the cushion with her hand. It felt soft. On either side of the settee stood silky jade sago palms in white porcelain pots.

Just ahead of Kendra, perhaps five feet or so, she saw a graceful Georgian archway which led to an elegant foyer. A black iron chandelier hung from a white ceiling. Palms potted in brass pots, flanked the entrance to the foyer.

At last, Gussie Rae Booker paused in front of a tall, heavy, mahogany door, with exquisite carving. She announced: "Dis is de liberry, Miz Applegates." She opened the door and stepped aside, so Kendra could pass through. "Ev'ryt'ing yo needs is heah. Efen it ain't, den it's upstairs en po' daid Miz Rogers' desk, en her baidroom/sittin' room. Her rooms is rites above dis heah liberry." She pointed to the ceiling.

Kendra looked upward and nodded, and then looked around the handsome room; she felt strangely shaken. Part of her trembling was from surprise; the other part was a strange feeling, almost like recognition. It was as if she had been here before. As if she knew there would be a library like this one.

The walls of the room were mahogany paneled, and separated by fluted pilasters. The wall facing the door had four, long, narrow, French windows draped in rose raw silk; two brass chandeliers hung from a high white plastered ceiling; and a deep rose oriental carpet covered most of the wide-plank floor, which was the color of golden honey.

Warm browns and creamy beiges created a restful atmospherefor this inner sanctum. The furniture was a mixture of rich brown leather and solid shiny mahogany. Brass floor lamps wore beige silk shades; jade porcelain table lamps, trimmed in gold leaf, wore creamy linen shades.

In the center left wall was a fireplace with a black marble mantel. Above the mantel, in a wide mahogany frame, was a large oil of two brown-and-white spaniels, hunting. The spaniels had paper white markings, glossy brown splotches, black noses that looked wet, and silky-flop ears. They were chasing a brown bunny with a white tail and a deer, who was flying over a wire fence.

To the right of the mantel was a mahogany-framed map of the world. A globe stood nearby. On either end of the mantel were bisque vases filled with red rose buds, a few peeling opening. Flanking the fireplace were an imposing pair of Louis the XVI carved bookcases, decorated with parcel gilt and classical masques. They reached the ceiling, and were lined with calf-bound books.

Groupings of brown leather wing chairs and matching ottomans stood on either side of the fireplace; a low, square, black marble-topped coffee table was placed in front of the fireplace. Waterford decanters containing sherry and brandy sat in the center of the coffee table on a large brass tray; delicate crystal glasses were set to the side of the decanters.

Across the front wall there were six tall French windows, also draped in rose silk, and these narrow windows extended to the floor, sliding straight up from the sill. These windows over looked the front gallery. In front of the middle window sat a round, rose marble-topped table with a big bouquet of bronze chrysanthemums.

Leather benches, with brass casters, were stationed around the room; a fat, tufted, tuxedo sofa, piled with chintz, cotton and linen pillows in colors of burgundy and teal, stood in the middle of the room, with a low table in front of it, pleasantly littered with magazines and, behind it a library table; there were several Pembroke dropleaf side tables, some with vases of cut flowers, some just with lamps; all with either silver or crystal containers holding cigarettes or cigars.

On the wall that faced the door, toward the right corner of the room, there was an 18th Century round rent table on a pedestal base. It was rich-red mahogany, and as smooth as still water. A leather host chair, on brass casters, stood behind the table on a thick sheet of hardwood.

A few feet from the chair and against the wall, was a mahogany double-filing cabinet with Queen Anne legs, gleaming brass hardware, and a top that lifted up for two sections of file folders; to the left of the filing cabinet, sat a portable Underwood; a brown wooden wastepaper basket sat next to the Underwood.

Across the back wall were carved sliding doors, separating the library from another room.

"Gussie Rae Booker, which room is beyond those sliding doors?"

"Mistah Rogers' steady," she replied, opening windows. "Naw dats better. Ah lit'l cooler en heah wit dem winders op'n. Yo kin wuks better when it's cool den when it's hots.

"I certainly can. Thank you." Kendra walked over to the rent table, which held a phone and intercom system, a stack of file folders, a fountain pen, a few pencils, a ream of white paper. She opened the table's center drawer and found a bottle of ink, blotter, stationery, letter opener and a magnifying glass. All the tools for reading and writing—and typing.

She took a sheet of typing paper, put it in the Underwood and, bending over, typed: *Now is the time for all good men to come to the aid of their country.* M'm—works good for a portable—Even has a new ribbon." She tried another typing drill, and then sat down.

"Miz Applegates," said Gussie Rae Booker, opening the last window, "Xariffa made ah pots uv dat dare pure coffee foah Mr. Rogers, end she's gots som' lef'. It looks as weaks as monkey pee and tastes likes it. But Mistah Rogers likes dat dare monkey pee. Me and Xariffa hates it. Dues yo likes dat dare pure coffee?"

Kendra made a face. "No. I drink Creole coffee. I'll bring us a pound of Community Coffee, tomorrow."

"No needs. Xariffa is gunna git sum fum Mistah Pasafuma. When dat slo' poke, Blucher Dawdle, brings dem dare groceries, Xariffa kin makes us ah good cuppa coffee.— Efen yo has times, after lunch, Ah'll shows yo ovah de house," she added, as an afterthought.

"I'll make time.— Gussie Rae Booker, have you worked for the Rogerses since they came to New Orleans?"

"Nome. Me and Xariffa has on'y bens heah six munts. We used to wuks for Mistah Sidney Omer—sweet Jesus, res' his good soul—till him up-'n'-died on usen. We wuked twenty-five years foah him. Him wuz nearly ninety, had him senses, end wuz en good health. Him went to baid one nights end nevah wokes up de nex' mawnin'.

"Mistah Omer had on'y one great-neffy who gots all him's money. Dat slick great-neffy, Willie Omer, dat's anodder huckleberry pas' ma persimmon, him on'y come 'round when him needed ah li'le cash. Naw, Mistah Rogers wuz Mistah Omer's good frien'. Visited him lots. No strings 'tached."

"Didn't Mr. Omer leave you and Xariffa a pension?"

"Mistah Omer tol' usen ah long times ago dat him rit dat down dat when him died we wuz to be fixed foah life. Me end Xariffa. Him put dat piece uv paper dat him rit dat down on en him's strong box. Him showed bof me end Xariffa dat dare piece uv paper. Me end Xariffa caint reads no rites, but we knows Mistah Omer wuz no liar.

"Dat dare great-neffy, Slick Willie, sez dare wuz no sech piece uv paper en de strong box. Dat dare great neffy, Slick Willie, give me end Xariffa $10 apiece, end den lef' usen go. We had no place to goes. Mistah Rogers tooks usen en, even doe dem Satoes wuz heah."

"Who are the Satoes?—They sound Japanese.—Where are the Satoes now?"

"Miz Rogers brung dem Chinamens wit her fum Caliphonia. Foah Japs, dats wat dey wuz." Gussie Rae Booker held up four fat fingers.

"I thought you said they were Chinamen."

"Dey has yaller skin. Dey all looks alikes. Chinamens/Japs. Ah t'inks de lots uv dem Chinamens is commonest, end efen dey don'ts watch outs, dat dare Mistah McCarty will ketch 'em foah sho. Sen' dem pinkos off to de jailhouse. Him's even after movie stars dat's commonest. Truckin' dem off to de jailhouse, lef' en rites. Don'ts makes him no nevah minds efen yo is ah movie stars or nots. Likes Ah sez, dem yaller peoples all looks alikes."

Kendra to herself: "White people are always saying colored people all look alike—now colored Gussie Rae Booker is saying all orientals look alike."

"As soons as po' Miz Rogers wuz daid, dem Chinamens got dare pensions en tooks off foah Caliphonia. Ah wuz glads to see de lot uv dem go. So wuz Xariffa. It wuz hard wukin' wit 'em dese pas' munts. Dey pretended dey didn't understan' usen. Dat ol' Josie Sato, jes' cause she wuz Miz Rogers' pursonal maid, t'ought she wuz hot stuffs, dat one. T'ought de sun shined on her, even when it rained."

"Where was Josie Sato when Mrs. Rogers died?"

"En her 'partment, ovah de garage. Po' Miz Rogers died jes' likes Mistah Omer. Her didn't wakes up. Dat Josie Sato founds her daid en baid. She went ah screamin' en ah hollerin' end ah whoopin' it up all tru de house till she woked up Mistah Rogers. Him cawled Doctah Lopez. Doctah Lopez zamined po' Miz Rogers, end sez she died en her sleeps uv heart failure. Sez she's bens havin' heart troubles."

"Mistah Rogers sez dat dare heart troubles wuz news to hims. Dat wuz also news to all uv usen. Enyways, Mistah Rogers tol' de medical zaminer, when him picked up po' daid Miz Rogers, him wanted ah autopsees made on him's wife. End de nex' t'ing we all knows is dat zaminer dun went end burnt up po' daid Miz Rogers b'foah him makes dat dare autopsees. Him sez it wuz by mistakes dat him burnt her ups."

"What did Mr. Rogers say about that?"

"Him went crazy. Him wanted to cause ah big stinks, but dat dare ol' Judge Edwards—him lives rites across de street at Greenwoods Manor—tawked Mistah Rogers outs uv it. De Judge sez ah big fuss won'ts brings back po' daid Miz Rogers' body, end woulds on'y makes her det looks suspicious. So dat ended dat. Ah didn't knows whether to hol's ma nose or puts ah cloespins on it."

"It smells like you could've done both. What did the Satoes think?"

"Dey didn't likes it needer. Efen dat dare Miz Farnsworth end dat dare Mistah Osborne wuz heah, dey might've puts up ah fuss, end dey might not uv needer. Miz Farnsworth lef" on her vacation on de 12th uv April; Mistah Osborne lef' de same day to goes to Buckley, Caliphonia, foah schools—imagine ah 27 year-old man still en schools. Po' Miz Rogers wuz found daid en baid on Friday, de 13th uv April."

"Gussie Rae Booker, I understand neither Miss Farnsworth or Mr. Osborne can be reached. Is that so?"

"Dats so. 'Cordin' to Josie Sato, Miz Farnsworth, ovah de years, hav' nevah tol' Miz Rogers, her boss, whar she wents on her vacation. Miz Farnsworth tol' Josie Sato de reason foah dat is efen Miz Rogers knew whar she wuz, she'd be ah-wurryin' her ev'ry five minutes.

"As foah dat dare Mistah Osborne, him tol' ev'rybody heah him wuz goin' to Buckley, Caliphonia, foah ah six-weeks seminar end, when him wuz tru wit dat dare seminar, he'd come on back heah. Well, Mistah Rogers end ev'rybody else dun went en cawled Buckley ah dozen or moe times, tryin' to gets en tech wit Mistah Osborne. Mistah Rogers, no nobody else, ain't caughts up wit Mistah Osborne yets."

"Well, did Mr. Rogers find out if there was a scheduled seminar?"

"Yas, dare is ah seminar goin' on rites naw, but dat dare protege, Mistah Kyle Osborne, ain't 'tendin' it."

"That's odd. Very odd."

"It sho is. Miz Applegates, ah'll tells yo somepin, efen yo promise nevah to tells ah soul."

"Cross my heart, raise my right hand and hope to die."

"Ah t'oughts maybees dat Miz Farnsworth, since she had ah big fights wit po' daid Miz Rogers, b'foah she lef' on her vacation, might've kilt her."

"But you said Miss Farnsworth left on the 12th of April— Do you know what the fight was about?"

"She did leaves on de 12th, dat's why Ah caint really pin nuffin' on Miz Farnsworth. Ah didn't heah de fights, but Josie Sato lissun en on parts uv it. It wuz ovah dat dare protege. Him's young en fine lookin', but so's Mistah Rogers. 'Cordin' to Josie Sato—I don'ts knows whether to believes her or nots—po' Miz Rogers sez Mistah Kyle Osborne belongs to her; Miz Farnsworth screams en hollers him belongs to her, end sez she can proves it. Dats all Josie Sato heards."

"Where did this fight take place?"

"Upstairs en po' Miz Rogers sittin' room. Likes ah sez, her rooms is ah baidroom/sittin' room com'nation. When she hav' company she shuts off her baidroom wit dem slidin' doahs."

"Then no one but Josie Sato heard the fight? Where was Mr. Rogers?"

"Dats rites. Mistah Rogers wuzn't home. Him wuz at him's office. De fight tooks place mid mawnin, end by noon Miz Farnsworth dun lef' on her vacation. Later dat evenin', po' Miz Rogers had anodder fights wit dat dare protege; but dey make it up, "Cordin' to Josie Sato. Josie Sato sez dat dare protege kiss po' Miz Rogers ah million times, tells her ten million times how much him loves her, end den sez when him comes back fum Buckley, him's gunna marries her."

"What did Josie Sato say Mrs. Rogers said to that?"

"Said she'd deevoce Mistah Rogers—goes offs to Reno foah six weeks—end afterwards she'd marries up wit Mistah Osborne. How yo likes dat bucket uv worms?"

"I don't like it at all. I think Mrs. Rogers' death needs to be investigated."

"End Ah t'inks yo is de one to gits de investigashun goin'."

"I think you're right, Gussie Rae Booker. I think after I clear up whatever work Mr. Rogers has for me, in these folders, I'll do a little snooping in that sitting room."

"Den Ah'll lets yo git to yo wuks. Ah gots my own to dues."

Gussie Rae Booker left.

Except for a brief coffee break, Kendra had been completely engrossed in her work. She wrote one thank you note after another until all were done. One folder down. She tackled another, which called for typing letters. The Underwood clicked, clacked, thumped and swallowed up sheets and sheets of paper she fed it, as her fast-typing nimble fingers pressed the round black metal keys, with white letters. Her work went well. She wasn't bored.

A couple hours later, she pushed a pile of papers away from her and, wincing, straightened her stiff shoulders. The back of her neck felt tight, and between her shoulder blades hurt. She stood up, stretched, sat back down, and looked around the room. For a few minutes, she sat wool-gathering; then suddenly she knew why she had been strangely shaken at first sight of the library.

Without a moment's hesitation, she leaped from her chair, raced to the door; ripped it open, darted into the hallway, sprinted through the rotunda and bounded up the spiral stairs, two at a time. She flew across the landing, took a left and dashed down the wide hallway.

Breathless, she halted at a tall door, grabbed its big, gleaming brass handle and stopped short. She thought she heard voices, indistinguishable voices, coming from within the room. She knocked. No answer.

Trembling, she opened the door, closed it behind her and rested her head against the door, feeling frightened and cold. Colder than she had ever felt in her entire life.

She stood in the powder-blue bedroom, the room she had dreamed of so many times, and everything was as she had seen it in her dreams; even down to the cream colored Persian rug, woven with an explosion of blue flowers, that now cushioned her feet.

The room before her was the biggest and most beautiful she had ever seen. Her heart raced as her brown-gold eyes swept the spacious room, which was divided by tall, magnificently carved, sliding white doors, whose details were delicately brushed with blue and gold.

The adjoining sitting room was accessible through these doors, which were only pulled out a couple feet from the wall.

Fear and excitement mingled in her blood. She felt the room, along with dead Carol Rogers had, all this time, been waiting for her.

Slowly her brown-gold eyes traveled up to the white ceiling, to an immense wedgewood chandelier, and then back down the blue walls, taking in a six inch carved molding.

The top half of the molding was white, delicately brushed with blue; the bottom half was gold leaf. Directly beneath the molding was a frieze of cottony clouds floating in a blend of blues, with twigs of white wisteria and blue birds in flight.

Next her eyes gazed raptly at a great black walnut four-poster bed, whose posts rose nearly twelve feet high; both the head and footboards were intricately carved. She walked over to the bed, caressed one of the posts, and then measured it, encircling it with her thumb and forefinger. It was as slender as her own wrists.

As she inspected the post, her eyes noted all the bedroom furniture was of black walnut, and that the crocheted ciel (tester), and counterpane were white, and lined with powder-blue taffeta. This contrasted beautifully with the dark wood.

Carefully she turned down the counterpane and examined the white linen scalloped sheets and pillowslips, which had a border of hand-painted pink and peach cottage roses with mint green leaves. The pillowslips bore a *CR* Monogram, in silk blue threads. She pulled up the counterpane.

Never had she seen such an exquisite bed. It had two mattresses, making it impossible to get in the bed, or sit on it, without using the bedside step stool.

Night stands flanked the bed, and held wedgewood lamps, which wore white silk shirred shades.

To the right of the bed was a black lacquered four-paneled oriental screen, filled with blue birds on a golden background. At the foot of the bed was a Queen Anne bench, wearing a white silk linen cushion. About six feet from the bench was a round table adorned in a white cotton skirt, embroidered with tiny blue flowers, woven with silk threads; flanking the table were two blue silk upholstered armchairs, with slender curving legs and white wood frames, tenderly brushed with gold leaf.

A dainty, white marble-topped table stood next to a blue silk slipper chair, that had six inches of blue fringe for its hem. To the left of the table and chair and fixed to the wall was a narrow, floor to ceiling beveled mirror, framed in gold-leaf; to the right, a pair of floor to ceiling windows, separated by white fluted pilasters.

Above the windows were arches of stained glass; muslin and lace curtains draped these windows; and framing them were swags of blue silk, slipped through golden rings.

Kendra opened both windows, which overlooked the tops of tall, swaying pine trees, whose summits, like the pines in front of the house, were tangled with cones of smoky purple wisteria. It was cloudy out. Quickly she turned her back on the dreary day, and surveyed the bright room before her.

Across the room and, against the wall, was a black walnut bureau, with a white marble top, button boxes and an oval, tilting mirror. On the opposite side of the room, facing the bureau, was a towering armoire, with an intricately carved pediment. Mounted to the door of the armoire was an inlaid beveled mirror.

For a second or so Kendra gazed at herself in the glass: she smiled, made a face, then opened the armoire and peeked in. Here, her eyes feasted on a very impressive wardrobe. She read dress labels such as Chanel, Dior, Balenciaga, and Lanvin.

She knew these famous designers from reading *Vogue*; however, it was one thing to see fabulous fashions featured in a magazine but quite another to come face to face with the real article. She was struck dumb by so much perfection and beauty.

She examined these heavenly creations. Their seams were beautifully finished, their hems even, their linings lovely. Kendra petted the dresses, and they felt exquisite to her touch. Finally she shut the armoire and moved on to the dividing section of the room, passing into the sitting room.

The furniture in the sitting room was also black walnut. Directly she opened the four floor to ceiling windows, which were also wearing muslin and lace curtains and blue silk swags. A blue silk velour rug, bound with blue satin and finished with silk blue fringe, covered all but a small border of the golden, honey colored floor.

In the center of the room, across from the windows, was a fireplace with an intricately carved white Georgian mantel. Above the mantel in a gold leaf frame was an oil of blue hydrangeas. An ormolu clock sat in the center of the mantel; and a French blue porcelain box to the right of it.

Flanking the mantel were bookcases to the ceiling, crowded with richly bound books. In front of the bookcases were two square tables, each holding white porcelain lamps on a gold base, with pale blue silk shades. Positioned in front of the fireplace screen, was a white porcelain pedestal, which held a blue-and-white urn, spilling over with pink and peach rose buds, their petals peeling open.

Five feet from the fireplace stood an oval, Italian-legged coffee table, which separated two blue-and-white flowery loveseats. At the end of each loveseat, there was a square table, and next to each table, at an angle, was a dainty, blue silk linen chair, with cabriole legs and a white wooden frame, touched with gold leaf. A Waterford decanter, filled with brandy, sat on the coffee table, along with a crystal cigarette container, lighter and ashtray.

Straight across from this seating arrangement, stood an elegant secretary, whose pediment was carved with flowers, birds, vines, swirls and scrolls. The secretary had double glass doors with gracefully curved mullions and gold lion heads for drawer pulls. Beneath the droplid were four drawers.

A ribbon-backed Queen Anne armchair, with slender curving legs and a white linen seat, was pushed up to the secretary. Kendra pulled it out and sat, drumming her fingers on the desk. She picked up an ivory letter opener, admired it, and placed it back on the desk. She stood, pushed the chair back in place and looked some more

To the left of the desk stood another circular white skirted table, covered with a glass top. This table held a blue porcelain lamp, with a white silk shade; a crystal vase, etched in silver, and filled with red roses; and in an oval silver frame was a smiling picture of a beautiful young woman.

Kendra picked up the picture and examined it."I bet this is Carol Rogers when she was nineteen or twenty," she said to herself. "Tante was right. We resemble each other." She put the picture back.

Ther were two other pictures, also in silver frames. One was of a handsome, elderly couple; the woman was smiling while the man, at her side, stood stiff and staring. "This couple must be Carol Rogers' parents," mused Kendra. The other picture was of a good-looking middle-aged man, smiling. "This lone gentleman must be a relative. Mrs. Rogers favors him. I wonder why there isn't a picture of Mrs. Rogers and her husband."

Kendra shrugged and continued her inspection. To the side of the table was a Reagency wing chair, upholstered in parchment-and-white sateen cotton stripes. Behind the chair was a lush green potted palm.

Across the front wall, French doors, with tiny brass knobs and curtained in thin muslin, opened onto the balcony. To the sides of the French doors, in the left and right corners, stood potted palms and boudoir chairs covered in parchment colored watered silk, with matching ottomans. Next to each boudoir chair stood a Pembroke side table and a brass floor lamp.

Kendra opened one of the French doors and walked out onto the terra cotta tile floor of the balcony. The blue sky was covered with black clouds. "It's going to storm," she said to herself, looking at the sky, then at the white wicker furniture. She noted the cushions and pillows of the settees and chairs were all cotton, woven in cool mint and soft beige, displaying fields of delicate white blossoms and lush blooming borders of pink and blue flowers. "I wonder if I should take these cushions in." Without warning, a blinding flash of lightning lit up the sky, followed by a deafening crash of thunder.

Kendra snatched up an armful of cushions and hurried inside, leaving the door open. She stacked the cushions in the corner, next to a potted palm; and, just as she started toward the open windows, a voice stopped her in her tracks: "Kendra Louise, the answers are in this room. Look for them, *now.*"

A shiver ran up and down her spine. She moved forward and turned slowly in a circle, expecting to see a woman. No one was in sight; however, she saw a mist. This mysterious mist floated over to the windows and shut them just as big drops of rain fell.

Soon the clouds exploded, and it rained hard. Wind—rain—lightning—thunder. It stormed as if the world was coming to an end. And while the storm raged Kendra stood in the middle of the beautiful powder-blue sitting room and stared at the shimmering mist, as if it were the second coming.

Chapter Eight

Kendra, chilled to the bone, stood transfixed, straining her eyes incredulously, as the mist substantiated itself into a solid form. A beautiful woman, shrouded in a misty blue halo of bright lights and wearing a French blue silk shirtwaist dress, stood before the fireplace. The woman was one and the same in the photograph that smiled from the silver frame.

A fresh downpour of rain beat on the roof and slashed the sides of the house; great gusts of wind howled and shrieked, while shock and horror filled Kendra, as she tried to scream. No sound came from her lips except that of a little mewling noise. The apparition, the ghost, or the spirit was that of the dead Carol Rogers. Carol Rogers sauntered over to one of the blue-and-white flowery settees, sat down and crossed her shapely legs.

Kendra tried to scream again; still no sound came from her lips. She was now freezing, although sweat was pouring from her armpits. The cream silk blouse, beneath her saffron colored linen jacket, clung to her. Her hands were clammy. She wanted to run from the room, but was unable to move. She tried to call out only to hear the sound of incoherent babbling coming from her lips; the rain and wind cut off the words in her mouth.

Although Kendra saw the rise and fall of CR's breasts, through the bright lights, and heard her quiet breathing, knew CR was not alive, not really breathing on her own. Her breathing was mechanical, unnatural and, as Kendra realized this, she had the terrifying sensation that the spirit only breathed when she breathed.

Suddenly the room felt close and airless, making Kendra's chest feel like a great weight was pressing against it, causing her breathing to become irregular. At that moment, she had the crazy feeling of oneness with a ghost.

"But that's impossible. CR's dead. Dead people can't breathe, can't do anything, let alone be one with another person—share parts of another person's body. I need to get out of here and stop imagining things," she said to herself.

She tried to move, but her feet were fixed to the floor. Glued. She was locked in with a ghost, while steel-gray rain furiously slashed the window.

Panic stricken and shivering, Kendra's teeth chattered, as she gulped for air and struggled to move. Her head throbbed. The room spun round and round. The floor came up toward her face and went back down like the waves of the sea. Dizzily, crazily she saw CR, through a blur, calmly riding out the storm, scrutinizing her with her sea green eyes.

"*That* green-eyed spook is sizing me up. But why?" asked Kendra, staring back at the spirit, mesmerized. "I wonder if she can speak, and if she will?" she asked herself, at last able to move her feet and back away from the apparition. Backwards she stepped until she stumbled into the secretary, groped for its chair, grabbed a hold of it for support, and slowly sat down, gasping for breath and trembling.

The wind was roaring around the house. Louder. Louder. A roll of thunder in the distance sounded, and then another, closer. Another—terrifying clap overhead. A blinding flash of lightning exploded on the iron railing that enclosed the balcony, instantaneously followed by a piercing peal of deafening thunder.

Kendra jumped; her amber colored eyes darted toward the blinding white flash that turned into a bluish ball of deadly electricity. The blue ball thundered across the red tile floor of the balcony, passed right through the open French door, into the sitting room.

The ghost, playing second fiddle to this scene, Kendra, in horror, both hands held up to her mouth, watched the sparking blue ball of lightning. It spit fire, as it rumbled around the floor, seeking out electrical outlets, zapping them upon contact. Exploding. Lamp plugs, before her very eyes, were blown from their fiery sockets, burning and blackening the white wall areas around the outlets; the melted lamp cords, burned black, sizzled.

Frightened and in shock, Kendra expected fire, and jumped up to flee for her life, only to whirl around and encounter CR blocking her way. She swallowed hard. Her mouth felt dry. She felt stifled. CR's dead lips spoke: "Stay where you are. The storm is slackening.The worst is over. See, there goes the ball of fire, heading for the balcony."

The flaming blue ball raced across the floor, over the threshold, and onto the balcony, sparks flying this way and that. It went up the iron railing, over the side and shot through space for seconds, before it zoomed smack into a tall pine, that was standing in the front yard, and exploded. The sound was deafening. The pine stood split in half and smoking. Branches and leaves torn from its limbs littered the yard.

Kendra gasped and shuddered. The spirit showed no emotion. "I war to talk with you, Kendra Louise," said the spook. She closed the slidin doors, shutting off the bedroom from the sitting room, and said: "I alway close off the bedroom when I have a visitor.— Come, let's sit by th fireplace."

Kendra sat across from CR; the coffee table between them. "W-w what do you want to talk about?"

"Me.—Do you know who I am?"

"You look like Carol Rogers, but she's dead."

"How do you know what Carol Rogers looks like?"

"You look like the photograph of the young woman in the silver frame and, since this is Carol Rogers' room, I assumed that's who you are except an older version. Also, my Aunt, Miss Applegate, who sewed for you, described you to me."

"Yes, I am Carol Rogers; and, yes, I am dead."

Kendra sucked in her breath. "W-w-what do you want with me? W-w-what does the dead want with me?—I'm alive."

"To function in a solid state, I need one of your lungs and half youι body."

"I knew it! When I first saw you take solid form, I became breathless and had trouble breathing. That's when you started syphoning off my air. Wasn't it?"

CR nodded. "You panicked and became breathless. You're breathing fine now."

"It seems so, but I don't want to share my lungs or my body with you, or anyone.— Living or dead."

"It's too late. I've already chosen you. My soul will join your soul. Two souls, one body. I will rely on your left lung; and my soul—it only weighs an ounce or two so you won't experience any discomfit or heaviness—my soul will nestle on the left side of your heart."

Kendra stared at this apparition, this ghost, this spirit, this spook, in total disbelief. "Why did you pick *me*? Was it because I came into your powder-blue bedroom when you happened to be haunting it?"

"No. Don't be so foolish. I picked you on the recommendation of your father. Through dreams, I introduced you to Willowwynn, and specifically to my bedroom/sitting room."

"Yes, I dreamed of this room many times; but how can you know my father? He's long dead."

"I'm dead. The dead know the dead. I know your father and your mother. I met them on the other side. They're happily married."

"There're no marriages on the other side."

"So everybody on this side thinks. That's why when a husband dies and a wife remarries, or vice-versa, when the remarried spouse dies and goes to the other side and meets up with his or her original mate there's a big fight. Terrible fight. Hell to pay.

"There's also a big fight when the spouse who is left doesn't marry again, finally dies, hoping to meet his or her mate on the other side and live together for eternity, finds that mate has already found, on the other side, a new mate."

"Are you trying to tell me there *are* marriages taking place on the other side?"

"Yes. I know. I've been there—"

"If you've been on the other side, why didn't you stay there—where you belong?"

"I can't until my earthly mission is completed. Until justice is served.— I've talked with your parents. When I told them I had been murdered and wanted revenge from the grave, your father told me all about your great desire to do detective work."

Kendra stood up. "You're lying. I'm leaving. I'm never coming back to Willowwynn."

"Sit down. It's too late. The dye's cast. My spirit—some might say soul—will take up space in your body, opposite your soul. You will have two souls in your young, strong body. Mine on your left side; yours on the right."

In slow motion Kendra sat down and listened, though her head now pounded, while surges of dizziness swept over her. She couldn't think straight. CR seemed far away.

"The reason I've chosen you is we're very much alike. You came to Willowwynn with an ulterior motive—to capture my husband—marry a rich man. Didn't you?"

"We're not at all alike. I'm alive. You're *dead.* As far as marrying—"

"Don't deny your coming here with marriage in mind. The dead know all the secrets of the living.— I admire a young woman who goes after what she wants. If you help me, Willowwynn is yours."

"I don't want Willowwynn."

"Yes, you do. All you have to do is help me expose my murderer and get even with my enemies."

Kendra felt so badly. Her awful headache—her dizziness— "How many enemies did you have; and who killed you? Your husband? *Tell me!* I'll go straight to the state attorney, and tell him who killed you."

"Do you think, for a moment, Hippolyte Delacroix would believe Carol Rogers' ghost told you who killed her? He'd say you were mad—batty, and ship you off in a New York second, to a nut house."

"You're right. I'm not thinking straight. Did your husband kill you?"

"If you find that my husband killed me, will you turn him in? Or will you close your eyes to the facts?"

"I'm a woman of principle. I believe in truth and justice. Nothing could prevent me from bringing a murderer to justice. *Nothing.*"

"Not even if it came to saving, say your aunt's life."

"That's stupid. *Nothing*, as far as I'm concerned, takes precedence over truth and justice."

"We shall see.— You came here to marry my husband, the master of Willowwynn, so if you turn him in, you can't marry him. You can't be rich. You can't be mistress of Willowwynn."

"You talk as if your husband and I are engaged. I haven't even met your husband."

"I know Clark finds you very attractive, and he's interested in you.— I wouldn't mind marrying a murderer, for money and a home like Willowwynn."

"You speak of money as if you never had any of your own. I thought you were the rich one, and your husband made himself comfortable off your money."

"I was. Money was my god. I loved money. Surprisingly, Clark didn't try to take my money. If he had, he wouldn't have gotten a cent out of me. I was very tight with my money."

"Sounds like money was your everything."

"And soon money will be your everything. You're going to marry for money, just as Jack Trenchard did." She laughed sneeringly.

To herself: "For God's sake, this dead demon even knows about Jack. Don't give her the satisfaction of uttering his name." Aloud: "Money will never be my everything. And I've changed my mind—I'm not going to marry for money. And another thing, no woman in her right mind would knowingly marry a murderer. And one thing more, stop talking as if I'm going to marry your husband in the next ten minutes.—"

CR shrugged indifferently. "For now we'll drop the subject."

"Good."

"Before I get around to divulging the name of my killer, there are many things you must first do for me."

"For instance."

"When I'm ready I'll let you know. Do you smoke? Drink?"

"No."

"I do." She took a cigarette from the container that was on the table, sat it, unlit, in the ashtray. Next she reached for the brandy decanter and poured herself a stiff shot.— "Remember I'll be living, off and on, in your body."

"For how long?" asked Kendra, a feeling of dread seeping into her bones.

"Until my murderer is brought to justice, and my enemies to their knees. So keep in mind that I intend to do everything I used to do when I was alive. Smoke—drink—and—*everything*. Take my pleasure while I'm earth bound."

"Are you saying I can't stop you from abusing my body with alcohol and smokes—and *anything* else?"

"Exactly."

"Are you going to live inside me day and night?"

"No. I'll pick and choose the times I need to be a part of you. During those times, I'll be your dictator."

"Just *you* try it."

"Don't fight me, Kendra Louise, you can't win. Relax and have fun. As you can tell, I'm not in you yet; but when this conversation is over, I'll dissolve into these lights that are outlining me, and then turn into a mist. That's when you'll absorb me—my soul. That's when I'll possess your body and mind. Now you know the plan."

"And if I fight you? Resists your habits?"

"You can't. You're a puppet on a string, and I hold the string. I'll jerk it when I choose."

"You plan to make my life miserable—"

"So much so you'll wish you were dead." She laughed a chilling laugh. "You'll wish you were dead so you could take out your revenge on some other *living* soul."

Kendra felt so badly. Her temples felt like someone was sticking needles in them.

"When I possess your body I am the boss," droned on CR. "Remember that and we'll get along fine. Also remember, when we are one, we'll mentally communicate."— Without warning, she dissolved into a foggy blue mist and disappeared into Kendra's quivering body.

At the mercy of CR's commands, Kendra sat there, alone, except for CR's soul inside her, and smoked her first cigarette for CR's pleasure and enjoyment. She felt sick. Next she sipped her first hard liquor. It burned her throat and took her breath away. She felt sicker.

In a short while Kendra felt a lot tipsy and a little less sick, and very talkative. She mentally communicated with CR. "You said earlier that a soul weighs only a couple ounces. How do you know that?"

"The dead know everything," answered CR's voice inside Kendra's head. CR's voice sounded deep, as if speaking from Kendra's belly.

"If that's so, then tell me what color is a soul?"

"Mine is blue."

"I would've guessed black. Where's Icelynn Farnsworth?" asked Kendra, changing the subject.

"To hell with Icelynn," replied CR through a smoke ring, blown by Kendra. "I hate her guts."

"Do you also hate Kyle Osborne's guts?"

"I loved him."

"Then you hated your husband?"

"I could never hate Clark. He was always wonderful to me. He understood me. He put up with my needs. My extremes."

"What were your extremes?"

"*Money* and *m-e-n,*" her voice spelled out. "I couldn't stop wanting more and more money, nor could I stop loving the men I had made strong emotional ties with, prior to my marriage. All I expected of Clark was to know this. He didn't know I expected this. I didn't know that he didn't know."

"So he was old-fashioned enough not to want you to bring past love interests and old male friends into your marriage. I side with your husband."

"You would. At first Clark couldn't get it through his head that my loving another man didn't make me love him less. He was young and naive enough to think he could supplant all the fascinating men in my life. You're frowning in distaste. Why?"

"Because I find what you say distasteful.— Your husband didn't try to stop you?"

"He insisted I see a psychiatrist. I did, twice a week, for eight years. Clark and I were married for ten years."

"Have you seen a psychiatrist since you moved to New Orleans?"

"No. There was no need. Dr. Brown told me my problem."

"Men?"

"Well, there's a name for it. Nymphomania."

"I call it another name."

"Don't be rude, Kendra Louise. Some women go to great lengths to seek glory while all I ever did was sit on mine."

"I can well imagine how you vamped men, but I can't imagine how you went about getting more and more money."

"I invested. I didn't give a penny away; I didn't go to church because church expected a tithe; I didn't donate to any needy cause; I never paid my way; I did, however, make a donation, once, to the Democratic Party. I'm a democrat, of course."

"Of course."

"I bet men like you. I can't imagine—"

"Don't try to imagine anything where I'm concerned. I'll gladly put your crude curiosity to an end. I'm a virgin."

"Not for long. Do you think for one minute I'm not going to take advantage of such a young, beautiful body—"

"You need to be talking to the devil, not me.—You said at first your husband objected to your loving other men. After you married your husband, how long were you faithful to him?"

"Two whole years. He knew when he married me, he wasn't the first; however, he thought he was going to be the last. He got fooled. When he found out I was seeing someone else—I can't even remember who it was—Clark went to pieces.

"It took him a while to realize that these brief encounters meant nothing to me, and that I'd always come back to him. We got along beautifully until Kyle came into my life."

"Where is your protege? I understand your husband has tried to contact Kyle Osborne, who is suppose to be at UC attending a seminar, but can't be reached. Do you know why?"

"Don't look for Kyle at Berkeley. Look for him beneath the sea."

"Do you mean he's *dead?*"

"Do you know of anyone who can live beneath the sea?"

"N-no. Was he also murdered?"

CR's voice made no reply. The only sound was that of the rain drumming hard against the window panes. Kendra's temples throbbed; and while she waited for CR to speak, she drank another drink; smoked another cigarette; and sat there guzzling liquor and puffing away on cigarettes. The scene was fantastic, absurdly fantastic.

"Was your protege murdered?" repeated Kendra.

Still no reply.

"I work for your husband, so I haven't got all day to sit around chatting. My first duty is to Mr. Rogers."

"No, it isn't," snapped the deep and gruff voice inside Kendra's head. "*I'm first! Don't forget that!*" A long pause followed. "I loved Kyle," began again the voice of CR, "and he loved me. We were going to be married right after my divorce from Clark was final."

"Do you mean to say you were divorcing Mr. Rogers when you died?" asked Kendra, incredulous. "No one mentioned the word divorce. If you were divorcing your husband, why did you leave him all your money?"

"I didn't."

"The *Picayune* said you did."

"That's Judge Exum Edwards' fault. I fired that bastard after I caught him cheating me. I failed to tell Clark I had fired Exum; and, after I died, the bastard played like he was still my legal adviser. He read my *old* will, leaving everything to Clark. My *new* will left everything to Kyle. Consequently, Exum gave the newspaper false information."

"I see. You said the Judge cheated you. How?"

"For the past two years, he acted as my legal and financial adviser.—"

"And lover?"

"You have a knack for knowing things."

"Did you terminate the Judge's services for cheating you, or for being a lousy lover?"

She gave a dry laugh. "The affair was brief. I didn't fire him when we broke off. I fired him about six months ago when I discovered he had been stealing from me. He begged me not to make it public, which would destroy him and his family. So I didn't. A big mistake on my part. I didn't even tell Clark, a bigger mistake."

"So you quietly fired the respectable thief?"

"Yes. As my financial adviser, Judge Edwards made investments for me, often doubling my capital; and then, without my knowledge, used *my* profits to speculate for himself. As soon as he'd make a profit of his own, he'd put my money back, sans interest, and would've continued this practice if I hadn't caught him. He stole a small fortune from me."

"Why, that's misappropriation of funds. You should've prosecuted him."

"I know. But he promised me $100,000 if I didn't blow the whistle."

"And you jumped at that?"

"Of course.— To get back to when I confronted him, he said using a client's money was a regular practice, and all financial advisers do it. I told him, regular practice or not, to put my money back pronto, and that he was fired. He said he couldn't put the money back until April 15th. I gave him until then."

"And then you conveniently died on April 13th? Holy Moses! Did Judge Edwards kill you?"

"In time you'll know who my killer is."

"You must have some plan doped out that you want me to follow. So tell me exactly what role I play in tracking down your killer, and getting even with your enemies? Who can I take in my confidence?"

"*No one.* You take no one in your confidence. You handle this *alone*, and do exactly as I say. Of course, when I'm in your body, you won't have any choice but to do as I wish."

To herself: "This dead she-devil has no hold on me. So why do I feel fettered—tied?" Aloud: "You've picked the wrong woman. You should've picked a woman more to your own temperament. One who drinks and smokes and one who sits on her glory."

The voice laughed out loud and demanded another drink, and Kendra accommodated her. "Karl Erpelding, a long-time family friend and lawyer, will be coming to Willowwynn in the next couple of days," said the voice. "He has no idea that I'm dead. That news will greatly upset him, but afterwards he'll want to get to the bottom of my death."

"You say this Mr. Erpelding is a long-time family friend and lawyer. Did he handle your affairs before Judge Edwards?"

"Up until I moved to New Orleans, and met Judge Exum Edwards, my thief-of-a-next-door neighbor."

"And you fired your long-time family friend and hired your new-found lover. What excuse did you make to Mr. Erpelding for giving him the ax?"

"Distance. I said I needed a lawyer here in New Orleans, not all the way off in San Francisco."

"And, of course, lawyer Erpelding saw through that."

"He did. We had a terrible blow-up, but we made it up toward the end."

"And so you turned everything over to your sterling lover. By the way, did your husband know the Judge and you were a twosome?"

"No. I think he was the only lover Clark didn't know about."

"Mmmmm—" Kendra was thoughtful. "Tell me a little bit about Karl Erpelding."

"After my father died, Karl took over all the money matters for my mother; and after my mother died, Karl took charge of things for me. Karl's the smiling gentleman in the photograph on the table."

"I noticed his photograph. He's a very handsome gentleman. I thought he might be a relative."

The voice made no reply to Kendra's statement. "The couple is my parents. My mother, as you can see, even in old age, still had some remnants of a real beauty."

"Your obit notice didn't name any brothers or sisters, so I assume you're an only child."

"That's why my mother adored me. Worshiped me. I was a wonderful daughter to her. My mother's sister, Aunt Sadie, also adored me. She left me everything. Her home—I sold it—her diamonds and her money."

"Your Aunt Sadie had no children?"

"None."

"And your father. Did he adore and worship you?"

"My father didn't take good pictures. Too stiff."

"I noticed. Did your parents know you had this problem with men?"

"My darling mother, who was 75, had all her faculties, could drive, could do everything, understood; my father didn't. Neither did Karl Erpelding."

"Did your mother approve of your having affairs with married men?"

"Judge Edwards was my first and only affair with an old married man. The Judge was ten years my senior. I went for much younger men. Clark was 27 when I married him; I was 37. If I had lived, I'd made, in June, my 47th birthday."

"Hmmmm— And how old is Kyle Osborne?"

"Twenty-seven."

"Yes, I can see where old Judge Edwards couldn't hold a woman who picks up her lovers at nursery school."

"Don't act smart with me, Kendra Louise. Let's get back to the Judge's schemes and scams. Judge Edwards was very adventuresome with my money; Karl Erpelding was extremely careful and conservative."

"What did Karl Erpelding think of your taking risks with, I assume, a lot of money?"

"He didn't like it at all. We had a terrible fight. As I told you, we just recently made it up—started talking again after a two-year silence."

"You broke the silence?"

"I had to when I discovered the Judge was double dealing me."

"So Karl Erpelding knows about the Judge."

"Yes. But the Judge doesn't know that Karl knows."

"So the respected Judge Edwards thinks he's home free."

"Yes. It'll be up to you and Karl to get my money back—"

"And give it to your husband?"

"Yes. Kyle's beneath the sea, and can't use it."

"What about Kyle's heirs?"

No reply. Silence. The room was now dark and full of shadows; and, without warning, Kendra felt her body go rigid, then quiver all over. A weight lifted from her chest. The ghost, the spirit, the soul of CR had ejected itself. Startled, Kendra watched the foggy mist before her eyes evaporate. Unable to think clearly, she stared blankly at the cigarette butts in the astray, and at the empty liquor glass.

How long she sat there staring and sobering up, she didn't know. "I wonder if all these shifting shadows have tricked me into thinking I smoked, drank and talked to a voice inside my head—a ghost?" she asked herself over and over, in disbelief.

"Miz Applegates," called out Gussie Rae Booker, separating the sliding doors and stumping through into the sitting room. She snapped on the over head chandelier. No lights. She couldn't see the cigarette butts or the unstopped brandy decanter.

"Why de 'lectric's offs up heah. Wat's yo doin' sittin' heah all alones en de dark. Dis heah room is dark—debble dark.Yo bens hidin' up heah whiles dat dare storm wuz ah blowin'? Me end Xariffa's bens hidin' en de pantree wit our aprons t'rowed ovah our haids, so de lightnin' wouldn't gits usen. Dat dare storm wuz ah reg'lar howler. Likes ah pack uv wil' witches hauntin' end ah hollerin'."

Kendra stood up, shaky legged.

"Dats aud we ain't gots no lights up heah. We gots 'em downstairs. Comes on down, Miz Applegates, Mistah Rogers is ah waitin' on yo en de liberry."

As Kendra approached the library, the door opened, and Mr. C.C. Bennett appeared.

Earlier that morning, Kendra had been planning to tell *this* man a faceful; however, after her encounter with CR, she had had a change of heart. She was just too happy to see someone she knew. A friend.

"Am I ever glad to see you," cried Kendra, in a slightly slurring voice.

"I thought you'd be ready to give me hell. Tell me how frightfully bored you've been."

"I haven't been bored for a single second, since I got here."

"Well, where have you been? Hiding from the storm? I'm surprised you let a little lightning and thunder frighten you. You look unwell—distraught."

"I wasn't hiding; but I do feel a little shaky. The storm was bad. Almost as bad as—"

"When you took shelter at the leper colony?"

"Y-yes."

"The wind was so strong it blew over three pine trees; lightning split a fourth. Where have you been?"

"I—I've been upstairs in the powder-blue bedroom, rather the sitting room," stammered Kendra, looking directly into his quizzing navy blue eyes that weren't twinkling. "Listen, I can't talk now. Mr. Rogers is waiting for me in the library."

"Where did you hear the words powder-blue bedroom?" demanded Mr. C.C. Bennett, almost roughly.

"I guess Gussie Rae Booker said them," shrugged Kendra.

"No, she didn't. *Where-did-you-hear-it?*"

His tone of voice spoiled the encounter, especially since they had been such comrades the day before. "If she didn't say it to me, then I must've either dreamed it or, after seeing the blue room, just made it up.— What difference does it make to you, the *yardman,* where I heard it?"

"It makes a great difference. Only *I* know that my wife referred to her bedroom as the powder-blue bedroom. So-how-do-you-know?"

"*Your wife,*" repeated Kendra, incredulous, sobering. "I thought you said you were the *yardman* around here."

"My name is Clark Charles Bennett Rogers, and I have been the yardman ever since Harry Sato left."

Kendra hiccupped. "Well, the truth to tell, my aunt and I didn't figure you for the Master of Willowwynn, but we *did* figure you for a man of means. One of them fancy landscape designers. You were much too dressed up, clean and high toned for a regular yardman."

"Congratulations on your astuteness."

"You deliberately lied to me," hiccupped Kendra.

"I did not lie to you. You were the *one* who said I was the *yardman.* I just went along with you."

"You should've set things straight yesterday afternoon when visiting," reprimanded Kendra, her face shame stained. "If I had known you were Mr. Rogers, I'd have never said the things I said."

"You wouldn't have accused me of murdering my wife for her money?"

"No."

"Miss Applegate, you should never say things about someone behind his back that you can't say to his face without being ashamed, if found out," rebuked Clark Rogers.

"You set me up. You were devious. I detest deceit. If you're not lying about your name, then you're eavesdropping in hallways listening in on conversations."

"Your aunt knew she was wrong, and apologized."

"If an apology is owed, it's *you* who owe it. You owe *two* apologies."

"And you owe me an apology. You said you didn't smoke or drink, and you're standing here before me smelling like a smoke stack on top a distillery. Did you find the key to the liquor cabinet?"

Kendra still tipsy, countered with: "You took me away from my boss, Mr. Prosper, under false pretenses. I told you—alias Mr. C.C. Bennett, *yardman*—that I didn't want to work for Mr. Rogers, and this morning Mr. Prosper informed me—"

"Is that why you had to go drinking, smoking and snooping in my wife's bedroom?"

"I went looking for an address," lied Kendra

"I left all the addresses on the rent table in the library."

"All except Mr. Karl Erpelding's."

"Karl is special. He doesn't get a note. I've been trying to call him, without success. Why did you think you would find his address in my wife's bedroom?"

"Gussie Rae Booker said your wife's address book was in her desk."

"Well, did you find Karl's name in my wife's address book?"

"I didn't get a chance to look. The storm blew up, and lightning struck the railing on the balcony, rolled across the floor, through the French doors into the sitting room.—There's quite a bit of lightning damage upstairs. I'll show you."

Upstairs in CR's sitting room,Clark Rogers followed Kendra around, as she pointed out burned lamp cords and blackened outlets.

"This must've been quite a frightening experience," observed Clark, shaking his head.

"Terrifying," replied Kendra.

"At least you weren't hurt."

"No. Just shook up."

"I'll have the repairman here first thing in the morning." He ambled over toward the coffee table; Kendra followed.

The stopper of the brandy decanter sat next to the cigarette box; the ashtray was filled with butts; the rim of the brandy glass, that Kendra had used, was sticky, and in the bottom of the glass was a little pool of brandy.

For a few seconds, Clark studied these articles, and then he picked up the ashtray. He fingered a few butts. "Do you still claim you don't smoke?"

Kendra stood there with burning cheeks. "I don't smoke or drink— voluntarily."

"Are you saying today you smoked and drank *involuntarily?"*

"Y-yes. I did; but I didn't. I'm not sure what happened."

Clark stood there peering at her—pinning her. She wanted to scream at him: "I was your dead wife's victim. She made me do it—"

"Are you going to tell me how you knew this apartment was called the powder-blue bedroom?"

"I dreamed it." She shivered.

"Are you cold, Miss Applegate?"

"A little."

"Let's go down. I'll have Xariffa make a pot of coffee."

"I wouldn't care for any of your monkey pee." slipped out before she could catch it back.

Clark laughed a short laugh. "Miss Applegate, you look like Anne Boleyn the day she got her death sentence; and could use a good cup of hot monkey pee to sober you up."

"I—I guess I could use a cuppa coffee."

To Kendra's great surprise, Xariffa had made her a cup of Creole coffee and a ham and cheese sandwich. Mr. Rogers brought it to her, and then went to his study.

While she sipped her coffee and ate her sandwich, she was preoccupied with thoughts of CR. Over and over she muttered beneath her breath: "It's stupid and senseless to dwell on the dead."

Kendra tried to concentrate on other things, but CR forced herself on her thoughts. "Did I really see a ghost, and did that ghost really inhabit my body? Possess my mind?—*N-no-o*—*Y-yes*-s," she argued with herself. "I spoke to CR—She spoke to me—*No-no-no.*—I know Mr. Rogers thinks I smoked those cigarettes and drank that brandy because I wanted to.— Any chance I might've had with him is gone now. He must think I'm an awful liar."

There was no balm for the shame and humiliation she felt. She was grateful that Mr. Rogers had gone into his study and had stayed there. After she finished eating, she returned to her typewriter, clacked a few lines and argued with herself, all over again, if she really and truly had seen the ghost of CR, or if it was all a delusion—A hallucination.

Again and again she asked herself: "CR, are you an absurdity that was born out of a stormy day and a dark shadowy room? A devil-dark room," until her head pounded, and she felt more confused than ever.

The rest of the afternoon went this way. She had become so engrossed with her delusion, her hallucination, that Gussie Rae Booker had to tell her it was, "Quittin' times. Pas' quittin times, Miz Applegates."

Kendra, thoroughly spent and exhausted, glanced at her watch. "It sure is. I'll just tidy up a bit, and be on my way."

Chapter Nine

At home, Kendra found her aunt in the kitchen, the gatelegged table already set and spread with two plates of red beans and rice, seasoned with pickle pork, and a side dish of panee pork chops.

"When did you cook all this? I'm only half an hour late."

"We lost the lights at work, so I came home early. Since this is Monday, Stella Dora made her usual big pot of red beans and rice, and shared them with us. I fried the poke chops. Holmes had pecan pies on sale, so I bought us one for dessert, but we can't eat it."

"Why not?— I think I hear Sholar Picarara yowling at the back door."

"Don't let him in the kitchen," warned Molly Primrose, darkly.

"You couldn't drag him in here. I've tried." Kendra poured some milk in an empty cream cheese carton. "I told you, when you said right before his face he couldn't come in the house because his mouth was full of seven deadly diseases, you insulted him. Hurt his feelings."

"Good."

Kendra took the milk out to the back steps where Sholar Picarara was. He wouldn't lap any of the milk. He just kept meowing, mournfully. She gathered him in her arms and hugged him. Then stroking him, said: "Nice kitty—Pretty kitty—Why are you so sad?—You been fighting with Motel, and lost?"She nuzzled her face in his fur, and then set him down. He stretched. "I've got to go in now, Sholar, so drink your milk.." He took a couple laps of the milk, and then washed his face. Kendra returned to the kitchen.

"Sholar seems sad. He hardly touched his milk."

"Wash your hands, Kendra Lou. Cats can't feel sad."

Kendra washed her hands, and then sagged into her chair.

"Don't you feel all right? You look tired."

"I'm all right."

"You don't look all right."

"Do you want me to stick out my tongue, like when I was a little girl, so you can decided if I need a dose of castor oil?"

Her aunt waved this away, sat down, said Grace and announced: "We can't touch that pecan pie because I've got some terrible bad news to tell you. Lolotte DuPuy called a little while ago to say her brother, Antlee Theaud, jumped off the Huey P. Long Bridge this afternoon in all that rain. He broke and battered his poor body to pieces. He mangled himself somethin' awful."

"*My God!*" cried Kendra.

"He jumped with Motel in his arms. He committed suicide and made his cat die with him. So we got to carry that pie, tonight, over to Lolotte."

"*My God!*" cried Kendra again. "If he wanted to kill himself, why drag poor Motel into the deal? I just saw Antley Theodd the other day, and he seemed fine. The same day I saw Antley Theodd, I saw Motel and Sholar Picarara in the DuPuy front yard, tearing round and round like two crazy cats; stopping only to start chasing their own tails. Antley Theodd should've never made Motel die with him. No wonder poor Sholar seemed so sad. He knows his buddy's dead."

"Cats can't tell when another cat's dead. Cat's don't grieve. —Lolotte said she saw her brother at breakfast this mornin', and he seemed fine. She said he was his reg'lar quiet self.— Here, put some butter on your bread while its good-'n'-hot.—Eat." Silence.

"It's a pity all right," went on Molly Primrose, cutting a piece of her pork chop and taking a bite of her bread and butter. "Antlee Theaud was a fine-lookin' young man. Only thirty-five. He was fine until he came back from the war. The war ruined his life. Some how he just wasn't the same after the war. Lolotte said he couldn't get satisfied. I hope his dyin', since he did it to himself, satisfied him."

"I guess, if he made Motel die with him, he was sicker than anybody figured."

"Five years in the Pacific fightin' them dirty sneaky Japs left their toll. Just before peace was declared, the guvment pronounced Antlee Theaud was sufferin' from shell shock, discharged him, and gave him a pension for the rest of his livin' life. Then he had to go and jump off the Huey P. Long Bridge. I used to wish he'd fine a nice young woman and get married, but now as it turned out I'm glad he didn't."

"I suppose the pension ends with his life."

"I'm afraid so. Poor Lolotte. You know, she depended on her brother's pension to help raise her two chirren. Well, Eddie Frank, as soon as he graduates from Fortier this June, plans to join the Army. So Miss Lolotte DuPuy won't have to worry about her son makin' a livin'."

"She'll just have to worry about the Army shipping her son over to

Korea. She'll have to worry about good-looking Eddie Frank coming home in a pine box like Kenny Joe did."

"That's a big worry all right." Aunt Molly Primrose was thoughtful. "Eddie Frank has everything his sister don't—smarts, good looks, personality. It's too bad that Lolotte didn't get *that* way by the same man when she conceived Edna Pearl. Lolotte was a beauty when she was Edna Pearl's age. Pretty hair and skin. Nice trim figure."

"Poor Edna Pearl. She sure is plain and stout—and mean mouthed."

"Yes, she is. That's the way of the world. They got plains and pretties, stouts and skinnies. Can't be helped. I used to hope Edna Pearl was gunna be like a bug: shed her shell and come out like a beautiful butterfly. Oh well, she's got two more years before she graduates from high school.

"Afterwards, I hope she'll find a good husband. But if you believe in like mother like daughter, then Edna Pearl won't get no husband. —Kendra Lou, stop playin' with your beans. You're makin' a mess of your plate. Cut up your poke chop. Eat! You're actin' like you don't feel good."

All the while Kendra had listened and talked, though her head ached and her stomach felt a little nauseated, half her mind was absorbed with the ghost of CR in the fear that she had imagined all.

"I'm not hungry. And I don't believe in like mother like daughter. It's too bad Miss Lolotte DuPuy couldn't make the men who got her *that* way pay child support for her children."

"No body knows who her lovers were, and Lolotte will never tell. Of course, it's too late to get any support for Eddie Frank. He's all grown up. But Edna Pearl is a horse of a different color. That's what Lizzie Slapp Springmeyer and Moochin' Mamie TuJax said."

"Did you see *those* two today?"

"No. I heard them over the phone when Lolotte cawled to tell me the bad news—oh, I almost forgot to tell you, AntleeTheaud landed feet first, and the impact of the fall forced his legs up into his chest; Motel was found dead in his arms. *Un*scratched.

"Just as Lolotte told me that, both Lizzie Slapp Springmeyer and Moochin' Mamie TuJax picked up the phone and stayed on the line lissenin' in.—Go on and cut up your poke chop."

"I wish *those two* weren't on our party line."

"If it wasn't those two, it would be some other busybodies.—At first Lolotte was mad with Lizzie Slapp and Moochin' Mamie for lissenin' in, but later she agreed it was better that way because she wouldn't have to make two more phone calls."

"That's one way to look at it."

"It woulda been OK if Lizzie Slapp and Moochin' Mamie hadn't got to fightin', and all because Lizzie Slapp kept sayin': 'Heh, what's that you say, Lolotte? Heh?...Heh?'... 'Turn up your hearin' aid, Lizzie Slapp,' yelled Moochin' Mamie. 'I don't wanna. It's turned up enough. If I had my way, I'd shut the blame thing off altogether...Tune out the world.' 'While you're tunin' out the world go ahead and tune out this here phone call.' 'Heh? What's that you're sayin'?' 'If you don't hear me and I'm yellin', then get off the line,' hollered Moochin' Mamie. I hated for Lolotte, with all her grief, to hear such goin's on."

"Those *two Biddies* are something else." Kendra cut a piece of her pork chop, chewed it up, swallowed and announced: "I've got some news myself. For the next six months, I'll be working at Willowwynn, for Mr. Rogers."

Aunt Molly Primrose's button blue eyes widened. She put her fork down. "How did that come about, Kendra *Louise*?"

"Well, to make a long story short, Mr. C.C. Bennett, the great liar, the great deceiver, turned out to be Mr. Clark Charles Bennett Rogers, Master of Willowwynn and owner of the Homestead. Mr. Prosper's boss. He simply called Mr. Prosper *Saturday evening* and borrowed me. Why he didn't mention this *yesterday* while he was charming you and making up to me, makes me mad."

"He must've forgot. Anyway, who ever woulda thought a *yardman* was the Master of Willowwynn and Mr. Prosper's boss? Not me. I knew he seemed like a man of means." Aunt Molly Primrose paused, and then: "Well, being Mr. Rogers and not Mr. Bennett is good news, because he don't have to go to Delgado, to take up no trade. I couldn't bear the thought of you marryin' a *yardman*, Kendra Lou."

"Tante, you sound like Mrs. Bennett in *Pride and Prejudice,* making matchess. I wish you'd stop talking like Mr. Rogers has asked me to marry him. He hasn't. Besides, I thought you didn't like the idea of my working for Mr. Rogers, let alone marrying him."

Her aunt's button blue eyes twinkled. "Now that I've met Mr. Rogers, I don't mind at all."

"Tante, you don't mind a man who says black is white and day is night?"

"Kendra Lou, stop mean mouthin' Mr. Rogers. It was *you*, my dear niece, who went to Willowwynn with a facefull of deceit. When you met Mr. Rogers, alias Mr. C.C. Bennett, *yardman*, the lies were flyin' thick-'n'-fast. Both ways. Remember you're just where you wanted to be to start with.— I know you must've toured Willowwynn so tell me what she looks like."

"Do you remember during my pneumonia bout I had that strange recurring dream about a mansion with a powder-blue bedroom?—"

Whenever Kendra mentioned the words *dream* and *ghost*, her aunt always shut up like an "erster." She nodded slowly.

"Willowwynn is the same mansion in my dream. The powder-blue bedroom is at Willowwynn."

Aunt Molly Primrose's button blue eyes clouded with doubt, but that didn't deter Kendra. She described Willowwynn, Gussie Rae Booker and Xariffa; and then finished up with that day's storm and the ball of lightning that rolled around the floor of CR's sitting room.

"Kendra *Louise*, I never heard the like of a blue ball of lightnin' runnin' all around a floor, explodin' lamps and sockets as it went. Sometimes I think your imagination gets the best of you. You got your good looks from both your parents; your imagination from neither." She sighed. "But I must admit it's aud that you dreamed of this powder-blue bedroom/sittin' room, and then found one to match it."

"I-didn't-imagine-any-of-it."

"By the way, since Antlee Theaud only has one moth eaten suit, Lolotte is gunna bury him in his green Army uniform," said Aunt Molly Primrose, changing the subject.

"If the coffin lid's closed—I'd think she'd want it closed if his body's battered—it won't matter if he's buried naked."

"I asked her if the coffin lid would be closed. She said she hadn't decided yet. I hope she decides in favor of a closed coffin, since his nice body is broken and battered somethin' awful."

"Tante, do you think the living can talk to the dead, or vice versa?" asked Kendra, out of the blue.

"Kendra *Louise,* I do declare you can come up with the strangest questions. Who ever heard the like of a such a question? Not me. To answer your question: *No*, the livin' can't talk to no dead, nor the dead to no livin'. I think it would be a sin to do so."

"Why a sin?"

"Well, I read somethin' in the Bible about a witch talkin' to the dead, and the Lord, soon afterwards, got in touch with that witch. He said: 'Witch, tomorrow, you'll be on the other side.' The next day the witch found herself on the other side."

"Do you think there're marriages on the other side?"

"Gawd save us! Everybody knows there—ain't—no—marriages on the other side. All religions teach that.— I think you need a good dose of castor oil."

"No, I don't. What if all the religions are wrong?" I think our religion is wrong saying it's a mortal sin, if we eat meat on Friday. I refuse to believe, if I eat a weenie and chili on Friday and die, I'll go to hell."

"Kendra *Louise,* we ain't gunna discuss *that* again. I already told you there ain't never gunna be no weenies in this house on no Fridays. We ain't Produstunts."

"Even if the Pope should say it's all right?"

"The Pope ain't never gunna say it's all right."

"Even if he did, you, and I don't know how many others like you, wouldn't accept it. You'd be more Catholic than the Catholic Church. Wouldn't you?"

"There'll *be no meat in this here house on no Fridays, and no missin' no mass on Sundays and holy days. Period.* And no Pope will ever say to eat meat on Friday and miss Mass on Sunday ain't no mortal sin." Aunt Molly Primrose, her apple cheeks blazing, took a deep breath. "We've been over this a hundred times."

"Some day one of the Pope's will say all that, and a lot more." persisted Kendra. "I hope whoever the Pope is will also tell us we don't have to pray for the conversion of Russia anymore. I don't even know what a Russian looks like, and every Sunday after Mass I spend ten minutes praying for people who hate America."

"One day the Russian conversion will come."

"I also hope that same Pope will tell us we can listen to the radio during Lent. Why, the Wheelerhands watched TV this past Lent."

"That's the Wheelerhands. Every day they're actin' more like Produstunts than good Catholics."

"Tante, changes in the Church are going to come. Some Pope will change the rules, substituting love and understanding for fear and guilt. Even divorce may become possible."

"Kendra *Louise,* divorce will *never* be possible. I hate it when you get on one of your tangents. I don't know who you take after for havin' such crazy notions. My dear brother never talked nutty, and, for that matter, neither did your sweet mother."

"Is it crazy to want things to be right— normal— just?"

"It's strange and aud for you to attack things the way you do. A few years back you got it in your head that some day we'll have instant food. Instant potatoes, of all things. That's never gunna happen. We're gunna peel potatoes and boil 'em just like our ancestors did before us. It's only natural. To go against bein' natural is to go against Gawd. You don't want Gawd to get mad at you."

"I'm sure God don't give a hoot-'n'-a holler if we peel potatoes or not."

"Please leave Gawd out of this instant food business."

"I believe God wants things easier for his children. Wouldn't it be nice to come home from work, open up a box of powdered potatoes, put them in a pot, add cream and butter, stir 'em up, and in a minute or two have mashed potatoes?"

"Eat your beans and rice that took Stella Dora all day to fix."

For a few minutes Kendra concentrated on eating, and then she put down her fork, looked her aunt straight in her blue eyes and asked? "Tante, do you think there's room in one body for two souls?"

This was too much for Molly Primrose. "Gawd save us!— I'll pour the coffee and get you a couple cookies," she replied, rising. A moment or two later she returned to the table, carrying a plateful of cookies. She poured the coffee, sat down, and sipped hers in silence.

"Well, if you can't answer that question, I have another. Where's the soul located in the body?"

"Kendra *Louise,* when you talk like that you worry the heart out of me."

"Tante, what color is a soul?"

"After we bring our pecan pie to Lolotte DuPuy and visit a little with her—you can stay as long as you like—I'll go sit with Rosa's twins so she can carry her cake to Lolotte. You know the twins are totterin' around. They're too young for that. I warned Rosa not to let them do that because they'll just make themselves bow-legged."

"Tante, I've got to tell you something that you're not going to like nor believe."

Molly Primrose gave her niece a look of boundless exasperation.

"Today, I talked with the ghost of Carol Rogers. She told me she was murdered, and demanded that I find her murderer. Until I bring her killer to justice, she's going to share my body, possess it when she wants. She's going to use and abuse me."

Molly Primrose gave Kendra a mildly scathing look.

"She made me smoke and drink, for her pleasure."

"Kendra *Louise,* you're of age and, if you want to smoke and drink, you don't have to make up no such wholesale falsehoods," replied her aunt, unemotionally. "I'm against those vices, but if you don't take them in excess, they can't kill you."

"I'm not lying."

"Kendra *Louise*, up until now, you've been in the habit of truthfulness. Durin' your teen years, I expected trouble; but there was no hooky playin'; no cigarette smokin'; no beer drinkin'; and very little sass out of you. And now this! Talkin' to ghosts. None of the Applegates talked to ghosts," she added, implying maybe Kendra's mother's people did.

"I didn't make it up. It happened."

"You imagined the whole thing. When you was little both you and Kenny Joe couldn't get your fill of ghost stories and ghost movies. Every time *The Ghost of Frankenstein* came to the Tivoli, you begged and begged until either I or Stella Dora took you and Kenny Joe. You and Kenny Joe never got tired of that old *Frankenstein guy*, though he never failed to scare the liver and the lights out of both of you.

"After we'd get home from one of them scary movies, I'd have to leave every light on in the house; look under your bed, my bed; check out every tiny noise: leaves rustlin', branches scrapin' the winders, cause you thought the ghost of Frankenstein was after you. When you finally went to bed, scared to death, it was in my bed, not your own.

"And right next door Kenny Joe, filled with fear, was puttin' his parents through what you was puttin' me through. Cryin'-'n'-carryin' on. I might've known today's storm, and your bein' in that powder-blue bedroom/sittin' room, was a perfect settin' for an imaginary ghost to make his appearance."

"So you think the storm made me conjure up the ghost of CR?"

"I do."

"These cookies"—they were bumpy with nuts and raisins—"taste good dipped in my coffee. Real good," simply replied Kendra, as she munched away."Mr. Rogers asked me if I drank his wife's liquor and smoked her cigarettes. I told him I did it involuntarily."

A scornful movement played around her aunt's lips. "Moochin' Mamie TuJax, point blank, asked Lolotte DuPuy how she was gunna make ends meet now that Antlee Theaud's pension would be cut off." said Molly Primrose, determinedly changing the subject. "She also asked if the guvment would bury him."

"That biddy, Mooching Mamie TuJax, has a lot of gall.— I'm not going to Miss DuPuy's house tonight. I just don't feel up to it."

"Why, Kendra *Louise*, you know whenever a neighbor dies on Starlight Street we all go comfort the family."

"I've got a headache. Just tell everybody I've got a headache."

"I don't need to tell the neighbors you got a headache, they'll know, if you don't show up, that's somethin's wrong; and they'll draw their own conclusions. They're like that," drily said Aunt Molly Primrose, rising and clearing the table.

Kendra stood up and started helping. "I'll wash and dry the dishes—there's only a handful," Tante. Afterwards, I might listen to Amos and Andy, and then go to bed."

"Of course, Lolotte will understand, even if I don't. You're as bad as Nell Miller. She and Lolotte DuPuy went all through Wilson School together, but Nell's goin' to the picture show tonight. If Nell's not watchin' her seventeen-inch Philco, she's runnin" off to the picture show. To see, of all the movies playin', *Joan of Arc,* starin' Ingrid Bergman, even though she disgraced herself with *that* Eyetalian—whatever his name is."

"I suppose Ingrid Bergman couldn't help falling in love with Roberto Rossellini."

"Well, as far as I'm concerned, if she wasn't already married to a fine doctor and had a child, she coulda fallen in love with the iceman. But now she's got herself *that way*, and by *that* Eyetalian. A foreigner."

Kendra shrugged.

"The wake'll start tomorrow; the funeral is Friday, if all goes well. "I'll be going directly to the wake from work. You can do the same."

"Let's get back to how Miss DuPuy's going to make ends meet now that her main support has committed suicide."

"She told Lizzie Slapp and Moochin' Mamie she'd have to rent Antlee Theaud's room, as she rents her other dead brother's room, to Miss Tea Burn. Tea is close to a hundred, and still got her mind. Lolotte says Tea just got in the habit of livin' and can't quit."

"I didn't know Miss DuPuy's other brother."

"You was a baby when Asa Earl, the motorsickle po-leeceman, died chasin' a man who ran a red light. Asa Earl tried to cut off the speeder, and the speeder ran right over him. Crushed Asa Earl to death, and smashed his motorsickle. Kendra Lou, you've eaten next to nothing for supper, and you look so skinny tonight. Have some more cookies, before I put 'em away. You said they were real good."

"They're delicious." She munched on a cookie while she filled the dishpan with hot soapy water; her aunt at her side. Pots and pans and dishes clattered, water splashed, they talked:"Both Lolotte's brothers have died tragically," remarked her aunt. "Of course, that Asa Earl was sorry dirt. A cocky little cop, he was. Threw his weight around."

"What do you mean?"

"Being a po-leeceman he figured all the merchants in town owed him a livin'. He never paid for a loaf of bread or a quart of milk. He strutted into any grocery store, like the banty rooster he was, helped himself and strutted right out. Did the same with liquor and smokes. Anybody else take merchandise, without payin' for it, would be arrested for stealin'."

"I've heard over half the cops get away with stealing."

"They do. Lolotte says they teach lit'le colored chirren to snatch white women's purses; give the chirren a dollar of the loot and keep nine for theirselves."

"Maybe some honest cop some day will step in and stop all those thieving cops, before it's too late."

"For the sake of the people of New Orleans, I hope so.—Asa Earl was always fond of sayin' 'I like a little sugar in my coffee.' Meaning he wanted everything free'n'-sweet."

"Well, he met a bitter end."

"He sure did. I often thought Asa Earl committed suicide. If he did, he'll meet up with Antlee Theaud, and the two will be lost in eternity. They'll never see the face of Gawd."

"Because they committed suicide?"

"Gawd can take you off the earth, but you can't take yourself off. People who do are lost souls, for eternity."

"Why do you think a man like Asa Earl, on the take, would commit suicide. He had a good thing going for himself. Why end it?"

"Unlucky in love. His wife left him. When she left he said he could never love another woman, and had no reason to go on livin'. Six months later he got killed."

"Who was his wife?"

"Esther, a young Jew girl. A real beauty. Esther gave Asa Earl a son, an ugly lit'le boy who didn't look like Asa Earl or Esther. Soon after the birth of baby David DuPuy, Esther ran off with Grace Lawler's rich neighbor, Buddy Boy Lyonnel, Jr., son of Buddy Boy Lyonnel, Sr., who was in the chicken business. That ol' chicken plucker's still kickin'."

"That's who we buy our chickens from."

Molly Primrose nodded. "Mr. Lyonnel, Sr. made a fortune raisin', killin' and pluckin' chickens. The Lyonnels just built a big red brick house behind Grace Lawler's old double."

"By now, David DuPuy should be a man."

"He is. As I said, he was an ugly lit'le boy who grew into an ugly-lookin' lit'le man. At first David lived with his mother, and when she died ol' man Lyonnel, Sr. bundled up baby David and dumped him on Lolotte's doorstep. She raised him. I think Buddy Boy, Jr. went along with dumpin' his baby on the DuPuy's doorstep, though he denied it."

"Well, how old was Esther when she died?"

"Esther must've been about fifteen when lit'le David was born. She'd have been a good twenty or twenty-two when she died of heart trouble. She died at the dinin' room table. The maid had just served the chicken soup; every day ol' man Lyonnel, Sr. made his whole family eat chicken soup, along with the other seven courses. Esther took a spoonful, had a heart attack, and fell face forward into her chicken soup. If she hadn't died of a heart attack, she'd have drowned. A month later her husband remarried."

"What a story. I think I know who David DuPuy is. He's a preacher. I saw his picture in the paper."

"He is. Lolotte said David bought himself a preachin" depluma through a mail order add. Paid fifty cents for it. She said he started preachin' in a tent, and a year later he built the biggest church New Orleans has ever seen. Lolotte says he built for the Second Comin'. He expects Jesus to land at his church. He's makin' money hand over fist.

"Lolotte says he's a no good so-'n'-so. A cheat, a thief, and the liar of the world, who, since he's took up preachin', has never worked a day in his life. A real smooth operator. A slick tongue."

"Maybe ol' 'slick tongue', since he's so rich, can help his aunt," said Kendra, washing the last dish.

"That's what Lizzie Slapp Springmeyer suggested, but Lolotte said that slicko preacher's got the first penny he stole. He's so tight, she said he squeaks when he walks.— Kendra Lou, you look *very* tired. I'm gunna dry these dishes."

Half hour later, Molly Primrose left for Lolotte DuPuy's; Kendra took a bath, put on her PJ's and went to bed. Sleep didn't come. What came were flashbacks of CR, wrapped in a foggy mist.

"CR is dead. Cremated," cried Kendra over and over to herself. "Her ashes are in an urn some where in San Francisco. Yet, when we talked, and we did talk, she seemed so alive."

This debate went on until Molly Primrose returned from Lolotte DuPuy's, and softly called out: "Kendra Lou, you sleepin'?"

"No. Come on in. How did it go?"

"The same as usual," replied her aunt, turning on the night lamp, and then sinking into the bedside rocker. "All the neighbors was there; and we talked on every subject we could lay our tongues to. Everybody asked for you. How's your headache?"

"Better."

"Good. I'm glad you didn't come, Kendra Lou."

"Why?"

"I haven't been in the DuPuy double since Lolotte's parents died. At that time, it was a neat and clean home. And now it's a disgrace. Lolotte's let everythin' go. She had to string sheets around the clutter and the dirt. She said she'd been meanin', for years, to go through all the useless things around the house: old magazines, yellowed newspapers, stacked to the ceilin' and everywhere, and throw them away; but didn't get around to it. She said Edna Pearl won't lift a finger to help her."

"I've never been in the DuPuy double, but just looking at unkempt Miss DuPuy—whenever I drive pass, mornin', noon or night, she's always sitting on the front gallery, rocking and picking her nose—no wonder nothing gets done."

"Poor Antlee Theaud. He was so neat and clean. Lolotte said he kept his room immaculate, and did all his own washin'-'n'-ironin'. It must've been torture, for him, livin' with all that filth.—Roaches all over the place."

"No wonder Antley Theodd jumped off the Huey P. Long Bridge."

"That might've been part of it. Anyway, Lolotte, after havin' *two* babies out of wedlock, no money, no prospects, and the neighbors judgin' her, let herself go, as well as the house." Molly P. shuddered.

"Today, the neighbors of Starlight Street, because of the death of her brother, forgave Lolotte those two illegitimate babies she brought into the world. Ordinarily Lolotte woulda had to die herself to be forgiven. Death always brings forgiveness. After a while everybody found seats, after sweeping the litter from chairs, and settled down with coffee and pie. Everybody wanted to know why Antlee Theaud jumped. Lolotte said she wished she knew."

"Tante, how's Miss DuPuy's taking her brother's death? Crying a lot?"

"Didn't get a chance to shed a tear, because she was too busy comfortin' and consolin' her friend, Blanche DeVieux,—Blanche is bent over so far she looks like a question mark—couldn't stop asighin'-'n'-asobbin' all over her second-best black crepe dress. From all them tears we thought Antlee Theaud had been her nearest and dearest; only for her to tell us she wasn't cryin' for Antlee Theaud, she was just cryin'. She said five years ago when she was forty-two she started cryin' a lot and sweatin'. She's now forty-seven. I suppose she'll cry-'n'-sweat until she's fifty."

"Why so long?"

"Everybody cries-'n'-sweats through the *change*, though I didn't. Blanche *really* cried when Lolotte took a flashlight and showed us Motel's grave in the back yard under the fig tree. Because Eddie Frank didn't know his uncle was dead, he went, after school, to the A&P to bag groceries. So Junior Foughtenberry volunteered to bury Motel. Junior got the box, dug the hole; Lolotte put Motel in the box, gave the box to Junior and he buried Motel. That was a big job, though Junior said the diggin' was nothin', cause the ground was so wet from all that rain. Don't you think that was real nice of Junior?"

"Real nice."

"Of course, everybody wanted to know why Antlee Theaud wanted Motel to die with him. Lolotte said because her brother loved Motel, and the cat loved him. Never before, she said, had her brother known a cat intimately and, because of that, Motel was a new experience for Antlee Theaud.

"She said Motel used to follow her brother all around, making little mewin' sounds like he was talkin'. He rubbed himself against Antlee Theaud's legs when he wanted to be petted, and he liked to hop up in Antlee Theaud's's lap, knead it, and then curl himself on Antlee Theaud's knees, purrin' contentedly. Lolotte said that Motel lent mystery and excitement to her brother's dull life. If her brother had to go and kill himself, he just had to take Motel with him, she said."

"I guess when it's put that way I can understand Antley Theodd's thinking."

"Everybody else said they understood, and didn't hold no grudge against Antlee Theaud for makin' Motel die. After that explanation, cryin' Blanche wanted to know why Antlee Theaud named his cat Motel?

"Lolotte said Antlee Theaud noticed Motel when he first came into the neighborhood as a stray. He knew Motel spent nights and days at various neighbor's houses, moochin' a saucer of milk here, a can of sardines there. Finally Motel spent a night at the DuPuy double, and both Antlee Theaud and the cat decided they wanted each other. So Antlee Theaud told Lolotte there was no better fittin' name for his cat than Motel.

"Lolotte told her brother to forget about takin' no nasty Tom cat in cause all cats carried seven deadly diseases in their mouths. But that news didn't frighten or faze Antlee Theaud; so Lolotte told her brother that Motel bore an even darker stigma, he had no pedigree. 'Good,' said Antlee Theaud, 'he'll fit in fine here.'

"Because Antlee Theaud and Motel loved one another so much, Lolotte asked Undertaker Shane if she could bury Motel with her brother. He refused, saying such an idea was insane. Cryin' Blanche DeVieux said she thought the idea was the sanest and soundest Lolotte had had in years.

Because of Undertaker Shane's refusal, Motel had to be buried beneath the DuPuy fig tree.— Oh, Kendra Lou, before I forget, there's trouble next door. Those two chicken hawks have got their claws in Stella Dora."

"Then their claws need clipping." Kendra sat up in bed, propped by two pillows. "What happened?"

"I overheard them tellin' Lizzie Slapp they want Stella Dora to buy a new tomb to put Big Joe and Kenny Joe in."

"But why? The tomb they're in is just fine. That's where Stella Dora and, I guess, those two chicken hawks will wind up."

"Wait till you hear this. The tomb next to the Wheelerhand tomb holds the body of a *madam*. On the street corner there's a signal light that throws a red light on the front of the *madam's* tomb."

"You're joking."

"No, I'm not. It's true. Everybody there confirmed it."

"Well, that red light doesn't have anything to do with Kenny Joe and Mr. Big Joe."

"The two chicken hawks don't want their brother and their nephew restin' next to no *madam*."

"To buy a new tomb because of a red light signal shining on a *madam's* tomb is foolish and senseless."

"Nothing shows the kind of fool you are quicker than your tongue. I hope Stella Dora can hold out against *those two*—"

"Rats. I wish I were a cat.— "

"Watch what you wish."

"Boy, I really got a headache now."

"I might as well tell you the rest of the gossip, and then give you two aspirins and a hot cup of milk, and then let you go to sleep."

"What's the rest of the gossip?"

"Bea-actress Pujowl, that misery-maker, became violent today. Everybody thinks it was that awful lightnin'-'n'-thunderin' that brought on her savage act against her daughter-in-law—poor Ruby Faye. The attack took place right on the Pujowl's back gallery."

"Today's storm is being blamed for all sorts of things. It made me see a ghost, and it turned crazy ol' Lady Pujowl violent."

"It was the Devil who caused it all. Nell Miller once told me the Devil wasn't born in New Orleans, but he grew up here. And all his live long life he's been making misery for the folks of New Orleans.

"Anyways, Bea-actress, screamin'-'n'-cussin', threw garbage all over poor Ruby Fay, and then shoved Ruby Fay's head in the garbage can, that was full of ol' stinkin' shrimp heads. The stench almost suffocated Ruby

Faye to death. They got to do somethin' with Bea-actress.You know, aside from bein' violent, she's taken to breakin' up the house."

"Maybe they better threaten her with the attic."

"Bea-actress ain't a-scared of no attic. Crazy people ain't a-scared of nothin', nor do they have no regard for other people's feelings.— Soon after Bea-actress attacked Ruby Faye, she saw Lizzie Slapp Springmeyer and accused Lizzie Slapp of stealin' her eyes. Lizzie Slapp said if she was gunna take anythin' off Bea-actress Pujowl, it would be her ears, not her eyes. As everybody knows, Lizzie Slapp is deaf as a post. She said that Bea-Actress Pujowl can hear a pecan fall on Claiborne Avenue.

"Anyways, when Lizzie Slapp denied stealin' Bea-actress' eyes, Bea-actress tried to gouge out Lizzie Slapp's beady blue eyes. Luckily, the rain came, and Bea-actress's ran inside. That storm saved Lizzie Slapp, this very night, from being eyeless."

"I think I need those aspirins."

Chapter Ten

At breakfast the next morning, Kendra, wearing a light green linen collarless dress, gold earrings and necklace, her mop of brown-gold hair piled on top her head in a pyramid of curls, tiny tendrils framing her forehead and temples, announced: "I'm not going to Antley Theodd's wake tonight because everyone will want to talk about my taking so long to get over Kenny Joe.

"They'll tell me not to skulk and mope. They'll tell me to find somebody and make a good match; get married and be happy. They'll dig at me, and I'm not up to being dug at. Besides, I've got to work late. So just tell everybody I'm working late." All this was said in a rush, as she sat looking ruefully at her aunt.

"Tell one lie you gotta tell ten. Green is definitely your color, Kendra Lou. I must keep that in mind when I make you somethin'. new. Well, if you can't make the wake, maybe, come Friday, you can slip in at St. Matthew's for the funeral mass; and slip out before anybody sees you."

Kendra nodded and smiled. "I'll drop you to work. Let's go."

Aunt Molly Primrose deposited at Holmes' side entrance; Kendra arrived at Willowwynn right on time, and was greeted by Gussie Rae Booker: "Good mawnin', Miz Applegates. It sho looks likes we is gunna gets som' moe rain todays. De ways de suns keeps ah goin' ens-'n'-outs. Efen it dues rain, Ah hopes it don'ts lightnin'-'n'-t'under, likes yesterday's storm."

"I hope not, too. Have the electricians fixed the lights in Mrs. Rogers' rooms?"

"Nome. Dey cawled end said dey bees heah en anodder hour or sos."

Kendra nodded. "Is Mr. Rogers in his study?"

"Nome. Yo jes' miss him. But him lef' ah lis' uv wuks foah yo."

"Then I better get to it."

"En ah lit'le whiles Ah'll brings yo ah cuppa coffee."

"I could use two."

"Ah knows wat yo means," laughed Gussie Rae Booker.

Kendra headed for the library. When she reached the spiral staircase she stopped, hesitated a moment and then a compelling desire came over her to see if CR was in her room. She bolted up the stairs, two at a time.

A few seconds later she stood at the door of CR's sitting room, trembling. Goose bumps rose on her arms and on the back of her neck. Her scalp prickled. She opened the door and walked in, as the sun hid behind the clouds, casting a black shadow across the room.

Shivering with fear, Kendra, over and over, softly called CR's name. The ghost was no where in sight. "She's not here. I guess she never was. Like Tante said, I must've imagined the whole thing."

Half Kendra wanted to believe CR was just a figment of her imagination while the other half cried: *"No!—I saw her—I spoke to her in this very room—She spoke to me—"*

From the sitting room to the bedroom, she prowled, her amber eyes searching, looking, expecting some sort of a sign that CR had been there. She checked the astray: "No cigarette butts," she mumbled,"and the brandy decanter is not unstopped—it's full. Well, even if she wanted she couldn't smoke or drink without me."

One more tour of the room she made before she noticed an off-white leather briefcase standing next to CR's secretary. The briefcase bore gold initials—*CR.*"This wasn't here yesterday." She picked up the briefcase, and snapped it open. It was empty. She noted its pretty blue suede lining. She sat it down. The sun came out, and lit up the room.

Next she tried the double doors of the secretary. They opened instantly, weightlessly. The top and second shelf was full of office paraphernalia; the bottom shelf held a small Dictaphone.

Every pigeonhole she searched, finding only a neat collection of papers and letters. On she hunted, discovering a few important papers pertaining to the Rogerses, marriage license and passports.

She pyrooted through the drawer beneath the writing table, and this produced a pile of insignificant papers. As she attempted to close the drawer, she somehow or other triggered a spring that caused the drawer to pop up a fraction of an inch.

"We-ell—what do we have here?" she mumbled beneath her breath. She pulled the drawer out as far as it would go, and raised the false bottom, which revealed two manila envelopes. A large and a small one.

The big yellow envelope contained several papers clipped together. A legal looking document and two letters. These she spread on the writing table of the desk, sat in the desk chair and scanned her find.

The legal document was headed *The Last Will and Testament of*

Carol Sloan Rogers, dated *April 5, 1950,* and signed by *CR.* "Holy Moses! CR wrote her will only eight days before she died. That's calling it close. Let's see who witnessed this baby. Josie and Harry Sato, the hired help—That's interesting—

"M'm—according to this piece of paper the bulk of CR's estate goes to Kyle Osborne, her protege, and not to her husband, just like she told me. Mr. Rogers told me he got his wife's entire estate. No wonder he's in no big hurry to get in touch with Kyle Osborne, bring him back to New Orleans—"

Kendra read and reread the will word for word. "Well, as Tante would say 'it ain't full of them whereases and wherefores.' She set the will aside, picked up the carbon copy of one of the letters, and read:

New Orleans, La.
March 20, 1950

Mr. Karl Erpelding
Attorney-at-Law
Suite 100 - Cliff House
San Francisco, California

Dear Karl,

I know you are retiring shortly and not accepting clients but, since you were my mother's best friend and have always acted like a father to me, I have a big favor to ask. Please don't take down your shingle until you can render me one more service. I fired Exum, as my legal advisor, for unethical actions, and want you to take over. I want to change my will—again.

As you know, in my original will, the one you drew up when I married Clark, he was to inherit, upon my death, all my holdings — now totalling 20 million. Of course, there were some legacies and pensions for the hired help and servants.

I now want to leave Clark nothing. All my holdings—20 million—will go to Kyle Osborne, my protege, soon to be my new husband. Icelynn Farnsworth's legacy of $25,000 is cancelled; Dr. Lopez' legacy of $200,000 is cancelled; the Satoes' legacy and pension are still in effect.

I know you are wondering why I've fired Judge Edwards and cut Icelynn out of my will. The reasons are I've lost all respect for Exum Edwards; I've come to hate Icelynn with a white hate; and I suspect Emile Lopez is in the Judge's back pocket. His private executioner. In these circumstances, as you can understand, I can't ask Exum Edwards to handle any legal matter for me, and especially this one.

I know you are wondering about Kyle Osborne and my wanting to marry him. Well, it's simple. I've fallen madly and hopelessly in love with Kyle, and we plan to marry on June 6th, in Mexico City, after I obtain a Reno divorce from Clark.

By the way, Clark and I are on the best of terms; however, he knows nothing of my plans to marry Kyle. I will tell him everything around the middle of April. That's when Kyle leaves to attend a special seminar in literature, at Berkeley. He'll be gone six weeks.

I know what you're thinking. 'Tell Clark now.' Don't waste your breath. I'm not going to tell him until Kyle goes to Berkeley, just in case Clark should act like a jealous husband. I don't think it'll happen, but I don't want to take a chance on any unpleasantness. You know how I hate scenes.

Besides, Clark is a very understanding man. After all he's lived with me for ten years, and has put up with all my extremes. Clark loves me and I love him, but we're not *in love* any more. Our husband and wife relationship has turned into a loving brother and sister kinship.

Another thing, don't feel sorry for Clark because I'm cutting him out of my will. His business ventures have been extremely profitable, and he has been very successful. Contrary to what most people think, including yourself, Clark does not live off my money. He's rich.

Of course, when Clark and I were first married I had to support him, as I'll have to do for Kyle, who is only twenty-seven and not established. So stop frowning, you old dear. I'm in love again, and I want *YOU*, of all people, to be happy and excited for me.

Oh, before I forget, I want my new will to be effective April 5, and in my possession no later than April 11. I want to show it to Kyle before he leaves for Berkeley on the 13th.

If you have any questions, call me. I always love hearing your voice.

All my Love
Carol

Kendra gave a low whistle, her hands trembling as she held this long epistle. "CR's will not only completely cuts Clark Rogers out the picture, but Icelynn Farnsworth and Dr. Lopez as well. M'm.—And she's fired Judge Exum Edwards for unethical actions. Wow! I wonder what unethical actions?

"Another thing, Kyle Osborne was suppose to leave for Berkeley on

April 13th. Gussie Rae Booker said he left on April 12th, the same day Icelynn Farnsworth left. Why can't Icelynn and Kyle be reached? Icelynn in the old will stood to inherit a pretty penny; Kyle in the new stands to inherit *all*.

"It sounds like Judge Edwards purposely read the old will, or didn't know a new existed. Is Judge Edwards in cahoots with Clark Rogers? All this is strange."

Kendra put this letter aside; picked up the other—Karl Erpelding's reply—and read.

Cliff House
March 24, 1950

My dearest Carol,

You sounded perfectly wonderful over the phone last night. You know my shingle is always out for you. I've changed your will. Your new will becomes effective April 5, 1950. I'll post same, via airmail special delivery, this afternoon.

When you receive your new will sign where I've put the pencilled Xs. Also, it is legal to have Josie and Harry Sato sign as witnesses.

As soon as possible, return to me the signed and witnessed will, so I can affix the official seal to the document.

Now that the legal ramifications of your new will are in the legal process of being taken care of, I want to get back to our telephone conversation.

Who exactly is Kyle Osborne? I know you told me he's a student, has no family, and that he's your protege—has been for the past two years —and that Icelynn brought his plight to your attention.

You also told me he will soon have his doctorate in English literature. Thanks to your generosity. But other than that I know nothing of him, except he's twenty years your junior, and that he, like yourself, also hates Icelynn Farnsworth. Why?

Forgive me, dear, for frowning, but I can't help but frown, because I care about you. Yes, I was very upset when you replaced me with Exum Edwards, giving distance as the flimsy excuse for my dismissal.

As you know, I have clients all over the world. But that's water over the bridge. My only care and concern now is for your happiness; however, I'm not at all sure you're going to find happiness with Kyle.

When you married Clark, who was ten years your junior, I was opposed. So was your dear mother. Of course, your marriage to Clark turned out very well—until now. Speaking of Clark, I think you do him a disservice not being open with him. He should know you've cut him out of your will, and are planning to divorce him. He should know you're planning to marry Kyle Osborne, and he should know all that *NOW!*

And while I'm on the subject of telling you to be open with Clark, you should be wary of Exum Edwards. Keep in mind Edwards is a liar and a thief. He abused a trust, and thinks himself above the law. A man like that is not to be taken lightly. I met him last summer, when he attended a legal seminar in San Francisco, and decided then and there I wouldn't want him for an enemy. At the time, I had no idea you were having an affair with him, though you say it was a brief fling.

I know you are forty-seven, and I'm chastising you as if you were a teenager— My only excuse is I love you, and your mother would want me to.

I have one more thing to mention about your new will, and then the subject, for the time being, is closed. I know Kyle Osborne is only twenty-seven, and I hope he will live to be ninety-seven; however, accidents do happen.

You've made no provisions if, God forbid, Kyle Osborne should die before you. He has no family, so, if anything should happen to him, then I think you should leave everything to Clark. Think it over. Call me, and I'll insert the clause.

Now, my dear, I can't begin to tell you how happy your invitation, to spend a few days with you, has made me. I wish I could come now, but that's not possible.

As I told you on the phone, I retire on March 29th, and on the 30th, close my office suite at Cliff House. On April 1st, I fly to Paris to conclude business for a client. I'll be there a week, and afterwards I'll travel about Europe for another two weeks. I should see you anywhere from April 25th—30th. I'll fly directly from London, to New Orleans.

Take care of yourself, my dear, and remember I love you.

Karl

"Holy Moses! Today's the 25th," exclaimed Kendra, "and Karl Erpelding could show up at the front door. And the poor man doesn't know CR's dead." She put the will and two letters back in the big yellow envelope, and then opened the small yellow envelope. The first item she fished out was a snapshot of a very dark and handsome man. A Mexican. He was in bathing trunks, stretched on the sand, at Pontchartrain Beach, showing off a brown hard body. The man looked about thirty-five to forty, had jet curly hair, black eyes and a bandit's mustache.

On back of the of the snapshot, in a scratch scrawl, was written, *To:*

Carol, followed by a couple lines in Spanish, which Kendra didn't understand, and ended with *Love, Emile.* She tossed the snapshot aside, and fished some more in the envelope. Out came a pack of love poems, tied with a blue silk ribbon, and no doubt left to fade. These were written in English, and in the most beautiful penmanship she had ever seen. Each poem was simply signed, *E.* Kendra read all of them. They were beautiful.

"Emile with his chicken scratch hand couldn't have written these poems. I wonder if Exum Edwards did? Whoever wrote them really had a bad case for CR."

Kendra put the poems and the snapshot of Emile back into the envelope, and returned all to the desk. She sat there, trying to piece the puzzle together. From reading so many mysteries, she knew the basic motives for murder were: love, jealousy, greed, hate, revenge, fear and convenience.

"Reciting motives for murder isn't going to help solve this case, especially when there's no body. If only a witness would come forward, and say 'I saw either Clark Rogers, Judge Edwards, Emile, Kyle Osborne, Icelynn Farnsworth, or whoever, give CR a shot, a pill, or a dose of poison, which caused her to have a heart attack.'

"Then the question would be asked: 'Why would Clark Rogers want his wife dead?' The answer: Because he found out his wife was going to divorce him, marry her protege and leave her millions to her new husband. The motives would then be jealousy and greed. Simple.— Too simple."

At that moment, Gussie Rae Booker, carrying a small tray, came into the room, startling Kendra. She tried to snap on the overhead chandelier. "Ah fogots. No lights. Dat dare 'lectrician cawled ah li'le whiles ago end sez him won't be heah today. Him'll come furst t'ing en de mawnin'. We gots lights all ovah de house, but not en dis heah room."

"I don't need the overhead light, with all this sunshine pouring in. I think the rain clouds have passed over us.—What you got on that tray?"

"Ah brung yo coffee end ah nice hot piece of brioche." She plopped the tray on the secretary. "Ah figgers, since yo wuzn't en de liberry, yo wuz ups heah doin' som' serious snoopin'. Efen yo is gunna snoops, yo needs to keeps up yo stren't."

Kendra laughed. "M'm—the coffee smells delicious"—She took a sip of coffee and a bite of brioche.—"That taste yummy. Thanks."

"Yo could also use ah li'le breeze blowin' tru. Ah better op'n som' uv dese winders end de doahs to de balk-knee. Yo needs to bees com'tibble whiles yo dues yo pryin'.—Ah shoulda op'ne dese winders early dis mawnin' when Ah came ups to do ma dustin'; but findin' de room all topsy turvy, likes de debble had ah nightmare en heah, Ah couldn't make it straights fas' enough to gits out. Even de cushions fum de balk-nee funiture was tossed all arounds. I don't knows how dem cushions gots en heah, but Ah's glad, cause dey woulda gots ruint en yesterday's storm."

"I put them in here, and forgot about them.You say you found *this* room upset?"

"Yaas, Ah sho did. Las' night Mr. Rogers has me comes ups heah to wash dem black smudges aways fum de outlets whar de lightnin' hits end burns, end to puts t'ings en order. Ah dids; end dis mawnin' dare wuz new disorder, likes Ah ain't dun nuffin. Ah tol' him jes' dat."

"What did he say?"

"Nuffin. Him jes' went offs to him's office. Efen yo ax me, Miz Applegates, dis heah room is haunted wit spooks."

"Maybe so. Er, don't bother to open the windows or the doors to the balcony. I'm fixing to leave, after I drink my last swallow of coffee and eat my last crumb of brioche. I want to look at Mr. Osborne's room, and at Miss Farnsworth's. Will you show them to me?"

"Sho. De quicker Ah gits out uv dis heah room de better Ah likes it. C'mon. Follows me. Ah'll shows yo."

Gussie Rae Booker, the coffee tray in her hands and her stout legs stumping toward Kyle Osborne's room, said: "Dis is de protege's room, end de nex' room is Miz Farnsworth's."

"Did Mr. Rogers say what time he'd be back?"

"Nome. Ah 'spect him'll bees backs foah supper. No earlier. So yo might as wells spen' de res' uv de mawnin' diggin'-'n'-delvin', pokin'-'n'-pryin', end den dues yo typin' wuk dis afternoon."

A smile played hide-and-seek around the corners of Kendra's mouth.

"Efen yo needs me, Ah'll bees rites downstairs." She left.

Kyle Osborne's room, spacious and handsomely decorated— armoire and bureau full of clothes—provided next to nothing until Kendra's keen eyes caught sight of a writing pad on top of a kneehole desk. The pad was pushed toward the back of the desk, half hidden. A note had been written, torn off and a very good impression left.

"M'm—what does this say: *DuPlessix Shipping Lines, S.S. Catherine Celene, departing New Orleans, April 13th, 6:30 a.m.; docking, London, April 20th, 7 p.m.* Below there was more: *Cambridge-poetry and literature experience. Six weeks.*

Kendra tore the slip of paper from the pad and put it in her pocketbook. "I guess the reason Berkeley has no record of Kyle Osborne is because he's not there. He's in England. Why would he lie to everybody, say he was going to California when he was going to England? Why would he lie to the woman he loved, the woman he was planning to marry? Why? Perhaps to throw her and everybody else off his track. Kill her—disappear, and later come back to claim his inheritance—No, no, no, that won't cut it—"

For a good five minutes, Kendra contemplated this new development, and then went to search Icelynn Farnsworth's room.

Another spacious, beautifully decorated room, but completely devoid of any slip of paper or scrap of evidence that Icelynn had been in possession of this room. Her armoire was empty, her bureau and dresser empty. Not an article belonging to her had been left behind. Icelynn Farnsworth was not coming back to Willowwynn.

At this point, Kendra made a decision. She left Icelynn Farnsworth's room and went back to CR's sitting room, hesitating a moment at the big door before opening it and going in.

Kendra, first looking around to see if CR were there and, finding she wasn't, then went directly to the secretary, found the spring in the center drawer, raised the false bottom, grabbed the two manilla envelopes and put them in CR's monogrammed white briefcase.

A couple minutes later she was in her Dodge, heading for a photostatic copying shop on Magazine Street. She only had enough money to make one copy each of the will, letters and the love poems.

Thirty minutes later she was back in the library, at Willowwynn, the two manilla envelopes returned to CR's desk; the photostatic copies in CR's briefcase, locked in the trunk of her Dodge. It was lunch time.

"Miz Applegates, Xariffa dun went end fixed yo ah bowl uv vegetibble soup end ah sof'-shell-crab sandwitch. Ah'll brings it to yo, end den Ah'll bees en de garage, wrenchin' out ah few t'ings."

"So that's where the wash tubs are."

"End de cloeslines is behin' de garage. Outs of sights. Miz Rogers said she didn't likes foah nobodys to sees her wash.— Enjoy yo lunch, Miz Applegates," she added, stumping off.

Kendra had just finished eating her soup and most of her sandwich when she heard the front door knocker. Knowing Gussie Rae Booker was working in the garage, out of earshot, she stuffed the rest of her sandwich in her mouth and gulped it down as she answered the door.

"Good afternoon," said a gentleman in an expensive blue silk suit and red silk tie, with diagonal navy stripes, "I'm Karl Erpelding. Mrs. Rogers is expecting me."

Kendra froze, as she listened attentively and wide-eyed to the man on the other side of the threshold. His voice was firm, authoritative and no doubt used to command.

Karl Erpelding looked just like he stepped out the silver-framed photograph in the powder-blue sitting room. He was tall and slender with great gray eyes that were circled from fatigue or lack of sleep. He had a wealth of white hair and a buttermilk complexion, with a touch of apple in his cheeks. He looked about seventy-five. In his left hand he held a black leather briefcase; a suitcase rested at his right side.

"Er—good afternoon, Mr. Erpelding—Er—come in, please. I'm Miss Kendra Louise Applegate, Mr. Rogers' secretary."

"How do you do, Miss Applegate. I had no idea Mr. Rogers had a secretary here at Willowwynn."

"I just started working for him yesterday. You may leave your briefcase and suitcase here in the foyer—"

"I'll leave my *grip* but not my briefcase. Where's Miss Farnsworth?"

"She's on vacation, and won't be back until sometime in May or later. Right this way to the library, sir."

"I'll wait here while you inform Mrs. Rogers that I'm here. Also have Harry Sato carry up my grip to my room."

"Sir, the Sato family no longer work here—"

"*What?* When did that happen? Never mind, Miss Applegate, just tell Mrs. Rogers I'm here."

"Mr. Erpelding, please come into the library and have a seat while I call Mr. Rogers. He's at his office."

"No, I do not, at the moment, wish to speak to Mr. Rogers. If Mrs. Rogers is not at home, I'll wait for her in my room."

Kendra took a deep breath and let it out slowly. "I have some bad news for you. Won't you come to the library and have a seat—"

"Bad news! Humph—I can take the bad news right here in the foyer as well as in the library. Out with it, young woman."

"I'm very sorry, Sir, to be the one"—Kendra faltered.

"Out with it—*now!*" demanded Karl Erpelding, losing patience.

"Mrs. Rogers is dead. She died on April 13th," blurted out Kendra.

Apparently this was not the sort of bad news Mr. Erpelding could take in the foyer. He fell at Kendra's feet, and banged his head hard on the marble floor. This was the first time anyone had ever fainted in front of Kendra and, for a few seconds, she stood paralyzed with fear. Mr. Erpelding's groaning brought her to her senses. Bending over him she asked: "A-a-are you all right? Can you sit up?"

He rubbed his sore head. "I think so. "I've got a bump on my head."

"I bet you do. Here, take my hand. I'll help you."

Now in a sitting position, his back propped against the wall, he looked ashen, like he might fall out again.

"You need some brandy. I'll be back in a minute."

Two minutes later Kendra, on her knees, held a double shot glass to Mr. Erpelding's slightly blue lips, while he sipped the amber liquid. A little color slowly creeping into his face.

"Sir, I think you'd be more comfortable sitting in a chair," suggested Kendra.

"So do I," replied a very familiar voice.

Kendra jerked her head around and looked into the handsome face of Clark Rogers. He was dressed in a made-to-order gray silk suit, his loose brown-gold hair, as usual, tumbled on his forehand and his navy eyes were filled with concern for the visitor.

"Oh, Mr. Rogers, I'm so glad to see you," cried Kendra, sounding relieved.

"I'm sure you are," he replied, his navy eyes never leaving Karl Erpelding's face. "I think you'd be more comfortable sitting in a chair, Karl, as Miss Applegate suggested."

"Help me up, Clark."

Assisted by Clark and Kendra, Mr. Erpelding stood up, stumbled the few steps to the hallway and then collapsed into the cane-bottomed, claret-cushioned settee, the one Kendra thought begged to be sat upon. "I'm all right. I just suffered a terrible shock. Miss Applegate told me—Carol's dead."

"I'm sorry you had to learn of it this way. I tried to get in touch with you, but couldn't. I even ran Carol's obituary notice in *The San Francisco Chronicle* and *The LA TIMES,* hoping you'd see it. When you didn't respond I figured you were still mad at Carol."

"I could never be *that* mad. I was very upset when Carol replaced me with Exum Edwards; however, this past March we patched up our differences. You couldn't get in touch with me because I've been in Europe. I've just arrived from London."

"I called your office only to learn you no longer have an office."

"I retired the end of March. I told all that to Carol."

"She didn't tell me."

"It must've slipped her mind; however, it's all in a letter I wrote her. Have you been through her things? Her desk?"

"I've been through her desk, but didn't find any letter. To be perfectly candid, I didn't find anything in her desk."

Kendra's presence, obviously forgotten, was thinking: "So, Clark Rogers doesn't know about the false bottom in his wife's desk."

"Well, I must say it's very odd that my Carol has been dead since the 13th of this month, and I haven't been informed of it. How did she die? An accident?"

"No. She died in her sleep of an apparent heart attack. Dr. Lopez, our family doctor, as you know, wrote the death certificate."

"When we spoke over the phone Carol sounded wonderful; said she felt fine. She made no mention of any health problems, especially a heart condition.— So did the autopsy confirm heart trouble?"

"There was no autopsy." Here Clark briefly told the whole tragic tale, and when he got to the part where Carol had been accidentally cremated, Karl Erpelding stared at him in horror.

"Who is your medical examiner?"

"Dr. Vincent Prestijockeymoe."

"A *Dago?* I hold him responsible."

"No, it wasn't Vince's fault. They laid the mix up of bodies on the poor assistant, Albert Lepardieux. Dr. Lopez had sent Carol's body to the morgue for an autopsy; there was a Karen Rogers, who had already had an autopsy and who was ready to be cremated. Somehow"—he shrugged— "Lepardieux got the bodies mixed up."

"That's what the investigation said?"

"Judge Edwards advised against a formal investigation."

"Who the hell is Judge Edwards to advise against a normal procedure? I hope you're not going to tell me Prestijockeymoe and Lepardieux have not been fired."

"They haven't."

Karl Erpelding looked at Clark with great disgust, which soon turned to fury. He fainted again.

In a few seconds he revived, and Kendra, in an aside, said: "Mr. Rogers, I think you need to call a doctor for Mr. Erpelding."

Clark nodded. He turned to Karl. "I'm calling Dr. Lopez."

"No. That won't be necessary. It's all these horrible shocks I'm getting, one after another, that's causing me to faint. What else do you have to tell me that will make me pass out?"

"Nothing."

"Good. Am I to assume I'm the only one who knows nothing of my Carol's death?"

"Icelynn Farnsworth and Kyle Osborne don't know. I can't locate them. Er—Karl, seeing you today is quite a surprise."

"Carol invited me here. She wanted to see me a lot sooner, but I had commitments I couldn't break. I called and told her I would be in New Orleans between the 25th and the 30th of April. She asked me here to discuss her new will."

Clark showed complete surprise. "She didn't have a new will. Judge Edwards, as her attorney and executor, has already read Carol's will, and taken care of all the legal matters pertaining to her affairs."

"Then I guess he'll have to untake care of them. Carol fired Edwards—"

"And no doubt rehired him five minutes later. That was her way. You know that, Karl."

"Not this time. She fired him, and rewrote her will. I have the will in my briefcase, and it's dated April 5, 1950. There should be a copy of that new will in Carol's desk."

For a second or so, Clark Rogers showed surprise. "Why did she fire Exum?— Does the new will contain major or minor changes?"

"She fired him for stealing. I'll tell you about that later. And she made major changes. She left the bulk of her estate to Kyle Osborne. Nothing to you. Nothing to Icelynn Farnsworth. Nothing to Dr. Lopez. The legacies and pensions to Harry and Josie Sato remain valid."

"That's crazy. Let me see that will."

"Certainly." Erpelding withdrew a key ring from his pocket and, when Clark handed him his briefcase, he unlocked it. "Here it is. I only have one copy. Carol has a copy."

"If she does, I don't know where it is. I went through her desk, and there was no will. The will that Judge Edwards read he got from Carol's· safety deposit box, and it was dated 1940."

"Haste makes waste. Edwards read the wrong will."

"Being a Judge he was able to push things through. Almost immediately. I already have Carol's 20 million bucks; Icelynn Farnsworth, when she returns from her vacation, a check awaits her for $25,000; and Dr. Lopez already has his $200,000; and Josie and Harry Sato have their pensions."

"I'm glad Icelynn Farnsworth hasn't received her money, because she, like Dr. Lopez, would just have to give it back."

"I can understand Carol casting Icelynn out of her will; but why Emile? He was her trusted physician."

"She claims Dr. Lopez is Exum Edwards' hatchet man."

"That's absurd."

Clark, *read* the will in your hand, *and* note the date."

Clark read the will, stared at it, and then read it again. "This will is preposterous. Mad!"

"Of course it is. I tried to talk Carol out of such a rash action. I tried to talk some sense into her stubborn head, but couldn't. I figured when I saw her, face to face, during this visit, I could convince her to tear up this new will. But I'm too late. She's dead," choked Karl.

"Then you intend to see that Kyle Osborne gets his inheritance?"

Karl looked at Clark with a critical eye. "Of course. You wouldn't want it any other way. Would you?"

"Kyle Osborne's a bastard."

"Bastard or not, the money's his." Karl Erpelding closed his eyes, as if he were going to faint again.

"Sir, wouldn't you be more comfortable resting on one of those big sofas in the library?" asked Kendra, bringing attention to herself.

"Perhaps so."

"That's a good idea," said Clark.

"Sir, do you think you could walk to the library?"

"*Certainly* I can walk to the library, *young lady.*"

"Then let's go.—"

Chapter Eleven

In the library, Karl Erpelding chose not to recline on the sofa, but sank into a deep leather wing chair close to the sliding doors that separated Clark's study from the library. He propped up his feet on the chair's puffy ottoman.

Clark sat in an identical chair, facing Karl; Kendra sat at the rent table, waiting to take in more of both men's conversation, who still seemed oblivious to her presence. Noiselessly, she shifted her lunch tray to the side; then shuffled papers, pretending to be busy and absorbed in her work, hoping to remain where she was, unobserved.

"I guess I better call Judge Edwards and have him come over to see this will," began Clark.

"Don't call him yet. I only have *one* copy of the will"—he nodded his head at Clark's hands—"and I'm sure Edwards will want a copy."

"That's no problem, I can send Miss Applegate to have some copies made. It won't take more than twenty minutes."

That remark brought Kendra's presence slap-dab center. Both men looked at her, and studied her for a few seconds. "Er—Clark," Erpelding nodded toward her—"I'll make copies of it, myself."— Erpelding reached out his hand for the will; and Clark gave it to him. He placed it in the briefcase. "Er—Clark, I have a few *personal* questions I'd like to ask you, *privately,"* he added, giving Kendra a hard look.

Instantly, she stood up before Mr. Rogers could ask her to leave the room. "These letters need your signature, Sir. I'll put them on your desk, and remain in your study until you need me."

Clark nodded.

Kendra opened the sliding doors just wide enough to slip through. She passed into the study and stood to the side of the open doors, eavesdropping. She could see and hear the men; they couldn't see her.

"I think we said too much in front of *her*," commenced Erpelding.

Clark shrugged."She's trustworthy. Loyal." He shrugged again.

"Let's hope so. Anyway, I want to know what happened between you and Carol? When did your problems start?"

"Right after her mother died our troubles began. Carol went crazy from guilt. You know, she told everybody her mother was in perfect health. Had all her faculties, when the poor old lady didn't know her ear from her elbow. She was senile, and everybody knew it. Poor Marian Sloan was putty in Carol's crafty hands.

"As soon as Carol got her mother to change her will—actually, my wife rewrote her mother's will—put the pen in her trembling hand and helped her sign the paper. Of course, the new will left everything to Carol and nothing to Jean and Gen, her sisters, though Carol didn't consider them sisters because they were adopted.

"As soon as Carol had what she wanted, she turned on her mother. Became mean and hateful. Bossed her mother something terrible. Wouldn't let the old lady spend a penny. Marian Sloan wanted a $2 pair of garden gloves—she loved pottering around the garden with old Blevins—and Carol wouldn't let her buy the cheap gloves. Blevins bought them. Carol wouldn't buy her mother anything, or take her any where. It was only a couple months after Marian signed over everything to Carol, that she took the big black Caddie—"

"That was a pity!" said Karl, shaking his head sadly. "Marian hadn't driven in over a year; and didn't need to drive. She had a driver. Sam chauffeured her where ever she needed to go."

"But Sam was off that day, and Carol claimed she had accidentally left the car keys on the coffee table." Clark shrugged. "I think Carol was ready for her mother to cash in, and I think Marian, when she snatched those conveniently placed car keys, was trying to run away from her daughter. Trying to die. She crashed. Killed only herself. Thank God."

Karl Erpelding shuddered.

"When the accident happened, both Jean and Gen were in Europe, with their daughters. Carol was going to bury her mother without letting her sisters know their mother was dead. I cabled them.

"Jean and Gen were shocked over their mother's tragic death. They were even more shocked to hear they weren't in the will. When they had left for Europe, the will had stated the fortune and the diamonds—Marian had many diamonds—would be equally divided three ways."

"Carol told me she had bought most of those diamonds."

"Carol hadn't bought *one* of those diamonds. Old man Sloan bought *all* those diamonds. Carol never considered either Jean or Gen her sisters because they didn't come out her mother's body, as she had. Therefore neither was entitled to any of the money. Any of the diamonds. Not even the granddaughters. Marian had promised each granddaughter, and it was in the original will, a diamond ring and a diamond bracelet."

"Too bad Marian, long before she died, didn't give the girls their rings and bracelets."

"The girls were content to wait until their grandmother died. They wanted their grandmother to enjoy her diamonds while she lived. Of course, Carol had *you* to make her thievery legal."

Karl winced."That still haunts me. Too late, I learned of what Carol had done. I'd give anything to right that wrong. When Carol replaced me with Edwards the thought had crossed my mind to tell the world how she had cheated her sisters; and how I, unknowingly, had aided and abetted her in her great swindle. Her thievery, as you put it."

"If you want to make things right, tear up the new will. I'll gladly share the twenty million with Jean and Gen."

"And what about Kyle Osborne?"

"For the past two years Carol's given him a home, paid his tuition, bought his books, supplied him with a Ford convertible and given him an allowance. *That should be enough.*"

"It's not; considering he should be getting twenty million dollars. I'm sure Carol told him."

"I'll set him up in style: a new Caddie, $10,000 cash, get him appointed to the staff at Berkeley and buy him a house. That should do."

Karl smiled a thin smile. "That won't do. Is Osborne here? I'd like to talk to him. Feel him out."

"He's not here. I don't know where he is. He was suppose to be attending a literature seminar, at Berkeley. He's not there."

"That's odd. Find him. After I speak with him I'll think about your proposal—"

"Keep this in mind while you're thinking. Now is not the time to cleanse your conscious by giving twenty million bucks to Osborne, because you helped Carol to do Jean and Gen Sloan dirt. And another thing, why should I be left nothing?"

"Carol wrote that you were quite successful with your brokerage firm."

"That has nothing to do with it. I was married to Carol for *ten* years. I loved her and tried to help her straighten out her life.— And now, after a two-year absence, you show up with a new will signed by my wife, saying all her money and property goes to her protege.

"This may come as a surprise to you, Karl, I wanted a divorce, but Carol wouldn't give me one. Louisiana, as California, has a community property law. If I could've gotten her to agree to a divorce, I'd have gotten half of everything. Oh, she wanted her freedom, all right, but she didn't want to share her money. Her property. I realize now she wanted somehow to finagle a way to keep it, so she could give it *all* to Osborne. A lazy good-for-nothing. *A bum. Don't* worry about Osborne. *Worry* about Jean and Gen Sloan. Clear up that piece of dirt. *Right that wrong!"*

"If I had cleaned up that piece of dirt when Carol fired me, I would've done it out of vindictiveness. I couldn't do it."

"And now?"

Erpelding took a deep breath. "I helped Carol steal her mother's estate and her aunt's, because she's my daughter. She never knew. She never suspected."

"This *is* a surprise. Many things crossed my mind, but never *that* one."

"Marian had just married sixty-year-old Sidney Sloan, one of the wealthiest bankers in San Francisco, when we met. Marian wanted children but, after a year of marriage, never conceived. So she and Sloan adopted two baby girls: Jean and Gen—"

"And a year after Marian and Sloan had adopted Jean and Gen—"

"Marian miraculously conceived— my child."

"As your daughter, Carol didn't have any legal claim to Sidney Sloan's fortune. Jean and Gen, the adopted daughters, had more claim than Carol, who was nothing to Sloan. She was just—"

"A bastard. My bastard."

"And didn't deserve a penny of old man Sloan's money, and got it all through legal tricks."

Erpelding slowly nodded. "All these years I loved Marian. I never married because I wanted to be available for Marian and for Carol."

"A bad mistake."

"I didn't think so then, nor now. Anyway, I got to watch my beautiful daughter grow up."

"And did you enjoy how she turned out?"

"A nymphomaniac, a liar, a cheat and a jealous woman who craved men, money and power so she could control people? A woman who made money her God?— N-no."

Both men were silent and thoughtful, and then Karl spoke: "Why did Carol chase off for New Orleans, after her mother died?"

"Guilt drove her, along with booze and the other two women in her body. Carol was a trinity. Three women in one. Carol No. 1, which seldom surfaced, was kind and loving; Carol No. 2 and No. 3 displayed an outward show of good will and an inward intention to back stab everybody opposed to her. In short, Carol No. 2 was a witch and a bitch;

Carol No. 3 was downright wicked and evil. Number 2 and No. 3 always surfaced simultaneously, and after they had done their dirt, No. 1 might peep up. If No. 1 did, then kind and loving Carol would send, whoever she had stomped, a single red rose. That red rose, in Carol's twisted mind, would wipe out any stain, any vileness.

"Because of this madness, Carol had no friends. And after what she did to Jean and Gen, she had no family. After she robbed her sisters of their fortunes, she sent them each a red rose. They told her where to stick that thorny red rose.

"Carol No. 2 and No. 3 were never accountable for anything. These two individuals, personalities, if you please, lied, cheated, denied all wrong-doing. I really and truly believe Carol No. 2 and No. 3, even in death, could return to earth, to perform wicked deeds."

"You frighten me, Clark, when you say such things. You sound as if someone would have to stick a stake in the hearts of No. 2 and No. 3 to kill Carol. Kill the trinity."

"I do."

"Do you have an example of how these two personalities did dirty deeds, and then denied wrong-doings?"

"A perfect one. Four years ago, when Jean's daughter, Carrie, married millionaire, Allen Rosenberg, you and I were out of town. Carol was invited to the formal rehearsal dinner, given at the St. Francis. An eight-course, sit-down meal was served. A lavish and very expensive affair.

"Carol sent her regrets. Then on the night of the rehearsal dinner showed up, got falling down drunk, put her feet up on the table, exposed herself and made a scene. Jean and Gen, who were seated at the head table with Carrie and the Rosenbergs, asked Gen to go take care of Carol.

"Gen went over to Carol and whispered 'Let's you and me go for a walk.' On the spot there was a big fight. Gen had to get the doorman, who had to drag Carol, from the banquette room, kicking, screaming and cursing. Gen, with the help of the doorman, managed to get Carol to the ladies room. In the ladies room, Carol bit Gen's thumb—"

"Did you say bit?"

"*BIT!* Blood went every where, but mainly all over Gen's beautiful white gown. Gen had to be taken to the hospital emergency room, where she got five stitches and a tetanus shot. Not knowing Gen was on her way to the hospital, Jean left the banquette room to see how things were going. She found Carol in the ladies room, crawling in and out of the stalls, snarling and snapping like a mad dog. She said she was looking for Gen, so she could kill her. Carol ruined Carrie's beautiful rehearsal dinner.

"The next day, Carol was confronted for what she had done; but denied she had put her feet on the table, exposed herself and bit Gen. Jean barred Carol from attending Carrie's wedding.

"Because you were in Europe, for six months, Carol got another lawyer and tried to sue Gen for defamation of character. The two lawyers got Carol and Gen together, and Carol dropped the suit; however, for two years she hassled and harassed Gen. When I called to tell Jean and Gen Carol was dead, both said 'Good.'"

"I can't believe such a disgrace took place at the St. Francis. Marian never said a word to me. Who told you?"

"Jean and Gen—later Marian. Marian wanted to spare you. The Rosenbergs kept the disgraceful scene out the paper; and the guests probably talked only among themselves. So the story didn't spread from one end of San Francisco to the other."

"How terrible."

Clark sighed. "That's just one example. I could go on and on. Anyway, after Carol got the Sloan estate, she started drinking heavily. Every day I came home and found her falling down drunk. One day I came home and she said new scenery, a new home, without memories, would help her; so I agreed to go wherever she wanted to go. She chose New Orleans.

"Then when we bought this house, she insisted on calling it Willowwynn, and turned it into a carbon copy of the mansion in San Francisco. She recreated the atmosphere and memories she was supposed to be escaping from.

"Living so far from San Francisco, enabled her to lie a great deal. She told everyone she was an only child; her mother adored her; her mother died in an automobile accident—the truth—and, after her mother's death, she was so grief ridden she couldn't stand to live in San Francisco, where she had lived so lovingly and happily with her dear mother. *All lies—"*

"She needed medical help."

"When we first arrived, I tried to get her to see a psychiatrist. She refused. She tried to talk Dr. Manning into giving up his fabulous practice in San Francisco, but he wouldn't. So she bribed Dr. Lopez, her medical doctor, into moving to New Orleans. She promised to build him a clinic. Doc is here, and the clinic's not built yet.

"She gave Doc only half the money she had promised. It's rumored Judge Edwards is financially backing the clinic. I think Carol figured sleeping with Doc would be the other half of the promised money. One thing about Carol, if she gave you money or loaned you money, she automatically figured she owned you. Told everybody who'd listen to her how she owned so-'n'-so. How she had so-'n'-so in her pocket. As soon as I could I got out of her pocket, I didn't take a penny from her."

Karl just shook his head. "I don't know how you stood it."

"Our marriage ended because Carol refused to be helped. She said she didn't want help. All she wanted was men and booze. She got lots of both. She said the only way to ease her grief was through sex; and, since she claimed to be all the time in a state of grief, she couldn't get enough sex."

"Too bad she didn't convince her psychiatrist to move to New Orleans, as she convinced her personal physician."

"Dr. Manning didn't have to move here. There are any number of good psychiatrists in New Orleans, and I begged her to see one. She refused. She went from man to man, bed to bed. The list of men in her life is too long: Judge Edwards, though she thought I didn't know about that one; Hippolyte Delacroix, the state attorney; Dr. Lopez; and I think she made a play for Judge Edwards' son-in-law. He turned her down, and she hated him. Those few names come quickly to mind. There're others."

"You forgot the main one. Kyle Osborne. She planned on marrying him."

"I didn't forget Osborne. I just can't believe it yet. For a long time he kept his distance. It's only been within the past six months that Osborne has fallen under Carol's spell. When Osborne dined with us, he chatted more with Icelynn than with Carol. I suppose that's why Carol cut her out the will. Jealousy. Osborne didn't even flirt with her. I guess Osborne had to sooner or later succumb to Carol's charm. Her allure. Her witchery."

"According to Carol, Osborne hated Icelynn."

"I don't believe that. Carol was a jealous liar, who of late, because of her excessive drinking, developed a bad memory."

"A great drawback to a liar."

"Exactly. Anyway, if men paid any attention to Icelynn, Carol was jealous. If there was any hate, I think it was on Carol's side.—Silence; then: "Carol flaunted her affairs in my face. She always invited her lovers and their wives to dinner. I couldn't stand sitting down to dine with my wife and a couple of her lovers and their wives. One big happy family.

"I finally asked for a divorce. She refused. She suggested a separation. So we lived these past two years as brother and sister. Nothing was ever said about her wanting a divorce so she could marry Osborne."

"She wrote me she was planning to marry Osborne this coming June, in Mexico City, after she got a Reno divorce from you. In that same letter she told me Judge Edwards, unbeknownst to her, had speculated with over half a million dollars of her money. She said she caught him red-handed. She said he promised to put the money back by April 15th."

"And did he?"

"I don't think so."

The two men exchanged thoughtful, knowing looks.

"If the Judge hasn't put the money back, then you're here to get it from him?"

"Yes."

"May I see Carol's letter."

"I didn't bring it with me."

"Because she bad-mouthed me?"

"On the contrary, she praised you. She just simply said she was madly in love with Osborne."

"Osborne is only twenty-seven, and a handsome devil. I was twenty-seven when I married Carol."

"At thirty-seven, you're not exactly Methuselah."

Clark grinned.

"Now if you don't mind, Clark, I'd like to go to my room. I feel tired."

Karl tried to stand, but fell back in his chair.

"I'm calling Dr. Lopez."

"Clark, that's not necessary—"

"Sorry, Karl, but you can't keep falling out every five minutes."

Clark walked over to the rent table, picked up the phone and gave the operator Dr. Lopez's number. He talked briefly, and then hung up. "Doc'll be here shortly," he said; then, using the intercom, buzzed his study: "Miss Applegate, I'll need you and Gussie Rae Booker to help me get Mr. Erpelding settled in his room."

"Yes, sir. I'll get Gussie Rae Booker."

Minutes after Karl was in his room, Dr. Lopez arrived. To Kendra's great surprise, Doc was *Emile*, the man in the snapshot, who wrote in Spanish.

Soon after things had calmed down—Dr. Lopez, at the other end of the room, burrowing through his black bag—Erpelding whispered loud enough for Kendra to hear: "Clark, two things: find Osborne—*fast*; and bring Lepardieux here. I want to talk to him."

"I'll do what I can to find Osborne, but I don't think Dr. Lopez would approve of your talking, just yet, to Lepardieux. Too much excitement. You'll have to wait a while."— Clark turned to Kendra.—"Miss Applegate, call it a day. I'll see you in the morning."

"Yes, sir."

In the hallway, Kendra glanced at her watch. It was four o'clock. She flew down to the library, Erpelding's words 'find Osborne, fast', ringing in her ears. She grabbed the phone and asked the Operator for the DuPlessix Freightline Company. A couple seconds later a secretary's voice came on the line. Kendra identified herself and said:

"I'd like to verify that the *SS CATHERINE CELENE* departed New Orleans on April 13th, at 6:30 a.m.; docked in London, on April 20th."

The secretary said that was so, and then listened to the rest of what Kendra had to say; put her on hold; came back on the line and said a Solicitor Dubonette would see her in twenty minutes.

Twenty-two minutes later, Kendra sat down opposite Solicitor Theodore Q. Dubonette. His office was handsome. The distinguished Dubonette was dressed in an expensive dark blue suit, made to order. He was probably seventy or seventy-five, and was of medium height, with an unbelievable headful of wavy white hair, keen blue eyes and pink-and-white skin.

"What can I do for you, Miss Applegate?"

"I'm here, as a shot in the dark. Mrs. Carol Rogers, my boss' wife, died unexpectedly on April 13th. Kyle Osborne, her protege, supposedly left on April 12th, we thought for a seminar at UC. Mr. Rogers has been trying to locate Kyle Osborne to tell him of this tragedy," explained Kendra.

"Mr. Rogers now thinks Kyle Osborne didn't go to UC but, instead, sailed to England on April 13th, aboard the *SS CATHERINE CELENE*. Can this be checked out?"

"I'm sorry to hear of Mr. Rogers' loss."—Dubonette paused and studied Kendra closely— "Miss Applegate, your shot in the dark has hit its mark. Mr. Osborne and his wife sailed for England on April 13th. Osborne purchased one round trip ticket for himself; a one-way ticket for his wife.

"Normally, I wouldn't give out this information, but there's been an accident. Osborne was drowned at sea, and Mrs. Osborne, who was discharged, yesterday, from a London hospital, wouldn't respond to any of our questions. We didn't know who to contact."

Although the ghost of CR had told Kendra, Kyle Osborne made his bed beneath the sea, it came as a shock to hear it from a living human being. "This is bad news. When did the accident happen?"

"On April 17th. Did you know Mr. and Mrs. Osborne?"

"N-no. I just started working for Mr. Rogers this week. I never met the Osbornes. I don't even know Mrs. Osborne's first name."

"It's a very unusual name. Icelynn—Icelynn Farnsworth Osborne."

"Icelynn," repeated Kendra. "That *is* different. I don't believe I've ever heard it before. How did the accident happen?"

"Captain Meyers, of *THE SS CATHERINE CELENE,* cabled that two crewmen observed Mr. and Mrs. Osborne, at the rail, early in the morning of April 17th, physically fighting. Both went over."

Kendra shuddered. "How horrible."

"It was indeed horrible. Only Mrs. Osborne was rescued. I understand physically she's recovered, but mentally"—he shrugged. "Neither the doctor nor our agent in London could get her to tell us anything about herself or her family."

"I assume all Osborne's identification was on his person when he went overboard."

"Correct. Mrs. Osborne and her pocketbook went over the rail. We had nothing to go on until you showed up, Miss Applegate."

"I'll give this information to Mr. Rogers. He'll want to talk with you."

"Yes; by all means." Dubonette rose and handed Kendra his card.

They shook hands and Kendra left. On the way out, she borrowed the receptionist's phone and called Clark Rogers. Gussie Rae Booker said he wasn't in, and didn't know when he'd be back. She also said Dr. Lopez said Karl Erpelding had suffered a slight stroke, and couldn't have any visitors. She hung up the phone, thanked the receptionist, and left for the morgue, to see assistant Albert Lepardieux.

Lepardieux's office was a small green, square room, with a white ceiling; the cement floor was partially covered with green and white linoleum, highly polished. Lepardieux sat behind a gray metal desk, cluttered with manilla colored folders. The file cabinet, to the right of his desk, was also gray metal. A tan nahaughyde armchair stood to the side of the desk. Dead silence reigned supreme.

"Hello, Mr. Lepardieux. I'm Kendra Applegate, secretary to Attorney Karl Erpelding, of New Orleans and San Francisco. I'd like to talk to you—"

"What do you want to talk to me about? I've got to file these folders, and then I'm off. You'll have to come back tomorrow."

Albert Lepardieux was a fairly young man, painfully thin, with thin lips, long nose, watery blue eyes and a shock of blonde, almost white, hair. He looked like a mop somebody had stood up in the corner.

"We can talk while you file. It's about your accidentally sending Mrs. Carol Rogers' body to the undertakers, without the autopsy that Mr. Rogers had requested. I'm told, because of you, she was accidentally cremated," said Kendra, coming instantly and bluntly to the point.

What little blood Albert Lepardieux had, left his thin body. "Er, sit down, Miss Applegate." He nodded to the tan naughyde armchair; Kendra sat; and the cushion on her chair made a noise like air escaping from a balloon. "Er, w-why would Attorney—w-what did you say his name was?—send you to see me? W-why not come himself?"

"Lawyer Erpelding has been in Europe for the past month. He arrived in New Orleans today, had a slight stroke and is unable to leave his bed. But he's anxious to know more about his client's cremation. That's why he sent me, his secretary."

Albert Lepardieux wilted. "I'm so glad Dr. Prestijockeymoe's not here. He said if there was any more stink about this matter, I'm axed."

"Lawyer Erpelding instructed me to talk to you and you alone about this matter. After all it was *you* who made the terrible mistake."

"Yes, oh, yes. Ever since it happened, I haven't been able to sleep or eat."—he coughed—"I've lost ten pounds, and I can't afford to lose one pound."—he choked—"My sainted mother says, if I don't gain some weight, I'm going to go right down the tub drain. What do you want to know? I told it all to Judge Edwards, who explained it to Mr. Rogers."

"Tell it to me."

"All right, I will, even though Dr. Prestijockeymoe forbids me to speak of it. He's furious with me." He took a deep breath, let it out slowly and began: "On the morning of Friday, April 13th, Dr. Lopez—he's a good friend of Dr. Prestijockeymoe—and two ambulance attendants arrived with Mrs. Rogers' body. Dr. Lopez said Mr. Rogers had requested that an autopsy be performed on Mrs. Rogers. I told him Dr. Prestijockeymoe was at a board meeting at Charity, and would be back within the hour.

"He said he'd wait. The ambulance attendants left. Dr. Lopez, who had been here on the previous day, working with Dr. Prestijockeymoe on another autopsy—a Mrs. Karen Rogers—asked if the undertaker had picked up Mrs. Karen Rogers' body. I said the undertaker was due shortly. I had everything ready. Mrs. Karen Rogers' toe was tagged."

Albert Lepardieux was now sweating, clenching and unclenching his hands, cracking his knuckles, coughing and choking. "Dr. Lopez said I should get Mrs. Carol Rogers' body ready for the autopsy, because he'd start without Dr. Prestijockeymoe. I did. I also tagged her toe.

"Dr. Lopez then said he'd sure like a cuppa coffee and some beignets, from the French Market. He said, if I'd go get it, he'd treat. He even loaned me his big Buick."

"How long were you gone?"

"Thirty minutes. When I got back, Dr. Lopez told me the undertaker had come and picked up Mrs. Karen Rogers body, for cremation. Doc then reheated our coffee, because he said it wasn't hot enough."

Lepardieux, using his right index finger, started rubbing his nose. "We then drank our coffee and ate our beignets. Still Dr. Prestijockeymoe hadn't come. So Dr. Lopez decided he wouldn't start the autopsy without Dr. Prestijockeymoe being present. Instead, he filled out forms on Mrs. Carol Rogers, gave them to me and I made a file folder for her. Doc said he couldn't wait any longer; and left, telling me to have Dr. Prestijockeymoe call him when he was ready to start the autopsy on Mrs. Carol Rogers."

Lepardieux still rubbed his nose.

"After Dr. Lopez left, I fell asleep. I have never fallen asleep on the job. *Never ever!* But I did that dreadful day. Dr. Prestijockeymoe found me sleeping. He had to shake me to wake me. He was very angry with me for sleeping on the job. You can imagine the verbal abuse I took. The fact that I had never fallen asleep before didn't matter to my boss."

"Did Dr. Prestijockeymoe, that same day, discover the mix up in bodies?"

"No. It wasn't until the next day."—He gasped for breath, still rubbing his nose— "I had put Mrs. Carol Rogers' toe tag on Mrs. Karen Rogers' toe, and vice versa. I even lost the file on poor Carol Rogers."

By now Lepardieux's long, thin nose was highly inflamed.

"I wasn't fired, only because of Dr. Lopez and Judge Edwards' intervened in my behalf. They talked Mr. Rogers out of pressing neglect charges, and then talked Dr. Prestijockeymoe out of firing me. Dr. Prestijockeymoe says if he hears one more word about Mrs. Carol Rogers, I'm gone. He said he'd blackball me for life. Miss Applegate, if that happens, no body will ever hire me. I'm the sole support of my widowed mother. If I lose my job, we'll be in the street.

"I've never before made such a horrible mistake. If only Dr. Lopez hadn't insisted that he wanted his coffee from the French Market, I'd been here when the undertaker came. I'd have never let the wrong body be taken away. I always double check before releasing a body."

"Where do you regularly go for coffee?"

"Just across the street, to Joe's Diner. Every time Dr. Lopez comes, he sends me to Joe's for coffee and jelly doughnuts. I'm gone five minutes at the most. This time Dr. Lopez said he wanted beignets, not jelly doughnuts. It's my fault for being away from my post so long."

"Maybe you're blaming the wrong person," quietly said Kendra, rising, her cushion expelling hissing air.

"Dr. Prestijockeymoe said it's all my fault, and predicted I hadn't heard the last of it, and he was right. Lawyer Erpelding is here, all the way from California, to press charges, get me fired. Isn't he?"

"I don't think Lawyer Erpelding is after your job. I don't think you have anything to worry about. Go home, Mr. Lepardieux, eat a good supper and get a good night's sleep."

They shook hands, and Kendra drove straight to Willowwynn, to inform Mr. Rogers of all these new developments. He wasn't in.

"Mistah Rogers is prob'ly still at him's office," said Gussie Rae Booker, "dough de staff leaves at five. It's naw ha'f pas' six, but dat don'ts means Mistah Rogers ain't still at wuks. Him'll bees comin' along.— Is dat rain Ah heah?"

"It just started to sprinkle when I parked my automobile." To herself: "Tante's at Antlee Theodd's wake, so I'm in no hurry to get home." Aloud: "I'll wait for Mr. Rogers in the library."

On her way to the library, as she was passing the staircase, Kendra stopped in her tracks and took a deep breath. "I'm not breathing right." Then she heard CR's voice's say, 'Come on up. I'm waiting for you.'

Drawn like a magnate by the sound of the ghost's voice, Kendra mounted the stairs. Midway up she stopped. "She can call me day and night, but I'm not going to her."

Slowly she walked back down the stairs and when she had reached the bottom step, the calling had become irresistible and insistent. An impelling curiosity sent Kendra racing back up the stairs and down the hallway.

As she reached CR's bedroom door, she came almost to a sliding halt. There she stood for a few seconds, and then walked on down the hall until she came to the door that led directly into the powder-blue sitting room. She stood there, breathless.

After a few seconds she made a decision:"I won't go in"; but CR's persistent calling rang loudly in her ears, and the need to see if this ghost really existed nagged. "I won't be cowed by a ghost," she said, as she opened the big heavy door and crossed the sill. The room was dimly lit. It felt close and airless, and unnaturally cold.

No one was in the sitting room. So she opened the sliding doors and stepped into the bedroom. She quickly looked around and, when her amber eyes rested on the great four-poster bed, she doubted her sight. She saw a blue mist and a gray mist. Two blurs.

Slowly one blur projected itself; and then the other followed. Two shadows materialized into substance. CR and a man were in bed. Asleep. CR's naked body was outlined in an aura of glowing blue, that sparkled with tiny flashes of white and pink; the sleeping naked man was outlined in gray, no sparkle. He was young. Good-looking. His blond head rested on a blue covered pillow. One arm was flung out, embracing CR. She looked ecstatic. He looked lustful.

"What am I seeing? Who is that gorgeous-looking guy? Kyle Osborne? CR said he made his bed beneath the sea; so what's he doing in the powder-blue bedroom?"

Kendra couldn't tear her eyes away from *those* two dead lovers who were still breathing. Softly, mechanically. With each breath CR took, Kendra felt a pressure in her chest, and heard her own deafening heart beating some where up in her throat; her ears loudly ringing.

"*Those* two are dead. Dead flesh. CR's flesh is nothing more than ashes stored away in an urn in some cold, dark mausoleum, in San Francisco; by now the crabs have eaten Kyle Osborne.

"I got to be pine black crazy to be standing here intruding on two naked dead lovers. I've never seen anyone naked, not even Tante. When I was little and Miss Stella Dora, that one time, had bathed Kenny Joe and me together, and Kenny Joe asked: 'Kendra Lou, where's your ding dong?' Miss Stella Dora quickly answered: 'Son, girls don't have ding dongs.'"

The golden guy blinked open his eyes, and reached for CR. His eyes were brown and bold. He oozed with confidence and arrogance. Both were now awake. Golden boy smiled an enthralling smile. Kendra caught her breath. Any second they'd turn her way. Catch her spying on them. "I've got to get out of here." She couldn't move.

The blue mist was slowly closing in on her, and she was powerless to stop it. She had lost her power to resist. She stood there, her hands clenched, sweating and staring, while Golden boy buried his face in CR's white breasts. They murmured softly. He ran his fingers through her hair. They whispered passionately. He cupped her breasts in his hands. He fondled her. He raised his golden head and pressed his mouth hard against CR's hungry mouth. Their eager mouths clung.

Kendra's lips felt warm and bruised and parted.

Golden boy mounted CR, and when it was over, Kendra felt undone, exhausted, satisfied. Shame washed over her, followed by revulsion "CR's lover is now my lover; CR being me, and me being CR. She's used me like she said she would. God help me!— CR," shrieked Kendra, "you've gone too far—You've burned your bridges! —I'll never bring your killer to justice, now—Who ever killed you, I thank him." The ghost of CR laughed a hideous laugh. Kendra stumbled from the room.

How she got downstairs to that small bathroom, off the hall, she didn't know. How her fumbling fingers turned on the water in the basin, she didn't know. All she knew for certain was she had somehow been violated. By a ghost.

Trembling and icy cold, she splashed water on her face, and then cupped her hands, filled them with water, and gulped greedily. She vomited—hair and dung. Afterwards, she washed her mouth and face. Dried herself and looked in the mirror.

The face that stared back at her was her own, as well as the face of CR, except her eyes were green and her hair was no longer piled on top her head. It was a mass of gypsy ringlets, tumbling about her head and shoulders. She kept staring at herself in the mirror.

"That face looking back at me belongs to both of us. I'm CR, and she's me. CR and I are one. That's impossible! I'm mad! I'd have to be insane to believe an evil soul has lodged itself inside my body. But it happened, I didn't imagine it *and* I'm not insane."

Weak and wobbly, she started for her Dodge. On her way out, she met Mr. Rogers on his way in. "Why, Miss Applegate, what are you doing here? I thought you left around four. It's now after eight"

"I came back to see you about something, you weren't in, so I decided to wait. But it got too late—"

"Well, I'm here now. Let's go into the library.

In the library, Kendra sat at the Rent table; Mr. Rogers on the arm of a nearby sofa, looking her over critically, his navy eyes questioning "I see you've let your hair down. I must admit I prefer the ringlets, though they need a good combing, to the severity of an upsweep."

Normally, Kendra wouldn't have let this remark pass without a retort but, at mention of her freed hair, she could see, almost feel, Osborne running his fingers through CR's hair; and, since she was CR as well as herself, his fingers had gone running through her hair, taking out the hairpins, as he caressed her curls. At that realization, she cried to herself: "My God, the hairpins are in the bed." She felt sicker.

"You look unwell, Miss Applegate. Almost as if you're frightened of something. Did you see a ghost?" He chuckled.

To herself: "I've been upstairs with your dead wife and her dead lover. We shared Osborne." Aloud: "D-do you believe in evil?"

"I believe in evil, everlasting life and goodness."

"D-do you believe in ghosts?—evil ghosts?"

"I've never seen one, evil or otherwise," shrugged Clark Rogers, "but

I've known reliable people who claimed they have."

"Gussie Rae Booker told me, this morning, she found the powder-blue bedroom a mess—"

"And you weren't here last night to mess it up.—I thought your eyes were brown with gold flecks, but I see they've changed color. They're green—sea green. Who do you think messed up the powder-blue bedroom?"

"Maybe Carol No. 2 and No. 3 is making visits to the powder-blue bedroom?"

He laughed a quiet laugh. "So you were eavesdropping and heard me tell Karl about Carol being a trinity, eh?" He laughed again. "Now tell me, what you wanted to see me about?"

Before Kendra could reply, she shivered from head to toe and felt breathless. In the next second, whoom CR was inside her, and the two were one again. Bubbly laughter rang out from Kendra's lips.

"Are you all right, Miss Applegate? You look frightened."

"Of course, I'm all right, darling," answered CR through Kendra's lips. "How nice to see you," she giggled, rising and moving toward Clark.

Clark rose, stood still and watched her come toward him, waiting. Kendra, controlled by CR paused, and then moved forward again. In the next moment, Kendra unable to control CR's actions, was in Clark's arms, passionately kissing him. Almost violently. Clark returned the kisses, kiss for kiss, in a reckless response. Quite suddenly he let her go.

Kendra stood very still, as though her stillness would prevent CR from ambushing her again. She felt cold and frightened and alone. Never had she kissed Jack Trenchard the way her mouth, CR's mouth, had kissed Clark Rogers. She was trembling with ecstasy.

"M-mr. Rogers, I didn't really kiss you," was all she could say.

"How disappointing."

Her feeling of ecstasy soon turned into shame, which turned into anger: "I'm glad your wife's dead; and I want nothing to do with anything that relates to her. I'm only sorry I concerned myself with the idea that she was murdered." To herself: "No sense telling him what I learned from Solicitor Dubonette about Kyle Osborne and Icelynn Farnsworth. Let him find out for himself." Aloud: "Knowing how I feel, do you still want me to work for you?"

"Yes."

"Then I'll see you in the morning."

Chapter Twelve

The next morning, Kendra, having had a bad night, felt tired and depressed. So to lift her spirits she chose to wear her for good sweetpea dress. A floral voile, splattered with colors of mauve, rose, blue and pink. The dress' square neckline and elbow-length sleeves were trimmed in cotton cream lace. Taking too much time dressing, she barely made it to work on time. She had worried needlessly and might just as well have been late, for Mr. Rogers wasn't in.

"Did he say when he'd be back?"

"Nome. Him's jes' sez hims had to goes to him's cottage en Bay St. Loois on bizzness. Sez hims would bees back by dark. Efen yo wants to cawls hims, Ah's gots him's foam number dare."

"N-no.Thanks any way.— Did you and Mr. Rogers check the powder-blue bedroom this morning?"

"Nome. Mistah Rogers dun it by hisse'f. Said ev'ryt'ing wuz OK."

To herself: "I bet he found those hairpins."Aloud: "How's Mr. Erpelding," she asked, changing the subject.

"So-so. Doctah Lopez wuz heah seben o'clock dis mawnin', wit en artlee. Mistah Erpelding gots som' medicine, den ah nice baf en shave, end den him's breakfas'. Doc'll bees backs tonites to checks on hims."

"Did Dr. Lopez say when Mr. Erpelding could have visitors?"

"Nome. Him jes' sez no visitors. No 'citement whatsoevah."

"Then wouldn't it be better and easier, on everybody, for Mr. Erpelding to be hospitalized?"

"Doc wanted to horsespittalize dat dare man, but dat dare stubbin man refused to go. Hims jes' wants to stays heah en keep us all wurried hims mights falls out agins, not to mention hims keepin' usen runnin' up-'n'-downs de steps, ah servin'-'n'-ah tentin' to hims."

"That's too bad. Well, I've got to get to work."

Kendra went to the library and found a few typing jobs that Mr. Rogers had left on the Rent table. She finished them off in no time. Afterwards, she sat, staring straight ahead into space, thinking of what had happened to her the night before in the powder-blue bedroom; thinking how, through CR's control, she had passionately kissed Mr. Rogers. Remembering that electrifying embrace, she relived the rapturous sensation and wondered if that feeling of rapture had been mutual. "I hope when I see him he won't refer either to the kisses or to the hairpins that he surely found in CR's big bed."

Then she began thinking that Mr. Rogers still didn't know Kyle Osborne was dead—drowned at sea; that Icelynn Farnsworth was married to Osborne and was just discharged from a London hospital; that Albert Lepardieux's story sounded as if he had been made a scapegoat, by Dr. Lopez.

Her thoughts suddenly shifted to her aunt, who, the night before, had gotten home just minutes before she had.

"Kendra Lou, when you said you couldn't go to Antlee Theaud's wake because you'd be workin' late, I thought that was just an excuse. But here you come strollin' in at ha'f pas' nine. Did you eat any supper?"

"No."

"Me neither. I picked up a shrimp po boy and a couple pieces of coconut custard pie."

"I thought you were going to eat at the wake."

"There was no wake. No money to buy the eats. Antlee Theaud's best friend, Tic Toc Tennenbum—that Tic Toc looks more Spanish than Irish to me, with that crow-black hair, dark eyes and skin, and that blade-like face of his—and his yeller-haired girl friend, Filacity Casabon, was just leavin' when I got there. Filacity was poured into a red jersey dress, that fit her like a tight green cornshuck wrapped around an ear of corn. Every one of her bumps-'n'-bulges showed.

"Lolotte said Tic Toc and Filacity spent the whole day at the track, playin' the horses, with her last money, tryin' to win enough to buy the eats for tonight's wake. They lost all Lolotte's money. Lolotte ought to know gamblin' is nothin' but chance and mischance."

"And horse racing is fixed nine out of ten times."

"Of course, it is.— Lolotte asked me to stay and help her tell everybody, who came, the wake was cancelled until tomorrow.She said her cousins from Cutoff; Amite; Bogalusa; Opelousas; and Mamou would bring the eats for tomorrow's wake. I'm glad I got this po boy. We can split it."

Kendra took a couple bites of her sandwich, and could eat no more. She did manage to drink a cup of coffee and eat her pie.

"Kendra Lou, you don't eat enough to keep a bird goin'; and tonight you so look tired and worried. What's wrong?"

"I can't tell you because you don't believe in ghosts—"

"That's right. Don't tell me nothin' about no ghosts tonight. I'm in no humor to lissen to no monkey foolishness."

Soon afterwards, the Applegates went to bed. A little after two, Kendra was awakened from a deep sleep, startled. Standing over her was the ghost of Carol Rogers, dressed in red. It was one thing to see CR at Willowwynn, but quite another to wake and find her standing over her at home.

"What do *you* want?"

"To tell you where you can find the evidence that will convict my killer."

"I already told you," hissed Kendra, "you burned your bridges in bed with Osborne, not to mention making me kiss your husband. I'm glad somebody killed you. I will not look for your murderer."

"And I'm telling you," snarled CR, "find those answers, or suffer the consequences. The answers are hidden in the walls of the powder-blue bedroom—*find* them."

The voices woke Molly Primrose, who, in a high-necked, long-sleeved, pink cotton nightgown, to her ankles, her white hair, falling to her waist in silky waves, came flying into her niece's room to investigate:"What is it, Kendra Lou?" she asked, her voice all atremble, as she snapped on the night lamp. "I thought I heard you talkin' in your sleep. Real loud you was talkin'. Are you all right?"

Kendra, in white PJ's, her mop of brown-gold hair a tumble of curls, and her sleepy eyes only half free of the vision of CR, blinked and sat up, in bed: "The ghost of Carol Rogers was here, standing over me, threatening me. She said if I didn't find her murderer, I'd suffer the consequences. She said the evidence, that would convict her killer, could be found in the walls of the powder-blue bedroom. She disappeared when you came in the room."

"Gawd save us! Who ever heard the like of a ghost in *this* house? Not me," asserted Molly Primrose, her sleepy blue eyes scanning the room.

"I tell you she was here."

"And did she tell you to tear out them walls, to get to them answers?"

"No."

Without another word, Molly Primrose hiked up her nightgown over her knees, got down on her hands and knees and looked under the bed. "Nobody under the bed," she muttered, rising, stiffly. Then she opened the armoire." Nobody in the armoire." Lastly, she sat on the edge of her niece's bed.

"There ain't nobody here, leastwise no ghost. None of the Applegates ever saw ghosts. You had a nightmare. It must've been that couple bites of that shrimp sandwich and that coconut pie. Too rich for your blood.— Well, I need my rest and so do you. If you like, you can sleep with me."

"That's OK, Tante. Thanks anyway."

"I'll leave the light on in the hall."

Back to the present. Still seated at her desk, still staring straight ahead, Kendra frittered the whole morning away, thinking of CR's remark: 'Find the answers or suffer the consequences.' "What more can she possibly do to me, aside from kill me?" she asked herself. "I can't get into those walls."

She talked to herself in this manner until noon. Instead of eating lunch, she went to the library and poured over books on alien spirits. Nothing came close to her situation; however, she checked out a book on the spirit world; and, because of the subject matter, tossed it in the trunk, discovering CR's white briefcase.

"*Holy Moses!* I forgot about this briefcase and the evidence I stashed in it. I better return it."

Back at Willowwynn, she typed for the rest of the afternoon, but didn't know what she had typed; and didn't care. After a while her conscious got to her, and she wrote a note to Mr. Rogers: *Must talk to you about Icelynn Farnsworth and Kyle Osborne. I have some ve-ry important info regarding these two people. KA.*

After writing that note, she left the office, at five.

As she parked in front of her double, she saw standing on her side of the front gallery the two white-faced chicken hawks and Lizzie Slapp Springmeyer. Lizzie Slapp's spiky pink hair was standing on end, as if she had stuck her finger in an electric outlet and got zapped; her blood red lipstick was smeared across her thin lips, grotesquely extending the lines of her lips. She stood holding up her full-skirted, cotton, chartreuse colored dress high above her knobby knees, looking, as usual, like a Mardi Gras on the verge of a court curtsey.

"What are those two chicken hawks and Biddie Springmeyer doing on my side of the gallery?" muttered Kendra to herself. "Those chicken hawks haven't spoken directly to me since Jackson."

Slowly she got out the Dodge, went around to the trunk and opened it to get her library book. To her disgust, there was CR's briefcase. "Dammit, I forgot to put that briefcase back—I'll do it tomorrow.—I better take it in the house, because if I leave it in the trunk, I'll forget to put it back." She jerked out both the briefcase and library book. She turned the briefcase so the initials couldn't be seen.

"Sugar," called out Lizzie Slapp, hiking her dress higher. "Lettie Lou wants me to tell you you've just missed Stella Dora bein' carried off to Charridy."

"You mean Charity's ambulance just left here with Miss Stella Dora? Is she sick?" demanded Kendra, hurrying forward and taking the front steps two at a time, excited and pale.

Lizzie Slapp let go her dress. "Just a minute, Kendra Louise, while I turn up my hearin' aid."

Breathless and tightly holding the briefcase, Kendra stood staring in amazement, alternately at Lizzie Slapp and then at the two chicken hawks, who were wearing navy blue voile dresses, with white lace collars, their faces thickly powdered with cornstarch, their meringue hair piled high, waiting for Lizzie Slapp to adjust her hearing aid.

"I can hear now."

"Good," sang out Effie Vi'let. "Lizzie Slapp, you know Lettie Lou and me don't speak to Kendra Louise no more, so you'll have to tell her it was a red autoe-moe-beel, with a po-leeceman drivin' and an intern, that took Stella Dora away. You got that?"

Lizzie Slapp simpered, curtsied and midway through stopped her recital, said: "Say again, Effie Vi'let. Where was I? What was I sayin'?"

The two chicken hawks prompted her, and she finally got it all out.

"Now, Lizzie Slapp," said Lettie Lou, "tell Kendra Louise that the intern said it was time to reevaluate Stella Dora's mental health."

Lizzie Slapp curtsied, opened her red mouth and said: "Precious," and came to a full stop. She turned to the chicken hawks. "What was it you wanted me to say, and who did you want me to say it to?"

"Mrs. Springmeyer, you were talking to me."—Lizzie Slapp looked blank and bewildered. Kendra turned to Miss Lettie Lou, looking ruthlessly into her Pekinese's.eyes, and blasted her with both barrels. "If you have something to say to me, *you* say it directly to my face and not indirectly. You don't need a go between. Speak for yourself."

"Well, since it was you who got Stella Dora released from Jackson, we thought it was *you* who had her picked up for her reevaluation."

"I had nothing to do with it. You mean to tell me you let Charity take Miss Stella Dora without finding out who initiated this, this reevaluation," lashed out Kendra, enraged.

"We thought it was *you,*" insisted Miss Effie Vi'let. "We was just ready to go catch the streetcar so we could go to Antlee Theaud DuPuy's wake, when Charridy's red autoe-moe-beel pulled up. We thought *you* was the one who sent Charridy here, didn't we Lizzie Slapp?"

"We did, Honey," verified Lizzie Slapp, still looking blank and bewildered, trying to keep up with everybody's lips while lifting her dress above her knees, curtseying and bobbing her pink head up and down, as if it were on a spring. Her long pink drawers showing.

"Why didn't you all go with her?" snapped Kendra, disgusted.

"They wouldn't let us."

"Well, c'mon let's go see what they've done to Miss Stella Dora."

"The intern said we couldn't come see her until after the evaluation, which should take a good two or three days," explained Miss Lettie Lou. "I'm not worried about Stella Dora. I'm worried about the bills she owes. It's time to pay your aunt the rent. The utility bills are due and the groceries have to be made. Stella Dora only had a ten dollar bill in her pocketbook, and that's not enough, to cover nothin'. She couldn't take any money with her, so I took the ten dollars."

"We just havta get our hands on her fat bankbook," said Miss Effie Vi'let, "so we can pay the bills and buy that new tomb for Big Joe and Kenny Joe to rest in, away from *that madam*. We coulda done it while Stella Dora was bein' reevaluated, if she hadn't acted hateful and hid the bankbook on us."

To herself: "What a pair of greedy grasping women. They think themselves just, and they're the two most unjust women I know. Aloud: "If you're so upset about not paying the rent on time, just put up your part of it and let my aunt worry about collecting Miss Stella Dora's share."

"Humph! We're not puttin' up a penny of the rent money until Stella Dora puts up hers."

Kendra took a deep breath and let it out slowly: "Well, that settles that. —As far as the bankbook goes, if you got your hands on it, you couldn't draw out any of the money, anyway. So stop troubling yourselves about Miss Stella Dora's money; forget about a new tomb; and, for a change, start worrying about your sister-in-law," added Kendra through tight lips.

"We're not about to worry about Stella Dora. We're gunna leave all the worryin' up to *you*," smirked Miss Lettie Lou, through her thin merciless lips. "Me and Effie Vi'let decided, since *you* got her out of Jackson, we'd let *you* get her out of Charridy. Come along, Effie Vi'let, Lizzie Slapp, we've got to go catch that streetcar so we can go to Antlee Theaud's wake. Have you been to the wake, Kendra Louise?"

"No."

"I assume your aunt's there. What time are you gunna pick her up?"

"She's there; but I'm not going to pick her up," replied Kendra and went inside, shutting the door behind her, leaving the trio gawking on the gallery, at the closed door.

Kendra went directly to her room, tossed the briefcase and library book on the bed, kicked off her heels, slipped out her sweetpea dress, unsnapped her garter belt, pealed off her stockings and tugged her slip over her head. All was tossed on the bed in a heap. "Phew! that feels better."

She threw her pink chenille robe on, pushed her feet into pink mules and click clacked to the kitchen, where she made herself a fried egg sandwich on white bread, with lots of mayonnaise and sliced tomatoes. Next she poured herself a glass of cold creamy milk, sat at the gatelegged table and bit into her sandwich, thinking of Kyle Osborne, CR's enthralling dead lover, also her lover.

Remembering his caresses—his face against hers—his kisses covering her face—her mouth. "CR said she'd only take up a small part of my body, and now, after what happened she has all of me. None of me is Kendra."

A couple bites into the sandwich, a horrible thought occurred to her. A ghastly thought. "What of Kyle Osborne's seed?" she asked herself. "If a cold dead man can make love, is his seed dead or alive? Can a dead man make a live woman pregnant? In all logic, could I have conceived?" She sat panic-stricken and wet palmed.

"What's ahead of me? If I—" she broke off. "Tante would never believe a ghost did it to me. No one on Starlight Street would believe it, either. For that matter no one anywhere in the whole wide world would believe it. If it's true, what am I going to do?"

She was so engrossed with this horrible absurdity that she didn't hear the knocking at the back screen door. The knocking went on as she sat there completely absorbed in her thoughts until she heard the squeaky screen door open and slam shut, getting her full attention.

She heard the floor boards of the back porch creak, as steps crossed them. She held her breath, as the knob on the kitchen door turned and the door opened.

Tall, slim, dark-haired and blue/purple eyed Jack Trenchard stood before her. Startled, Kendra slowly stood up and jerked her robe more securely around her. To herself: "God he's beautiful! I can't believe his good looks still have such an effect on me." Aloud: "If you wanted to scare me to death, you did. How dare you walk in on me without knocking? What do you want?"

He held a small suitcase in his right hand. "I practically knocked the door down, but you wouldn't answer. I knew you were home—the Dodge is out front—and I had to see you. By now, I thought you'd be through with supper," he said, momentarily shifting his blue eyes from Kendra's face to what was left of her sandwich and milk.

"I'm through." She pushed the sandwich aside.

"Where's your aunt?"

"She's at Antley Theodd DuPuy's wake. Our neighbor."

"Isn't that the guy who jumped off the Huey P. Long Bridge?"

"Yes," answered Kendra, seating herself. "What do you want?"

Uninvited, Jack sat across from her, the case at his side. "Why are you working at Willowwynn, for Clark Rogers? Have you replaced Icelynn?"

"Who told you I'm working at Willowwynn?"

"I called your office, and Clio Calliope said you were no longer Mr. Prosper's secretary; that you were working at Willowwynn, for Rogers."

"Clio Calliope is *dumb-dumb-dumb*. Her brains are in her big bust. I'm still Mr. Prosper's secretary. I'm temporary help at Willowwynn. Why are you so thin and tired looking?"

Jack shrugged. "Are you at Willowwynn to keep an eye on me?"

"Don't flatter yourself," flared Kendra. "I'm working at Willowwynn because Mr. Prosper loaned me to his boss, Mr. Rogers. I *told* you I'm temporary."

Jack whistled. "I didn't know Rogers owned the homestead."

"I suppose there're a lot of things you don't know. So why are you here?"

He took a deep breath and let it out slowly. "Two reasons. First, Judge Edwards sent me to collect a favor you owe him. Secondly, I've got to talk to you about *us*. Allison is pregnant," blurted out Jack.

"Well, don't look so sad. What does that have to do with us? I'm glad for you. B-but— I thought you said she couldn't have children."

"That's what I was told. Judge Edwards made the whole thing up. Neither Allison nor her mother knows what he did."

"You mean Allison doesn't have a deadly blood disease?"

"No. She's fine. I accidentally found out about it."

"Did you have the guts to ask that low-down Judge why he lied?"

"He said he did it because he couldn't stand for Allison to be jilted by Claremont. She had her hope chest, her wedding dress. Everything—"

"But a groom. Why didn't Claremont marry her?"

"When Allison became engaged to Claremont, the agreement was she'd bring a million bucks to the marriage. When the time came to turn over the money to the Claremonts, all the Judge could come up with was $800,000—"

"And he told the Claremonts he'd get the rest of the money, a mere couple hundred grand, in a few months; but the Claremonts wouldn't go for it."

Jack nodded. "I've been had. Claremont wouldn't settle for $800,000 to take Allison off the Judge's hands—"

"And you jumped at $300,000."

"He got me cheap."

"I hope, for the rest of your life, you're not going to go around singing that time-worn refrain, 'I've been done wrong.' Besides, $300,000 isn't cheap. You're just mad because Claremont turned down the baggage for $800,000 and you snatched it up for $300,000, and ran with it.. Now that you know about the $800,000 you're feeling greedy-minded. At the time, you threw everything to the wind for that $300,000."

"By everything you mean our love, not to mention all the hurt and pain I caused you. The degradation of being jilted—"

"Yes," murmured Kendra, her eyes misting. "The loneliness and the loss." Silence. "What's done is done. Look at it this way, you got what you wanted. Money, a half partnership in the Judge's law firm, a mansion to live in with your beautiful, talented and charming wife, who's not going to die; and a child on the way. You got it all. What more do you want?"

"What I agreed to. Judge Edwards said Allison would be dead in a year or so, and after she died I'd be rich and free—to marry you."

"You took a chance and you lost. You thought you were going to have your cake and eat it too, but it didn't pan out for you. Did it?"

"Not quite. Judge Edwards lied to me—I trusted the Judge—He betrayed me."

"Just goes to show you you can't trust a Judge."

Neither spoke for a while, and a loud awkward silence followed before they commenced chatting again. Rather than get back on Jack's betrayal, she skimmed the surface of safe subjects: the weather, Antley Theodd's death, Aunt Molly Primrose.

At last Jack got the conversation back on track. "The second reason I came to see you concerns Karl Erpelding, Carol Rogers' former attorney. As you probably know, Clark Rogers came to see the Judge, announcing that Erpelding is at Willowwynn, stirring the pot."

"Erpelding is too sick to stir any pot. He's suffered a slight stroke."

"That slight stroke's not stopping him from ordering an audit of the Sloan Endowment Fund."

"And that audit makes the Judge squirm and sweat a little, eh?
Jack shrugged.

"Do you want to know what I think?"

"Not really. But being the determined woman you are, you're going to
tell me, aren't you?"

"I think Erpelding suspects the Judge of dipping his sticky fingers into
the Sloan Endowment Fund—SEF. I bet the audit will prove that
$800,000 is missing from the fund, and that missing money can be found
in Judge Edwards' pocket, less $300,000, which is in your pocket, for
having married the Judge's daughter.

"I also think the real reason the Judge got you to marry Allison is he
needed a scapegoat, if an audit of the SEF was pulled by anyone but
himself. It's being pulled now, and you're the scapegoat. The Judge has
already, some how or other, fixed it so the embezzlement finger points
directly to your face. Have you spent any of the $300,000?"

Stunned, Jack slowly shook his head. "N-no."

"Then I think you're going to have to give it back to the Judge, so he
can put it with his $500,000, and give it all back to the SEF."

"I had nothing to do with Carol Rogers' financial affairs. The Judge
handled that. I doubt the combined efforts of Erpelding and his army of
auditors can prove that the Judge stole a dime."

"Then why did the Judge send you to see me, if he doesn't want
something covered up? And whether you admit it or not you're worried
about your $300,000 being stolen money. Aren't you?"

"It'd be hard to prove. Let me explain a few things. During the past
two years when the Judge handled Carol Rogers' financial affairs he
speculated with some of her profits—"

"Without permission and for himself, of course. No doubt hoping to
make enough money so that Allison could marry into the Claremont
family."

"He might've had Allison's dowry in mind. I don't know. Anyway, to
speculate with a rich client's money is an acceptable practice. Most
lawyers do it."

"They do it, if they can get away with it. If lawyers make a practice of
using their rich clients' money, without their permission, chances are a lot
of those rich clients die never knowing their lawyers have stolen money
from them. Their heirs are cheated."

"A gamble."

"I guess a lot of lawyers gamble and win all the time; however, I think
the Judge just lost," said Kendra through tight lips; "and he's about to go

down; and you're going to sink all the way to the bottom with him."

"How do you figure that?"

"I think before spy-eyed CR—that's what I call Carol Rogers—died she caught the Judge red-handed, skimming money from the SEF, and threatened him with public exposure, if he didn't put back all her dough.

"The Judge, fearing scandal and disgrace, agreed to put it back, plus a little lagniappe, like a hundred thou or so, for CR not blowing the whistle on him. But then CR up-'n'-died, and the Judge felt safe in keeping *all* that money, until now. Until Erpelding surfaced."

"You're fishing. Supposition's not hard evidence."

"If you and your father-in-law don't wanna go to jail, I suggest you tell him to slip that $800,000 back *now*, before the auditors start digging and delving."

"He doesn't have enough money to do that."

"Then you already suggested that avenue to him."

Jack didn't answer. He just looked sheepish.

"I think the *honorable* and *respectable* Judge Edwards is going to gamble again.— I'm going to do a little guessing here. I think CR told the Judge nobody knew what he had done and, if he'd put the money back by such and such a date, she wouldn't blow the whistle on him. The *respectable* Judge agreed.

"CR died, and the *respectable* Judge figured, since no body knew what he had done except God and dead CR, he'd keep the money. And now Erpelding shows up ordering an audit, and the Judge is worried sick that CR, before she died, might've blew the whistle on him. Blew that whistle all the way to San Francisco. To Erpelding's big ears."

"You have an uncanny way of coming straight to the point."

"A gift. You know, Jack, when you came to see me right after your honeymoon, you were flying high. Money, position and power were yours; and now, not even a year later, you're in trouble. You know, you could be accused of collusion, or masterminding the whole thing."

"I'm neither in trouble nor have I done anything to be accused of collusion; and I didn't embezzle money. What the Judge did he did on his own. Also, what he did is done all the time. It's just one of those things that lawyers do; so don't go calling Judge Edwards a *thief.* And another thing, stop saying the word *respectable* with a sneer."

"I think the audit will prove the Judge *is* a thief, and a *thief* needs to be sneered at. He betrayed you...lied to you...tricked you, and I think, if it means saving some of his own skin, he'd let you take the rap." She paused for a second to let what she said sink in. "You know it's said that during revolutions, the first to be shot are lawyers and judges, so why defend somebody who should be shot?"

"I'm not defending the Judge, just his position. The position of all lawyers and their rights."

"*Bull.* In my book, to help yourself to someone else's dough is no right, just plain out stealing. I'd say $800,000 is a big bundle not to have to put back. I can well understand why the *respectable* Judge is worried.—You're worried, too. Worry is written all over your face."

"I'm not worried. Neither is the Judge. He, he just wants to—"

"Cover his backside."

"He wants to make sure Erpelding doesn't have anything in writing. We must protect the family name, especially with a baby on the way."

"Not to mention protecting your $300,000. The Judge should've thought of the family name before he stole CR's $800,000."

"All he wants is to make sure Erpelding doesn't have anything in writing. The audit, without written proof, can't convict him."

"I wouldn't count on it. So what does the Judge and *you* want me to do?"

"As you guessed, the Judge wrote a note to Carol saying he'd pay back all monies owed the SEF, by the 15th of April. He wants you to find if that note still exists."

"How does he want me to do that? Walk up to Lawyer Erpelding and say 'Did CR send you a note written by Judge Edwards saying he stole $800,000 from the SEF, and agreed to pay it back by April 15th, interest free? If so, give me that note, so I can turn it over to Jack Trenchard, my ex-boyfriend, who has been bought for $300,000, by Judge Edwards, his *honorable* and *respectable* father-in-law.'"

Jack squirmed in his chair.

"I guess after the Judge gets his grasping hands on that note, he can then tear it up and flush the pieces down the toilet. Is that what *you* and the *respectable* Judge have in mind? coldy asked Kendra.

"Find that note. The Judge is 15 days late with the payment."

"I haven't seen any note saying the Judge would cough up that stolen $800,000, by the 15th of April, and I've been all through CR's things; however, I did come across a packet of love poems, written by the Judge to CR—real mush stuff. Do you think he wants those poems back?"

"The Judge didn't write Carol Rogers any love poems. He wouldn't touch that bitch with a pair of tongs. He's glad she's dead."

Kendra forgot she wasn't hungry, grabbed the cold egg sandwich and took a big bite. Chewed it up and swallowed. "If I had stolen $800,000 from someone, and then that person up-'n'-died and nobody but the dead person knew of the theft, I'd be glad, too."

"You make it sound sinister."

"Maybe it is sinister. Did it ever occur to you that CR might've been murdered, and the Judge might've done the murdering? He had enough motive.— Remember, Jack, you've got a chunk of that stolen money, that might be tainted with blood."

"That's crazy talk, Kendra, and you know it. Your aunt always said you read too many ten-cent detective stories." Again he squirmed in his chair. "Anyway, Carol probably threw the note away—"

"Or sent it to Karl Erpelding."

"Whatever has happened to that note, the Judge expects *you* to find it."

"Because you told him you had an inside source—namely me."

"I told him I had recently ran into my friend, Miss Molly Primrose, the lady we had helped to get her tenant, Mrs. Stella Dora Wheelerhand, released from Jackson, and she told me her niece was working at Willowwynn. I suggested to the Judge, since Miss Applegate owed us a favor, we should collect. The Judge jumped at it. It's time for you to repay the favor, Kendra."

"What do you want me to do? Kill Erpelding?"

"No. Just go through his briefcase. The note may be there. Also, make copies of any documents that he has pertaining to Carol Rogers."

"And give it to you so you can give it to the Judge, so he can destroy it all, so he can save himself?"

"Y-e-s."

Kendra laughed out loud. "Tell the *respectable* Judge Edwards, if he wants all that dirty duty done, do it himself." Kendra laughed again.

"Why are you laughing?"

"Because I can't believe you're going out on a limb for a man who lied to you. Told you his daughter was dying from a blood disease. How low can you get?" She paused. "Jack, why don't you just hand over the $300,000 and walk away from the whole stinking mess?"

"I can't. I like the money and the high living. And if Allison knew all this, it would destroy her. I can't hurt Allison."

Silence. The two looked deeply into each other's eyes. "But you can destroy me—Hurt me—Use me—That's OK, eh?"

"Life is full of cruelties and injustice.— "Well, Kendra?"

"Well, go to hell, Jack."

"Kendra, you owe the Judge."

"Go back and tell the Judge the Applegates said to go to hell."

"If you don't do this favor, then Stella Dora Wheelerhand goes back to the insane asylum."

Stunned, as if Jack had struck her a dizzing blow, she blurted out with icy rage: "That's blackmail. It was that *respectable bastard, liar* and *thief,* Judge Edwards, who had Miss Stella Dora picked up today and sent to Charity's mental ward, for a reevaluation. On what authority did he do that?"

"I told you the Judge was a powerful man. When the Judge pulled strings to get Mrs. Wheelerhand released from Jackson, he had her freed under *his* recognizance, not her own."

"You told me she was released on her *own* recognizance."

"Judge Edwards instructed me to tell you that."

"So you *lie* for him, too, eh?"

"You have three days to find that note. When you find it, Stella Dora Wheelerhand comes home."

"Dammit, Jack, what if CR *did* throw the note away?"

"Then you're going to have to prove that it doesn't exist. If you can't, Mrs. Wheelerhand goes back to Jackson for extensive shock treatments. You needn't look so crushed," quietly said Jack, rising. "I told you when the Judge got Mrs. Wheelerhand out of Jackson, he never did anything for nothing. You agreed to those terms, and now you *owe* the Judge."

"I don't owe that *thief* a damn thing. And another thing if you hadn't told the Judge Miss Applegate's niece works at Willowwynn, I wouldn't be on a spot. You *sicked* the Judge on me. How could you, Jack?"

"He'd found out sooner or later. Just cooperate with the Judge, and everything'll be all right."

"You cooperate with the bastard. He's your father-in-law, not mine." Then more to herself than to Jack: "In order to keep Miss Stella Dora safe I've got to be in league with a *lying, thieving, blackmailing* Judge. I got to help the bastard legally steal $800,000 dollars from Clark Rogers, my employer."

"Don't worry about Rogers. He inherited millions. He can afford to lose a million or so without fear of falling into the pit of poverty."

"That's not the point. And another thing, poor Miss Stella Dora shouldn't have ever been sent to the crazy house in the first place. It's a damn shame. I told you I've already been through all CR's papers and all I found were those love poems, signed with a big *E.*

Jack knitted his brow. "You'll have to show me those poems. I can't imagine the Judge getting mixed up with Carol Rogers, courtesan-at-large.

"Both Rogers and Erpelding knew the Judge and CR were lovers. I understand the courtesan-at-large even had a fling with you."

"*No she didn't.* She tried—"

"But you wouldn't touch her with a pair of tongs."

He glared at Kendra. "Let's get back to the issue at hand. If you want to save the Wheelerhand woman, I suggest you go through Carol Rogers' things again. I suggest you find *that* note—*and fast.*"

Kendra nodded slowly.

"I know I said I came to see you for two reasons, but there's also a third. I need your help. I've got $150,000 cash with me, and a cashier's check for $150,000."—He jerked up the suitcase, placed it on the table and snapped it open. Kendra's eyes popped.—"I want you to keep this money for me in case the Judge gets caught." He closed the case and put it back down on the floor.

"*Are you crrracy?* I can't keep *that kind of money* here. *Where* do you suggest I hide it? Under my pillow? Or under my mattress?"

"That's up to you."

"I can't do that, Jack. Give it to Allison. Let her hide your loot.—*Jackkk,* you had to draw all this money out because you got a tip the Judge is going to ask for it back. Right?"

"A friend of mine, Beverley Reynolds, head teller at Claremont's bank, made me a copy of a signature card, showing the Judge's name on my account."

"That's fraud. So you drew the money out before the Judge could?"

He nodded. "That's why I need your help. You're the only person I trust." His blue/purple eyes pleaded. "This money is for us. I'll get a quickie divorce, we'll get married and leave town."

"What about Allison and your baby?"

"That's the Judge's worry. He lied to me. I was suppose to be free in a year. Free to marry you."

"Well, in order for you to marry me, we got to run away, eh?— But in the meantime, if you're caught and this money is found here, I'll be implicated."

"Trust me. I won't let anything bad happen to you."

Kendra looked away, and said to herself: "He's using me again."

"Well-ell."

Without warning stinging tears sprang into her eyes and streamed down her cheeks. Jack walked over to her, pulled her to her feet and gathered her in his arms. "Darling, don't cry. Look at me." He kissed her hard. "I love you, Kendra. Do this for me, my darling.

"*Hm-mh! Excuse me,*" said Clark Rogers, standing in the kitchen doorway. He was wearing an oxford blue short-sleeved shirt, open at the neck, khaki pants, and brown penny loafers, gleaming with polish. His brown-gold hair was tumbling on his forehead, and his navy eyes were peering hard at them.

Startled and trembling, Kendra stared back at him through teary eyes; Jack stepped away from her.

"Miss Applegate, I came over because I couldn't reach you by phone. This note," he waved the piece of paper, "you left said you had some very important information for me.— I hope I'm not interrupting anything."

"You're not," choked Kendra, reseating herself.

"I knocked at the front door and got no answer; I knocked at the back screen door and got no answer. I knew you were home—"

"Because the Dodge is parked out front," hiccupped Kendra.

"That, and because I heard voices." He put the note in his pocket.

Jack stepped forward and extended his hand. "I—I was just leaving."

Clark regarded him quizzically, shook his hand and asked: "Is that your overnight case?"

"No," answered Jack.

"*Take it with you,*" cried Kendra.

"*No.*"

Jack left without looking at Kendra.

"What's all that about?" demanded Clark.

"N-nothing."

"Here's my handkerchief. Stop crying. Tears never solved anything. Where's your Aunt Molly Primrose?"

Kendra wiped her eyes, returned the handkerchief and stared at the suitcase that held $150,000 cash, plus a cashier's check for the same amount. "My God!" she said to herself, "this money belongs to Mr. Rogers, and he's standing right next to it. What am I going to do?"

"Where's your Aunt Molly Primrose?" repeated Clark Rogers.

"Attending a neighbor's wake. Antley Theodd DuPuy—he jumped off the Huey P. Long Bridge."

I read about it in the paper. Do you usually entertain Jack Trenchard, wearing only a robe, and when your aunt's away?"

"Are you *nuts?* I wasn't entertaining Jack Trenchard. He walked in on me, just like you did. This is a heavy cotton chenille robe, not a thin see-through negligee. Do you want me to change?"

"Only if you put on a thin see-through negligee."

Kendra stuck out her tongue at him. "I'm sure I *said* in my note for you to *call* me, not come over here. Doesn't my note say that?"

"It does. I tried to call you, but all I got was a busy signal."

"I haven't been on the phone. We're on a three-party line, and the phone stays busy a lot. Even if you had gotten through, I couldn't have told you everything I wanted to, because, as I said, we're on a party line, and someone's always listening in."

"And because Jack Trenchard was here. Are you going to tell me what Allison Edwards' husband was doing here, kissing you?"

"No, I'm not."

"Last night you were kissing me; tonight Trenchard."

"I kissed you involuntarily."

"And Trenchard?"

She stuck out her tongue at him.

"Finish eating your sandwich."

"It's not fit to eat. It's cold. Can I fix you something?"

"No, thank you. I've had supper. What do you have to tell me about Osborne and Icelynn?" Clark sat down.

"I went snooping in Osborne's room, where I found a pad, with an impression on it. The impression read: DuPlessix Shipping Company, *S.S. Catherine Celine, sailing for London on April 13th.* Since Osborne wasn't at Berkeley, I figured he might've gone to England. I called the DuPlessix Shipping Company, and was given an appointment to see that Company's solicitor—Dubonette. I learned from Dubonette that Osborne *and his wife, Icelynn Farnsworth Osborne,* had, indeed, sailed for England."

"Icelynn—Osborne's wife?"

"Yes."

"What else did Dubonette tell you?"

Kendra repeated Dubonette's tale of how Osborne shoved Icelynn over the rail. "I told Dubonette you'd get in touch with him."

Clark nodded. "How horrible. It's hard to believe Kyle is dead, drowned at sea; was married to Icelynn and tried to kill her. When did you find all this out? And why didn't you tell me you suspected Kyle had taken a cruise instead of attending that seminar at Berkeley?"

"I found it all out yesterday, the same day Karl Erpelding arrived. After we got Mr. Erpelding settled in his room, you said for me to call it a day. I didn't call it a day. I did some investigating and, right after I had all this information, I drove straight to Willowwynn to tell you."

"And I wasn't home, so you decided to wait for me in the powder-blue bedroom."

Kendra started to deny that. "Don't deny it. After you left last night, I went to the powder-blue bedroom and found that Carol's bed had been slept in. I also found a handful of brown hairpins in the bed. He took the hairpins out his pocket, and handed them to her. She got up and threw them in the garbage.

"Are you going to tell me what went on in Carol's bedroom?"

"No. I can't." She sat down, taking a long breath. "I really don't want to tell you about Osborne and Icelynn, but it wouldn't be right not to. As I said last night, anything that concerns your dead wife—and Osborne and Icelynn concern her—I want no part of. But I got to thinking it over and decided it might be days before Dubonette caught up with you; so I wrote the note. So what do you think of Osborne and Icelynn being married?"

"I never dreamed those two were lovers. There were such differences: Personalities. Temperaments. Age."

"Well, Carol was twenty years Osborne's senior."

"Yes, but she didn't look or act it. I want to see their marriage license."

"I suppose your friend, Hippolyte Delacroix, the state attorney, can have the Marriage License's Department, of the States of California and Louisiana, run a check for you. Maybe they're not married. Maybe they just wanted to take a cruise together, as Mr. and Mrs. Osborne."

"I intend to check it out."

"You know, if they were married, Icelynn, as Osborne's widow, inherits all his worldly goods and wealth. That is if Karl Erpelding shows the court that new will."

Clark gave Kendra a hard look. "For not concerning yourself with my wife's affairs, you sure got your nose in her business."

Kendra smiled sheepishly. "Of course, there's another angle. I don't believe CR—that's what I call your wife—knew Osborne and Icelynn were married. I think those two somehow schemed to get CR to rewrite her will, leaving everything to Osborne."

"Yes—but Osborne had promised to marry Carol."

"That was no doubt part of the plan, plotted by Icelynn. All Osborne had to do was make CR fall in love with him, talk her into rewriting her will, and then kill her. Then Icelynn and Osborne could live happily ever after on CR's millions."

"Oh, come off it, Detective Applegate. That's too farfetched. Besides, Osborne left on the 12th."

"*The SS Catherine Celene* sailed at 6:30 a.m. on the 13th."

"And Osborne boarded the ship on the 12th. Carol died in her sleep early on the morning of the 13th. She died of heart failure."

"You don't know that. You're just repeating what Dr. Lopez, one of CR's ex-lovers, who only got half his clinic money, said. What if Osborne sneaked back to Willowwynn, slipped CR some sort of a poison potion that stopped her heart, and then beat it back to the ship? There's your means, motive and opportunity."

"You've been reading too many detective stories. Why, you've even thrown suspicion on Dr. Lopez, a man dedicated to saving lives, not taking them."

"Perhaps." Kendra was thoughtful for a second or so, and then went on: "I also visited the morgue. I spoke with Albert Lepardieux, Dr. Prestijockeymoe's pitiful assistant. I think Dr. Lopez is to blame for sending CR to the crematorium before she got her autopsy."

"Now you're talking as if Lopez set-up Lepardieux."

"I think he did. You didn't bother to talk directly to Lepardieux. Why?"

"Because Judge Edwards recommended that I didn't. I was too upset so Judge Edwards interviewed Lepardieux, and was satisfied that it was Lepardieux's neglect that caused Carol to be cremated before she got her autopsy."

"Did Judge Edwards tell you that Dr. Lopez had sent Lepardieux all the way to the French Market for coffee and beignets? Lepardieux is usually sent right across the street to Joe's Diner, for coffee and jelly doughnuts.—

"Did the Judge tell you Lepardieux wasn't there when the undertaker came for the body of Karen Rogers and got Carol Rogers' instead? Lepardieux also said Dr. Lopez knew that an autopsy, the day before, had been performed on a Karen Rogers, and that the undertaker was coming for her body that day—to cremate it."

"Whoa! Nothing was said about Lepardieux not being there to give the undertaker the final OK, or about a Karen Rogers."

"I didn't think so. — And did Judge Edwards tell you that Dr. Lopez thought the coffee that Lepardieux brought back wasn't hot enough, and personally reheated it? And that poor pitiful Lepardieux, after drinking some of it, fell asleep on the job, for the first time in his career. He even lost the file on your wife. To this day, he can't remember where he put it."

"Well, Detective Applegate, if you wanted to make me suspicious of Icelynn, Kyle, Lopez and Edwards, you've succeeded. Next you'll be telling me all four had had a hand in Carol's death," said Clark, darkly.

"Why not? I overheard everything you told Karl Erpelding about your wife. If all those things are true, then Icelynn, Kyle, Lopez and Edwards no doubt knew her as you did, and probably hated her. They might've gotten together to rid the earth of a crawling critter."

"She was a spider," mumbled Clark.

"And the only way to get rid of a spider is smash it; however, when both the spider and the smasher have two legs the law calls *smashing* murder, and some body's got to pay."

"All your theories are very interesting—but, if as you say, Osborne and Icelynn were in cahoots to get Carol's money and then kill her, why did Osborne try to kill Icelynn? Did the thought suddenly occur to him, as he was sailing along, for jolly ol' England, to pick a fight with his partner in crime, and shove her overboard?"

"Something like that. I think Osborne used Icelynn, and once he knew lots of money was waiting for him, he didn't need a wife any more, especially an old wife. He had his youth, his free education, lots of money and his whole life ahead of him. He wanted to wipe the slate clean and start afresh. Find a young woman."

"I must be out of my mind to sit here and listen to you, my secretary, the-would-be-female-detective, and think what you just said could've happened.— Tell me why do you suspect Dr. Lopez?"

"Money. I think he might've been obligated to Judge Edwards, and as a favor tampered with the time your wife died, or worse yet made sure she died. Money is a great motive for murder. Ask *Karl Erpelding* about that. I also think that audit of the SEF will find the *honorable* Judge Edwards guilty of stealing $800,000."

"I told the Judge that Karl is instigating an audit of the SEF, and he thought it was a good idea. Does that sound like a worried man?"

To herself: "If you heard Jack Trenchard, you'd know the Judge is sitting on the hot seat, squirming and sweating." Aloud: "Maybe you ought to call in your friend Delacroix, let him put the pieces of the puzzle together and see what he comes up with."

"I intend to."

"Before you call him, I think you should have Icelynn Farnsworth Osborne brought back to Willowwynn so you can question her; and then call in Hippo Delacroix."

"Must I remind you that I already have Karl Erpelding, a stroke victim, staying with me; and now you suggest I take in a near drowned victim. Do you want me to turn Willowwynn into an infirmary?"

Kendra shrugged. "I'd confront Icelynn with your suspicions—"

"Your suspicions."

"And then threaten her with you're going to turn her over to Hippo

Delacroix for further investigation. That ought to loosen her tongue a little."

"And when her tongue's good and loose and she asks to see Carol's will—"

"Laugh in her face. An accomplice to murder gets the chair, not millions. And while you're pulling Icelynn back to Willowwynn, I think you should drag the Sato family back. I think Josie, as CR's personal maid, might've seen something. Did Delacroix question Josie Sato?"

"No. He talked to her, but he didn't grill her." Clark took a deep breath. "Kendra"—this was the first time he had called her Kendra—"Kendra, I can't seem to get across to you, no one, not a soul, thought of Carol's death as murder."

"Did Delacroix, who also had an affair with CR, tell you that?"

"Are you now suggesting the state attorney had a hand in Carol's death?"

Kendra shrugged. "Who knows. CR might've got under his skin, and he, too, is now relieved that she no longer exits. Only her ashes remain in an urn, way off in San Francisco. Nothing to go on."

"Hippo was satisfied with Dr. Lopez' report."

"The report that Lopez turned over to drugged Lepardieux, who is blamed for losing *that* report."

"You don't know that Lepardieux was drugged. The report was rewritten, and it stated the same. Death due to heart failure."

"If you were so satisfied with Dr. Lopez' cause of death—heart failure—why did you order an autopsy?"

"Because in California it's automatic and, being a Californian, I ordered an autopsy. Hippo didn't even know I wanted Carol to have one."

"And when Hippo Delacroix found she was cremated instead and the cause of death—wasn't confirmed—what was his reaction?"

"Shock. He was shocked and sorry about the mix-up, because of my feelings, of course. Not because he suspected foul play."

"Of course. I don't suppose he told you that without a body the State has no case?"

"If Hippo had suspected foul play, he'd have investigated."

"Not necessarily. Remember no body, no case. He might've thought it would be a waste of the taxpayers' money to pursue the impossible."

"Why are you so sure that my wife was murdered? When I first met you, you told me you thought *I* had killed her for her money."

"I told you all that stuff, because I thought you were Mr. C.C. Bennett, the yardman, not Mr. Rogers. I was just speculating then."

"Last night and tonight you've told me you want nothing to do with anything pertaining to my dead wife. Yet—"

"I don't. But that doesn't mean I won't share the info I have with you, so you can pursue the investigation, if you want."

"So you no longer have me under suspicion?"

"I haven't completely ruled out that angle."

"Thanks."

" You asked— You seem to be fighting the facts, tooth and nail, that point to murder. The longer you wait the colder the trail gets."

"You're making it warmer. However, there are no hard facts. Everything you said so far smacks of circumstantial evidence."

"Maybe.—CR was *murdered*. I know it for a fact."

"Then, *you,* go give that fact to Hippo Delacroix."

"I can't. He wouldn't believe me. Besides, I've washed my hands of CR."

"I repeat, if you have a single fact, give it to me now."

"Kendra *Lou-u-u,*" called out Aunt Molly Primrose, the front door slamming behind her. "Where are *you-u-u?*"

A long pause, and then: "In the kitchen.— Mr. Rogers is with me."

Chapter Thirteen

Molly Primrose, wearing her wake-going black suit, black accessories and a white blouse, a relief, was groping her way toward the kitchen, clicking lights on as she went, called out: "You didn't even leave the gallery light on for me. The whole house is in darkness."

"I got a light in the kitchen," called back Kendra.

"A lot of good that's doin' me," grumbled her aunt, finally entering the kitchen.

"Good evening, Miss Applegate," smilingly greeted Clark Rogers, rising and bowing deeply.

Upon seeing the handsome visitor, Molly Primrose's irritation quickly disappeared."Why, good evenin', *Mr. Rogers*. What a surprise. The last time we met, I believe you called yourself *Mr. C.C. Bennett, yardman*," she reminded, smiling.

"I can tell you're pleased that *that yardman's* out of the picture."

She smiled broadly, her button blue eyes shiny bright and her apple cheeks glowing, expressed her delight. Then she turned to her niece, who was also standing and, of course, wearing only a robe in the presence of a gentleman caller, gave her one of those looks, that said *I raised you better*— Then she turned her eyes to the table. "I don't see any cups out. Would you like a cup of hot tea, *Mr. Rogers*?"

"I was just leaving; so I'll have to take a raincheck. Good night, Miss Applegate," again bowed Clark; then to Kendra: "I'll see you in the morning." He turned to go, heading for the back door.

"Mr. Rogers, you must go out the front door. It's too dark to tramp through the alley, to the front; or did you come in the back?"

"He came in the back," answered Kendra, before Clark could.

"Well, Mr. Rogers, you'll have to go out the way you came in. It's bad luck to come in one door and go out another."

"I'm not superstitious," chuckled Clark, "I'll go out the front."

"Well, don't forget your case."

"That case doesn't belong to me. Jack Trenchard left it."

"Was Jack Trenchard here?" asked Aunt Molly Primrose, her white eyebrows mounting high, her button blue eyes, narrowing.

"Yes," answered Clark. "He left as I arrived."

"I'll show you out," said Kendra through tight lips.

Molly Primrose watched the couple pass from the kitchen into Kendra's room. Minutes before, she had snapped on her niece's overhead light, not noticing the pile of articles on the bed. Now, standing in the kitchen doorway, she saw a pool of light shining brightly on Kendra's slip; garter belt; library book; and the briefcase, bearing the gold initials *CR*.

Clark, as his navy eyes spotted the briefcase, looked askance.

Molly Primrose, at first, only noticing her niece's slip and garter belt, looked embarrassed. It was bad enough that Kendra was dressed only in a robe, before a man; and now this. To the old maid's mind, a gentleman caller should never see such personal items, so she quickly snatched them up, hid them behind her back and retreated to the doorway.

After the unmentionables were safely out of sight, a brief silence followed, and then Clark frostily demanded:"How did my wife's briefcase get on your bed?"

Before Kendra had a chance to answer, her aunt, noting Mr. Rogers' icy tone of voice, reproachfully repeated the question: "Yes. How did Mrs. Rogers' briefcase get on your bed?"

"Obviously I put it there. I borrowed it."

"Who gave you permission to borrow Carol's briefcase?" angrily demanded Clark. "What's in it?"

"No one gave me permission.Papers that wouldn't fit in my purse."

Clark stepped over to the bed, snapped open the briefcase and pulled out a copy of his wife's will, along with the letter she had written to Karl Erpelding, his reply, and lastly, the love poems written by *E*.

"Where did you get these?" he demanded, waving all in Kendra's face. "Where are the originals, and what were you going to do with them? Blackmail me?"

Aunt Molly Primrose, twisting and twisting the slip and garter belt, behind her back, opened her mouth, but nothing came out; however, her eyebrows formed two question marks.

"Blackmail's not my style. I took them from your wife's desk yesterday, a little before Mr. Erpelding arrived. The center drawer of her desk has a false bottom; that's where I stumbled on the papers. I made photostatic copies. I put the originals back in the desk."

"*But why did you take them?*"

"I grabbed them on impulse because they're evidence that could help prove your wife was murdered." She shrugged. "Since then, I decided not to pursue your wife's killer."

"The coroner's record shows my wife died of natural causes. So who asked you to look for evidence to prove my wife was murdered?"

"No—one. I—er—"

By now Molly Primrose's button blue eyes were about to pop out her head, but her tongue was back in working order. "Mr. Rogers, my niece is young and full of foolish fancies. I'm sure she meant no harm."

"The truth to tell, I forgot about the briefcase being in the trunk of my car until today. I brought it inside to remind me to return it in the morning. I was going to tell you about the hidden drawer and the, er—evidence."

Clark, brow knitted, stuffed the papers back into the briefcase.

"Don't frown, Mr. Rogers," mumbled Aunt Molly Primrose, "you'll hurt your good looks."

Clark smiled a small tight smile; Kendra raised her eyes.

"Tomorrow, Miss Applegate, when you come to work, do you recommend that I lock up all desks and cabinets; the silver; the liquor and loose cigarettes?"

Kendra made no reply, but gave him a look that if looks could kill, Clark Rogers would shortly be at the undertakers. "Tante, show Mr. Rogers out."

"No. You show me out. I came to see you, and you'll show me out, or I'll find my own way out. Who knows, on my way to the front door, I just might bump into a few more items belonging either to my wife or to Willowwynn."

"Not in this house," icily replied Kendra through clenched teeth, reddening.

At the front door. "Miss Applegate, disregard anything we shared a short while ago," said Clark with curt finality.

For a second or so she stood quietly, her eyes blank and inward-looking, and then she drew her brows together and looked at him with a puzzled expression before she asked: "Did we share something?"—A knife turned in her heart.—"I don't think so. Good night, Mr. Clark Rogers."

A strange empty numbness washed over Kendra, as she closed the door. She took a deep breath and let it out slowly. "Well, that's that. Whatever might've been between Clark Rogers and me now will never be."

She returned to her room, where her aunt sat in the bedside rocker, silent and stricken, waiting for her.

"Tante, go on and jump me and be done with it.—I'd like to tell that Mr. Rogers where to get off at."

"*Kendra Louise Applegate*, tell me what's goin' on? I never heard the like of takin' Mrs. Rogers' briefcase without permission; and lookin' for murder evidence when there ain't been no murder committed. Of all things."

Kendra flopped on the bed, her back propped by pillows, her knees drawn up and, leaning forward, her chin on her knees, answered simply and truthfully: "I borrowed it. *I didn't steal it.* I know you believe if a person lies, he steals; and you think I lied about CR's ghost standing over my bed, telling me the answers are in the walls; her ghost forcing me to smoke and to drink."

Molly Primrose shook her head slowly and doubtfully. "Kendra *Louise,* I'm past my patience with that ghost business. So don't start. I'm not up to it tonight."

"I'm being open and honest with you. I *borrowed* the briefcase."

"All right.— Just tell me what Jack Trenchard's brazen face was doin' here? And you in your robe, visitin with' him, and later with Mr. Rogers." She shook her head. "Is that Jack's case in the kitchen?"

Kendra gasped. "*My God the case!*"

She jumped up and flew from the room, returning shortly, lugging the case with her. She flung it on the bed, and sat beside it. "I'll tell you about this, after you tell me what went on at Antley Theodd's wake."

"Don't put me off, Kendra *Louise*. What's in that case?"

"First, I want to hear about the wake. I have a feeling something bad happened tonight. Did it?"

"Humph! Somethin' bad happened at the wake, all right, but I also have a feelin' somethin' bad happened right here in my own house," she sniffed, all the while suspiciously eyeing the case.

"You tell me first, and then I'll tell you." Kendra scooted farther into the bed, her right leg under her; her left dangling over the edge; her aunt sat straight and stern looking.

"You're side-steppin' me, Kendra *Louise*. You're tryin' to hide somethin' beneath chitchat and gossip. If it takes that to get to the root of all this, I'll play your game." She cleared her throat.

"In a nutshell and in this order, shiny nose, Lolotte DuPuy, without stockin's or girdle and in her second best black dress, her white slip showin', said she was savin' her best black dress for the funeral, smelled of camphor and looked worn with worry and grief. She looked white as wax and colorless as lard; and more forlorn than usual. My heart ached for her. Then:

"Elderly Miss Tea Burn, Lolotte's boarder, surprised everyone by speaking. She said men and women are born into this world without permission; and when they die, that's usually without permission, except in Antlee Theaud's case. And death is always at an inconvenient time, for the dead person and for those who have to see to the dead person."

"That makes sense."

"Yes, it does. It was a lot for Tea to say. After Tea's recital, Ruthie Hartman and her son Giross arrived. Ruthie's still moaning' about movin' all the way to Met-tree. She misses not being able to borre the Wheelerhands' broom; and not gettin' cut roses from me. She asked for you. She said Giross was still crazy about you. She still says she thinks her son would hand you his head, if you'd have it."

Kendra winced. "Giross better hang onto his head. He might need it, if he wants to keep being Maison Blanche's *head* floor walker."

"Oh, she also said she heard that red-headed Annie Beaujolais, that young wider woman, with the twin boys, who lives around the corner next to Blanche DeVieux, is just crazy about floor walkers with boutonnieres in their lapels. By the way Blanche DeVieux was cryin' buckets, and I guess all those tears relieved her, but it didn't help Lolotte or the rest of us. While all this cryin' was goin' on Elmyra Foughtenberry butted in and said she'd never let her Junior marry no wider woman with twin boys.—Junior, for a few minutes, stopped by the wake on his way to work. He said hello. —Did I ever tell you how Leonidas Foughtenberry, Gawd rest his soul, determined to have the last word accomplished the almost impossible."

Kendra started laughing. "A hundred times, but tell it again."

"Leonidas Foughtenberry, ailing for years—Elmyra never believed him when he said he was sick—so unbeknownst to Elmyra, Leonidas found himself a stonecutter and had him chisel into the Foughtenberry's tomb tablet: *I said I was sick.*'" Both women laughed until tears came to their eyes.

"I'll never forget the expression on Elmyra's face when she buried Leonidas, and saw, for the first time, them words, *'I said I was sick'* carved in stone beneath her husband's name. Everybody who passes the Foughtenberry tomb laughs. Oh, before I forget, Elmyra also said if you knew how much money Junior made, you'd forget about dead Kenny Joe and go steady with her Junior, a real catch."

Kendra's mouth, eyes and nose all screwed together. "Tante, you know how I feel about homely Junior Foughtenberry, the sniffer and the spitter *and* the draft dodger. If he were Rumplestilkins weaving thread into gold, I wouldn't go out with him, let alone go steady with him."

"Well, Rosa Ganucci put both Ruthie and Elmyra in their places. She said Junior and Giross would have to get in line behind her handsome Sonny, now that Kenny Joe's dead. She said when Sonny comes home from Ko-reah she expects you'll be changing your name from Applegate to Ganucci. Does Rosa know somethin' I don't?"

"No. Sonny and I are *just* good friends.— Who else was there?"

"Ol' moochin' Mamie TuJax. She forgot her teeth, but didn't forget to wear her wider's weeds, from head to toe, which blended in with her knot of tar-black hair and beady black eyes.

"Shrouding herself all in black, that away, didn't help her yeller complexion, though it did make her look a little less plump. She sat next to Lolotte, sniffin'-'n'-a-cryin' about her dead Oscar. TuJax's been dead forty years, and Mamie said Antlee Theaud's wake brought to mind her own sad grief. She carried on like he just passed yesterday. Oscar was a bad husband, but in death Mamie's made him a saint.

"Mamie said she was grievin', this day, more than ever for Oscar. It seems her cousin, Camilla Mae Moutee, from Mamou, Loosieanna, who's been visitin', left today, but not before thankin' Mamie for puttin' that giant mayonnaise jar of ashes back of the toilet. Camilla Mae said she heard that ashes was great for brushin' your teeth.

"Mamie said Camilla Mae had been with her ten days, and used up a good cup of Oscar. She was just sick over it. Lolotte told her if she had buried Oscar, like a good Christian wider woman shoulda done, a cup of Oscar wouldn't have been used up for no toothpowder.

"After that, Mamie quit lamentin' losing a cup of Oscar, and started on how she loved Antlee Theaud, like a son. You know, I can't figure out why Mamie, her age against her and no money, ever thought she had a chance with Antlee Theaud."

"Well, Mrs. Springmeyer, in the same boat as Mamie TuJax, was also after Antley Theodd. I often thought each was praying for the other to die, to lessen the competition."

"I'm afraid you're right. Now I guess they'll have to go after ol' Otis Peckinpaw and his pension check, though they consider him too old to cut the mustard and soon a casket case. They say Otis, like ol' Tea Burn, just got in the habit of livin' and don't know how to quit. Anyway, Mamie repeated she loved Antlee Theaud like a son, and said Lizzie Slapp loved him like a gran'son. I'm glad Lizzie Slapp wasn't there to hear that."

"If Mrs. Springmeyer had heard Mamie making her a granmaw to Antley Theodd, there'd have been a row."

"None to match it. Finally, Mamie went to the dinin' room to eat, and discovered Lolotte had forgotten the pet cream and the mayonnaise her cousins had brought, from up the country. So she and everybody else had to eat dried baloney sandwiches on stale bread, and wash them down with strong black Creole coffee.

"Nobody minded except Mamie, though she kept peevishly sayin' 'Eatin' dry sandwiches and drinkin' black coffee makes me no never mind.' She kept goin' on about it until Lolotte reminded her that she was not only a vegetarian but allergic to milk and cream and mayonnaise, and to remember that respect she has for her insides."

'"Not at wakes, I ain't,' grumbled Mamie. 'When I'm home, I've got great respect for my insides, but once I cross the threshold of my double I lose all respect for my insides. I get a powerful craven for meat, milk and mayonnaise.'

"Why didn't Lolotte send Edna Pearl home to pick up pet cream and mayonnaise? You could've called me."

"If I'd have cawled you, you couldn't have come, with Jack Trenchard here, and Mr. Rogers showin' up on his heels. Besides, I told everybody you was workin' late. Tell one lie, you gotta tell ten."

"What about Edna Pearl?"

"Whinin' Edna Pearl—gettin' over a case of carbuncles—was complainin' about everythin'. Even the weather. She refused to go home and get those items for her mother. She said she couldn't bear leavin' Georgie B. Jonas, her husband-to-be."

"When did whining Edna Pearl get engaged? She's only sixteen."

"I don't know when Georgie B. Jonas popped the question. All I know is she announced her engagement at her Uncle Antlee Theaud's wake, and everybody, not usin' a lick of sense, made a big fuss fawnin' over her and her engagement ring."

"Who the devil is Georgie B. Jonas? How old is he? Seventeen?"

"Georgie B. Jonas is a quiet bachelor who is about thirty-five, but looks fifty-five. He's a long tall drink of water—all knuckles and knees—and has greasy, stringy brown hair. A nice mannerly type man—too good for Edna Pearl, if you ask me. It's just too bad Edna Pearl didn't take a little after her momma. Lolotte, when she was young, had buttermilk skin and beautiful wavy auburn hair. Now, of course, it's faded gray and wiry. Red hair gone gray is never pretty. I think Edna Pearl's daddy must've been a Jew. She's so dark, and has that big nose."

"I think you're right. What does her boyfriend do for a living?"

"Accordin' to Lolotte, he's a junkman who drives around in a nasty, ol', fallin' down, rusty red truck, collectin' junk. After Edna Pearl marries him, she's gunna become a junkwoman. Help him collect trash. They plan to marry this June, right after Edna Pearl finishes her sophomore year, which Lolotte thinks is plenny education for a girl."

"Lolotte DuPuy probably only went to the eighth grade."

"The sixth. Anyway, Lolotte's homely cousin, Bride Doppe, from

Cut Off Loosieanna—a little dark woman, with lit'le beamin' black eyes and a mouth brimmin' with buck teeth—a nothin', accordin' to Lolotte, a-puffin' one cigarette after another, makin' a stink and a stir. She kept tellin' everybody that she gave the pet cream and the mayonnaise, that Lolotte forgot to bring.

"After Edna Pearl announced her engagement, Bride Doppe proudly let everybody know that she had just remarried her husband, *Leeeeroy*, for the fifth time. Divorced him four times. Who ever heard the like of marryin' the same man five times? Not me.

"Any way, Bride told me and Beevie Tootey, from Bogalusa, another of Lolotte's cousins, another nothin', who brought the baloney and the stale bread, that it didn't matter how many times you married, because when you died there was no marriages in heaven. She said when she died she was just gunna be an angel. No wife to no man.

"BeevieTootey didn't buy that. She told Bride Doppe she might not turn out an angel on the other side. She just might turn out to be a little devil. Then Beevie Tootey asked Bride Doppe to tell her where that angel passage was in the Bible, chapter and verse. Bride Doppe said she didn't know where it was, but it was there; and then she fiercely turned on Beevie Tootey and snapped: 'You been married five times already yourself, so what you squawkin' about?'"

"'Yes, but all of mine died. I never divorced a one of 'em. Besides, I gotta plot that'll hold ten.' "

"'And the way you're goin', joined in Lolotte,'you aim to fill it.'"

"Everybody laughed. Soon after this outburst, Bea-actress Pujowl, her son, Poochie and his wife, Ruby Faye, arrived. They paid their respects and headed for the dinin' room to eat some of them dried baloney sandwiches and drink that black coffee. Bea-actress, that misery-maker, refused refreshment, gruntin' she didn't want no field hand grub. Lolotte said Bea-actress would no doubt grunt in glory."

"So what kind of misery did she make?"

"She went moseying over to the coffin, and right off started monkeyin' with it. She poked on the lid and started swearin'. When she finished, you'd thought she'd cursed her tongue out. 'Lolotte,' she hollered, 'this is a cheap coffin—weak.You shoulda made the guvment pay for a strong one. This is gunna crumble before Antlee Theaud does.'"

"'The guvment gave me enough money for a better coffin, but I went a different route.' replied Lolotte, sulkin' 'I had no choice.'

"'Being a fulltime cheapskate, you bought a cheap coffin so you could pocket the rest of the money, didn't you?' You always been on the look-out to see what's comin' to you. And takes what's not.'

"Lolotte mumbled somethin' about needin' every penny, and then Bea-actress shrieked: 'Lolotte DuPuy, open this heah coffin up so I can see Antlee Theaud's face. I don't believe you got your brother in this heah cardboard box. I think you're hidin' somethin'.'

"'I ain't hidin' nothin',' hollered back Lolotte. 'And even if I wanted to open that coffin lid, I can't. It's sealed. Go on and have a cuppa coffee with your son and nice daughter-in-law.'

"'I ain't havin' nothin' with Ruby Faye, that big heifer, with all her gums, throwed all her fat on me, that bitch.'

"'That ain't no nice way to talk about little Ruby Faye. She can't he'p it if she's got more gums showin' than teeth. And another thing she's been big as a minute for all the years I knowed her, so she couldna throwed no fat on you. If you ax me, you could use a little fat throwed on you. I bet soakin' wet you ain't more than 75 pounds.'"

"'Don't you tell me what I weigh, Lolotte DuPuy.' Then in a furious state shouted 'You done went and laid down with two different curs, and each time you got up you caught flees all over your horsey body and a baby in your big belly. Two bastards you brung into the world and, bein' the bitch you are, you won't tell who them two curs is.' Everybody got real quiet, cause they had forgiven Lolotte her sins, but was still mad at her for not tellin' her business."

"And that's something the good people of Starlight Street will never forgive, will they?"

"Never. She ought to name them men and be done with it. After that to do, I tell you it was some uncomfortable in that wakin' parlor. So we just ignored Bea-actress."

"Sounds like you all had a lot of comforting conversation. Did anybody go after Poochie Pujowl to see if he could get his momma under control?"

"Lolotte did, but Poochie said he couldn't do a thing with his 'crazy momma.' He said she'd pick a fight with the holy angels and the sacred saints, if she could see 'em.' Who ever, in his livin' life, ever heard of fightin' with the holy angels and the sacred saints—"

"Not me," said Kendra before her aunt could.

"Poochie also told us he's got just enough money saved up so he can take his momma to see Sister Elvira, that ol' voodoo witch. Sister Elviar, he said, is a horror to look at; but she knows her onions when it comes to gettin' rid of devils-'n'-demons."

"Maybe she can exorcise the soul of CR's ghost from my soul."

Aunt Molly Primrose gave Kendra a withering look. "Accordin' to Poochie, Sister Elvira kills and bleeds about 75 to 100 chickens, and lets their blood drip into a big bathtub, that's in her back yard.

"When the tub's full, she dunks her client into a blood bath. The blood forces out devils-'n'-demons, and purifies the possessed client. Poochie said he's now got enough money to buy all them chickens, so Sister Elvira can bleed 'em; and then plunge his momma into that purfyin' blood bath."

"Yuck! Poochie is going to have to gag and hogtie his momma before he'll get her into that tub of blood. She won't jump in on her own, that's for sure. What if old lady Pujowl, after her blood bath, is still raving?"

"Then Sister Elvira will anoint her with herbs, and then beat the tar out of her with a branch from a chinaberry tree, whose leaves will suck out the evil spirits."

"If you ask me, the whole scheme sounds pine black crazy."

"It does. Anyways, the next thing we all knew Bea-actress Pujowl who, all this time, had been monkeyin' around with Antlee Theaud's coffin, caused the bier the coffin sat on, to collapse, though she swore up and down she didn't do it. The coffin hit the floor with a terrible thud and the lid sprung open, and poor Antlee Theaud rolled out, barefooted, onto the rug. And who rolled out behind him was his cat—*Motel*. It scared us all nearly to death, and capped the evenin'."

"*I guess so.* But I thought you said Junior Foughtenberry dug a big hole under the fig tree, in Lolotte's back yard, and buried Motel."

"Lolotte dug him up. She said she got to thinkin' about how much her brother loved Motel and decided, before the coffin was sealed and whether Undertaker Shane liked it or not, to slip Motel in with Antlee Theaud. Lolotte said it hadn't occurred to her that a cat needed to be embalmed, same as a man. Motel was matted with maggots."

Kendra shuddered. "Well, what did they do with poor Motel?"

"They threw him, and as many of his maggots as they could scoop up, in the garbage can. Afterwards, Elmyra Foughtenberry, pitched a fine fit, because she said her Junior had worked in the rain to dig a grave for Motel but, in the future, she'd make sure that her Junior would never ever dig a big hole to bury another cat for Lolotte."

"Lolotte, and soon the rest of us, begged Elmyra not to tell Junior about Motel. She finally agreed. Anyway, Antlee Theaud looked dreadful on that red rug in his wrinkled, moth-eaten green army uniform, on his way to meet St. Peter and Gawd Almighty. Who ever heard of a coffin breakin' up like that before it rotted? Not me; though Bea-actress Pujowl said it would crumble before Antlee Theaud did.

"Lolotte said she hadn't bothered to press or mend her brother's drab uniform, because the lid would be closed and nobody would see Antlee Theaud except those on the other side; and she was sure 'spirits don't notice wrinkles and holes.' Alive or dead, I think Antlee Theaud, who was always well-groomed, would want to look his best.

"Anyways, Lolotte had to go get Undertaker Shane and three other men to put her brother back in his coffin. While this was goin' on moochin' Mamie TuJax must've forgot we all forgave Lolotte her sins, and started lecturin' her on sin and the sad sorrow it brings. She started to quote text, but Undertaker Shane interrupted, sayin' he could either tie up the coffin with big ropes or glue the lid down. Lolotte said she didn't mind her brother goin' to his reward barefooted and in wrinkled clothes, full of holes, but she objected to him goin' tied up with ropes.

"So in front of us all, Undertaker Shane glued the lid down. It took three big bottles of paste, which Lolotte had to pay for. Lolotte said, not her, but Poochie Pujowl had to pay for it, since his momma caused it. Poochie Pujowl said he couldn't pay, because all the money he had was tied up in them chickens for his momma's blood bath.

"Lolotte told Poochie before he left the wakin' parlor he better untie that money, forget about them chickens and pay up or else. Hearin' this, Otis Peckinpaw, dressed in his seersucker suit, mismatched socks and holdin' his Panama hat in his hand, came to the rescue. Without a word, he passed that big Panama hat of his, so everybody there could help pay for the paste, savin' a big row."

"I think Poochie should be responsible for his crazy momma's actions," muttered Kendra. "Don't you agree, Tante?"

"Poor Poochie told me he feels the same way, but his momma's breakin' him with plumbers. She keeps stoppin' up the toilet with big sheets of newspaper, pots of cooked grits, buckets of sand, gobs of garbage, or whatever she can get her hands on.

"She lives to stop up the toilet, the face bowl, the kitchen zink and even the tub drain. The plumber's at the Pujowl double nearly every day. Who ever heard of a woman gettin' her kicks over a stopped up toilet? Not me. All the women I know, except Bea-actress, feel sick when their toilets get stopped up."

Kendra shook her head. "No wonder when you say old lady Pujowl's name, people say: 'Oh, Bea-actress Pujowl,' and then shut up."

"Lately, everybody says Bea-actress Pujowl is pine black crazy, and provin' it every day.— Oh, before I forget, Otis Peckinpaw, later on in the evenin', brought bad notice to his quiet, respectable self. He spoke more than two words—eleven altogether, and directed them eleven words to his good neighbor, Miss Lavinia Gervaise. One of them eleven words was an ugly one."

"Mr. Peckinpaw's not a talker. I've never heard him waste words."

"Well, he picked a fine time to get wordy at a wake. Of course, in a way it was Miss Lavinia's fault. She told Otis Peckinpaw in her mush-mouthed way that she was sick of pickin' up poops, from her front yard, belongin' to his hound, Henry. Henry, she claimed, made pyramids of poops.

"She said she knew her dainty Miss Magnolia Blossom didn't do it, because Miss Magnolia Blossom's poops were tiny dainty piles. She said she got a special stick just to measure them poops. Who ever heard of measurin' dog poops?"

"Not me," again said Kendra before her aunt could.

"Then Miss Lavinia Gervaise elaborated on Henry's piles of poops. She said those poops were the biggest and the tallest she had ever seen on all Starlight Street. That's when Otis Peckinpaw piped up with his eleven words. 'Miss Lavinia, who made you the sh-- sheriff of Starlight Street?"

Kendra laughed out loud.

"While this hubbub was goin' on the two chicken hawks showed up, along with that reg'lar Mardi Gras, Lizzie Slapp. I must say Lizzie Slapp brought color to the wake. I learned tonight that Lizzlie Slapp is real tender hearted. She fell on her knees at Antlee Theaud's coffin and cried-cried-cried. She stopped suddenly, and asked who was dead in the coffin. From now on we all decided to call her Lizzie Slapp, the tender hearted, instead of the Mardi Gras.

"While Lizzie Slap cried her heart out, the two chicken hawks took over Antlee Theaud's wake, turnin' it into their late brother's and nephew's wake. They recalled every detail of Big Joe's death, and how Kenny Joe, the spit of Big Joe, was killed in action. To get them off that subject, I asked where Stella Dora was, and they told me and everybody else that Chariddy picked her up for mental reevaluation. I was shocked to hear it. They blamed it all on you. Said you had her picked up, which I know is a lie; so tell me what happened."

Kendra brought her aunt up to date on Stella Dora's reevaluation; and then her aunt said: "Now I want you to open Jack's suitcase."

Kendra snapped open the suitcase. "All this money—there's $150,000 cash here—is Jack's. He left it for me to hide. Also, that envelope on top the money, holds a cashier's check for $150,000."

Aunt Molly Primrose, pop-eyed and trembling, sat there as if paralyzed. Her tongue felt dry and heavy. She opened her mouth perhaps to say, 'Gawd save us', but no words came, because she was too stunned to speak.

"If Mr. Roger's hadn't walked in on Jack and me, I'd have forced Jack to take this money with him. This is stolen money from CR. The money now belongs to Mr. Rogers. Judge Edwards stole $800,000 from CR, and gave $300,000 of the stolen money to Jack, to marry his supposedly dying daughter.

"At the time, Jack had no idea the money was stolen. Right after his honeymoon, Jack came to see me. He asked me to wait for Allison to die, and then he'd marry me. We'd be rich."

"Gawd save us!" cried her aunt, finally finding her tongue. "Kendra *Louise*, get that money back to Jack as quick as you can. You could be clapped in jail for conspirin' with a thief."

"Jack's-not-a-thief. I'm afraid we're stuck with it tonight."

"No one in the Applegate family ever hid, under the mattress, more than $25.00. I'm terrified, with all that money—$150,000 cash! And that cashier's check! And stolen!" Molly Primrose blessed herself.

"Tante, please calm down. I'm not going to keep this money a second longer than I have to. I'd have gotten rid of it tonight, but in the circumstances I couldn't make a big stink in front of Mr. Rogers."

"No-o-o-o—no," she agreed. "If Mr. Rogers finds out, your chances with him are lost forever."

"I think my chances ended when he discovered his wife's briefcase on my bed. I'm surprised he didn't sack me on the spot."

"Well, what's done is done. We'll hide the money tonight in my armoire—it has a key; and tomorrow you make sure Jack comes and gets his money. Until this money is out of my house, it's gunna worry the heart out of me."

"I'll take care of it tomorrow."

"Well, see that you do.—Close that suitcase. Just lookin' at *that* stolen money makes my heart thud like a drum. Put it under the bed until I find the key to the front door. My parents, your dear grandparents—Gawd rest their souls—never had a key for the back door, but there's a strong bolt on it."

It took both women a good half hour to hunt up the old house key. It was big and slightly rusty; and when Molly Primrose put that rusty key in that rusty lock, it turned stiffly and with a groan.

Kendra pulled the back door shut with a bang and shot the bolt, while her aunt, despite the warm night, closed all the windows except those in their bedrooms and in the kitchen.

Jack's suitcase was then placed in Aunt Molly Primrose's armoire, which they locked, and the key they hid in the top bureau drawer. Afterwards the two women, though it was late, sat at the gatelegged table and had a cup of coffee.

"Tante, I know all this has been quite a shock to you, but there's more. You know I believed Mrs. Rogers was murdered, and wanted to bring her killer to justice. I still believe she was murdered, but no longer want anything to do with it."

"Thank you, Lord! Why don't you want anything to do with it?"

"Because she's used me in an abominable way. She's evil, and her killer did everybody a favor. I'd like to send her to her torture—hell."

"I know you have a flare for fiction, so don't tell me about ghosts."

"I won't speak of ghosts, but I will tell you something of the case. Attorney Karl Erpelding, CR's former attorney, of San Francisco, is at Willowwynn. He's CR's real father; CR died not knowing this. Mr. Erpelding, upon hearing CR was dead, suffered a stroke."

"Gawd save us!"

"Then there's CR's secretary, Icelynn Farnsworth, who was secretly married to CR's protege, Kyle Osborne. The two embarked on a secret voyage to England; and Osborne shoved his wife Icelynn overboard. He went over the side with her. She lived; he died."

"Gawd save us!"

"The papers I took from CR's desk and stashed in her briefcase say she was planning to divorce her husband and marry Osborne. She left all her money and property to Osborne, not to Clark Rogers, who has already inherited all his wife's money and property. Thanks to Judge Edwards reading the wrong will."

"D-d-did that will in the briefcase say that Osborne was to get all; Mr. Rogers, nothing?" asked Molly Primrose.

"Yes."

"Then the money belongs to Icelynn, not to Mr. Rogers. No wonder he don't want you snoopin' in his affairs."

"Yes. If Icelynn and Kyle didn't kill CR, and if Erpelding makes the new will public knowledge, Icelynn will be a very rich woman. Clark Rogers is trying to talk Erpelding into tearing up the new will."

Molly Primrose quivered all over. "Who ever heard the like of all this? Not me. I begged you not to get mixed up in any of this. I knew the day you went to Willowwynn somethin' bad would happen. And it has. And now you're in the middle of it. Gawd save us!" She moaned, paused and then went on: "When it comes right down to it, rich people don't go to jail. They buy their innocence. If that don't work, they frame some body—"

"I'm not going to jail; and I'm not looking for CR's murderer."

"D-d-do you think that dear man, Mr. Rogers, did it? I was so in hopes that you two would marry."

"Besides Mr. Rogers, I have another suspect in mind—I think Judge Edwards, a fake and a phoney, who fleeced $800,000 from the SEF, might also be a murderer. CR discovered he had been secretly and systematically stealing from her all along, and fired him. He promised, in writing, to give back the money by April 15th, if she wouldn't blow the whistle on him. He hasn't put it back; and Erpelding's here to prove he stole from the SEF.

"The Judge sent Jack here to blackmail me. He wants me to go through CR's desk and look for that note—I told him I already did that, and found nothing—and now he wants me to pyroot through Erpelding's briefcase, looking for that note. If I find it, I'm to turn it over to the Judge. If the Judge doesn't get his thieving hands on that note within three days, he sends Miss Stella Dora back to the crazy house—forever."

"Who woulda thought it was Judge Edwards who had Stella Dora picked up. Gawd save us!— Kendra *Louise*, you are going to go through Mr. Erpelding's briefcase, and see what you can come up with? For Stella Dora's sake."

"I can't do that. The Judge must come up with that $800,000, because Jack's not going to give him a penny of that money that's in your armoire." Kendra reached across the table and patted her Tante's ice-cold hands. "I've got more to tell you." She told all about Dr. Lopez and how he used Albert Lepardieux; she even mentioned Hippo Delacroix being one of CR's lovers.

"Any one of them coulda killed her," murmured her aunt. "I pray it's not that nice Mr. Rogers. I did so want him for you, Kendra Lou."

"It would've been nice. But not if he killed his wife.—"

"Like you, I don't condone cold-blooded murder. I wish Mrs. Rogers had died like the paper said, of natural causes.— We shoulda had lemonade instead of coffee. It's warm in here—downright hot."

"I know. I feel like I'm going to melt. I've got a couple more swallows of coffee, and then I'm off to bed."

As Kendra lifted her cup to her lips a sudden icy blast blew through the hot house, howling and rattling the windowpanes; the kitchen seemed to shiver and shake from the cold wind. As she was about to take a sip of her coffee, the cup tore itself from her hand, floated toward the ceiling, exploded in mid air and fell to the floor. Smashed to smithereens.

Startled beyond belief, the two women jumped up in a fright only to experience more of the same phenomena. Before either could utter a sound, the sugar bowl and cream pitcher were swept, by an invisible presence, from the table to the floor, exploding into a tiny million pieces. The teaspoons leapt from the table and floated around the room.

Slowly the two women, dumb and numb, sank back into their chairs, only to see the icebox open, and eggs, milk, butter, bacon and all manner of food, carried out, as though, by some unseen hand. Food, pots and pans and other objects sailed through the air before them, propelled—as far as they could see—by no human being. The lot went flying through the air crashing into the ceiling, walls and floor, upon contact, staining and slopping all; some almost bashing into Kendra. She ducked, and the hurling missiles smashed into the wall.

The very air in the kitchen swarmed with a sense of evil, as an icy red mist floated about; and soon that mist materialized into the foggy form of CR, who looked wild and fiendish. Seeing the ghost of CR confirmed Kendra's worse fears, and left her horror-stricken and breathless.The blood around her heart froze, as she eyed this terrifying evil thing of darkness and moving shadows.

Clark had said his wife was a trinity, three persons in one, and Kendra had never seen this wrathful person. This dead creature looked wild and angry. Foaming at the mouth mad. She couldn't speak, but her aunt, startled and shivering, her white plaits practically standing on end,whispered: "W-who are you?" Her words were barely audible.

"You know me, Miss Applegate," muttered Carol Rogers in a deep, almost masculine voice, which had a withering effect.

"I recognize your voice, Mrs. Rogers, but your head's turned into a goat," nervously murmured Molly Primrose. "I don't know what a dead goat wants with us."

CR waved a hand in a dismissing gesture, and turned to Kendra: "You see what power I have; so, unless you want more of the same, do as I say. Call Clark; Dr. Lopez; Judge Edwards; Eleanor Edwards; and Hippo Delacroix, and have them, in half an hour, gather in the music room, at Willowwynn, so you can question them about my murder."

Although Kendra was stunned that CR had the power to transform herself into an animal, and to make objects fly through the air, she didn't give into that power:"You burned your bridges when you used me to receive Kyle Osborne. I can't and I won't help you."

CR's head was still that of a goat; her hands and feet hoofs."You didn't tell me any such thing," yelled CR, with savage vehemence.

Frightened and overwhelmed by CR's display of such evil power, Kendra decided to try a different tact. "It's almost midnight—too late for me to call anybody. Even if I did call these people, I haven't got any overwhelming evidence against them. It's all circumstantial."

Without warning, she transmuted her head into a snake's, and she hissed; then she her turned her head into a fox's, and she barked; then her own head returned.

"Why, she's as smart as the Devil," whispered Aunt Molly Primrose, "and if the two met, the Devil would be morn-'n'-likely to get out of her way, then she out of his."

Kendra, her eyes never leaving CR's face, nodded slowly.

"I told you the evidence is in the walls of the powder-blue sitting room. The walls flanking the mantel," said CR, her voice a whiplash; her eyes blazing. "I want that evidence *now*. I want you to get into those walls *right now*. If you don't do as I say, then you will suffer the consequences."

Having seen the horror and terror and danger that swept through the kitchen, CR's dominating force in action, her body taking on different animal forms, Kendra wanted nothing further to do with *more of the consequences.*"How do I get inside the walls? Use a pix ax? I'm sure your husband wouldn't go for that; but tomorrow I'll find a way to search the walls," she added in a conciliatory voice.

"You can't get in them walls without Mr. Rogers' permission," whispered Aunt Molly Primrose. "You're dealin' with a ghost and a ghoul, so don't make no promises you can't keep.— I'm freezin', Kendra Lou, shut the winder."

She got up to close the window; it slammed shut on its own. At that moment, Kendra realized the evil spirit's soul had entered her body; and whatever CR had in mind, she was helpless against. CR was the cat; she the mouse. Kendra spun around and faced the cat.

The twomentally fought. After a long, one-sided argument, things began to happen. Slowly, CR's vindictive personality worked through Kendra's body; her hands trembling, as if in palsy; her face wrathful and distorted in pain; her eyes blinking and blazing. CR's dominating force, a vindictive force, compelled Kendra to do evil and destructive things against her will.

And what happened next, before Molly Primrose's startled eyes, was no longer strange, no longer impossible. It happened; therefore it was true.

Kendra, possessed of CR's supernatural force, became an ugly, terrifying, evil thing. Propelled by CR and against her will, she swept her aunt's beautiful old china coffee cup and saucer off the table to the floor, breaking it to pieces; while her aunt, freezing, watched in horror.

Next she easily lifted the heavy gatelegged table over her head and hurled it, with such force, against the window, that all the panes were knocked out. Still in a rage, she bashed the table, what was left of it, against the stove, breaking off three legs. The table was now horribly defaced and deformed.

From Kendra's lips came rapid mutterings, in a deep, masculine voice. This was CR muttering vile curses and blasphemies against Christ. Still cursing, CR, being in command of Kendra's body and armed with supernatural strength, lunged at the kitchen cabinet and convulsively shook it until all the cherished china crashed to the floor. The blue-and-white willows, castles and bridges were no more.

Molly Primrose, now knowing and believing that her niece was possessed, compelled and propelled by CR, stood by helpless, while her precious niece, pushed and driven by CR, wrecked and rampaged their kitchen.

CR's hands, inside Kendra's, ripped and gutted the beautiful petit point seats of the chairs belonging to the gatelegged table. Even the chair Molly Primrose sat upon was snatched from under her and gutted. Without warning, CR suddenly left Kendra's body with an explosive gush. The icy red mist, hovering before Kendra, savagely punched her in the stomach, before brutally shoving her to the floor. With these last ferocious and exhaustive acts, CR threatened Kendra, as she lay limp, at her Aunt Molly Primrose's feet:

"If you don't do as I say, I'll destroy this house, room for room and, in the end, burn you to the ground. Those are a few of the consequences."

Fear took on a whole new meaning for Kendra, as it sent a shudder of cold horror through her, all the way to her soul. She looked up at her aunt and saw she was gasping for breath; and knew if CR's bizarre behavior continued, it would surely kill her aunt.

"You win," conceded Kendra, and stood up, with shakiness and weakness. She felt as if she had just climbed off a merry-go-round and couldn't steady herself. The floor was spinning, and through turning shadows, she saw her aunt had fainted.

It was all a nightmare. Kendra knelt at her aunt's side and rubbed her cold hands, pleading: "Wake up, Tante, it's OK. It's over."

After a while Molly Primrose blinked open her button blue eyes, and slowly rolled them around the kitchen. "Kendra Lou, where's that evil spirit?" she asked, pale cheeked and short of breath.

"That devil's gone.— Tante, God must've been really some mad at me when he let me go to Willowwynn and meet up with the ghost of Carol Rogers."

"This is the Devil's doin's, not Gawd's. I told you Nell Miller told me the devil wasn't born in New Orleans, but he grew up here."

"Don't talk. You're icy cold and sweat's pouring from you brow. Here, let me help you to bed."

Seated in her bedroom rocker, Molly Primrose stammered: "Kendra Lou, what I saw strengthens your case in favor of ghosts, and weakens mine. You look white as a sheet, and your hands are icy cold and bloody. You look sick bad."

"I'm all right. And you?"

"My heart's beatin' so fast, and I can't catch my breath.— "

"I'm calling Dr. Herbert."

Half hour later, Molly Primrose Applegate was taken, by Dr. Herbert, in his black Roadmaster Buick, to Touro Infirmary, for treatment of a mild heart attack. Kendra followed.

At the hospital, Dr. Herbert said Molly Primrose would remain hospitalized two weeks or longer, depending on how she did. He also said she couldn't have any excitement or visitors—and then sent Kendra home. It was 3 a.m.

Chapter Fourteen

Filled with anguish and grief, and deeply depressed, Kendra, feeling weak and drained, stood like a wilted flower, swaying on a slender stem, in the middle of her battered and broken kitchen, surveying the damage and disorder.

Seeing the broken blue-and-white china, her aunt's treasure, and some day to be hers, along with the smashed gatelegged table and chairs, and the kitchen cabinet, all ruined, not to mention her aunt's heart attack and, knowing she had had a hand in it, felt like her heart was being torn to pieces by a wild beast with cold claws.

How long she stood there, sick and swaying, she didn't know. Finally, sheer exhaustion drove her to bed; and she fell into a fitful sleep until meowing woke her. She raised up on her elbows, blinking her eyes, and saw Sholar Picarara seated in the bedside rocker, rocking and watching her with glowing green eyes, like two jewels set in his narrow face; his plumy tail was wrapped around his front paws.

"Thank you, Sholar, for coming in." Before she could say anymore, the telephone rang; and she got out of bed, groaningly, and slipped one foot into a slipper, the other slipper she couldn't find—it had to be under the bed and she didn't feel like wriggling under the bed and wriggling out—so, wearing one slipper, she limped to the phone. It was Nell Miller calling.

"Kendra honey, where's your Aunt Molly Primrose? It's ha'f pas' nine, and she ain't at work yet. She's never been late before."

"My aunt's in Touro with a heart attack," sleepily explained Kendra, adding: "she can't have visitors for a few days."

Nell expressed her shock and sorrow, and then put Molly Primrose's boss on the phone. Mr. Straveinia said he was sorry, but quickly reminded Kendra that her aunt wouldn't be paid for time lost. He also said if she was out too long, he couldn't hold her job. To this, Kendra reminded Mr. Straveinia that her aunt had given Holmes forty good years, and that this was her first major illness.

Mr. Straveinia said he was well aware of that, and then put Nell back on the line. Nell said when she did visit Molly Primrose she wouldn't say anything about the possibility of her losing her job. Kendra thanked her and hung up. Before she had a chance to limp away, the phone rang again. It was Clark Rogers. "Miss Applegate, aren't you coming in today?"

"No," exploded Kendra. "My aunt's in Touro with a heart attack, and it's all your vile wife's fault." She slammed down the phone, limped to the bathroom and, using the jelly glass that she kept her toothbrush in, drank some water. She refilled the glass, went back to her room and set the glass on the night stand. Sholar was sleeping in the rocker. Noiselessly, she crawled back in bed, and almost instantly fell asleep. She dreamed of Jack Trenchard and CR fighting on a landing at the top of a broad staircase.

The argument intensified, and what happened next was quicker than a cat could blink an eye. CR picked up Jack and hurled him over the railing. Kendra screamed. Her own scream wakened her. When she opened her eyes, she screamed again.

Sauntering into her room was Clark Rogers. He was wearing a light gray business suit, a crisp white shirt and a navy tie with red stripes, his brown-gold hair was tumbling on his forehead.

"I didn't mean to frighten you," he said, with a smile.

Sholar Picarara was on the nightstand drinking Kendra's water.

Kendra raised up on her elbows, blinking and stammering: "H-how did you get in here?" she demanded, her eyes dark and smoldering.

"I knocked and knocked. I knew you were home because—"

"The Dodge is out front." She gestured with an air of exasperation.

At that moment Sholar took a flying leap from the nightstand onto the rocker, causing the cushion to slide askew. He kneaded the crooked cushion, and then curled up on it and watched Clark closely.

"I tried the front door—it was open—so I let myself in. I figured you were in the kitchen. I had no idea you were still in bed. It's almost noon. I thought you said your aunt didn't want that Italian cat in her house." Sholar gave him an insolent look.

Kendra fell back on her pillows, stifled a yawn and pushed a tangle of brown-gold ringlets out of her pale face. "Since my aunt's in the hospital, Sholar must've figured I needed company. I'm glad he's here. What do you want?" she mumbled scathingly, as she pulled up the sheet close to her neck, covering most of her pale pink PJ's.

"I want you to explain that cockamamie statement you made over the phone about my dead wife causing your aunt's heart attack."

Frowning, Kendra turned over and buried her face in the pillows.

"Don't frown, you'll ruin your good looks."

"Go to hell," came the muffled reply; "and while you're at it look at the kitchen."

In a few minutes Clark returned. "So you've been vandalized. That shouldn't keep you from working. Turn over and look at me."

Kendra rolled over, sat up, propped her back with the pillows and glared at Clark. "The lone vandal was your dead wife," was her icy reply. Then she began to sizzle: "CR turned her head into a goat; then a hissing snake; then a barking fox; then she broke all our beautiful china, tore up the kitchen. I bet if she'd have broken your precious *Spode*, you wouldn't have whined *I've only been vandalized.*

"You know what that china and the gatelegged table *meant* to us. My aunt's heart couldn't take seeing your demon wife destroy our treasures. Your vicious wife even punched me in the stomach and knocked me to the floor. She threatened to wreck the rest of our home, if I didn't do what she wanted—bring her killer to justice."

His navy eyes narrowed the faintest trifle. "I'm sorry all this happened to you; but I haven't got time to indulge your ghost fantasy. No doubt you've been reading about the Middle Ages."

"This is no ghost fantasy. Whether you like it or not, there's something demonic about what went on in my kitchen, and your wife was behind it. She wanted me to call a gathering of her enemies to Willowwynn, and question them about her murder. I tried to put her off by telling her it was midnight—too late to call people, but she wouldn't go for it. She became violent and vicious. She went berserk."

To himself: "When Carol's violent personality surfaced, no one could put her off." He cleared his throat. "Surely, Miss Applegate, you and your aunt imagined—"

"*Your wife* as our destroyer. No way. Your dead wife, Mr. Rogers, is still on earth. Her spirit is so corrupt and tainted and polluted with wickedness and lust that the Devil won't open the gates of hell to let her in. She's got to die again, die a second time, to get into hell."

"Have you seen and talked with my dead wife?"

"*This very day.—*"

"Was that the first time?"

"*No.* My first day of work, the day it stormed, I met your wife face to face in her sitting room. She told me she had been murdered, and instructed me to find her killer. She said, as soon as I found her killer, she'd pass on to the other side."

"Did she say who killed her?" asked Clark, obviously disturbed.

"No. I did, however, ask her if you had killed her, but she wouldn't answer. She wouldn't name her killer."

He sneered. "I didn't kill her."

"That same day, she also told me she needed a young body to inhabit. She took over my body; and when she enters my body we share a mental oneness. Through me and by using my body, she gets her pleasure by proxy. *.But no more."*

Clark looked incredulous.

"I saw CR again, on my second day of work, in bed." She made no mention of Kyle Osborne being in bed with his dead wife. "The third time I saw her she was in my bedroom, standing over me, yelling all the answers were in the walls of the powder-blue bedroom. She said if I didn't get these answers, find her killer, I'd suffer the consequences.

Early this morning, midnight to be exact, was our fourth encounter. This visit, as I told you, she demanded I call a gathering of her enemies, to Willowwynn, or suffer the consequences. I called her bluff, and suffered the consequences. She took over my body, and savagely tore up our kitchen."

"Then you were a party to this debacle?"

"A controlled party. When CR enters my body we are one, and she's in control. She makes me do things against my will. The first time we met and talked, she smoked, via my mouth, one Camel after another and guzzled liquor. When she finished I was drunk. I thought for sure you'd fire me."

"I almost did. Did she cause your hands to get all those scratches?"

"Yes. My hands are scratched up from CR forcing me to rip the seat covers off our chairs. It's not just my hands that are hurt. I've had a bad shock."

"And money can soften a shock. You expect me to believe this fantastic tale, plus pay for the damages, don't you?"

She stiffened and her eyes flashed darkly. "Money can't soften what happened to me and my aunt. To our home. Yes, I expect you to pay for your dead wife's dirt. Also, I think my transformation, before my aunt's eyes—she saw I was CR and CR was me, and then CR turning herself into all those animal heads, and the violence that took place in our kitchen—caused her to collapse. I think you should pay damages."

All this time, because Sholar had the rocking chair, Clark had been standing, a ferocious frown on his handsome face. "That cat's listening to every word I say—"

"Well, you don't have to worry about Sholar repeating anything."

"I'm not so sure about that.—Come, Sholar, it's time you went out."
He picked up the cat and dumped him out the window.

"Come back anytime, Sholar," called out Kendra.

Clark sat in the rocker, lit a cigarette and inhaled deeply. "The court
would call your story rubbish, and deserving of nothing but contempt.
You wouldn't get a penny." He took another drag.

Her bottom lip trembled, and she stammered: "We can't replace those
things. They belonged to my grandmother." Tears filled her eyes. It took
a few seconds for her to calm herself.

Meanwhile a long ash formed on Clark's cigarette. He knocked it off
in a dish that was on the bedside table. "I'll make some coffee."

"There're no cups to drink out.— Why didn't you fire me? I know
you smelled the smoke and liquor on me."

"Because when I looked at you, you were Carol all over again. Even
your eyes had turned green; and, when you said you had smoked and
drank involuntarily, I knew something was wrong. I guess deep down I
suspected Carol had a hand in it. I half expected you either to kiss me, ask
for a cigarette or a drink.

"Carol always kissed me after she had done something disgusting.
That kiss was suppose to turn her bad deed into a good one. After she'd
bestow her redeeming kiss, she'd ask for a cigarette and a drink"

"The other night I kissed you, or rather Carol kissed you." To herself:
"She didn't have time for a kiss and a drink, Osborne was upstairs waiting
for her."— Aloud: "If you suspected Carol had a hand in my smoking and
drinking and kissing you, you shouldn't have any trouble believing what
went on here last night. And another thing, I overheard you say to Mr.
Erpelding 'I really and truly believe Carol No. 2 and No.3, even in death,
could return to earth, to perform wicked deeds.'

"'You frighten me, Clark,' said Mr. Erpelding, 'when you say such
things. You sound as if some one would have to stick a stake in the hearts
of Carol No. 2 and No. 3, to kill Carol No. 1.—Kill the trinity.'"

"And you said, 'I do believe it.' "

He ran his hand through his hair. "When I checked the powder-blue
bedroom/sutting room this morning—I've been doing that since the day
of that bad storm—I found it, as usual, a mess."

"That should tell you your dead wife's still hanging around, haunting
Willowwynn and having temper tantrums. After she destroyed us, she no
doubt went home and did a number there."

Clark stood up and paced. "Gussie Rae Booker refuses to be alone in
Carol's rooms, so I have to stay with her while she cleans up. It was

almost noon when she finished, and you hadn't come to work yet. So I called."

"I didn't get home from the hospital until 3:00 a.m., and then, for I don't know how long, I just stared at the kitchen. I just couldn't make it to work to day. Besides feeling frightened and emotionally drained, I feel too weak to move. I'm sore and bruised from being battered by CR. I feel too sick even to go see my aunt. I know she's going to have a lot of questions, and I don't have any answers."

"Don't worry about your aunt. I'll check on her."

"She can't have visitors."

"*As her nephew, I'll see her*. Right now I'm going to call Xariffa and have her make up a thermos of coffee and a tray of food for you. It'll be ready by the time I pick it up. While I'm gone, take a hot shower, comb your hair, get rid of those childish PJ's and put some lipstick on," he ordered, and left.

When Clark returned, Kendra, bathed, barefooted and seated on the edge of her bed, was wearing a white cotton nightgown, with pink silk grosgrain ribbon encased at the waistline. The neckline yoke, all pin-tucked, was fastened in the front with six tiny pink pearl buttons, and the collar was embroidered with pink rosebuds. The rest of the embroidery on the gown was six inches deep all around the hem. Her aunt had made this for her twenty-first birthday, and she had put it in her hope chest, expecting to wear it for Jack Trenchard.

No longer having any hope of a husband and because eagle eyed Clark Rogers had made that smart alecky remark about her PJ's being childish, she chose this beautiful gown.

She looked lovely in it despite her pallor. Her brown-gold hair was piled on her head in a pyramid of curls, some escaping at the nape of her neck, while a million tiny tendrils framed her pale face. Her amber eyes were sad and circled.

"You look pale but pretty. —I stopped at Touro and saw your aunt. She has color in her cheeks, that's more than I can say for you. I told her I was taking care of you, and with a couple days rest you'd be good as new. She was relieved, and said she wanted you to rest and not to visit her until you really felt up to it.

"She made no reference to last night's scene. Nurse Cramer, ran me off, saying your aunt needed her rest. Now relax and eat your lunch."

Kendra ate, from a mahogany luncheon tray, a roast beef sandwich, with lots of lettuce and tomatoes and mayonnaise; and, for dessert, a dish of hot bread pudding, with a whiskey sauce. She drank two cups of steamy Creole coffee. Clark sat in the bedside chair and watched her.

"That was delicious. Thank you. I feel much better." She looked at her tray. "You shouldn't have brought your good Spode."

"It's not my Spode any more. It's yours. I know it can't replace your blue-and-white willows and castles, but it'll have to do for now.— By the way, Delcie Doty, a cousin of Gussie Rae Booker, forty times removed, will be here shortly to clean the kitchen. Also, Louie Winner, who has a refinishing shop on Freret Street, will pick up the pieces of the gatelegged table, the chairs and the kitchen cabinet."

"I don't think all the kings men and all the kings horses can put the gatelegged table back together again."

"Louie can. He's also bringing a Duncan Phyfe table and chairs for you to use until your table has been restored. Oh, yes, and a small buffet, oval shaped, all glass front and sides."

Kendra looked stunned. "T-thank you very much."

"Now that all that's out of the way, how about telling me why you really came to Willowwynn, and how you knew Carol's apartment was called the powder-blue bedroom?"

Kendra, still seated on the edge of the bed, took a deep breath and let it out slowly. "My aunt always says there's never a wrong time to do the right thing. So I'm going to do the right thing, right now, and if you fire me, that's my tough luck." She took a deep breath, and began again:

"The first time I came to Willowwynn was to get my foot in your door. I tried to deliver your wife's suit, which, as you suspected, wasn't the suit, but turned out to be a boxfull of paper. I vowed to meet and marry a rich widower, because Jack Trenchard had gotten himself a rich wife."

'Ahhhh, I know when I first saw you. It saw the day Allison Edwards married Trenchard. I was hurrying to her wedding—Carol was already there—and you were running away from the Edwardses' patio, crying. You fell in the street; and I helped you to your Dodge."

"So, after nearly a year, I finally know who the kind man was who helped me."

"I wanted to drive you home, but you wouldn't let me."

"I had to be alone."

"Why were you running away from Allison's wedding. What's Jack Trenchard to you?"

"The exact same day and hour that Jack was marrying Allison, he was suppose to be marrying me. When he didn't show up, I thought he had been detained by Judge Edwards, his employer, so I went looking for him.

I found him promising to love, honor and cherish Allison, when he was suppose to be making that promise to me. It was a jolt."

"I'd say that was quite a jolt."

Kendra nodded slowly.

"Then you were never engaged to Kenny Joe?"

"Never. He loved me and I loved him—like a brother. The same day Jack jilted me, I had another jolt. A telegram came saying Kenny Joe had been killed in action. Kenny Joe's father, after reading that bad news, dropped dead."

"I'm so sorry. That must've been horrible for you."

"I don't know how I got through it. Anyway, when I did get through it, I decided to marry a rich man. A widower, without a family. I watched the obituary notices, and finally stumbled onto you."

"And you knew Willowwynn was bigger and more beautiful than Greenwood Manor; and was next door to where your Jack lived. Easier for you to thumb your nose at Trenchard, eh?"

Kendra flushed. "Something like that."

"And where did your Aunt Molly Primrose stand in this scheme?"

"Out of it completely."

"A very wise lady.—Now tell me where you heard the words powder-blue bedroom? Did Carol, when she was talking to you, making you drink and smoke, tell you?"

"No. Right after Jack married Allison, Kenny Joe's mother, Stella Dora Wheelerhand, was committed to the State Insane Asylum, at Jackson—"

"Your aunt told me about that raw deal."

"Well, after that trip to Jackson, I got pneumonia. My fever went high and, in my delirium, I dreamed, every night for a week, a haunting dream of a mansion, only the inside, not the grounds. If I had seen the grounds, I'd have recognized, when I brought that box full of paper, Willowwynn as the mansion in my dream. Anyway, a voice in the dream, which I now know to be CR's, kept saying 'All the answers can be found in the powder-blue bedroom.'

"So, by mid-morning, of the first day I went to work for you, I recognized Willowwynn as the mansion in my recurring dream. Knowing the floor plan, from my dream, I ran upstairs and found the powder-blue bedroom/sitting room. As I already told you, that was the day CR entered my body. She goes and comes at will—she uses my left lung to breathe. My body, at her choosing, is host to her soul.—"

At this point in the conversation, there weren't enough adjectives to describe the shock and horror that mingled in Clark's navy eyes.

"CR's soul lodges itself a fraction to the left of my heart." Kendra placed her right hand in the middle of her chest, a little to the left, and pressed hard, as if she could feel CR's soul. "My soul is on the right." She dropped her hand in her lap.

"Er—what does Carol's soul look like?"

"Misty. Tiny. Weightless. Oblong shaped."

Clark was very thoughtful.

"I can tell you don't believe me. Neither did my aunt until—"

"I don't disbelieve you. I believe if anyone could come back from the dead, it would be unpredictable Carol. Let's get back to your jilting. Did Trenchard ever tell you why he married Allison?"

"Yes. He came to see me soon after his honeymoon, and told me Judge Edwards had paid him to marry Allison, because she'd soon be dead from a rare blood disease. He said, after she died, he'd marry me. We'd live happily ever after—rich. I told him to get lost."

"Well, I'm glad you're not sitting around waiting for Allison to die. According to the gossips, the only illness that plagued Allison would end in nine months. A few weeks before she married Trenchard she lost Claremont's baby. She's still seeing Claremont. The child she's presently carrying also belongs to Claremont."

Kendra sucked in her breath. "It sounds like Allison is mad for Claremont; so why didn't the Judge force him to marry his daughter. Why pick on poor Jack?"

"Claremont wanted his bride to bring him a million dollar dowry; and he's not going to marry until he finds a girl with a million bucks. Allison was pregnant and needed a husband in a hurry; the Judge talked Trenchard into marrying his daughter—for peanuts."

Kendra felt sick. She wanted to scream: "The $300,000 is your money, and it ain't peanuts." Aloud: "Are you sure the baby Allison is now carrying isn't Jack's?"

"Claremont claims it; though he was drunk at the time."

"God save us! as my aunt would say. Jack just found out that the Judge lied to him about Allison having a rare blood disease, and that really hit him hard. The poor guy has no inkling that Allison was in on the scheme, nor does he suspect she's not carrying his child. He's so protective of her, though he claims he doesn't love her. I pray he never finds out the truth. It would destroy him."

"You seem overly concerned for Trenchard's feelings. He did you wrong, remember?"

"I'm only concerned because I don't think he can handle this kind of betrayal."

"What he can handle and what he can't handle is not your worry, unless you're still in love with him."

Their eyes met and held. Kendra dropped hers first.

"Last evening, when I walked in on you two, you were kissing."

"He was kissing me." She raised her eyes.

"Are you over him, or are you carrying a torch?"

She shrugged. "For a while I hated him, but now I feel terribly sorry for him. He's been badly used."

"In this case, I'd say what goes around comes around."

"You're right, of course." Kendra was thoughtful for a few seconds. "There's something else: Jack got Judge Edwards to get Mrs. Wheelerhand released from Jackson. I thought on her own recognizance; but, I've learned it was under the Judge's recognizance."

"*Wow!* Exum Edwards does nothing for nothing."

"At the time, Jack told me that, but I didn't think it possible that a bigshot Judge would ever need a favor from a peon secretary."

"What does he want?"

"He's just had Mrs. Wheelerhand picked up and sent to Charity for a mental reevaluation. If I don't find the note he wrote CR telling her he'd pay back the $800,000 he stole from her, and return it to him in the next couple days, Mrs. Wheelerhand goes back to Jackson."

Clark opened his mouth to speak, and then shut it.

"If I find the note, I'm turning it over to Mr. Delacroix. And another thing, Mr. Rogers, I *didn't* steal your wife's briefcase. I borrowed it."

"So you could fill it with evidence against me, that I killed Carol."

"No. Who ever the killer was. Not just you. You know, I bragged to you and to my aunt about my being able to be a detective. Crack any case. Well, anymore, I don't think I'm such a hotshot sleuth.

"In fact, I've got my fill of being Sherlock Applegate. All I ever wanted to do was go some place and have a good time. I was forever dreaming of being a detective or a secret agent—chasing spies all over Europe, meeting people, never being broke, eating exotic foods—seemed so romantic. So exciting. In a sense a social.

"Of course, I've learned dreaming is wonderful; reality is horrible. I want out; but the only trouble is I can't stop now. I told CR I wouldn't bring her murderer to justice, but I've got to. If I don't, CR stays on earth to plague me forever, not to mention she might destroy the rest of my aunt's home. I wish another ghost would kill CR."

Clark took Kendra's hand. "We'll work this nightmare out. We'll bring Carol's killer to justice, and then you'll be free of her, if I have to stick a stake in all three of her evil hearts."

She looked up at him from under dark lashes, and her eyes were sad but beautiful. "Then you believe me; and I'm not fired?"

"I believe you; and you're not fired."

They were both silent and thoughtful, and then Clark began again: "I want you to know Carol was a thoroughly rotten wife. Living with her, these past two years, has been hell. After she died, all I felt was a secret relief. I often told myself if I ever got free of Carol, I would never ever become seriously involved with another woman.

"And then you came along. I had to get to know you, and what a better way than to have you work for me. So I took you away from that old poop, Henri Prosper. What I'm saying, Kendra, is our friendship could easily blossom into something beautiful. What do you think of that possibility?"

"I like that possibility more so than my aunt."

They both laughed. "She really didn't like the idea of my being a yardman, did she?"

"No. She was going to try to talk you into going to Delgado, to learn a trade."

They both laughed again. "Kendra, last night, I noticed you tried to make Trenchard take that suitcase. What was in it?"

"I—I can't tell you—yet."

Clark stood up. "But you will tell me some day?" He pulled Kendra to her feet, stepped back and looked at her. She was tall and lissome and graceful. A breeze blew through the window, and the air was soft and sweet with the breath of honeysuckle and roses. She brushed back a stray curl from her face. He drew a deep breath. "Do you know how lovely you are?" She smiled; and he pulled her to him. His arms tightened around her and his mouth found hers— When he released her, she was breathless.

"Now I want you to rest," softly ordered Clark.

For the next few days, Kendra rested. During this interval, Delcie Doty had whipped the kitchen back into shape; the gatelegged table and chairs and the kitchen cabinet were carted off to Louie Winner's refinishing shop; the Duncan Phyfe dining table, chairs and buffet were put in place; Clark came with picnic lunches; Aunt Molly Primrose made progress; and so did Kendra, especially where Clark was concerned. Daily he lavished her with gifts; and by the end of the week, he had proposed. They'd marry in October. He'd give her an engagement ring, a round saphire with diamonds, after her aunt came home from the hospital.

On the Monday after CR's ferocious attack, Kendra, dressed in a pale green silk dress, a gift from Clark, her hair a mop of brown-gold gypsy ringlets, her amber eyes clear and beautiful, her cheeks, no longer pale, but stained the color of a rich rosy pearl, looked the picture of health, and was feeling much better.

She was ready to leave for work when she had a phone call from Jack Trenchard. He said he was on his way over, and before she could say, *"No,* I'm on my way to work," he hung up.

In a few minutes a knuckle knock sounded at the front door. "Come in," said Kendra, standing in the doorway. "You must've been just around the corner when you called. What' s wrong? You sounded terribly upset. You look ill.—Sit down."

Handsome Jack, wearing a navy sports coat, light blue shirt, cream silk pants, no tie, and navy loafers, sat in the occasional chair, where proud peacocks walked among red poppies; Kendra on the blooming sofa. "You look gorgeous."

"You didn't come here to tell me how I look. What's wrong?"

"I've had a terrible jolt. A bitter jolt. And it's all come about through my own stupidity. I could kick myself for being such a fool."

Kendra braced herself. "Tell me what happened, Jack?"

"Allison told me she knows her father gave me money to marry her. She also knows I've withdrawn that money from the bank."

"Who told her?"

"Cameron Claremont. His father owns the bank. She demanded I put the 300 G's back today, or she'll tell her father."

"So you're here to pick up your money—give it back to the Judge."

"Hell, no. That money's *mine,* Kendra. I earned it. When I got that money, I had no idea the Judge had stolen 800 G's from Carol Rogers, and my 300 G's was part of that stolen money. Later, I accidentally came across a secret file and learned that the Judge had embezzled all that money from Carol Rogers. As you pointed out and suspected, right off the bat, the 300 G's he gave me was taken from the stolen money. It was too late to holler fire, because I was already married to the Judge's charming, well-educated daughter."

"Who turned out to be Allison the terrible—anything but charming and appealing, eh? And to think she's an aristocrat, a debutante."

"Don't rub it into the bone. The debutramp laughingly told me the baby she's carrying belongs to Claremont. From the beginning the Judge had plans for me. He used me two-fold. First, to give his whorin' daughter's baby a name. Second, to take the rap, if Erpelding's auditors prove embezzlement."

"It sounds like he planned it early on."

"Before he even took me into his law firm he was forever telling me how lucky I was to be an orphan. I disagreed. I wanted a mother and a father. I wanted to know who I was. He said that was silly, because if I ever got in trouble, there'd be no family name to drag through the mud. I guess when he found me he thought he had the perfect scapegoat, to save his *good name.* I've been betrayed. Used. Terribly used. You can't imagine how that feels."

"I think I can," replied Kendra, with a terrible terseness. "I'm sorry, Jack, really sorry. So what are you going to do about all this?"

"I'm flying tonight to Mexico City. I want you to go with me, Kendra darling."

"What!"

"I love you, Kendra, I've always loved you. I only married Allison to get the big bucks so, when she died, we could marry and be rich —have a beautiful life together. You always talked about wanting to go some where and have a good time. London. Paris. Vienna. You wanted to travel and meet exciting people. Well, I wanted that, too; and now we can do it.

"Two days ago I got a Mexican divorce from Allsion, by proxy. Alfredo Galvez, of Mexico City—I'll be working in his law firm—handled the divorce. I told Alfredo I'd be bringing my bride with me; and for him to have the paperwork ready. All we have to do, when we step off the plane is sign a paper and we're married. I did not give Alfredo your name, because if anything goes wrong I don't want your name dragged through the mud.

"After we pick up our marriage license, the next day we'll fly to Eurpoe. When we return to Mexico City, I'll go to work for Alfredo, Alfredo and Trenchard, for $10,000 a year."

Kendra whistled.

"With my salary, plus $300,000 bucks in the bank, we can live like kings. Have a palace, with servants. You can have your six kids. Say you'll come with me, darling."

Kendra flamed. "Do you honestly think, after *what you did to me*, I'd marry you?" she challenged.

"Yes," he replied, all his heart in his eyes. His eyes that morning reminded her of purple pansies, soft and velvety. "You love me. I love you. We belong together. We were meant to marry. I was never happy with Allison. You were always on my mind. I know you haven't forgotten me, cause I couldn't forget you. Why, to forget you would be like forgetting myself. Not to love and want you would be like not wanting to love myself. I want to make it up to you, darling. I want to give the rest of my life to you. Come with me, and love me again."

This declaration instantly created a storm in Kendra's heart, along with sunshine. Her head was spinning like a crazy top. She was engaged, to Clark; but the killing thing was she hadn't forgotten Jack. It was like he said. To forget him would be to forget herself. And she *did* love him. She had never stopped loving him, even though he had humiliated her; had caused the bottom of her world to fall out. Had caused her a grief that was on the same par as losing her parents before she got to know them. In spite of all this, he had a hold on her. She loved him, and love conquered all.

Jack stood up and removed a tiny blue velvet ring box from his coat pocket. He then sat beside Kendra, took her hand and slipped the ring on her left finger. The diamond solitaire was set exquisitely in thin gold filigree, and flanked by sapphires and pearls.

"It's five karats, darling. I hope you like it."

Her startled eyes stared at the ring, and then met his eyes, and he was smiling at her. She couldn't speak, nor could she jerk the ring from her finger, as her mind told her to do; and then tell Jack he was too late because she was already engaged to marry Clark Rogers.

She sat still and stared into his eyes, and then down at the ring. "It's beautiful," she murmured, raising her eyes to his. He put his hand beneath her chin, and his eyes swallowed her up. Blue/purple clung to brown gold. In the next moment she was in his arms, their faces pressed together, and then they kissed. After their lips met she wasn't sure of anything.

"My darling, I love you," he murmured, and then kissed her again..

"And I love you," whispered Kendra, feeling ablaze and reckless and ready for anything. "I'll go with you, darling."

"Our plane leaves at midnight. I'll be here at ten. I have two briefcases to carry the money. We'll divide the cash."

"Darling, slow down. You're going too fast for me. I'll go with you, but I can't fly away tonight and leave my aunt. She's in the—"

"Bring her with you."

"I wish I could. She's in Touro with a heart attack, and probably will be there another ten days. And another thing, I'll have to give Mr. Rogers notice." To herself: "God! How is Clark going to take this!"

"To hell with Clark Rogers.— I'm sorry about your aunt. She always seemed so healthy. When, when did her heart attack happen?"

"Oh, a few days ago." Kendra made no mention of the circumstances surrounding her aunt's heart attack.

"I'm truly sorry to hear that. —Darling, you'll just have to get private nurses for her. When she's well, she can come live with us."

"Jack, you know my aunt would never leave Starlight Street, let alone move away from New Orleans. New Orleans is the world!"

"Then she'll have to learn to live without you, because I'm not going to live another day without you."

They were back in each other's arms, kissing, whispering words of love, and kissing again. "I think my aunt will understand."

"She will, darling. Stop worrying. You said yourself she'll be in the hospital another ten days. She's in good hands. Besides, you can't do anything for her until she comes home. I tell you what. We won't go on our honeymoon until she's released from the hospital. You can fly home and get her settled. Then we can go on our honeymoon."

Everything Jack said was sensible. Slowly, Kendra, her emotions all in a jumble, gave in. They kissed again. Then: "Well, darling, you've dispensed with my aunt; so what do I do about clothes? I'll need a new dress for my first plane ride, and a trousseau."

"Wear the dress you've got on. You're a knock-out in green."—

She wasn't about to wear Clark's dress to elope with Jack. "Oh, no. I'll come up with something else," firmly replied Kendra.

"Whatever you wear, I'll love. When we get there, I'll buy you a trousseau—anything you want. But for the flight, pack *only* your toothbrush. I'm not taking anything but my shaving gear, and it's in the trunk of my car. I'll leave it with you. I didn't want to take any chances being seen leaving Greenwood Manor, with a suitcase, by the Judge's henchman, Dom Puttuci.

"Allison as much as told me, if I don't put that money back, by morning, she's going to sick that spy, Puttuci on me. She also told me my convertible belongs to her father. I have a phoney title."

"I suppose your partnership in the Judge's law firm is also phoney?"

"You got it. I don't ever want to hear the name Edwards, nor do I want the Edwardses ever to know where I am and who I'm married to."

"I don't blame you. Jack, has the Judge forgotten about that note he wanted me to steal for him?"

"I did that on my own. The Judge knows nothing of you. I had Mrs. Wheelerhand picked up, using the Judge's name. I've arranged for her release—tomorrow."

"*Jack-k-k,* how could you?"

"Lawyers do whatever it takes. Yesterday, Dr. Lopez gave Erpelding a knock-out shot, opened his briefcase and found the note the Judge had written to Carol, promising to pay back the money by the 15th of April."

"Erpelding told Clark Rogers he didn't have that note."

Jack shrugged."Obviously Erpelding was playing games with Rogers. I'll get my shaving kit and the briefcases."

"I'll get the case with the money."

Moments later, Jack returned with his shaving kit, briefcases and a box of chocolates covered with white parchment paper and tied with silver ribbon. "For you, darling."

Kendra tore open the box and popped a chocolate in her mouth while she watched Jack divide the cash: $75,000 went in her case; $75,000, plus the cashier's check for $150,000, went in his case. "I'm also putting our tickets, my will, the file folder, that can put the Judge under the jail, my diary and everything else that can hang him, in my briefcase. If the Judge should try to implicate me in any way, I'll turn over all these items to Delacroix. These items are my savior."

"Let's hope and pray the Judge won't move against you."

"I'm ready for him, if he does.— All done."

They put both briefcases and Jack's shaving kit in Molly Primrose's armoire and locked it; and then kissed long and lovingly. "I wish I could stay right here, holding you, until it was time for us to leave for Moisant."

"I'm for that."

"Can't, darling. Got to clear up a few things at the office."

Moments after Jack left, Clark phoned. "Is everything all right, darling? I thought you'd be here by now. In five minutes I'm leaving for Bay St. Louis to clear up some business. I've left you a stack of typing. but if you'd rather come with me—"

"*You know I'd love to go with you,* but I think I better go see my aunt, and then head for Willowwynn. Type my fingers to the bone."

He laughed. You make me sound like a slave-driver. I should be back in town around ten. I'll call you."

"Yes. Call me. That'll be fine."

"You sound odd. Are you sure everything's all right, darling?"

"Everything's just fine. I'll see you when you get back."

Trembling, Kendra hung up. "It's like Tante says, 'tell one lie and you gotta tell ten.' I'm not going near Willowwynn. I'll write him a note and mail it from the airport."

Kendra finally left home and went directly to the hospital, dreading telling her aunt that she was leaving that evening for Mexico City, with Jack. To her relief, she found her aunt asleep; and therefore only stayed long enough to read the card on a beautiful bouquet of flowers, sitting on the bedside table. They were from Clark.

To herself: "How thoughtful and sweet of him."—Her aunt turned over. Kendra held her breath. "She's still sleeping. Good. I'll write her a letter and explain everything." Softly and tenderly she blew her Tante a kiss; and a few minutes later she was seated behind the wheel of her Dodge. She pushed in the clutch, turned the key on, pressed the starter button and floored the gas pedal. Nothing happened. With the choke out, she tried it again. Still nothing happened. She tried it one more time before glancing at the gas gauge. It was below *E*.

"Dammit, I'm out of gas. How stupid of me."

An hour later, Kendra, with a full tank of gas and five dollars less in her pocketbook, threw the Dodge in gear and headed for a leather shop on Canal Street. She bought a small overnight case; then she went home to get ready to leave for Mexico City.

Chapter Fifteen

At home she packed her new overnight case, and then tried to write a note to her aunt and to Clark. She balled up half a dozen sheets of paper before she decided she'd just wire her aunt from Mexico City; the five-line note she wrote Clark took forever to compose, and it still wasn't good enough. She put the note in her pocketbook, to be mailed at Moisant.

A few moments later the florist delivered a corsage of brown orchids, from Jack. She kissed the corsage, and put it in the icebox.

The day dragged on and on. Time wouldn't budge. She put some records on; even Frank Sinatra couldn't distract her.

So she read the file that Jack had boasted could put the Judge under the jail. "He'd be a fool to go after Jack, with such incriminating evidence against him."

Next she read Jack's diary and found two odd entries: *Beverley Reynolds, a love, but so glad she's married; Maria Galvez, thanks to her pulling strings, I now have a partnership in her brother's law firm. Mexico City here I come.*

She closed the diary, returned it and the file to Jack's briefcase, just as the phone rang. It was Jack. "Are you all set? Did you get the orchids?"

"Yes, darling. They're beautiful." It was on the tip of her tongue to ask why he was glad Beverley Reynolds was married; and what kind of strings had Maria Galvez pulled for him; and the cost? Instead she said: "How did you know to send brown orchids? They go perfectly with the cream suit I'm going to wear."

"I'm clairvoyant." He laughed— "Is your toothbrush packed?"

"Yes, darling."

"I love you. I'll be there in about five hours. I'm coming in a cab, so have the briefcases in the parlor."

"I will, darling—"

"By the way, old Father Landry, the priest who ran the orphanage where I grew up, is waiting in the outer office to see me. I always take time to see him. He's got a middle-aged woman with him, by the name of Mary Placide, who looks like a penny waiting for change."

"What do they want?"

"Probably some free legal advice.— I'll pick you up at ten. Then we'll be together forever, my precious love." He made a kissing noise, and so did she; and then he hung up.

Five minutes later the phone rang again. It was Clark, calling from Bay St. Louis. He had no idea she hadn't worked that day. He just wanted to talk. She had a devil of a time getting rid of him. The next time the phone rang it was the hospital. The night nurse said her aunt was restless, and suggested that Kendra come for a five-minute visit, even though it was eight o'clock and visiting hours were over.

Quickly she slipped out her wrapper into street clothes and left.

"Tante, what is it?" asked Kendra, breathless and on pins and needles to get back home. She kissed her aunt, and sat down.

Molly Primrose studied her niece closely. "You got high color. There's light and laughter in your eyes. Mr. Rogers droppin' by later?" she asked, approval shining in her button blue eyes.

"Shoot no. It's eight-thirty."

"Kendra Lou, are you eatin'? You look like you fell off. What did you have for supper?"

"I'm eating fine. I haven't fallen off. I ate two sandwiches, for supper," she lied. "Tante, what's on your mind besides my eating?"

"That ghost. I always told you there was no such things as ghosts; but I saw the ghost of Mrs. Rogers change her head into different animal heads. I saw Mrs. Rogers, inside you, wreck-'n'-ruin our kitchen. I saw her knock you down. My dahlin' niece, I'm so sorry I doubted your story about the ghost of Mrs. Rogers appearin' to you, makin' you smoke-'n'-drink." She took a deep breath. "Knowin' what an imagination you got, I thought you imagined it all. Please forgive me," she pleaded.

Aunt Molly Primrose's apple-cheeked face was the color of skim milk—bluish. Kendra stood up. "There's nothing to forgive, Tante."

"I've tried to forget it, but I can't. I'm feelin' terribly guilty about how I went around with my eyelids sewed up and my ears stopped, regarding that ghost business. As you know, I believe in the vengeance and justice of Gawd. That ghost's is gunna get hers."

"Tante, please forget it. This kind of talk isn't helping your heart."

"I know. I've been a bundle of nerves all day over a feelin', a premonition that somethin' bad's gunna happen, and you're gunna be in the center of it.—"

"*Me-e-e-e?* That's ridiculous, Tante, I'm not going to be in the center of anything bad. Now stop worrying. I love you." To herself: "It's uncanny how she knows when I'm up to something she doesn't approve of."

Before Molly Primrose could continue, the nurse came in with a glass of warm milk for her patient; Kendra waited while her aunt drank her milk, kissed her good-bye and left. On the way home, she dropped the note she had written Clark into the mail box in front of Katz & Bestoff, instead of waiting until she got to the airport.

She drove home, got undressed and redressed, slipping into a burnt orange silk blouse and a cream colored shantung suit, her fast-beating heart hammering away.

"My God! Jack'll be here in ten minutes.—*The corsage*!" She dashed to the icebox, got the orchids and sat them on the parlor table, along with the tickets. Next she peeped out the front door. No sign of Jack. She paced; she left off pacing and sat on the sofa, the briefcases at her feet. All aflutter, she waited breathlessly for Jack, in an agony of anticipation.

The phone rang. She nearly broke her neck running for it. It was Clark, saying he had just driven in from Bay St. Louis, and wondered if she were still up? She said she was in bed. In that case, he said he'd see her in the morning. She hung up and muttered: "Well, by mid-morning he'll have my note. Know I'm in Mexico City, with Jack."

She waited for Jack. She peeped out the door; Sholar Picarara slipped in, almost unnoticed. She paced; Sholar sat in the occasional chair, with the proud peacocks and red poppies, and watched her. She prayed. By eleven o'clock, she knew he wasn't coming, and the night turned blacker than it was. By midnight, she knew he had humiliated her for the second time.

Feelings of anger, shame, hurt and disgust assailed her. She vomited. Afterwards, she put the orchids back on ice, the tickets in her pocketbook and the money in the armoire; and then, still wearing her shantung suit, sat in her bedside rocker, Sholar, curled at her feet.

She hadn't been seated five minutes when she heard hideous laughter. Laughter that sounded like it came from the mouth of a demon cast into the depths of hell. Laughter that shrieked of triumph. Laughter that threatened more consequences, if CR's killer wasn't brought to justice. Laughter that told her that wicked and wild CR was in the room with her. Evidently, Sholar also heard the laughter, for the fur stood up on his back. He yowled; then leaped through the open window.

The laughter abruptly stopped. Kendra, looking around expecting CR to appear, was greatly relieved when she saw nothing. So she rocked on. And between rocking convulsively, crying, calling herself a fool, and dozing, the black night passed.

A little after six, the phone rang. It was the hospital. Her aunt wanted to see her right away. Heartsick, Kendra, still in her shantung suit, undressed and redressed; and went to Touro; the night's turmoil written all over her face.

When she walked into her aunt's room she found her rigged to an oxygen mask, the green cylinder tank standing to the side of the bed. A frightening sight. The pallor of her aunt's face had a strange tinge to it. "Tante, a-are you having trouble— breathing?"

Molly Primrose lifted the mask. "A little; but not enough to need this contraption. What's all this costin'?" she asked, a little breathless.

"Don't worry about the cost," murmured Kendra, as she leaned over and kissed her aunt, and then sat in the bedside chair, frowning at the oxygen apparatus.

"Don't frown, Kendra Lou, you'll hurt your good looks. You don't have a drop of color this mornin'.—I can't help but worry about the cost—*and* about *you*."

"Remember, Tante, you're here to get better not to fret about money or about me. Please put that mask back on. I want you to live to be a hundred."

"I'll probably do that. I'll probably live to have another heart attack," she said, scornfully.—"Did you notice the pretty bouquet of cut flowers Mr. Rogers sent me?—not the roses—they came yesterday afternoon, and they're from Jack Trenchard. I wonder how he found out I was in the hospital?" she asked, suspiciously.

At the mention of Jack's name, Kendra started trembling. "The flowers are lovely," she said unsteadily. "Tante, put your mask back on, and tell me why you had Nurse Pearce call me here this morning?"

Molly Primrose, her blue eyes thoughtful and troubled, looked hard at her niece, and realized the young woman had suffered a new wound, and it was deep. "Kendra Lou," she faltered, "a-are you still hopin' for Jack?"

Kendra shuddered. She had shuddered before, but this shudder would lead to a series of shudders that would shake and shatter her very soul. She made no reply.

"So you still care." There was a sorrowful and sympathetic pause. "All these months you've been pretendin' you forgot your loneliness and your loss. Pretendin' you were over him, haven't you?"

Salty tears rolled down Kendra's face and crept into her trembling mouth.

"You can thank your lucky stars you've been shut of him," said her aunt in a low soft voice, her button blue eyes all seeing. All knowing. "I've got some bad news for you," she went on in a mournful tone. "Not long after you left me last night an amberlance brought in Jack."

At first Kendra was too stunned to speak. It had never occurred to her the reason Jack didn't show up was because he was sick. Her relief broke in a little laugh, as she dried her eyes. "Tante, how do you know that?—Are you *sure* it was Jack?—What's *wrong* with him?"

"The night nurse told me Judge Edwards' handsome son-in-law was across the hall, seriously injured. The aud thing about it, she said, none of the Edwardses came with him, not even his wife. Of course, she's about to have her baby, so that must account for it."

"Tante, please, what-happened-to-Jack?"

"This is the strange part, Kendra Lou, Nurse Pearce said the Judge told the amberlance Doctor that Jack tried to commit suicide, because he was about to be arrested for embezzlement. He said Jack, at the top of the stair landing, threw himself over the bannister; but Jack told the Doctor a different story. He claimed he was picked up by a red mist and pitched over the bannister. He said, as he went flyin' through the air, he heard the voice of Carol Rogers laughin' like a demon. Nurse Pearce said the doctor called Jack's tale 'insane.'

"If Jack dies and can't defend himself, the Judge will get away with pinnin' that embezzlement rap on him.— Do you have any idea why the ghost of Carol Rogers wanted to kill Jack Trenchard?"

Kendra looked stricken, and shuddered again; however, this time the blood around her heart froze, as she said a silent prayer. "Please God, no! Don't let Jack die. You know how much I want him." Aloud: "I don't know why she'd want him dead." To herself: "Except to stop me from getting away from her. I knew when I heard that triumphant laugh she'd had her way again." Aloud: "The Judge is lying, but I won't let him get away with it. Is Jack conscious?"

"Off and on. He's bleedin' inwardly. When he comes to he's quiet. When he's out of it, he screams for, brace yourself,— *Kendra dahlin'*; not for his wife. A dyin' married man callin' clearly for a single young woman, a virgin, looks bad, real bad on her part. Like she's his woman," said her aunt in an indescribable mournful tone.—

"You know, Kendra Lou, you're not bone of my bone or flesh of my flesh, but you're still mine, and can tell me anythin' and everythin'. Do you have somethin' to tell me?" she asked, her button blue eyes full of expectation and suspicion.

Kendra shook her head negatively.

For a while, Molly Primrose didn't pursue it. She changed the subject. "Just thinkin' of that horrible night and what went on in our kitchen scares the lights and the liver out of me. Have you done anythin' to find Mrs. Rogers killer?"

"No—not yet. Forget that night. I told you our kitchen, thanks to Mr. Rogers, looks like new. So forget about it."

"I can't forget about the kitchen, and I can't forget about what's goin' on across the hall. The nurses are in deep discussion—winkin'-'n'-wonderin'—who *Kendra dahlin'* is. The nurses only know you as Miss Applegate, so you're safe unless he starts yellin' his head off for *Kendra Dahlin' Applegate.* If he does, you'll be branded a loose woman, and your chances for a husband, especially Mr. Rogers, are all over. So don't go near him," she cautioned, darkly. "Promise?"

"Cross my heart and hope to die. I won't," mumbled Kendra. She stood up and took her aunt's spidery fingers in her hands.

"Oh, Kendra Lou, your hands are still full of bo bos from that hateful ghost." She brought both hands to her lips and kissed them. That's when she noticed the ring. "*Oh, my, what a beautiful ring!* Are you and Mr. Rogers engaged?" she asked, beaming.

Before she could answer a terrible cry came to their ears. The voice crying out belonged to Jack Trenchard: "Kendra darling...I love you...I'm coming...Wait for me!...I got to talk to you...."

"*You see, you see! There he goes again! Did you hear that?*" whispered Aunt Molly Primrose, her button blue eyes full of bewilderment and suspicion, the ring completely forgotten. "I never heard the like of a married man carryin' on like that toward a girl who's not his wife. He should be yellin' his head off for his wife. There'll be talk about this," she added darkly, nodding her head.

"Tante, put your mask on, and don't worry about anything."

"You're not leaving already, are you? You just got here."

"I know, but I've got to get to work." She kissed her aunt, put the mask back on her and left. Once outside her aunt's door, she stood tense, cold shivers running up and down her spine, and waited for Jack to call her name. Soon he screamed "*Kendra,*" and, judging from the sound, she knew which room to enter.

A moment later, she crept cautiously into that room. Long-limbed, handsome Jack lay inert and limp, his feet extended beyond the bed. Even battered, broken and gasping for breath, he looked gorgeous.

Kendra swallowed hard. Her throat was dry. She went to his side and bent over him. She could feel his heart beating against hers, and the pulse was irregular and weak."My darling," she softly whispered, "I'm here...Can you hear me?"

Jack fluttered open his blue/purple eyes, and it took a little while for him to focus on her. With trembling lips, she ever so gently kissed his forehead, eyes and mouth, murmuring over and over: "I love you, my darling. I always will."

"My precious one, I was so worried you might've thought I left you in the lurch again," feebly murmured Jack, in an almost inaudible voice. "I knew you'd find me. I knew you'd come."

"What happened, darling?"

"The ghost of Carol Rogers, with the strength of an ox, picked me up and hurled me over the bannister so hard, that when I landed below on the marble floor, the impact crushed my insides and broke my back. No one believes dead Carol Rogers did this to me."

"I believe you."

He had a coughing spasm. "Kendra—"

"Don't try to talk, darling. Rest."

"I can't rest until you know what to do. I want you to give my diary and the file I have on the Judge to my lawyer, Maria Galvez. I want Maria to tackle the Judge, not you. She knows how to handle the big boys, and the Judge is one of those big boys. When she gets through with the Judge, Johnny'll walk free."

"*Who's* Johnny?"

"You must go see Father Landry and Mary Placide"—his voice drifted away.

"You mean the priest and the woman you saw yesterday?"

He nodded. "Promise me you'll go to St. Matthew's rectory today, see Father Landry, and then give Mary Placide the money she needs."

"Who is Mary Placide? Why does she need money?"

"She'll tell you. *Promise!*"

"Cross my heart and hope to die. I promise, darling."

"Good.— Kendra, we're not ever going to Mexico City."

"*Yes, we will. You'll get better.*"

"No, sweetheart. Dr. Lopez, my doctor, is in the Judge's pocket; and, even if I could make it, the Judge, all the Edwardses, want me dead; the Edwardses always get their way." A deadly silence followed.— Finally Jack broke it: "I want you to take the money and go some where and have a good time. Forget your troubles."

Tears welled up in her eyes, and a knife twisted in the pit of her stomach. "I can't have a good time without you," she choked.

"You must."

"Please, Jack, don't give up. Don't leave me here to dream alone. *Please!* I love you too much. I want you with me, *always.* "

"You don't know how much I'd love to stick around and dream with you, but it can never be, my precious one." Silence. Then: "Carol Rogers did me a favor," he said more to himself than to Kendra. "Stop crying and kiss me. That's better." He was quiet for a few minutes.

"Remember," he began again, "the money's yours; but give Mary Placide what she needs. Don't give the Edwardses a penny. *Promise!*"

"*I promise...I promise!*" choked Kendra, her eyes brimming.— "Tell me how dead Carol Rogers did you a favor?" she prompted.

"Make sure Johnny goes free, even if you have to sacrifice my good name," was the last thing he said before he slipped into unconsciousness. Kendra couldn't rouse him. So she just kissed and caressed him until she heard the voice of Dr. Lopez in the hallway, say: "He's the same, Exum." — She hid in the closet.

The two came into the room. "How long does he have?" asked Exum Edwards.

"I think he's going to make it. If he does, he'll be in a wheelchair for a while; then his old self again."

"Allison doesn't want to be chained to a husband in a wheelchair, even for a little while. She had planned, after the baby was born, to divorce Jack and marry Cameron. Death is preferable to divorce. Jack's an orphan; his passing won't grieve anyone. Actually, we'll be doing him a favor by giving him a shot. You needn't worry about an autopsy, Allison won't request one.—By the way, Emile, I meant to tell you Robichaux construction, this minute, is pouring the foundation for your clinic. Let's go see it."

The two left the room, and Kendra, soul sick, was conscious of nothing but a bleak emptiness and a sepulchral silence. She kissed Jack good-bye, and soon slipped, unnoticed, from his room. How she made it to her Dodge and slid behind the wheel, without collapsing, she didn't know.

With fumbling fingers, she unfastened the gold chain with the locket that dangled about her neck, took off her diamond ring and slipped it on the chain, next to the locket that held her parents' pictures. She refastened the gold chain around her neck; and now both the locket and the ring would bang her heart—*forever.*

Grief and a sore sense of outrage mingled inside her, she drove to Canal and the river, parked the Dodge close to the wharf and watched a banana boat being unloaded. Soon tiring of that, she took the Canal Street Ferry across. The day was hot and humid, and the river breeze, that cooled her face, smelled damp, cemetery damp. She rode the ferry back; and then drove to the French Quarter—Jack's favorite place. The sun was shining and she was freezing.

She parked the Dodge and walked from one end of the French Quarter to the other. As she went along, she continually asked herself: "When will Dr. Lopez give that shot? If only I could stop him."

Suddenly it hit her. "I promised Jack I'd see Father Landry. I'll go to St Matthew's rectory. No, I better telephone the rectory and make an appointment.".

As she pulled up at her double, she saw an elderly priest, knocking at her front door; a woman with him.

Seeing them filled her with a sense of foreboding that increased when they were seated in the parlor, the introductions over. Both were from the bayou country—St. Catherine's Parish.

Father Landry and Mrs. Placide sat on the sofa where peonies bloomed brightly. They were smiling kindly at Kendra, who sat across from them in the peacock and poppy-covered occasional chair, that was placed next to the window; a sweet breeze floated through, billowing the curtains.

Father Landry, a black briefcase on his lap, was a dark slenderly-built man, with white hair and black eyes. "Miss Applegate," he softly began, "early this morning I anointed Jack Trenchard."

"I was with him," added Mary Placide, who had lots of curly inky hair, streaked with silver, and blue/purple eyes, soft as pansies. She was both plain and pretty; thin and weather worn. About fifty or so.

Kendra to herself: "I know this woman from some where."

"I am Jack Trenchard's mother," slowly and quietly went on Mrs. Placide in a very soft voice, almost inaudible, wringing her hands..

A palpitating silence followed this revelation, which took Kendra's breath. She couldn't speak. She sat still as stone, staring incredulously at the woman who called herself Jack's mother; then at the priest; then back at the woman. Bewilderment and dismay clearly carved on her pale face.

"I was seventeen when Jack was born, out of wedlock. Findin' myself PG, I went to Father Landry, for guidance and help."

"The nuns at St. Catherine's," contributed Father Landry, "took care of Mary Trenchard until her baby was born. When the baby came, I arranged for him to be taken into the orphanage I run."

"Soon after my baby Jack had been placed in the orphanage, my drunken daddy died; my momma was long dead. I returned to my daddy's houseboat, and fished for my living. I still do."

"W-why did you wait all these years to make yourself known to your son?" asked Kendra, flatly and tonelessly. "Jack longed to know who his parents were and if they were alive."

"I was afraid my son wouldn't want nothin' to do with the likes of his uneducated fisher momma, who lived on an ol' houseboat. I was sure he'd be ashamed of me. I didn't want to blacken his chances. Through Father Landry, who kept track of Jack, I kept up with my son. Last evenin' when I told Jack who I was and how I lived, he wept and kissed me all at the same time. Had I thought for a minute he might try to kill hisself over me makin' myself known to him—"

"Don't torture yourself over that, Mary," softly said Father. "We now know the real reason Jack wanted to die."

"Jack didn't want to die. He was pushed over the bannister," mumbled Kendra; then to herself: "And Dr. Lopez is going to kill him with a shot, because the Judge wants him dead."

Father Landry raised his eyebrows, but made no comment. Mary Placide evidently didn't comprehend Kendra's remark. "I came to see my son to ask him to defend his brother, Johnny, who's in jail, right here in New Orleans, for murder, though it was self-defense. Been in jail a couple months, cause I couldn't raise the bail money. Johnny needs a good lawyer. Naturally, I thought of my son, Jack. I felt, if Jack knew the facts, he could save his baby brother."

Kendra now knew who the mysterious Johnny was.

"Who did Johnny kill?"

"Anton Delachaise, Judge Edwards' cousin's son. Johnny was at a bar in the French Quarter, and Anton picked a fight with him. The bartender will swear to that. Anton knocked Johnny down; and when Johnny got up he knocked Anton down—Anton never got up."

The blood around Kendra's heart froze."Oh, my God!"

"That's what Jack said when I told him. Jack said he heard the Judge talk about the case, and how he was goin' to lock up Johnny Placide and throw the key away. Revenge his cousin."

"Judge Edwards, the trial judge. What bad luck."

"Another judge was goin' to preside, but Edwards bribed him so he could be the judge. When I came to New Orleans, I didn't know Jack's father-in-law was such a powerful and dangerous man. Jack hates him, and is hated in turn."

"The Judge is one of the big boys, all powerful, who can kill and get away with it," murmured Kendra. A deadly silence followed.

"Anyway, we met with Jack late yesterday afternoon," rejoined Father Landry. "Before we stated our business he told us he was leaving for Mexico City, that night, to become a law partner in the firm of Alfredo Galvez. After Mary told him who she was, and about his brother being in trouble, Jack said Judge Edwards must never know that Johnny was his brother. He also said he'd defend his brother, and that his first move would be to get the Judge off Johnny's case."

"Jack was catching a midnight flight for Mexico City. I can hardly believe he'd change his plans because of a brother that he just learned existed five minutes before—"

"He said he'd make arrangements to handle the case through Galvez' New Orleans law firm, which is in the Maison Blanche Building. The firm's run by Alfredo's sister, Attorney Maria Galvez."

"Jack had a flight reservation," persisted Kendra.

"That reservation meant nothing when Mary told him his father was Thomas Jack Applegate—"

A deafening silence settled over the room. There was no mistaking what Father had said, and Kendra wanted to scream: "*That's a dirty lie!* Thomas Jack Applegate is *my* father," but her voice froze in her throat. She was smothering.

"To that piece of news, Jack reacted almost insanely."

"If he was goin' to carry on so, I'd have thought it would've been about me being his momma, not Tom. Tom was educated—a fine man. That's where my boys got their brains, from their daddy."

"It wasn't until early this morning, after I gave Jack extreme unction," softly said Father Landry, " that we learned why he carried on so. He confessed he had divorced his wife, by proxy, and was taking *you* to Mexico City with him, to marry *you*, his half sister. I guess rather than face you with such news, he took the easy way out—he *wants* to die."

Kendra shivered with misery.

"I knew your daddy before he married your momma," remarked Mary. "After Gen Rose died, your daddy got TB. I learned of his condition, came to see him while his sister was at work. The young lady next door, who had a lit'le boy, was mindin' you. Please don't look so hurt. Your daddy had nothing to do with me after he married your momma. I knew him again, after your momma died."

Kendra heard birds beneath the window sill quarreling.

"I talked Tom into goin' to a TB sanitarium, which was close to St. Catherine's parish, so he could get help and we could see more of one another. Every other month or so he went home to New Orleans, by train, and visited with you, his baby daughter, and with his sister."

A cricket chirred, chirred, chirred. A chirring cricket meant death, so Nell Miller had told Aunt Molly Primrose, who had told Kendra.

"He never knew I had Jack until after he got the TB, and we got back together again. When your daddy learned he had a son in a home, he wanted me to go get his boy. But, at the time, your daddy was too sick and barely had enough money to take care of hisself. I made just enough to keep him in the sanitarium.

"I soon got pregnant with my Johnny. A week before Tom died, I gave birth to Johnny, another half brother of yorn. Yorn aunt knew nothin' of Jack or Johnny.

"After Johnny's birth, John Placide, a fisherman and friend, that just lost his wife in childbirth, came to me. He said if I'd be mother to his infant daughter, baby Victorine, he'd marry me and give my son, Johnny, a name. Fearing, if he knew of Jack in the orphanage, he wouldn't have me. I kept quiet. John died last year. Victorine's married and got a pretty lit'le girl. She calls her Mary, after me."

A mocking bird landed on the window sill, and sang a sweet song.

"Johnny's twenty. He's the spit of Tom Applegate: chocolate eyes, skin the color of honey, hair, like yorn, brown-gold, tall, slender, fine-boned, like yourself. Johnny could pass for yorn twin. Jack favored me morn than his daddy."

To herself: "To think I was forever telling Kenny Joe I couldn't love him because he was too much like a brother. And the man I loved and wanted to make babies for turned out to be my brother. Some times life plays tricks on you." She felt hysteria rising in her throat.

Father Landry snapped open his briefcase and took out a faded manilla envelope and a new one. "These are the birth records of Jack and Johnny. The originals are in this old envelope; the copies I made for you are in the new." He handed both to Kendra.

Carefully she read them, sickeningly convinced that everything that Mrs. Placide had revealed was the truth. She handed the original documents back to Father Landry, without comment; she put the copies in her pocketbook.

"When I saw Jack this morning," slowly began Kendra, "he said you needed money. How much do you need?"

"We need $5,000 bail, plus whatever lawyer Galvez is goin' to charge us," softly replied Mary. "Since Jack can't defend his brother, he wants his good friend, Maria Galvez, to defend Johnny. Jack said if Judge Edwards is removed from the case, Maria and Alfredo can save Johnny; even if they havta buy his innocence. But that ain't necessary, cause Johnny's innocent."

"What was Johnny doing in New Orleans?"

"Workin' his way through Tulane medical school. Top ten in his class; but the dean told him, even if he gets off, he can't come back to Tulane. A real pity cause Johnny always wanted to do doctorin' in the bayou country, where doctors is needed."

"First, let's get Johnny out of jail, clear up this murder rap, and then we'll worry about medical school."

Kendra stood and walked with leaden legs to her aunt's armoire, pulled out one of the briefcase's and filled a brown grocery bag with $25,000, and returned to the parlor. She handed the bag to Mary Placide."There's enough money in this sack for Johnny's needs, and maybe a little left over for you. If you need more, let me know."

Mary Placide wept softly. "I just told Johnny about Jack. He don't know he's got a sister. Do you want me to tell him?"

"I'll, I'll have to let you know. You see, all these years I've thought of myself as an only child, and now I find I have two brothers. One's dying and one's in jail. I've got to come to terms with that, and I've got to break all this to my aunt, who's in the hospital with a heart attack."

"Well, I don't wanna cause you, or Tom's sister no trouble."

"One other thing, never tell anyone, even Attorney Galvez, where you all got this money," warned Kendra, changing the subject. "Jack *earned* this money I've given you."—

"Thank you, Miss Applegate, and God Bless. We'll be staying at the rectory a few more days; Mary at the housekeeper's apartment. Right now we're going back to the hospital to see Jack, and then to see Attorney Galvez, and give her the $5,000 bail money. When Johnny's free on bail, we'll go home to St. Catherine's Parish, returning for his trial. Jack requested, in the circumstances, that his mother not stay."

"Jack's afraid if the Judge finds out I'm his momma and Johnny's his brother, he'll make sure he crucifies Johnny. I wish I could stay and hold my son's hand until the end. The doctor said Jack can't last much longer. I can't bear the thought of him dyin' alone."

"I'll sit with him," offered Kendra—"

"*No!* You bein' with Jack would tempt and torture him. You should be on your knees thankin' Gawd that we got here in the nick of time to save you from elopin' with your brother."

To herself: "Lady, you just murdered me with this news, the same as if you stuck a knife in my heart. You destroyed me; and you want me to thank God for my death and destruction?" Aloud: "Mrs. Placide, you must remember I never knew Jack as my brother before now. I won't be saying prayers of thanksgiving for your saving me."

Both Mary Placide's and Father's lips puckered into a line of disapproval. Mary spoke: "In all this big city, how brother and step-sister ever met is beyond me."

"My aunt would say a mad quirk of fate decided by the devil. Did you all know the devil grew up in New Orleans?"

Mary Placide and Father Landry stood, sober and straight. "We got to go now," quietly said both.

After they left, Kendra knew where she had seen Mary Placide. She opened the back of the shabby family album, and found the envelope with the snapshots. She could hear her Tante telling her when she was little: 'Kendra Lou, I found these pictures in your daddy's wallet. I don't know who that pretty woman is, or anything about that houseboat; but I can't throw them away cause it must've meant somethin' to your daddy. He had them in his wallet.'"

Kendra took the pictures out. One was of a young and beautiful Mary Trenchard, on her houseboat, standing next to an older man, probably her daddy, Jack's Grandfather Trenchard; the other was of handsome Tom Applegate, also on the houseboat, his arm around Mary Trenchard. She put them back, and closed the album.

Kendra felt blank and bewildered, and overcome by an unbearable sadness. She sat heedless of everything but Mary Placide's story. A hundred or more thoughts crossed her mind, but the most unthinkable was the horrifying idea that she came so close to marrying her brother.

Mentally and physically exhausted and emotionally drained, Kendra collapsed on the sofa, and slept. She dreamed of CR, and saw the conclave of killers who murdered her; saw where the proof was hidden. She woke in a panic, recalling every detail of her dream. She lay there, feeling swaggery, staggery and with a nasty brown taste in her mouth. Slowly she sat up and looked at her watch: "It's two. I've slept over an hour, and I'm still tired.

Dazedly, she went to the bathroom and washed her face and brushed her teeth, the unsettling dream too vivid before her mind's eye, to ignore. I've got to go to Willowwynn and check it out."

In record time, Kendra was standing in front of the white Georgian mantel in CR's sitting room. She lifted the lid of the French blue porcelain box that sat next to the mantel clock, and saw a pool of white powder in the bottom of the box, as in the dream. She poured some of the substance into an envelope and sealed it. She tossed the envelope on CR's desk. "I'll drop this at the chemist's, and see if it really and truly is chloral hydrate."

Next she ran her nimble fingers along side the bookcase, to the left of the fireplace, and touched a button. Almost instantly the bookcase swung out, revealing two shelves. On one shelf was a tape recorder, a tape in it, and stacks of tapes next to it. Kendra pressed the rewind button on the recorder, then the play button, raised the volume and listened in horror. The entire murder scene, as it happened in her dream, was on this tape. At the end of the tape, she rewound it and also placed it on CR's desk; she closed the bookcase.

Then she moved to the right of the fireplace, ran her fingers along side the other bookcase, found the button and pressed it. That bookcase also swung out, revealing two shelves, filled with folders. She pryrooted through the folders until she found the one labeled Judge Edwards. She read the contents of this folder and found it basically contained the same info Jack had in his special file, plus a copy of the note the Judge had written CR, promising to pay back the embezzled $800,000, by April 15th. She read the note twice, put it back in the folder, placed the folder next to the tape on CR's desk; then closed the bookcase.

She left the sitting room and passed into the bedroom. Following the scenario of her dream, she tapped the panels behind the big fourposter until she heard a hollow sound. She parted both panels, and found another tape recorder. She listened to the revealing tape that was on the machine—CR's voice and various lovers in the throes of passion. She turned it off, closed the panels and returned to the sitting room. She sat at CR's secretary, staring at the incriminating tape and folder on the desk, thinking what to do next.

Finally she reached for the phone and called Hippo Delacroix. "This is Miss Foughtenberry," said Kendra talking through her nose, "I'm Attorney Erpelding's assistant. Mr. Erpelding is too ill to speak with you, and asked me to call you. He has a tape of the voices of CR's killers. He wants you to listen to that tape on Sunday, at 3 p.m., at Willowwynn."

Dead silence on the other end. "Er, Miss Foughtenberry, Mrs. Rogers died of natural causes; but I'd like to listen to that tape," muttered Delacroix.

As soon as Kendra hung up the phone, the intercom on CR's desk buzzed, causing her nearly to jump. Slowly, she picked it up, expecting to hear Clark's voice.

"Miss Applegate, or rather Miss Foughtenberry, my assistant," strongly said Karl Erpelding's voice, "I accidentally picked up the phone while you were talking to Hippo. I'm on my way to Carol's sitting room, to listen to that tape."

Two minutes later Karl Erpelding, wearing gray slacks and a white shirt looked surprisingly fit. Kendra opened the bookcases to the left of the fireplace, placed the incriminating tape on the recorder and pressed play. At its conclusion Erpelding looked white and weak.

Next Kendra handed him the folder with the note the Judge had written CR promising to pay back the embezzled $800,000."I believe you had the original of that note—"

"I did; but it disappeared. I suspect Dr. Lopez, after drugging me, took it and gave it to Judge Edwards."

"I also think that's what happened."

Karl read that note twice and the rest of the contents in the folder. "Miss Applegate, how did you know, and not Clark, where to look for this evidence?"

"The ghost of CR told me the answers were in the wall; I dreamed of her today and she showed me her killers and how to get into the walls."

He looked stunned. "I don't believe in ghosts," he shrugged."I want you to keep the tape and this folder in your possession, and present it at Sunday's inquisition. I'll inform Clark of this bad but good news, and we'll make sure the killers are here, so Delacroix can collect them for the Grand Jury. What's in the envelope?"

"I think it's poison. I'm going to take it to a chemist for analysis, and afterwards make photocopies of the papers in this folder."

"You'll need a briefcase. Use Carol's. It's right there by the desk."

Kendra put the powder envelope, the tape and the folder in the white briefcase. "I'll keep it in the trunk of my Dodge. It'll be safe." She looked at her watch. "Jeez, it's four o'clock. Both the Chemist Shop and photocopying shop close at five.—Er, Mr. Erpelding, please be very careful what you say to the killers, because they're dangerous. Also, don't take any pill or powder prescribed by Dr. Lopez. And whatever you do, don't let him give you a shot. I've got to go now."

The chemist said the substance, as CR had said in the dream, was chloral hydrate, never to be taken by a heart patient. Kendra left the chemist's for the photocopying shop. There she made copies of Jack's diary, skipping the pages pertaining to Beverly Reynolds and Maria Galvez; the contents of the file folder that could put the Judge under the jail: papers on how the Judge had used CR's money to speculate with, along with a list of other clients he had used in the same way; a copy of the phoney title to Jack's convertible; the phoney law partnership; the secret signature card that allowed the Judge to withdraw the $300,000 from Jack's bank account; and the note he had written to CR saying he'd pay back the $800,000 by April 15th.

Altogether she had made four photostatic sets of this evidence. She dropped off two sets at Willowwynn: one she put in the middle of Clark's desk; the other she gave to Karl Erpelding; the third, she left with Attorney Maria Galvez' secretary; the fourth she locked in the trunk to give to Hippo Delacroix.

Since it was way past supper, Kendra, on the way home, picked up a hot roastbeef po boy sandwich, sopping with gravy.

Ten minutes later, she wearily climbed out the Dodge, thinking she'd eat her po boy and relax. Try not to think about the taped voices of CR's killers; the lethal shot awaiting Jack; or the heartbreaking revelations of Mary Placide. As she slammed the car door, Poochie Pujowl, standing on his gallery, called: "Kendra, I thought you'd never get home. I've been watchin' and waitin' for you."

Poochie Pujowl was a middle aged man, short and stout, with a mop of gray-streaked brown hair, soft brown eyes and a warm smile—a teddy bear.

To herself: "I wonder why he's been watching for me?"

"How's your Aunt Molly Primrose?" inquired Poochie, striding across the street. "I was shocked to hear about her heart attack. I figured you was visitin' at the hospital, cause it's almost dark"

"She's doing pretty good. Why were you watching for me?"

"I need a favor."

Kendra gave him a questioning look, and started to trudge toward the house; Poochie went with her. "I guess you know I've been savin' up to get Sister Elvira, that voodoo witch, to chase off them demons that's livin' inside my momma."

Kendra nodded.

"I've got the money together, and this afternoon Sister Elvira sent word that she's ready to do voodoo on my momma. I have to carry my momma to Jefferson Parish, where the voodoo will take place."

"Well, what's the favor?"

"Sister Elvira said we couldn't come in no cab. Kendra, can you drive us there?"

"Tonight?" said Kendra in a shocked voice. She stopped in her tracks.

"Yes. If I don't go tonight, I lose my money. You see the messenger said Sister Elvira's already started killin' them chickens-'n'-bleedin' 'em. I gotta go tonight. Please don't turn me down.— Kendra, have you ever been so close to gettin' somethin' you want, only to miss it by an inch?" His voice was filled with frustration.

She managed half a smile, and started walking again. *"Yes,"* she sighed. *"*I know the feeling." To herself: "I'm in no condition to go anywhere, let alone to a voodoo ritual. She felt like screaming at him: "I almost married my brother, who's in the hospital and Dr. Lopez will kill him soon with a deadly shot; my other brother's in jail; and I know who killed CR."

Instead she tried to brush him off, gently. "Poochie, you'd have to hogtie and gag your momma to get her in my Dodge. She'd never let me drive her all the way to Jefferson Parish, and then let Sister Elvira plunge her in a bath of chicken blood, without her killing you and me both."

"Oh, yes, she would. Sister Elvira's messenger brought a potion with her. I put the concoction in momma's coffee and, for a change, she's actin' like a lit'le lamb, not like a lion. I can han'ler her."

To herself. "Well, I really don't have anything to do but worry if Dr. Lopez has done in Jack, yet; if Johnny's bail's been posted; if Mr. Erpelding will go after the bad guys; if CR's murderer will be punished. Maybe this ride to Jefferson Parish might, for a little while, make a miserable situation bearable. Anyway, what's a neighbor for, if not to drive another neighbor to a voodoo ritual?" Kendra drew a deep breath. "All right, I'll take you; but first I've got to eat."

"Sure. By the way, Ruby Faye ain't goin'. She said she can't take seein' no voodoo; but she's all for it."

To herself: "Neither can I take 'seein' no voodoo'; and I'm not for it." Aloud: "See you in a little while."

Kendra hurried inside; the phone was ringing. It was Attorney Galvez, who said she had the packet of evidence, and she could now make a deal with the Judge. Johnny would get justice. Kendra cautioned her not to mention names because of the party line. She told Kendra, when the deal was made, she'd let her know. End of conversation. Kendra then called the hospital. "This is Miss Wheelerhand, Mr. Clark Rogers' secretary. Mr. Rogers wants to know the condition of his cousin, Jack Trenchard—I see—no visitors—thank you." She hung up. "Well, I wonder what Lopez is waiting for. Maybe, he's caught a case of conscience." She went to her room.

Sick and numb, she kicked off her heels; tossed her pocketbook on the bed; shed her stockings and unhooked her garter belt. Next she quickly freshened up and changed to a plain, green cotton circular skirt and white blouse, then slipped her bare feet into a pair of old white ballerinas.

She felt dressed good enough for a voodoo ritual, which she thought would be nothing more than a lot of hocus-pocus, abracadabra and mumbo jumbo. She'd be home by 9—9:30, at the latest.

The phone rang. *"Kendra darling, where have you been?"* said Clark's anxious voice. "I've been out of my mind with worry. I've been phoning every half hour or so."

To herself: "He didn't get that horrible note, telling him I was marrying Jack." Aloud: "I just left Willowwynn a couple hours ago. "Did you find the packet I left on your desk? Have you spoken with Karl Erpelding?"

"Yes; and I must speak with you."

"Kendra Louise," interrupted Mooching Mamie TuJax, who just picked up the phone, "I understand you're takin' Poochie and his momma to see Sister Elvira, that voodoo witch, against Ruby Faye's wishes."

"Mrs. TuJax, please hang up."

"Kendra Louise,"chimed in Lizzie Slapp, who evidently was also on the line, "I know they say Sister Elvira knows how to cast spells and how to take off spells, but I don't believe it. Who am I talkin' to?"

"What's all this about a voodoo witch?"demanded Clark.

"I'm giving a neighbor a lift to Jefferson Parish; I should be home by nine. I'll talk to you, then. This phone has many ears."

"I'll see you around nine. Where does this voodoo witch live?"

"Way off in Jefferson Parish," supplied Mrs. TuJax.

"That's right, Mrs. TuJax, you answer my caller's questions," angrily replied Kendra. "I'll talk to you later, Clark." She hung the phone up, rigid with rage against those two, for listening in on her conversation. She went to the kitchen.

Standing at the sink, she gulped down half her po-boy sandwich, and drank a cold glass of milk. She grabbed an apple, and just as she crunched down on it, Poochie's impatient voice called from the back porch: "Kendra, are you ready to go?"

"I'm ready," she hollered back, her mouth full of apple. "Go on and get in the Dodge, I'll be right there."

Kendra had always kept a good distance from old lady Pujowl, and now, on this warm windy evening, she was going to be driving that wild, crazy woman all the way to Jefferson Parish, while her brother, the man she loved, was being made to breathe his last.

Carrying her apple in one hand, her car keys in the other, her pocketbook slung over her left shoulder, Kendra, nervous and heartsick, dashed to the Dodge. She slid behind the wheel, rolled down her window, and twisted around to face the back seat, where Poochie and his skinny, shrivelled momma, who was wearing a neat dark suit, sat in a stupor. Her white hair was pulled into a ball on top her head.

"Good evening—there's room up front for us all."

"Me and momma better stay back here," said Poochie.

Kendra turned back to the wheel and drove off, the Dodge bucking for half a block before it got smooth. As she drove she munched her apple while Poochie acted like a tourist guide."We just crossed Carrollton and Claiborne," he called out. "We'll be drivin' alongside the Carrollton Canal until we hit the Jefferson Parish line, so don't get too close to the edge of the road, cause we don't wanna fall in the canal."

"We won't." Kendra switched on her lights. They drove on for a while before Poochie spoke again. "Over there, on the left, is the water works. We'll soon be leavin' the canal behind. I'm glad."

On swept the Dodge. Kendra finished her apple and tossed the core out the window; it rolled into the canal. All of a sudden Poochie cried out: "We've just crossed into Jefferson Parish."

"Are we goin' to KB, Poochie?" asked old lady Pujowl, coming out her stupor.

"No, momma. You just relax and enjoy this nice ride. You're gunna be just fine when we go home."

Kendra drove for another ten minutes before Poochie alerted: "Make a right."

She left the highway for a-black-as-pitch, narrow, bumpy, deserted dirt road that was lined with thick woods, draped in eerie beards of moss, and full of scary night noises. Bushes grew in the road, so she had to concentrate on dodging both bushes and bumps.

On and on Kendra drove, until the road dead ended.

"That's it!" cried Poochie. "That's it on the right—Pull over, Kendra—You can park just beyond that dead end sign—Pull over!"

Kendra swerved the Dodge toward the gutter's edge, and brought it to a sudden stop. Poochie jumped out and held the door for his momma. "C'mon, momma. It's time to get out."

Before them—from what Kendra could make out, from the gutter's edge, assisted by the moonlight, a sickle moon in a vast star studded sky—she could dimly discern Sister Elvira's sagging shack. Closer up she saw it was surrounded by a falling down wire fence, pierced by a wooden gate that hung by the top hinge.

The place was shrouded in shrubbery, tall trees, vines, moss and honeysuckle, all crowded together in a tangle of weeds and debris. Piles of trash littered the front yard.

"C'mon, let's go round the back," impatiently cried Poochie.

"I wish I had a flashlight," muttered Kendra.

"We don't need no flashlight. The moon's out. Follow me."

Poochie led the way to the back part of the house; his momma followed and Kendra came up the rear. Four fiery torches lit up the yard. Beyond the torches loomed dark dense woods. In front of the torches, toward the left corner of the yard, stood an iron barrel belching flames and shooting sparks high into the sky, giving off a good deal more light and lots of heat, and filling the air with the sickening scent of burning chicken feathers.

A garden hose, a trickling stream flowing from it, lay close by the burning barrel. A few feet from the fire stood a footed bathtub. Smoking vapors shot up from this sinister tub of blood, producing vile odors. Over the tub was strung a wire line, from which hung, by their feet, a dozen or so headless chickens, dripping their blood into the tub.

Behind the tub was a rickety wire pen crammed full of frightened chickens who were in a panic, flapping their wings, squawking, butting their heads against the sides of the pen, and trampling one another.

This commotion was caused because of a dull, gray grizzled haired, stout, slow and sluggish nigger woman in a blood spattered white gown, who was snatching at their feet.

Next to the chicken pen stood a scarred white table that was splashed with fresh blood and caked with old dried blood turned brown. A hatchet lay on top it.

After many tries, the chicken-catching nigger woman nabbed a hen, and handed it to another stout nigger woman of the same caliber, also dressed in white. The chicken snatcher then went back to grabbing at chickens, and soon she seized another one.

Each woman in a dismal voice shrilly chanted some mumbo jumbo before wringing the chicken's neck. The dead chicken, while it quivered and writhed, was then handed over to a tall, ugly-featured, cadaverous nigger woman, with a sunken mouth and jutting jaw, that brought her chin up close to her beaked nose. She had twisted lips, no teeth and wild, stringy, white hair that hung down her back and in her bugging bloodshot eyes. Her fingernails were a good four inches long. She wore a narrow white calico gown to her feet, and her face was painted with chicken blood. She looked like a gargoyle from hell.

That scary lookin', witchlike nigger woman is Sister Elvira," whispered Poochie. "I can't introduce you, cause that was her orders."

"That's OK," whispered Kendra, already in a panic.

"C'mon, momma, let's go see Sister Elvira."

Poochie handed over his momma to the horrible gargoyle, and then returned to Kendra's side.

Sister Elvira stood old lady Pujowl beside the guillotine table. Next she snatched up a chicken, held it down on the blood spattered white table and, in a blood-curdling voice, chanted over it. Afterwards, she chopped off its head. Blood went every where.

Old lady Pujowl didn't mind this primitive, savage act; but Kendra did. Trickles of cold sweat ran down her forehead and temples.

The stout, dull nigger woman who had handed over the chicken, took down one of the bloodless chickens that was hanging over the tub, and tossed it in the fire; sending an uproar of crackling sparks and licking flames up into the darkness.

Next she grabbed up the chicken that had just lost its head, by his feet, and hung it on the line to bleed. The other nigger woman did the same thing. This process was repeated until every chicken in the pen had been beheaded and bled. The last three chickens to be guillotined, not only lost their heads but their feet as well.

Having expected only a lot of hocus pocus, Kendra, feeling cold and sick to her stomach, had enough. She had already been through purgatory that day, so why exit into hell?

She was ready to leave; but the voodoo witch, blood on her face, on her hands and in her wild hair, came over to Poochie and told him no matter what went on or happened, no one was to interfere or leave. Then she striped naked, and her two draggle-tailed assistants dressed her in a snowy gown, and gave her a cup of chicken blood to drink.

In the meantime, old lady Pujowl, still standing by the table, asked if she was at K & B and, if so, she was thirsty for a malted milk.

Sister Elvria, hearing this, dipped a cup of chicken blood from the tub, mixed in some quickly grounded up leaves, and gave the nasty drink to old lady Pujowl, who drank it down.

Kendra dived behind the nearest tree and lost her po boy sandwich and apple. Trembling, she found the water hose and washed her mouth out while Sister Elvira striped old lady Pujowl and stretched her out on that scarred white table where all the chickens had been killed.

The ritual began. Sister Elvira took up a chicken foot, dipped it in the tub of blood and dragged it across the now pale old lady Pujowl's forehead, nose and chin, scratching and scraping her something awful. She bled; and her blood mingled with that of the chicken's blood. Old lady Pujowl gasped and groaned in an alarming way.

"Your momma's going to get blood poisoning," said Kendra through stiff jaws, "you better end this."

Her blood's already poisoned. I want it to go on."

Sister Elvira picked up another chicken foot and dipped it in blood. She now had a bloody foot in each hand, and used both to scratch and scrape pitiful old lady Pujowl all over her tiny body while the other two nigger women, in the full pitch of their voices, wailed and pulled their grizzled gray hair. Coughs and gasps came from the table.

Each nigger woman had a turn at old lady Pujowl's tiny wrinkled face and shrivelled body until every inch of it had been gashed. She was a bloody mess. Under such an assault, old lady Pujowl's pale face grew mottled with a rush of blood.

Kendra, feeling wilted and weak in the legs, knew she had to sit down or fall on her face. She sat on the ground, amid dirt and debris and critters. Vaguely she saw lightning bugs winking. A flying roach smashed into her face. She screamed. No one paid any attention. "I've got to get out of here. —Poochie, let's take your momma home. This is horrible. Barbaric. Just look at your momma's face."

Poochie gave Kendra a crooked grin. "My momma's horrible and barbaric. If this can knock it out of her, I can stand it." He managed a weak laugh.

Kendra heard an owl give a hoot; another answered. A mosquito lit on her elbow. She slapped it. It left a glob of smeared blood where it died.

Meanwhile, Sister Elvira and her draggle-tailed assistants broke branches from a nearby chinaberry tree, dipped them in blood and beat the hell out of coughing, panting, quivering old lady Pujowl, as she lay on the table. Sweat and blood now streaked her muddy face.

"That good beatin' was to stir up them demons," explained Poochie in a hoarse whisper. "It's time for them demons to show theirselves."

On tottering legs they stood old lady Pujowl. She collapsed. They stood her up again, and this time a red froth flowed from her mouth. Following this froth came the horned head of a donkey in miniature size. Filth flowed from its braying mouth.

Sister Elvira, her eyes bugging and fierce, choked, clawed, cursed and pummelled the donkey's head until he retreated back down old lady Pujowl's throat, choking her. Sister Elvira's horribly thin face showed satisfaction with the results. Next her chanting caused a miniature lion, with the roar of a jungle cat, to shoot out old lady Pujowl's left nostril; its hindquarters remained lodged in her face and throat, bulging grotesquely. By now, old lady Pujowl had passed into a violent agitation. She was wildly thrashing about her with both fists, fighting savagely.

Poochie laughed feebly. "Momma's not fightin' Sister Elvira," he remarked, licking his lips. "She's fightin' them demons. They don't wanna come out."

When Sister Elvira's fists, claws and chantings couldn't best the beast she used the blood-soaked berry branches on him while the other nigger women chanted and tossed bloodless chickens into the fire.

Suddenly, to Kendra's horror, Poochie was caught up in the contagion of the tumult and, with his hands locked behind his back, started rocking back and forth, whistling *Jeepers Creepers*.

Right then Kendra knew it would be up to her to get the Pujowls and herself out of there. But how? Suddenly the wind grew stronger. It picked up the sparks from a kindled chicken feather and carried it into the woods. A small fire ignited.

Kendra staggered to her feet and grabbed the hose, but there was too little water pressure and too much wind, to fight even a tiny flame. She tried, but couldn't snuff out the fire. The flames, fanned by the wind, grew and grew and finally spread from one dry patch to another. Soon the woods were ablaze.

"Poochie, we got to get out of here—Leave now—If we don't, we'll be trapped in a full-fledged fire."

He stopped rocking and whistling long enough to whine: "Aw, stop frettin'-'n'-worryin'.We ain't gettin' trapped by no fire." He started rocking and whistling again.

"Come on, Poochie, get your momma. The place is on fire! The flames are shooting high as the sky. I bet they can be seen from the highway. We don't want to be around when the fire department and the cops come. Let's go. Hurry!" cried Kendra, throwing down the hose. "Hurry before we all burn up!—Get a move on!"

At that very moment, old lady Pujowl vomited up the miniature donkey and, when he landed at her feet, he turned into a full-sized wild animal. Braying, snorting and kicking up his heels. He ran headlong into the woods.

For a few minutes, this occupied Kendra's full attention; and, when she started nagging again, 'let's go, Poochie,' old lady Pujowl sneezed, and the lion came flying out her left nostril.

Instantly the lion turned into a fierce jungle beast, roaring; and he, like the donkey, went crazy and fled to the crackling woods. The third horrible animal, to be born out of old lay Pujowl's body, came from her right nostril. It was a piglet. It was black and vicious and, for such a tiny thing, fought like the devil himself.

Kendra, her eyes enormous, stood there and shivered violently. "Your momma's going to die, and you're going to let her, aren't you?"

Poochie stopped whistling and gave a helpless shrug. "My momma died the day them demons got insider her." He started whistling again.

At this juncture, while the woods were an inferno and flames licked the air, the three nigger women carried old lady Pujowl—the little piglet hanging half out her nostril—and placed her frail body into the big bathtub of blood. They pushed her head under. Pulled her up, and ducked her again and again. Then they lifted her out, bloody white hair straggling, the little pig still hanging from her nostril, and stood her on her wobbly legs.

Promptly she keeled over, rolled around the ground and clawed at the little pig, trying to jerk him out her nose. While this was going on Sister Elvira and her assistants chanted and spat on the little pig.

To Kendra's horror, obscenities flowed from old lady Pujowl's mouth in a voice belonging to someone other than old lady Pujowl. Sister Elvira and the little pig were now fighting for old lady Pujowl's body and soul.

The scene was a nightmare. No one could imagine such a fight. Suddenly the little pig was completely out of old lady Pujowl's nose and at her feet, a full grown, wild black boar with razor sharp tusks.

Two pistol shots rang out. Wild confusion reigned as Kendra spun around and faced Clark Rogers and a policeman, who growled: "Make room for the firemen." Kendra's face brightened with relief.

Just as the firemen invaded the back yard, the black boar, pawing, snorting and slicing the ground with his sword-like tusks, charged straight for Poochie Pujowl and knocked him off his feet.

The swine, in a flash, trampled and gored Poochie in the face and head; the policeman cocked his pistol to shoot the hog, but couldn't, because he might accidentally shoot Poochie.

Sister Elvira came to Poochie's rescue. She threw a bucket of blood in the boar's horrible face, and the chicken blood maddened him. He fled to the woods and leapt into the burning flames. While he burned all manner of violence took place in that fire. It sounded as if there were ten demons fighting and cursing one another. Then utter silence. Utter horror.

Kendra, unable to move, stood there flushed and ashamed. Clark stood next to her, holding her hand. Old lady Pujowl, a stark naked bloody mess, stood next to Clark. She seemed fine. She stood smiling. Poochie Pujowl was dead.

Chapter Sixteen

It was nearly daybreak Saturday and sprinkling rain when Clark dropped Kendra home. Once inside, she went straight to the bathroom and turned on the tub's water spigots and waited for it to fill, listening to the hot water pipes regurgitating, as she striped. She put her clothes, underwear and ballerinas into a paper sack, and trashed the lot. She never wanted to wear those clothes again or see them.

In the tub, she scrubbed her soft body with strong Octagon soap, even her pretty hair, because it smelled of dried blood and burnt chicken feathers. After cleansing herself of any remnants of the voodoo ritual, her body clean, her soul dirty, she felt exhausted. Limp with misery, she went to bed and stared at the ceiling, thinking of two tiny words, *if only,* which nagged her despairing mind.

"*If only* Jack wasn't my brother, he wouldn't want to die, he wouldn't let the Judge have him murdered—*if only* CR hadn't hurled him over the bannister, we'd be in Mexico City right now; and Poochie Pujowl would be alive. *If only* I had some how made Poochie leave, Ruby Faye wouldn't be a widow today; and she wouldn't be so mad at me." Tears stung Kendra's eyes. "One good thing came of this, old lady Pujowl's cured; but that's little comfort or consolation to Ruby Faye."

On and on she whipped herself until she made her mind messy. Had she known her thoughts, in sleep, would turn into nightmares, she'd never closed her eyes. But she fell into a fitful doze and dreamed a series of horrible dreams. In one dream, Sister Elvira had chopped off CR's head and hung her by her feet, from the Wedgewood chandelier in the powder-blue bedroom, to bleed on the blue rug. She woke up startled and to a slapping down rain. She fell back to sleep.

This time she dreamed of the crazy house, and the lunatics were either braying donkeys, roaring lions or wild, snorting hogs—all in an uproar, shrieking, yelping and mauling one another.

From the crazy house, her mixed up mind went to the leper colony, where the lepers were drinking Poochie's blood, and he was vomiting demons and savagely fighting for his life. Somehow or other Mary Placide was in the dream screaming at her: "*No-no-no! Jack's your brother! You can't sit with your brother.*" She woke up to the shock of remembering Poochie had died a violent death. She was shaking and sweating and her mouth felt dry. She got a drink of water and came back to bed, trembling. It was still raining.

She tossed, turned, dozed and heard a loud ringing in her ears and a roaring in her head. The ringing sound was the phone. It stopped.

Unable to move, she lay there in what seemed to be a prolonged panic, sweating and trying to gather her wits about her. Her head pounding. She looked at the bedside clock, and its black hands said it was noon. She had slept six hours, but felt she hadn't slept a wink.

She heaved a heavy sigh. The stress and strain and tragic events of the previous day and night were crowding her mind thick and fast. She sighed again. "I got to plan my strategy for tomorrow's inquisition, but before I do that I got to see Jack, whether Tante or Mary Placide like it or not. God, please don't let me be too late—"

With that resolve, she got up, washed and dressed, choosing a tan linen suit and a light blue silk blouse, another gift from Clark. She did all this in slow motion, weighed down by grief and sorrow.

She ran the comb through her mop of sweet-smelling hair that hung to her shoulders in a soft shower of brown-gold waves, and pulled it into a pony tail. Then put on some lipstick. Except for the circles around her eyes, she looked pretty good, considering what she had been through. "Now all I need to get going is some hot coffee," she said to herself.

After breakfast, she climbed into the Dodge—the rain had quit and the sun was busy sucking up steaming street puddles. As she drove away, she looked at the Pujowl double and shuddered. "Poor Poochie," she murmured to herself, heading for the hospital.

Perhaps because she was still feeling numb, she made a wrong turn and wound up at the back of the hospital, at the Emergency Entrance. She stopped the Dodge to get her bearings, and that's when she noticed the hearse.

A moment later, two attendants wheeled out a sheet-covered body, of an unusually tall person, whose legs were too long for the stretcher. The attendants heaved up the stretcher, shoved it into the hearse, and then went back into the hospital.

Unable to move and hardly daring to breathe, she sat straight and rigid, trying to think what to do. Slowly she got out the Dodge and crept close to the hearse, her head and heart pounding. She opened the door and crawled in beside the body.

Trembling she pulled down the black rubber sheet and looked into the beautiful rigid face of Jack Trenchard, her brother. His blue/purple eyes were glassy and staring blankly. She closed them, then tenderly kissed his forehead, and murmured: "I met your mother, and I gave her $25,000 to help our brother, Johnny, get out of trouble. When he's free I'll see that he goes back to medical school. I also see that Father Landry gets some money for his orphanage."

Softly she caressed his face: "The sharpest sting about us is, even if you had lived, we could never be lovers— *never*. How God could've played such a trick on us, I don't know. But I'll always love you, and I'm only sorry there's no way to get even with the ghost of CR. But I intend to have a hand in bringing down the Edwardses and Dr. Lopez, disgracing them, and letting them know I, your sister, with the help of Maria Glavez, caused their downfall and disgrace, for what they've done to you." She looked longingly at his mouth, but kissed only his forehead, before drawing the sheet over his face. She climbed out the hearse.

She got back to her Dodge just as the attendants returned and drove off with Jack's body. As she sat silently watching the hearse, as if in a dream, little by little reality returned. "Now that Jack's dead, the Judge'll be looking for his money; and if Jack left a trail to Starlight Street, I've got either to erase that trail or make impossible obstacles.

"God, please give me the strength and the ability to out-maneuver Jack's enemies—now my enemies. Help me plan my strategy, because I've got a feeling the Judge'll be sending a caller today."

She sat there a while longer, trying to think what to do, trying to think out a plan. As soon as it came to her, she cranked the Dodge, and with fits and starts it bucked away.

To implement her plan she stopped at the first grocery store she saw, and bought crayolas, milk, bread, eggs, Vienna sausages, potted meat and spam, totalling twenty-four cans in all; a bottle of cold *Orah C Cola;* and all the moon pies the store had. Three dozen.

The grocer, upon her request, packed her purchases in a big strong box, and she drove home.

In the kitchen, she plopped the big box of groceries on the table, and quickly put the perishables in the icebox. Then she went to her aunt's armoire and grabbed up the two briefcases. One case contained $50,000, for she had given Mary Placide $25,000; the other, the one Jack was to carry, aside from the $75,000, also held the $150,000 cashier's check. She snatched a fistful of money, about $5,000, and stashed it in her big shoulder strap pocketbook, which was big as a satchel.

Jack's briefcase, along with his shaving kit, she touched tenderly, and then put them in the empty grocery box; her briefcase she put on top of Jack's. She then stuffed wads of old yellow newspapers, she had gathered from the back gallery, around and over the two cases.

On top this nest, she placed cans of Vienna sausages, potted meat, spam, and all the moon pies, save one for herself. The box packed, she tightly tied it with string and wrapped it with heavy brown paper. Lastly, she took a black crayola and printed in the upper left-hand corner of the box, *FROM: MISS KENDRA LOUISE APPLEGATE, 3022 STARLIGHT STREET, NEW ORLEANS, LA.*— In the center of the box, she printed, *TO: PFC SONNY GANUCCI, APO BOX 140, SAN FRANCISCO, CALIF.* She also listed the contents of the box: *VIENNA SAUSAGES, POTTED MEAT AND MOON PIES.—MAY BE INSPECTED.* She figured by putting *MAY BE INSPECTED* on front of the box in big black letters, it wouldn't be inspected.

"All it needs now is to be secured with heavy twine, and taken to the post office on Monday.— Now I must write a letter to Sonny."

The letter she wrote said a big box was on its way, carrying lots of money and moon pies; and nobody on the face of the earth knew about the money except the two of them. She begged him to take care of the money for her. To keep it in his footlocker until he went on his next R&R to Tokyo, and then deposit it in both their names in a bank with the highest interest rate; or, find a good investment, that would also be OK.

She instructed him to take half the interest, and send her the other half. When he came home to the States, he was to leave the money in a bank or investment house in Japan. When he was discharged, she'd buy him the biggest pizza parlor in all New Orleans.

In case of his death,"God forbid," she promised all his family would be well fixed. She ended with, hoping he was doing as best he could in the circumstances, and that she was looking forward to hearing from him.

The letter written, sealed and stamped with two seven-cent airmail stamps, to insure sufficient postage, she put it in her pocketbook and breathed easier. Next she dashed into her room, pyrooted through her vanity drawer until she found the picture of Jack that she had planned to tear up, ever since he had jilted her, and put it in her wallet. She then looked for the picture Sonny had given her in his uniform, taken right after boot camp. She wrote on the photo toward the bottom right side: *TO KENDRA, WITH ALL MY LOVE—SONNY.*

On her bedside table there was a framed picture of her aunt. She put Sonny's picture in front of her aunt's. All completed, she dropped her automobile keys in her suitcoat pocket, went back to the kitchen, popped the cork on her *ORAH C COLA,* and took a long swallow. She tore the wrapper from the moon pie and managed one big bite before that expected, foreboding knock was heard on the front door.

She put the soft drink and the moon pie in the icebox, slung her pocketbook over her left shoulder, grabbed up the heavy box and lugged it to the front room, where she plopped it on the parlor table, with a thud. "Ugh! that's heavy," she muttered to herself, placing her pocketbook next to the box.

A louder knock sounded. She opened the front door. Two men stood before her. "What can I do for you?" she asked in her most pleasant voice.

"Good afternoon. I'm Hippolyte Delacroix, the state attorney." He handed her his credentials. "This is Mr. Dom Puttuci, a representative of Judge Edwards."

Kendra nodded, glanced at the credentials and handed them back.

Hippolyte Delacroix was tall and uncommonly handsome, with fair skin, dark hair and eyes, and full lips, as red as a youngsters. He wore an expensive navy suit, white shirt and navy and red tie.

Dom Puttuci, the Judge's henchman, had sallow, brocky skin, crow-black porcupine hair, the body of a weasel and the face of a fox, with beady black eyes, and squirrel teeth. The fox wore a dark zoot suit, and looked like he was on alert.

If Kendra had been an actress, she would've gotten an academy award for her performance. She looked from one man to the other, arching her eyebrows. "Well, gentlemen, what can I do for you?"

"Are you Miss Molly Primrose Applegate?" asked Hippo Delacroix, the splendid.

"No. That's my aunt. She's in the hospital, with a heart attack. No visitors. I'm Kendra Louise Applegate."

"May we come in?" asked Delacroix.

"S-sure."

"A nice parlor you have," remarked Delacroix, taking everything in with a sweeping glance, including the wrapped box.

The Fox made no comment. He just looked at Kendra long and scrutinizingly.

"Ahh, I see you've got a big package here," went on Delacroix, reading the address. "Going all the way to Ko-reah, eh?"

"Yes. My boyfriend's on the front lines. All he gets to eat is phoney food; so I'm sending him some canned goods. His favorites: Vienna sausages, spam, potted meat and moon pies."

Delacroix chuckled. "I like all that myself, especially moon pies. Ahem—Miss Applegate, since your aunt's in the hospital, maybe you can help me. I'm here on official business that I hope can be conducted in a not-so-official way."

"Mr. Delacroix, I can't imagine in the whole wide world what kind of business you'd have with my aunt. But I'll try to help, if I can."

"How well does your aunt and you know Attorney Jack Trenchard?" asked Delacroix, coming straight to the point.

Kendra looked blank. "*I* really don't know him at all; however, my aunt once used his services, but that's been a year ago."

"What service did he perform for your aunt?"

"He got our friend and neighbor, Mrs. Stella Dora Wheelerhand, released from Jackson."

"He couldn't do that on his own. He had to use the Judge's influence," curtly clarified Puttuci, the fox.

"All I know, it's been almost a year ago, since she was released."

"Your aunt was no doubt very grateful to Attorney Trenchard for getting her friend released, wasn't she?"

"Yes," agreed Kendra, still looking blank. "So why are you here?"

"Because Trenchard stole $800,000 from the Sloan Endowment Fund, and $300,000 bucks from Judge Edwards' personal account; and the Judge thinks he gave *that* $300,000 to your aunt to hide for him."

"That's preposterous. I suggest the Judge ask Attorney Trenchard about *that* money, not my aunt," fumed Kendra.

"Trenchard died today," replied the Fox, "and the thieving' bastid can't be asked nothin'," he added with withering contempt.

Despite that nasty remark and the awful strain on her nerves, Kendra didn't flinch, didn't betray any feelings. Her voice remained calm and cool. "Well, I'm very sorry to hear that. My aunt said Mr. Trenchard was a young man. What happened? An accident?"

"He attempted suicide and died from those self-inflicted wounds,," rejoined Delacroix. "He knew the Judge would expose him, as an embezzler, and killed himself. The reason this concerns your aunt is Mr. Trenchard left his insurance and burial policy to her—"

"There's got to be some mistake," cried Kendra, incredulous. "Mr. Trenchard hardly knew my aunt. So to make her his beneficiary would be—stupid."

"Of course, it is," muttered the Fox, again carefully scrutinizing

Kendra's pretty face, as if he could find the answer written on it.

"I can't speak for my aunt, but if you're here to ask her to let you tear up Mr. Trenchard's will, I'm sure she won't object."

"We want more than to tear up the will," surlily said the Fox, a sharp sly look in his beady eyes. "Since it's sooieside, your aunt won't get a penny of the insurance, ten gran'. The Judge ain't interested in that ten gran'. He wants the $300,000 that Trenchard stole from him; Rogers wants the $800,000 that Trenchard stole from the SEF. We think he got your aunt to hide that money in return for his insurance."

"My aunt's sixty-two. She'd never collect on a young man's life insurance. No body would fall for such a foolish deal."

"They say a fool's born every minute."

"My aunt was born on the second," quipped Kendra.

Delacroix laughed.

"He made the will leavin' all to your aunt right after the Judge threatened to expose his thievery. He did it, knowing he was gunna kill hisself. That vindictive bastid would rather see strangers get the money. That bastid, Trenchard, was an orphan. No maw, no paw. If they was known, I'd bet both was thieves. Bad blood tells."

It was hard for Kendra to keep from making an angry retort. "If my aunt dies, who inherits Mr. Trenchard's money?" she calmly asked.

"That Spic, Galvez, his attorney and bride, says you do," replied the Fox. "A few days ago, that sneaky bastid, by proxy, divorced pregnant Miz Allison, and married on his death bed, by proxy, *that* Spic. He musta had to do it. The bastid run out of time, died; couldn't change his will."

This news nearly toppled Kendra, but she held on.

"Don't slander Miss Galvez," cautioned Delacroix.

"Can't help but slander her.— C'mon, Hippo, quit your pussyfootin' and let's search this dump."

"*What!*" cried Kendra.

"This is no dump," snapped Delacroix; then, in his most urbane voice, "I have a search warrant, Miss Applegate."

"Warrant or not, the whole thing sounds pine black crazy. A lowly lawyer stealing from a hoity-toity Judge; my old aunt hiding his loot, in return to be in his will.— How did this lawyer, Trenchard, pull it off? Put a loaded pistol to the Judge's head and one to my little aunt's?"

A curious smile played around the corners of Delacroix's mouth; while the Fox gave her a quick, shrewd glance, no doubt trying to read her unreadable mind.

"I don't know how he convinced your aunt to be a part of his scheme.— I understand he simply took the $300,000 out of a dual bank account."

"If it were a dual account, both Trenchard and the Judge would have to sign. Yet, you tell me Trenchard, on his own, drew out all the $300,000. So the Judge is only looking for his half, $150,000, right?" she added in an even, mechanical tone of voice. They looked hard at each other. "I'd say it's the bank's fault for letting Trenchard withdraw the money; so the bank's got to make it good."

"Miss Reynolds, head teller, didn't know it was a dual account."

"To me that smells like rotten cat fish. Sounds like hanky panky going on at the bank."

"The bank's fine; Trenchard's trash," brusquely replied the Fox before Delacroix could answer. "We're lookin' for *all* that dough, and if we don't find it here, the Spic's got it; and we'll search her place."

Kendra recoiled in horror, as if the Fox were a loathsome snake.

"I'm sorry, Miss Applegate, but I must search this house."He handed her a piece of paper. "That's not a regular official warrant, because I'm doing this as a favor for Judge Edwards; and I'm trying to do it quietly to keep the newspaper from getting wind of it."

Kendra studied the *unofficial warrant*. "H'm—I think I better call my boss, Mr. Clark Rogers, and see what he thinks of this."

"Why, Clark and I are friends. I had no idea you worked for him."

"I just recently started working for him."

"You can call the King of England, for all I care," barked the Fox, "but we're gunna search this house today."

"I can't call the King, since England has a Queen," flippantly replied Kendra, looking directly at Delacroix, who was smiling. "I guess you might as well begin your violation right here in the parlor."

Instantly, the Fox turned up all the sofa and chair cushions, and then went fishing inside the sofa. He brought up a nickel; a quarter; a dime. The big chair, with the peacocks and poppies, produced two pennies and three nickels. He silently handed all to Kendra, with a muttered oath.

"Thanks. I usually do my digging on Thursday nights, trying to scrape up enough lunch money for Friday." To herself: "I've got to get them out of here, away from the box and my pocketbook." Aloud: "Maybe you all ought to dismantle my aunt's bedroom next. She's been known to hide things under the mattress and in her armoire. "

They searched Molly Primrose's room, and then went from room to room, peering under beds and mattresses, poking and plundering in drawers, desks and armoires. The shrewd-looking Fox, prowling from room to room like a sly-stepping cat, sneaking, even searched the bathroom.

In Kendra's room, Delacroix picked up Sonny's picture. "So this is the young man you're sending that box full of meat and moon pies to. He's lucky to have such a thoughtful and beautiful sweetheart."

Kendra smiled her prettiest smile.

The Fox, his face full of hate, muttered an oath each time he met with failure. "Give me your keys, Miss?" he gruffly demanded.

Kendra reached into her suitcoat pocket, pulled out her keys and handed them to the Fox.

"These are your car keys. Where's your house key?"

"It was that big key in the top drawer of my aunt's bureau. My aunt and I never use it. No body on Starlight Street worries about his house being broken into—or *searched*. That is until today."

"Here's your car keys back. Do you have a safety deposit box?"

Kendra laughed a rippling laugh. "I wish I did, then maybe I'd have some jewels to lock up.— I got a small savings account."

"Your aunt? How much you and the ol' lady got stashed away?"

"That's none of your business."

"You might as well tell us, Miss Applegate, because I can check it out," quietly said Delacroix.

"Then check it out.—Oh, well"—she shrugged indifferently—"my aunt's been saving all her life, and she's got about $2—3,000 bucks in the Hibernia Bank; and you saw her $500 burial policy when you went through her desk. I've got about $250 bucks in the same bank."

The Fox, looking like the fiend he was, turned to Delacroix. "Be sure and verify that."—Delacroix nodded—"We've got to search under the house," he added, "but I don't wanna get dirty. You'll have to call a flunk from the Force to crawl under the house."

"A lot of folk on Starlight Street put their savings in coffee cans and bury them under the house," interjected Kendra, "but my aunt's not one of them. Well, while you two are trying to get somebody to flunk for you, I'm leaving. I've got to go see my aunt for a few minutes, and then drop by Willowwynn. I have some typing to do for Mr. Erpelding."

"I'm afraid you won't be doing any typing for Karl Erpelding," softly said Delacroix. "Early this morning the housekeeper found him dead in bed. Dr. Lopez said he had another stroke."

The blood around Kendra's heart froze.

"Yeah, that Erpelding," muttered the Fox, "he's the one who got the

Judge suspicious of Trenchard. Erpelding got an audit started on the Sloan Endowment Fund; and while that audit was goin' on, the Judge soon discovered that Trenchard had embezzled $800,000. He confronted Trenchard, and the guilty jerk jumped over the bannister; and then at the hospital said a ghost shoved him.— A bastid, thief and a *liar.*"

"What I've seen from Mr. Erpelding's preliminary audit, proves the suspected embezzler is Judge Edwards. Of course, it would be to the Judge's benefit to blame his dead son-in-law, if he can get away with it."

Delacroix whistled; the fiendish Fox looked more alert than ever.

"You know, Mr. Delacroix, you should not only be searching for the Judge's money, but for Mrs. Rogers' killer as well— She was murdered, you know. According to Mr. Erpelding, he had evidence to prove Mrs. Rogers was murdered. Of course, he's dead now; but maybe his assistant, Miss Foughtenberry might have that evidence."

The two men looked at each other, startled. Delacroix spoke: "This mysterious Miss Foughtenberry—no one at Willowwynn's ever heard of her—called me yesterday and told me Mrs. Rogers was murdered. Do you know how I can get in touch with Miss Foughtenberry?"

"No. I just heard Attorney Erpelding refer to her as his assistant."

"I'll have to check further. Anyway, Mrs. Rogers wasn't murdered. She died of a heart attack. And another thing, Trenchard told the Judge where $500,000 of the $800,000 was. The Judge as soon as he gets his hands on that $500,000 will return it. So only $300,000 is still owed the SEF. But the Judge couldn't get Trenchard to say where he hid the $300,000. Personally, I think he gave it to Maria Galvez, his new wife."

To herself: "What a bunch of lying conspirators." Aloud "That makes more sense than giving it to my aunt to hide. I understand Mr. Erpelding came here to recoup the late Mrs. Rogers' money, and find her killer. He's dead, but the truth isn't.—Now when you two are finished pyrooting under the house, make sure my doors are shut before you leave. As I said no body on Starlight Street locks his doors, but they do close them." Then with her prettiest smile: "Mr. Delacroix, would you mind putting that big box in my automobile?"

"Not at all. You know it's too late to mail it today. The post office closed at noon."

"I know. I'm going to mail it Monday, but I've got to strap it with strong twine, first. There's lots of twine at Willowwynn, and I'm sure Mr. Rogers won't mind my taking some."

The two left the Fox on the back gallery going through the old icebox. Delacroix got the package, and Kendra opened the passenger side of the

Dodge. "Just sit it on the seat." He did.— "One moment, Mr. Delacroix, I've got an envelope in my trunk that I want to give to you. Do not show the contents to Puttuci."

She got the envelope and handed it to him. I hope you're not in the Judge's pocket, but even if you are, it doesn't matter, because Attorney Galvez and Clark Rogers both have this same information."

"I'm my own man," coldly replied Delacroix.

At that moment the mailman walked up to the Dodge. "Ah's got yo mail, Miz Applegates." He handed her several letters.

"Thanks, Ezra." Without looking at her mail, she slipped it in her pocketbook. Then to Delacroix: "I'd like to be with my aunt when you question her." She smiled prettily.

"I won't question her until her doctor says its OK. Who's her doctor?"

"Dr. F. Herbert."

"Small world. That's my family doctor."

A laugh bubbled out from between her lips. "It sure is." Delacroix nodded; and Kendra drove off. Her nerves a wreck; her mind in a whirl."Did I outwit Delacroix and the Fox? Or will they be back? If only the post office wasn't closed, the money would be on its way today."

As she approached the corner of Starlight and Claiborne Avenue, she saw Junior Foughtenberry, the sniffer and the spitter, standing at the streetcar stop, holding his black lunch box. She was home free. She halted the dodge along side the streetcar stop, blew her horn, waved and cheerily called out: "Junior, where you headed? How about a lift?"

Junior, his blue eyes blinking, his Adam's apple bobbing, his nose sniffing, spit before he answered: "I'm going to work, Kendra Louise."

"Get in. I'll take you— Oh, you'll have to move that-nuisance-of- a-box to the back seat. I'm sorry."

"That's OK." Junior moved the box, and observed: "I see you're sendin' that big box to Sonny Ganucci."

"Oh, I'm not. My aunt is. Without thinking I put from me on the return address. My aunt, just before she took sick, bought a lot of potted meat and moon pies for Sonny. You know, he's on the front lines, and only gets powdered food; and that bothers my aunt something awful. Anyway, every time I go to the hospital to see her she ask me if I packed and shipped that box off to Sonny.

"I finally got around to packing it today, but it's too late to mail, cause the post office closed at Noon. I guess I'll just have to *drag that big box* around until Monday morning. Besides, even if the post office was open,

I couldn't mail it today, because I got to tie it up with twine."

"Oh, Kendra Louise, I can take care of that for you. I have lots of twine and tape at the post office. There's a plane leaving at seven tonight, and I'll make sure Sonny's package is on it."

"That would be wonderful. You won't get in trouble doing this, will you, Junior?" asked Kendra, sounding very concerned.

"No, indeed. *I'm the supervisor*. I can do what I want."

Kendra smiled her prettiest smile.

At the post office, Junior taped and tied the box; weighed it. "That'll cost you $5.00, Kendra Louise.

"Is that airmail?"

"No. All packages, to Korea, go by plane as far as San Francisco, and then by boat, which takes about a week. To send this package airmail, all the way to Ko-reah, would cost close to—let me weigh it again—$15.00. Sonny would get all these goodies by Monday or Tuesday at the latest."

"I think that would make my aunt feel better."

While Junior plastered the box with airmail stickers, Kendra rummaged through her pocketbook for a $10 and a $5 bill.

"Sonny, you really know how to tape and tie a package real good. I'm now sorry that I wrote *MAY BE INSPECTED*. I just hate for those inspectors to rip open your *neat* work."

Junior beamed, blinked, sniffled, and almost spit on the floor, but caught himself in time. "I can fix that." He took a black marker and obliterated *MAY BE INSPECTED*. Then he grabbed a big rubber stamp, pressed it on an inked pad and then on Sonny's package. Big red letters appeared on the package—*INSPECTED*.

"Junior, I do believe you *are* the smartest supervisor the post office has or ever will have."

Junior simpered and sniffed.

"Junior, I have a letter in my pocketbook going to Sonny and, if you have a spare envelope, I'm going to rip it open and put a P.S. on it. Let Sonny know, because of your helpfulness, he'll be getting these goodies a week or two earlier than usual."

"Oh shucks, Kendra Louise, you don't have to do that. But I got an envelope you can have; and I can peal off the stamps from the old envelope and glue 'em on the new envelope."

Kendra opened the letter and wrote the P.S. A few minutes later the package and the letter were in the process of being on their way.

"Kendra Louise, you know I'm in the Gawd now; and when I'm not working here, I'm training," proudly remarked Junior.

"Yes. The Guard's the safest place for you, unless your unit gets shipped over. Then I'd have to be sending *you,* at the front lines, a big box of canned meat and moon pies. Bullets buzzing over your head, left and right, while you're trying to bite into a Vienna sausage."

Junior shuddered. "You're right. Absolutely right. But the reason I mentioned how busy I am is I should be getting a weekend off soon, and I'd like to take you to the picture show, if my momma will let me."

"What makes you think your momma won't let you?"

"Well, it's this way. She was all for us datin' until this mornin' when Miss Lettie Lou and Miss Effie Vi'let Wheelerhand came for a visit. They said Ruby Faye said you took Poochie, against her wishes, to a voodoo ritual. —And you got Poochie killed. But I don't think you did that, Kendra Louise."

"I didn't. Poochie begged me to drive him and his momma to Sister Elvira's place. He said his wife was for getting the demons out of his momma, but didn't want to see the ritual."

"I thought it might be like that. That bein' the case, I'm gunna ask my momma if I can take you to the picture show. You got a partic'lar picture you wanna see?"

Kendra knew Elmyra Foughtenberry monitored her son's movies, and would never allow him to see: "*Joan of Arc.* I'd like to see that."

Oh, I'm sorry, Kendra Louise, my momma won't let me see that one, because Ingrid Bergman disgraced herself."

"Well, how about *All About Eve,* with Bette Davis. She hasn't scandalized herself lately."

"That's also on my momma's *NO* list."

"Cinderella and Pinocchio were just at the Tivoli. Both should be coming back in a year or so."

"That's fine. By then I know I'll have changed my momma's mind about you."

"Well, just let me know. Thanks for everything, Junior—now I got to run. My aunt's waiting for me."

Kendra found her aunt sitting up in bed and no longer hooked up to oxygen; her cheeks had a little apple in them; her white silky hair brushed and drawn back into a neat knot at the nape of her neck; her blue eyes were stern looking.

"Tante, seeing you without the oxygen is a wonderful surprise," said Kendra, bending over and kissing her. "You're looking a lot like yourself."

"I guess I'm lookin' better cause Dr. Herbert put a name to that pain in my chest—angina, though I never heard tell of it. He also says it's not so much my heart givin' me trouble, as my gallbladder. My gallbladder he says is the real troublemaker—it's full of stones—and if it keeps actin' up, he'll havta cut it out. I hate the thoughts of surgery. If I live through that surgery, I'll be lucky; if I don't, I'll be dead."

"Well, what's Dr. Herbert going to do to make it stop acting up?"

"He says he may be able to cure me with diet; and, if that works, I can go home in couple days."

"That's the best news I've heard all day, Tante."

"Have a seat, Kendra *Louise*,"—she sank into the bedside chair—"You just missed Lettie Lou and Effie Vi'let. They called the hospital to see if I could have visitors, and Dr. Herbert had just taken that restriction off. So they came to see me. They came to tell me a big hawg killed Poochie Pujowl—

"Why folks ain't recovered from Antlee Theaud jumpin' off the Huey P. Long Bridge, and now Poochie's dead. Death can get you away from some folks and get you back to others. I hope Poochie gets a nice long rest before his momma joins him on the other side.

"Anyways, they said it's all your fault Poochie's dead. They said Ruby Faye begged you not to carry her husband and his momma off to Sister Elvira's place, but you didn't pay her no never mind.

"They said the po-leece brought you home early this mornin'. That's a terrible awful disgrace bein brought home by the po-leece. The po-leece never have come to my door, or my parents' door."

"The only exercise those two biddies get is running their mouths and jumping to conclusions," muttered Kendra.

"The po-leece bringin' a young girl, or anybody, home at the crack of dawn would make talk anywhere. Lots of talk—and all bad."

"Clark Rogers brought me home, not the police. One policeman drove my Dodge; another drove home ol' lady Pujowl in a patrol car. My driving Poochie and his momma to Sister Elvira's place against Ruby Faye's wishes is an out-'n'-out lie. Poochie *begged* me to drive him. I thought Sister Elvira would chant a lot o mumbo jumbo over old lady Pujowl, and then anoint her with chicken blood, and that would be the whole kit and caboodle.

"But it turned out to be an orgy of diabolical acts. I begged Poochie to come away— If he had listened to me, he'd be alive today. After Poochie had been killed and old lady Pujowl and I were taken to the police station—Clark knew exactly what to do at the station, and he did it quietly and expertly—I wasn't capable of driving home. If Clark hadn't driven me home, I'd have begged a policeman to."

"Kendra *Louise,* it's your monkey-foolishness that's makin' my trouble more my heart than them stones in my gallbladder."

"I'm sorry, Tante, I really and truly am sorry. I have some more bad news. Jack is dead and—"

"I suspected as much, because I didn't hear no ravin' goin' on across the hall. I am so sorry, my dahlin' niece. How did you find out?

"By accident." She briefly told her aunt how she had crawled into the hearse, pulled back the sheet and looked into Jack's face.

"Gawd save us! Who ever heard the like of crawlin' into a hearse? Not me. Go on with the rest of your bad news."

"I just left Hippolyte Delacroix, the state attorney, and a Mr. Dom Puttuci, Judge Edwards' henchman, a real fiend, at our house. They searched inside, and they're now waiting for a flunky to come crawl under the house and see if he can find Jack's $300,000."

"Gawd save us! Who would've ever thought the state attorney would be pyrootin' inside my house and under my house? Not me."

"Tante, did the chicken hawks say they were going straight home? I'd hate for them to see that search party."

"They're goin to the movies, to see *Joan of Arc.* Nell Miller raved so much about it, yesterday, at Antlee Theaud's funeral, I believe everybody attendin' the funeral's goin' to the movies today. They told me you didn't attend the funeral."

"Truth to tell I forgot about it. I'm sorry."

"No matter what's on your mind, I'd think it'd be hard to forget a funeral." Molly Primrose paused and changed the subject. "Kendra Lou, I'm so thankful Jack picked up his money. I wonder what made the state attorney and that other man come lookin' for the money at our house?"

"They said the Judge told Jack he was going to expose him as an embezzler; and Jack, knowing he was going to be unmasked, decided to kill himself, but not before he made a deal with you to hide the loot. In return Jack promised you the $300,000, plus his insurance, which, because he committed suicide, is not collectible."

"*Meeee! in all of this!* That's pine black crazy talk. I'm surprised the state attorney's so dumb."

"He may be playing dumb. Right now he's on the Judge's side, but I hope when I finish presenting the case I have against the Judge, he'll be on my side."

"Then you're going after the Judge?"

"Yes. I know Jack didn't want the Judge, or any of the Edwardses, to have a nickel of his money, nor did he want them to know about me. He used your name, in all transactions, to throw the Judge off my trail."

"Do you think the Judge will link Jack to you?"

"Yes. And soon."

"Oh, there goes that angina. I tell you, today, it's more angina than them gallstones. Kendra Lou, you're gunna worry the heart out of me before I get home."

"No, I won't. Listen carefully to me, Tante. I think I'll have all this cleared up before Delacroix and possibly Mr. Puttuci, can question you. If they do, I need you to play dumb. Say you knew Jack, but I didn't. Say you knew nothin of the money or insurance policies.'

"I don't know *nothin'* about no insurance policies."

"Well, that's one lie you don't have to tell.—"

"I'll say whatever you want me to say."

"Good. Tante, I know you said, after that trip to the crazy house and the leper colony, you never wanted to leave New Orleans again; but, when you get home and this is over, you and me are going to go some where and have a good time. Forget our troubles. We'll fly to Mexico City."

"Of all places, Mexico City. You talk like Mexico City is across the street or around the corner. Besides, this is the first time I've heard you say you wanted to run off to no Mexico City. You can't speak Spanish and neither can I. We couldn't have no good time with all them Mexicans, babblin' their heads off, in Spanish. All those colored people. We're already smothered to death with colored right here in New Orleans, why fly way over to Mexico City, to be smothered to death with more colored people."

"Spanish are white. You can't equate Spanish with colored."

"Kendra *Louise,* I just want to go home to my double and live happily ever after on Starlight Street. I don't wanna leave New Orleans, for no Mexico City. Besides, I'm afraid of airplanes.— Anyways, where was you gunna get the money to take me to Mexico City?" suspiciously asked her aunt, her button blue eyes very wide and very wondering. "Jack—did—get—his—money?"

"I mailed the money and some moon pies to Korea—today. To Sonny." Quickly Kendra told her aunt how Junior had helped her.

Mere words couldn't describe the horror on her aunt's face. Molly Primrose clutched her chest: "It's monkey-foolishness like this that's causin' my angina"; then she clutched her stomach: "It's monkey-foolishness like this that makes it feel like somebody's in my gallbladder using them stones like bowlin' balls. If Junior gets fired over this; if Sonny gets a bad discharge over this, not to mention Poochie bein' dead and

Ruby Faye sayin' it's all your doin's, we'll *havta* move to Mexico City," moaned her aunt in a dungeon-dark tone.

Kendra stood up. "Tante, I've got to go."

"Before you go, I got another question. How come Clark Rogers to know you were at Sister Elvira's place?"

"I told him over the phone I was driving neighbors to Jefferson Parish; and I'd be home around nine. Mrs. TuJax and Mrs. Springmeyer were listening in, and they told him where Sister Elvira lived. They must've gotten it from Ruby Faye. Clark came over at nine and waited on the gallery for me. When I didn't show he came after me with the Jefferson Parish Police. I'm very grateful he showed up."

"I would say so. Is he put out with you for going to such a place?"

"Yes, he is. He said it was a stupid thing for me to do. He was right, of course, but I had a terrible day and a worse night. So when Poochie asked me to give him a lift, I thought the drive might help me forget some of my troubles. If I hadn't been so exhausted when Clark dropped me home, I'd have told him where to get off at instead of letting him tell me Starlight Street was an extension of the crazy house.

"However, I'm grateful that Clark drove me home, and found out from the police that Sister Elvira put a substance in her fire that made me hallucinate. The only real things I saw were the chickens and the wild boar, and it came, not out of anybody's body, but out the woods, and sliced Poochie to pieces."

"Kendra Lou, Clark Rogers has been comin' to see me most every day he's in town, and I know he's in love with you—"

"I doubt if we'll marry now."

"Jack *is* dead; so don't be stingy with your love. You're too young not to love again. To love only once in a lifetime because someone dies is a waste. Don't waste any chances at love and happiness. Right now you feel certain Jack would've been your best love, but you can't be sure. Maybe the best is yet to come.

"When my William Kavanaugh died, I acted stupid and selfish, refusing to love again.— Whatever you and Jack were plannin', and his accident prevented it, can never be now."

Their eyes met in a long, wordless understanding, and Kendra thought, "She knows."

"Do not apologize or be embarrassed for what you was cookin' up with Jack. There's nothin' to forgive and nothin' to be embarrassed about, when it comes to love and bein' loved."

"Yes. But I don't think you'd feel that way if you knew the whole story. Clark Rogers had asked me to marry him and I accepted. Then Jack, just this past Thursday came to see me, and that's when I discovered how remarkable the healing power of true love is. He said he had obtained a quickie Mexican divorce, by proxy; was free, and asked me to marry him. I agreed.

"We were going to elope that very night to Mexico City. I loved him in spite of all his faults and failings, his sins and secrets. I still love him. I wrote Clark a note.—Oh, that terrible note. Oh, God—By now he's got it. Even if I hadn't written that note, I couldn't possibly marry him, without telling him."

"Kendra Lou, I got some good free advice for you: Never, never tell *everything* you got stored in your head and your heart to any living soul— Now go home and get some rest, so you can go to early early morning Mass. *Don't-forget-Mass.*"

"There's more, Tante. On his deathbed Jack married Maria Galvez. Now, Tante, don't look like that. Believe me, it's for the best. I think the Judge, since Delacroix and Puttuci didn't find the money at our house, is going to go after Jack's wife."

"When Jack Trenchard was across the hall being delirious your name was forever on his lips. And when he woke up, you mean to tell me, that gutter grass married some body else. Bad blood tells. His was tainted, spoiled and rotten. His parents must've been murderers or highwaymen."

"Jack's parents weren't murderers; and they haven't been highwaymen in a hundred years. Tante, how much can your heart take?"

"My heart can take everythin' and anythin' except not knowin' what monkey foolishness you're up to."

"Jack's one of us. He's my brother; and I have another brother, Johnny Placide. He's in jail for killing a cousin of Judge Edwards'. It was self-defense. I met Jack and Johnny's mother, Mary Trenchard Placide; their daddy is my daddy. Tom Applegate. There're several pictures of my daddy and Mary Trenchard in the back of our album. You said you found these pictures in my daddy's wallet, though you didn't know the woman, but figured my daddy did. So you kept them.

"On the very day Jack and I were to elope to Mexico City, he found out I was his sister."

Molly Primrose suddenly looked very small and fragile; even her hands looked thin and worn. Seeing this, tore at Kendra's heart. "Tante, say something. Even if it's only: 'Gawd save us.' I've got proof, if you want to see it. Father Landry, from St. Catherine's Parish, up the country, gave me copies of Jack's and Johnny's birth records."

"Spare me the sordid details."

"They're not sordid. My father knew Mary Trenchard before he knew my mother; he took up with Mary again, after my mother died."

"D-don't show me nothin' now, Kendra Lou. If you show and tell me all the bad news now, there won't be nothin' to show and tell when I come home. Another thing, Kendra Lou, you can't let the Judge think Maria Galvez, my dear nephew's wife, has that money."

"Don't worry about Maria; she's a lawyer and knows how to fight dirty. Tante, some day would you like to meet Johnny?"

"Of course I want to meet my dahlin' nephew. Johnny's one of us. He's sealed of our tribe; and so's precious Jack. I always said Jack looked like a handsome Applegate, didn't I?"

Kendra kissed her aunt. "Yes, you did. I love you, Tante. I better go now. You need to rest. I'll pray for us at morning Mass."

Chapter Seventeen

ATTORNEY JACK TRENCHARD, SON-IN-LAW OF JUDGE EXUM EDWARDS, IS DEAD AT 27.

The headlines of the Sunday morning paper darted up at Kendra as she sipped coffee and ate toast, that took four slices of bread to make two edible slices. Her eyes traveled swiftly down the column. Attorney Jack Trenchard, son-in-law of the honorable Judge Exum Edwards, died from injuries sustained in a suicide attempt. This past Thursday, Trenchard attempted suicide after his father-in-law threatened to expose him for embezzling $800,000 from the Sloan Endowment Fund, plus stealing $300,000 from Judge Edwards' personal account.

"I allowed Jack Trenchard, a penniless orphan, to marry my daughter"; read Kendra, "I gave him a partnership in my law firm; a home to live in; food to eat; a brand-new automobile, all the luxuries of life; and his thanks was to steal from me and a client of mine. This is proof-positive that bad blood tells."

Kendra read this quote twice, and started on a third reading, but a loud banging at the front door took her eyes from the printed page. Her lips trembled as she pushed the paper aside, adjusted her white wrapper, and answered the door.

"Miss Applegate?"—Kendra nodded—"I'm Attorney Maria Galvez," said the striking Spanish woman, who was about thirty, tall, dark and slender, with enormous velvety brown eyes. Her cheeks were rosy red, like her full lips, and her thick jet hair was worn in a French twist. She was dressed in an orange silk artist smock, a forest green silk blouse and a navy linen skirt. Jack's bride was vivid and beautiful.

"Come in. How about a cuppa coffee?"

As soon as Maria was seated and served her coffee, she abruptly announced: "I married your brother, Jack, by proxy, a few hours before he died."

"I didn't know Jack had divorced Allison," lied Kendra, playing cagey. "When?" She arched her eyebrows in surprise.

"A couple days ago. He divorced her by proxy, through my brother's law firm, which is in Mexico City. When I called my brother and told him Jack had an accident—"

"It was no accident," interrupted Kendra. "He was hurled over the bannister by the ghost of Carol Rogers."

Maria gave Kendra a look that implied *I don't believe in ghosts, so don't talk to me of ghosts.* "Anyway, when I told my brother that Jack was dying, he was shocked. He said he had recently talked to Jack and, acting as his lawyer, had the Mexican court grant him a divorce, by proxy. On the same day of the divorce, Alfredo drew up a proxy wedding ceremony, sans the bride's name. He said Jack wouldn't tell him the bride's name, because he wanted to surprise him.

"Jack also told Alfredo he and his bride would be arriving Mexico City, last Friday morning, 6:30, on Delta Flight 213. Alfredo said he was certain I was the girl Jack was bringing to marry, so Alfredo put my name on the license and performed a proxy marriage ceremony for Jack and me. I'm carrying Jack's child."

Kendra's startled eyes met Maria's. "I suppose lawyers and judges can do anything. Did Jack know he married you before he died?"

"Yes. He seemed pleased." Her eyes misted. "I called Moisant to confirm if Jack had two reservations for Mexico City; and the ticket agent said he had. One ticket for Jack; the other, the agent wouldn't tell me the name. D-did Jack say anything to you about marrying—*me?*"

Kendra to herself: "Flush both tickets." Aloud: "Yes. You don't have anything to worry about. You were the girl.— "Well, sister-in-law, you married into a family with a lot of trouble: your husband, according to this morning's *Picayune,* is branded an embezzler; your brother-in-law, Johnny, a murderer—"

"Whose now been denied bail. Judge Bosco had set Johnny's bail at $5,000; but when Judge Edwards bribed Bosco—I understand Edwards gave him 10 Grand for the case—Edwards said no bail."

"Does Jack's mother know?"

"Yes. Ever since Johnny's been in jail, she's been frantically trying to raise bail money. Last evening, I told her not to worry about money, because I was Jack's wife and I'd take care of Johnny's bail and defense."

"I suppose she was really relieved."

""Ve-ry. But I could tell she was stunned about Jack and me." She shrugged. "There's more bad news, the bartender who witnessed the fight between Johnny and Delachaise and, who can swear Delachaise provoked it, was found floating in the Mississippi River, shot in the head."

"Then the Judge knows Jack and Johnny are brothers. How?"

"The Judge has many spies."

"And to carry his grudge against Jack beyond the grave, he's going to fry Johnny—send him to the chair."

"That's his plan. Exum Edwards is a vindictive man. Jack told me to go after the Judge; and made me promise not to let you, his baby sister, get involved."

Kendra to herself: "God, *baby sister.*"

"Jack made two bad mistakes," went on Maria, "one, he beat the Judge to the $300,000; two, he divorced *precious* Allison and married me, before she could divorce Jack and marry Cameron Claremont. That set the old boy crazy."

Both were thoughtful; then Kendra asked: "Have you read this?" She shoved the headlines across the table."I thought I gave you enough evidence to ruin the Judge, not let the Judge ruin Jack."

"I read it. Ordinarily the kind of evidence you gave me would've put any man, except the Judge, under the jail. Judge Edwards is a *powerful* man. I confronted him, in the presence of Hippo Delacroix and Clark Rogers, with all the evidence you left with my secretary. The upshot: Rogers cut a deal with the Judge.

"The Judge agreed to pay back Rogers the $800,000 he stole from the SEF, but Jack must take the fall. The pay back is scheduled for eleven, this morning, at Willowwynn. Thus the article in this morning's paper, blackening Jack's name; praising the Judge for being such a good father-in-law, was agreed to by the deal-making parties.

"In turn, Clark Rogers insisted that the missing $300,000, that Jack had allegedly stolen from the Judge, be written off. The Judge agreed. I don't understand why Rogers did such a thing, other than he thinks I've got the money, that I'm pregnant and need protecting. The Judge then turned to me and said 'enjoy your stolen money, *Mrs. Trenchard.*'— I repeated I didn't have the money."

Kendra to herself: "Clark knows I've got the money, and he's protecting me." Aloud: "Yesterday, the Judge thought my aunt had that money. He had Delacroix and Puttuci search this house. They didn't come up with a cent, because my aunt doesn't have that money. —Too bad you didn't ask Jack what he did with his $300,000."

"Over and over I did. He just said it was still in the bank."

"I can't believe Clark Rogers and Hippolyte Delacroix let the Judge off the hook so easily."

The phone rang. Kendra dashed to the hall and took the call. It was

Mary Placide. "Kendra Louise, there's no bail and no lawyer fee. When can I bring you this paper sack back with what you gave me?"

"Never," whispered Kendra. "It's for you and Johnny. And it's still a secret. It'll always be a secret. Do you understand? I can't talk any more."

"Yes. Thank you and good-bye."

"It's not good-bye. We'll all get together soon. I want to meet my brother and my aunt wants to meet her nephew. I'll get back to you."

Kendra went directly to her room, removed the chain from around her neck and took the diamond ring Jack had given her and placed it in its tiny ring box. She refastened the chain around her neck and returned to the kitchen. She handed Maria the ring box. "When I visited Jack in the hospital he told me in his coat pocket was a ring for his girl, Maria. He didn't say he was already divorced."

With tears in her eyes Maria slipped on the diamond ring. "It's a little tight, but it's so beautiful."

"Yes, it is.— As I was saying, I can't believe Delacroix and Clark Rogers let the Judge off the hook."

"I can," replied Maria, lifting her eyes from the ring. "Both men are smart. Delacroix—the Judge made him state attorney—knows he has nothing to gain by exposing Edwards, and everything to lose. On the other hand Rogers isn't indebted to the Judge in any way, so I don't know why he didn't expose the Judge for the thief he is, or why he let Jack take the fall for the Judge. He's protecting some one and, in this case, it's not *me*.

"There's another possibility: I think Rogers believes the Judge is responsible for Karl Erpelding's death and, by letting the Judge off the hook, will end further killing. Hippo told me Rogers said Erpelding called the Judge and told him he had hard evidence linking him to a conclave of killers who murdered Carol Rogers.

"The Judge simply sicked his killer-doctor friend, Emile Lopez, on Erpelding, who received a lethal shot; and died a quiet death."

"Is anyone else aware that Dr. Lopez is Judge Edwards' needle man? I think he gave Jack one of those lethal shots."

"I'm sure he did. Certain circles in this city know for a fact, when Edwards says kill, Lopez jabs a needle in some victim's arm or butt. Anyway, Hippo and Clark searched Erpelding's room for that alleged hard evidence to back up Erpelding's calling the Judge a killer. All they found was a folder containing the same info you gave to me, to Hippo and to Clark. If only Erpelding had kept his mouth shut and presented his evidence against the Judge, Johnny wouldn't have to fry for killing in self-defense."

"The hard evidence Erpelding spoke of is on a tape; and *I have* that incriminating tape. The conclave of killers' voices, including Judge Edward's, along with the others, are recorded. Step by step their voices tell how they killed Carol Rogers."

Maria sucked in her breath. "Then give me that tape now, and I'll blackmail the Judge into releasing Johnny."

"It's not that simple." To herself: "I can still hear CR saying '...Will you close your eyes to facts?'

"'I'm a woman of principle. I believe in truth and justice. Nothing could prevent me from bringing a murderer to justice. *Nothing.*'

"'Not even if it came to saving, say your aunt's life.'

"'That's stupid. *Nothing,* as far as I'm concerned, takes precedence over truth and justice.'

"'We shall see,'" was CR's reply.

Still to herself: "I won't be cowed and subdued by a ghost. Johnny is my brother; he comes before you, CR, and justice." Aloud: "Another thing, Maria, have you considered Clark Rogers' feelings? I'm sure when he learns who his wife's murderers are, he'll want me to turn that tape over to a grand jury, not use it as a blackmail tool, to free Johnny."

"I knew Carol; and she was a bitch and a slut. She deserved to die. To be killed. We must make Clark see that—"

"I don't think anybody deserves to die. To be killed. No matter how much a bitch or a slut she is." Kendra looked at her watch. "I've got to get dressed now, if I'm going to bump into the Judge at Willowwynn and play my tape for him—blackmail him into setting Johnny free."

"I'm going with you. I promised Jack—"

"No, you're not. Your presence, the girl Jack divorced *precious* Allison for, won't help our cause. Believe me, I can handle this. Before I hand over that tape, Johnny will be released. All charges dropped. Stay home and wait for my call telling you to pick up Johnny, from Parish Prison."

"Good luck," said Maria, rising. "By the way, I can tell you and Jack are related, but Johnny could be your twin. I'll find my way out."

As soon as Maria left, Kendra went to her room, emptied her pocketbook on the bed and found the two tickets to Mexico City, along with the letters postman Ezra had handed her the day before.

"My God! here's my note to Clark, returned for postage. I mailed it without a stamp." She laughed and cried and tore it to shreds, along with the airplane tickets Jack had bought to Mexico City, for him and her. She flushed the pieces. Then she read the other letter, from Sonny Ganucci.

Sonny said, in about ten days, he'd be in Tokyo on R&R, and while there he'd marry rich Lily Rose Saki, a beautiful Japanese opera singer. Lily Rose's father owned a brokerage house. He said his future father-in-law would loan him the money to open a pizza parlor in Tokyo; and when he had paid the loan back, he'd open one in New Orleans, again using borrowed money from Mr. Saki.

"My God! Sonny's getting married to a rich Japanese girl. How wonderful for him; how horrible for his parents. Rosa and Tony and all the Starlight Street folk will never understand or accept a mixed marriage. They can't because they never go about. They think New Orleans is the world.—Well, Sonny should get the money and the moon pies by Monday. I suppose I'll hear from him when he goes to Tokyo. I think Jack's money will be in good hands."

She put the letter back in her pocketbook and dressed. She slipped into the same dress she had worn to Mass: a cool creamy white muslin, with a mandarin collar and full skirt. Because the day promised to be a scorcher, she piled her shiny mass of brown-gold gypsy ringlets on top her head, allowing a few curls to escape.

She glanced in the glass and said: "You need to look your best for this encounter." She leaned closer to the mirror and, with a critical eye, noted her honey-colored skin was soft and dewy and her high color was that of a pink rose. The overall picture was perfect.

Twenty minutes later she had reached Willowwynn; and found Clark in his study, in deep conversation with Hippo Delacroix. Both men gave a sudden start when she entered the room. Both stood. Clark was wearing white flannels and a navy knit shirt; Hippo, a dark suit.

"This is a pleasant surprise," said Clark. "Hippo, I believe you know Miss Applegate."

"Yes, he does," answered Kendra. "He and Puttuci, using a fake warrant, searched my house yesterday, looking for the $300,000 the Judge gave Jack to marry Allison. They didn't find it."

The fiery gleam in Kendra's amber eyes showed the intensity of her feelings; however, she took the hand held out, as Delacroix came forward and softly said: "The Judge now believes Mrs. Maria Galvez Trenchard is in possession of her husband's money, and has written it off. Now, Miss Applegate, you'll have to excuse me. I was just leaving." He turned to Clark and, with a significant nod, said: "I'll find my way out."

As soon as Hippo was out of sight, Clark came forward and hugged her hard. He was really glad to see her and, having some one really glad to see you, makes a great difference. She lost some of her stiffness.

"Kendra, I'm expecting Judge Edwards and his wife in a few minutes. Our business won't take long, then we can talk in the library."

"No. I know the Judge is coming here to return the $800,000 he stole from the SEF. The Judge is the thief, though he blamed the theft on Jack Trenchard, so said this morning's *Picayune*. After you get your money, I want you, the Judge and his wife to come upstairs to CR's sitting room. I'll be waiting for you there, to play an audio tape of CR's murder. I've got it in this briefcase. Didn't Karl Erpelding tell you about the murder tape?"

Clark looked surprised. "I didn't get to talk to Karl, but Hippo did. According to Hippo, Karl called the Judge and said he had hard evidence implicating him in Carol's murder. Earlier, a Miss *Foughtenberry,* claiming to be Karl's assistant, called Hippo, telling him to come to Willowwynn on Sunday afternoon, at which time Carol's murderer would be exposed. I told Hippo I wasn't aware that Karl had an assistant, here in New Orleans. Do you know a Miss *Foughtenberry?*"

"No," quickly lied Kendra, reddening.

"Anyway, after Karl's death, Hippo and I searched his room for that alleged evidence. We came up with nothing. Now you say you have that hard evidence in the form of a tape. You should've said that to Hippo before he left."

"No. I don't want Hippo in on this. When I'm through, you'll understand why."

"I'm looking forward to knowing *why;* however, to put your mind at ease, Hippo's on your side"; then he looked at CR's briefcase. Kendra gripped it in her left hand. "I see you borrowed it again."

"Yes. Karl Erpelding gave me permission. I suppose you've turned over Karl Erpelding's body to Lopez and Prestijockeymoe, so they can cremate him before an autopsy can be made. Then, afterwards, blame it on Albert Lepardieux."

"Kendra, there's no need to talk snippy and sarcastic. Dr. Lopez said Karl died of complications from his stroke. I've had Karl's body flown directly to San Francisco, where an autopsy will be performed."

"You trust Dr. Lopez and Dr. Vince Prestijockeymoe so much you sent Karl's body straight off to San Francisco, for an autopsy, eh?"

"I just don't want any slip ups. Hippo's on his way to see Vince now."

"Kind of late for that, isn't it?" She didn't wait for an answer. She changed the subject."Why are you letting Jack take the rap for the Judge's theft? By not coming forward with the proof I gave you, you've let the Judge ruin Jack Trenchard's name."

"Trenchard didn't have a name. I suppose, in your love for that bum, you've closed your mind to any consequences being visited upon your aunt."

"Is—my aunt—in—danger?"

"With Judge Edwards, it's the unexpected you must expect. By getting him to write that $300,000 off, and letting that story appear in this morning's *Picayune,* I may have saved your aunt's life and yours; and thrown Maria Galvez' life in jeopardy. The Judge hates Maria, not because he believes she has the money, but because of her death-bed marriage to Trenchard.

"I hated to involve Maria, but you left me no choice. I'm certain *you* have that $300,000. I think the money was in that case Trenchard left with you the night I interrupted the two of you. I let Trenchard take the fall, I let the Judge think Maria's got that money, because I care about what happens to you."

"If you care about me, then have the *Picayune* write a retraction to this morning's story. If the blame can't be laid at the Judge's door, lay it at the SEF's. Simply say the SEF made a terrible mistake when it reported $800,000 missing. Say the money was found in a separate account; and publicly apologize to Jack Trenchard."

"Forget about a retraction. Forget about an apology. I made a deal with the Judge, and I intend to live up to every pencil point of that deal. There are many things you can't imagine, and more you don't understand. Trenchard messed with the Judge, and got the axe. Let it go."

"And Karl Erpelding messed with that powerful crooked Judge, and also got the axe. There's just no stopping *that* axing Judge, is there? And another thing, Jack wasn't a bum. He was my *brother.*"

"*Your brother,*" repeated Clark, taken aback. "And you almost"—he swallowed the rest. "W-when did you learn this?"

"As you started to say, yes, I almost married my brother. I learned this news from Mary Placide, Jack's mother, the same day I drove Poochie Pujowl to Sister Elvira's place—to the voodoo ritual."

"You poor kid. I was such a beast that night. I had no idea that you were suffering so. I was overcome with jealousy because of a funny feeling I had that you and Trenchard were a twosome again; and you and I were history. I was also furious that you had allowed yourself to become involved in such hideous goings on, at a voodoo ritual—Pujowl's death. You could've been killed, and that made me so angry. No one has a right to play so carelessly with his or her life when he or she is beloved.— Do you have the money? No, let me put it this way, do you know where the money is?"

"Why are you so worried about Jack's money? You've got yours back."

"I'm not worried about the money. I'm worried about you. Carol did underhanded things. Carol was a great betrayer. I some how can't believe you're in her league."

"I'm not. I don't have the money, but I know where it is. Jack, on his death bed, said the money was mine and made me promise to keep it out of the Judge's greedy hands."

The front door knocker sounded.—"That must be the Judge," muttered Clark . "We'll finish this conversation later."

"I'll see you all upstairs."

Upstairs in CR's sitting room, the heat was oppressive. Kendra quickly threw open all the tall windows and the French doors leading to the balcony. Next she drew the chair, belonging to the secretary, close to an open window and sat in it facing the white Georgian mantel. And while she waited, a breeze, blowing in and out, brought into the room soft fragrances of magnolia and honeysuckle.

A quarter of an hour passed before Clark, Judge Edwards and his wife appeared. As they grouped around the oval coffee table in front of the mantel, Kendra sized them up.

The Judge, sporting a good tan, was dressed in a light suit, and looked stately and splendid. He was tall, with piercing blue eyes, and a head of steal gray finger-waving hair. He looked like a man accustomed to deference and respect. He didn't look like a thief, or as Aunt Molly Primrose had said 'a bad apple—worm eaten.'

He shook Kendra's hand, and the blood around her heart froze. Quickly she turned toward Eleanor Edwards, who was wearing a soft gray silk shirtwaist dress. Mrs. Edwards reminded her of one of those *Modess Because* models. She was tall and slender, with Bette Davis eyes and champagne blonde hair, which she wore in a French twist. She was lithe and graceful in her movements. She must've been a real beauty in her heyday, but now her fifty years were showing a bit, along with the spite and malice that now shone in those big eyes. She didn't shake hands, but said in a syrupy thick southern drawl:

"Why, Miss Applegate, how pretty you are—for a secretary."

After that bitchy remark, Mrs Edwards and the Judge sat down in the blue-and-white loveseat. Clark sat across from them.

"Clark says you've got a tape that alleges dear Carol was murdered," drawled Eleanor Edwards, "and you want us to hear it. I thought stenos were suppose to type, not be clever and keen witted, as Clark says you are. You best play your tape now, because we can only spare a few minutes— We're anxious to get to the hospital to visit our brand-new grandson."

"This is going to take more than a few minutes, Mrs. Edwards," replied Kendra, leaving her chair to stand center front of the mantel. "You see, I've decided not to play the tape, but to tell you a story, and then let you listen to the tape."

Before the Edwardses could object, Kendra plunged on: "Once upon a time there was a rich and beautiful married woman, who had many lovers and who did many bad things. She stole husbands from wives; she dumped lovers, with the greatest of ease. This bad woman was Carol Rogers; and she wound up murdered."

"And you think one of us killed Carol?" laughed Eleanor.

"No, not one killer. CR's murder was committed by a conclave of killers; but it wasn't planned or plotted—or premeditated. There was no conspiracy to murder. It just happened that this conclave of killers, each acting on his own, got the same idea on the same day—to kill CR."

Clark frowned; Eleanor yawned; the Judge acted indifferent.

Kendra continued: "I met the ghost of CR in this very room. We sat where you and your husband are now seated, and she told me she had been murdered, and couldn't cross over to the other side until justice was served. She said If I didn't find who killed her, she'd stay on earth and haunt me for the rest of my life. I believe she made a contract with the devil, to do just that."

The Edwardses laughed; Clark didn't. "Miss Applegate, as I said, my husband and I are in a hurry to visit with our new grandson; we really don't have time to listen to ghost stories."

Kendra ignored Eleanor. "Tyrannically CR uses my body—my organs as her own property. She possess me and controls me."

The Edwardses laughed again, and this time the sneer that ran through their laughter and the contempt and mockery in their eyes would've squashed a less determined young woman, but Kendra, unruffled, told what CR had thus far done to her and to her aunt.

"I'll spare you the harrowing details, for they are indescribable. The effect, however, sent my aunt to the hospital with a heart attack. I only tell you this, because I expect CR to show up today; and, if she's in the form of a red mist, you can be assured of violence. It was a red mist that pitched Jack Trenchard over your bannister."

"Miss Applegate, I think part of your mind is missing," said Eleanor Edwards with bland, icy politeness. "You don't need to talk to us; you need to talk to a psychiatrist. And as far as Jack being pitched over the bannister by Carol, we'd like to thank her for the deed."

The Judge nodded vigorously. "My daughter, my wife and I are glad Trenchard's dead."

Kendra, her cheeks red with indignation, was not deterred, continued: "I recently dreamed of CR; and, in that dream, she showed me how to open those bookcases"—she nodded at the bookcases flanking the mantel—"where the tape was that recorded her murder."

"I don't take much stock in dreams, but if the ghost of Carol Rogers can speak, I'd like to hear her," laughed Eleanor Edwards.

"You just might get that chance." Kendra then ran her right fingertips behind the left bookcase, found the latch, pushed on it until she heard a click, and the bookcase swung out, exposing built-in shelves, a tape recorder and stacks of tapes.

Clark gave a sudden start; the Edwardses sucked in their breath; and Kendra crossed the room to her chair, where CR's briefcase stood. She snapped it open, took out a tape, walked back to the recorder and placed the incriminating tape on its wheel.

"I had no idea that that bookcase hid shelves built into the wall," exclaimed Clark, rising and shaking his head in disbelief. He seemed mesmerized and hypnotized by those shelves. "Did you know?" he asked, his navy eyes sweeping the Edwardses, as he approached the exposed shelves.

"No," was their simultaneous reply.

"I assume the other set of bookcases also open, do they? And what do they hide?" asked Clark.

Kendra opened them. "These shelves hide the file folder containing the written proof that Jack Trenchard did not steal $800,000 from the SEF; but you did, Judge Edwards"

"That money, young woman," sternly said the Judge, has been returned today, to Clark, and it's none of your business."

"That's right," seconded Clark, frowning fiercely.

"Then I better mind my business, and get back to what's on that tape." She pointed to the tape she had just put on the recorder. "The voices on the tape, your voices, not yours Clark, produce blatant facts that verify what CR told me. It's all on *that* tape; so don't interrupt me, by denying things." —She pointed to the tape again.—"I believe CR taped every conversation she ever had in this sitting room; and also taped the voice of every man who made love to her. Those love-making recordings are hidden in the panels behind her bed.

"Of course, Dr. Lopez, his voice is on the killer tape and the love-making tape, isn't here to listen to himself; and Dr. Prestijockeymoe, who isn't on this particular tape—he's on the one in the bedroom—isn't here either, to listen to himself begging Carol to make love to him; and her telling him she'd rather die than make love to a man with three chins and a face like a bull frog, and a belly like a beer barrel. Unfortunately, there's one recorded lover who can never listen to himself—Kyle Osborne. He's dead. Drowned at sea."

Eleanor Edwards, now looking like a ve-ry pale *Modess Because* model, said: "I don't believe you—"

"Kyle's dead," confirmed Clark. "Kyle and Icelynn, man and wife, were sailing to England when he fell overboard and drowned."

"How horrible," echoed the Edwardses. "He told us he was going to Berkeley—alone. Instead he sailed for England with, of all people, *Icelynn Farnsworth*. When did he marry *Icelynn, of all the women on earth?"*

"Four years ago," replied Clark." She's here," he added.—Everyone looked surprised— "She came in late last night. She said she'd explain things today, and be off tomorrow, for California. I'll go get her now."

While waiting for Clark to return with Icelynn, Kendra sat in her chair by the window, and watched the Edwardses: Eleanor looked at her manicured fingernails; the Judge at the ceiling. To herself: "The Judge is smooth and suave; his wife, calm, cool and collected. They're a confident, sure-footed pair. They're not worried."

Clark returned with Icelynn, who wore a black broadcloth skirt and a white blouse. She was a nice-looking woman, not pretty but who, as the saying goes, could pass in a crowd.

She was of medium height, and wore her short blonde hair in a pageboy with a full fluffy bang across her forehead. She was excessively thin and pale, and dark circles were burned around her restless ice-blue eyes. She looked haggard and acted nervous.

Clark placed a chair next to Kendra's, for Icelynn, and then introduced them. Icelynn sat, clenching and unclenching her hands.

"Would you like a drink," offered Kendra.

"Y-yes— Thanks."

Kendra bumped the coffee table and made the liquor decanter and glasses rattle. The Edwardses glared at her. She poured the drink and handed it to Icelynn, who gulped it down. Kendra took the glass, put it on the table, sat down and waited.

"Kyle was twenty-four and I was forty when we married. He was a student, who worked part time. After we married he never worked another day in his life. No one knew we were married. I rented an apartment for Kyle and visited him on evenings and weekends.

"When Carol moved to New Orleans, Kyle came up with a plan to use Carol. He knew I hated her and said this would be a way to get even. The plan was simple. I'd move to New Orleans with Carol, and a few weeks later tell her that it had come to my attention, via the president of Tulane, of a worthy student in need of a benefactress. I knew I could convince her to become Kyle's benefactress, because she adored handsome young men. And Kyle was a beautiful young man.

"It worked. For the past two years, Carol paid my husband's tuition, bought his books, clothes, automobile, gave him pocket money. She refused to rent him an apartment; so Kyle lived at Willowwynn. We had to sneak around to be together until you, Eleanor, rented an apartment, so Kyle could make love to you."

Eleanor looked at Icelynn with that's a-lie-air. "Kyle was Carol's lover. He told me so," she coolly added.

"Carol told you so, *not* Kyle," submitted Kendra. "Would you like to hear the tape. Hear Carol telling you so is on the tape."

"Don't play the tape," said a very sobered Judge, his piercing eyes fixed to his wife's calm but chalk white face.

"Go on, Icelynn," prompted Kendra.

"Kyle made love to Eleanor every Wednesday afternoon, and she gave him $250 a week spending money. Kyle and I, unbeknownst to Eleanor, used her apartment on weekends."

Eleanor gave Icelynn a disgusted look.

"About six months ago, Kyle and Carol became lovers. Kyle becoming Carol's lover was part of a new plan my husband had come up with to get control of her money, all her assets—by simply marrying her.

"Kyle proposed to Carol and she accepted. Soon afterwards, she changed her will, at Kyle's coaxing, cutting Clark out the picture; leaving everything to Kyle."

"You didn't object to Kyle divorcing you?" asked Kendra.

"He wasn't going to divorce me. No one knew we were married. He was simply going to marry Carol—"

"And commit bigamy."

"Yes. He'd live with Carol a year and then kill her. After he killed her, he'd come back to me, his wife, and we'd live happily ever after—rich. At first I went along with Kyle's plan, but as the time grew nearer, I could see the plan was beyond comprehension. I begged Kyle to forget it.

"He wouldn't. He wanted that twenty million dollars. He lied to Carol, to all of you, saying he was going to Berkeley to attend a literature seminar, for six weeks, leaving early in the morning of April 13th. —The night before, on April 12th we boarded *The S.S. Catherine Celene,* and sailed at 6:30 a.m., April 13th, for London— Carol would leave on April 15th, to start her six weeks' residency in Reno; and then obtain a Nevada divorce from you, Clark.

"It was all part of Kyle's plan. He bought cruise tickets to London for us, with some of the money you had given him Eleanor. I found out later, in a London hospital, he only bought a one-way ticket for me, because he had planned to kill me. Shove me overboard. And he did. We both went over the side. I was rescued; Kyle drowned." She sat the cigarette holder in the ashtray on the coffee table, and returned to her seat.

Eleanor Edwards closed her big eyes, as if in deep pain; Clark kept his eyes on Icelynn; the Judge showed a slight interest.

"According to that tape, Kyle didn't kill Carol," said Kendra.

"No, he didn't kill her," cried Icelynn, grabbing her temples with both hands, as if she had a bad headache. Then she dropped her hands into her lap. "It's all my fault that Kyle's plan was thwarted. You see, around seven on the evening of April 12th, I came to this very room to tell Carol I was leaving on my vacation. That evening she was her usual cruel self, only more so. She had a way of teasing and taunting me until I felt smirched and defaced. I told her good-bye, and she laughed at me, saying 'I suppose you're going to hole up in some cheap hotel, read dime novels and pretend you're the whore.'

"She laughed at me, and her laugh was so horrible and degrading, I snapped. I flung out at her I was sailing to England with my husband, Kyle Osborne. It was my turn to laugh; and I laughed and laughed, thanking her for providing my husband with bread and butter —and even jam these past two years. I said now that Kyle had his degree, we no longer needed her money. Naturally, after my revelation, all hell broke lose. Carol screamed every dirty name in the book at me, until she turned blue in the face.

"I left this very room, Carol's curses ringing in my ears, got my bags, called a cab and went to the ship. I knew Kyle was at your apartment, Eleanor, telling you good-bye, which meant another $250 worth of spending money for our vacation."

Eleanor winced.

"Anyway," went on Icelynn, "Kyle came aboard ship around eight, and we had a terrible fight, as I expected. He said, because of me, he and Carol had had a big blow-up, but had made it up. He said the plan was on go again, but he didn't trust Carol. He said while we were away, he wouldn't put it past her to change her will again, making Clark the inheritor. Because of that he said he had to kill her before we sailed. He left the ship close to midnight, to kill Carol. I was glad."

"Whoa! We're getting ahead of ourselves," put in Kendra. "Let's back up two years, when CR first came to New Orleans. At that time, she brought Dr. Lopez with her, promising him $400,000 to build a clinic. Before they left San Francisco, she gave Doc $200,000 up front and told him he'd get the rest of the money when he reached New Orleans, and settled in. After he got settled, she reneged and told him he was in her will, and he'd get the other $200,000 when she died. At the time, CR was only forty-five and in good health. The clinic project was pushed to the back burner until just recently, when the Judge underwrote the project. No doubt in exchange for a lot of needle."

Kendra paused, hoping to get a rise out the Judge. Nothing; so she commenced again: "Six months ago, Lopez discovered, doubtless to his delight, CR had developed a heart condition and, knowing he was in her will, decided not to mention this serious problem. Probably, hoping she'd soon have a nice neat heart attack, and he'd inherit his—$200,000."

"That's pure conjecture," sternly stated the Judge, "you can't say that. Emile's not here to defend himself."

"It's not on *that* tape, but it's on one of them. If you like, call Lopez. I'm not going to call him doctor any more, he doesn't deserve that title, and I'll say the same thing to his face. Go on and call him."

"Hippo is talking with Emile," right now," responded Clark, looking at his watch. Hippo will escort Emile here; then we can hear his story."

Kendra looked surprised, paused a second and then resumed: "On the evening of April 12th, the day Kyle and Icelynn were to board the ship for England, which sailed the next morning, at 6:30, Carol was having chest pains. These pains were no doubt brought on by learning that Kyle, her protege and lover, and Icelynn, her secretary, who she hated with a white hate, were married and had conspired to use her. A blow. A staggering blow, because CR *used* people; people didn't *use* her.

"This knowledge, coupled with the furious row she had had with Icelynn, worsened her condition.— As Icelynn said, Kyle left your arms, Mrs. Edwards, and went directly to Carol, to spend some time with her, because he was supposedly leaving for Berkeley too early the next morning, to say good-bye.

"CR told Kyle the game was up. She knew he was married to Icelynn and they had bilked her for two years. She told him she knew the two of them were sailing in the morning for England. He said the only reason he was sailing any where with Icelynn was so he could kill her—shove her overboard.

"He said as soon as Icelynn was out of the way and Clark divorced, they could be together forever, because he only loved her. He said he had come to her room especially to tell her about Icelynn and his plan to kill her. He was just sorry he hadn't told her sooner. He begged for forgiveness; they kissed and made up. Kyle then left for the ship, where you, Icelynn, was waiting for him."

"And never suspecting he was planning to murder *me.*"

Kendra nodded. "And in the meantime, you, Mrs. Edwards, came to Willowwynn to see Kyle and, finding he wasn't in, figured he was with Carol in her sitting room. You had no idea he had boarded a ship that would, in the morning, sail for England. You thought, as everyone else, he was leaving early in the morning for Berkeley.

"You went to CR's sitting room, just as that clock on the mantel" —she pointed to the clock—"chimed nine strokes, clearly recording those nine strokes on the tape. Kyle wasn't there. You found CR breathless and in a terrible emotional upheaval. You called Lopez, and he came over right away. He listened to CR's chest and told her, at last, how bad her heart was. He told her if she didn't calm down, she'd have a heart attack.

"Hearing, for the first time, that her heart was bad, only excited CR. She raved even more, demanding to know when her heart trouble started. Lopez insisted, that six months before, he had told her of her heart condition. CR screamed he hadn't. Lopez left. But before he left, he tossed a handful of powdered tranquilizers, on this very coffee table, and cautioned CR to take only half a powder in warm milk."

Eleanor began to fidget. She sat there, twisting and twining her fingers.

"As you all know, CR reveled in the admiration of men; but that night of nights she needed the confidence of a woman. So after Lopez left, she told you, Mrs. Edwards, how much she loved Kyle Osborne, and that they had planned to marry.

"It must've been awful for you hearing Kyle was not yours exclusively. Finding out that CR and Kyle had actually set a wedding date, stirred you to insane jealousy. You were so jealous that you decided, on the spur of the moment, to cause CR to have a heart attack. Then Kyle would be yours.

"So when CR said she couldn't stand the chest pain any longer, you suggested that she go to bed and take half a tranquilizer powder, that

Lopez had left. You said you'd get Josie Sato to make her a nice cup of cocoa, and add the powder to it.

"You helped CR to bed; then you went back to this very sitting room and emptied four of the five powders into that blue porcelain box, sitting right there on the mantel, next to the clock." Kendra got the blue box, opened it and showed Eleanor and the others, the pool of powder in the bottom of the box. She returned the box to the mantel, saying: "You must've put the empty wrappers in your dress pocket; then you had Josie Sato make the cocoa. You personally brought it to CR. You tore open the one packet of powder and, before CR's eyes, emptied half into the cocoa. Stirred it; and CR drank it.

"By this time, jealousy had gnawed you up. CR had shared your husband, and you hated her for that. And now you just learned you had been sharing Kyle, with the woman you hated. A terrible blow. You had to kill CR, and what better way than to cause her to have a heart attack. Minutes after CR drank her cocoa, you calmly told her that Kyle loved you and was going to marry you.

"CR went into a tirade. She screamed you were nuts. She said you were a bore and a bother and no body loved you, not even your husband. This drove you over the edge. You took one of the empty packets from your pocket and reminded CR that Lopez had said only to administer half; more than half, you said, would cause a person with a good heart to have a heart attack. CR said she had only taken half a packet.

"That's when you threw that half empty packet along with the rest of the empty packets in CR's face, laughing like a lunatic and crying: 'You're dead, Carol, *dead*. Kyle's mine.' CR cried 'Kyle belongs to Ice—' But in your jealous state, you didn't even hear what CR said.

"CR had a heart attack, not from that powder that was in her cocoa, but from your power of suggestion. You called Lopez; he came and, when he saw all those empty packets of sedatives, he jumped to the conclusion that CR had overdosed on his prescribed powders; and you let him think that.

"Lopez cried: 'She's killed herself.' That's when you reminded him that your husband was building his clinic; and that $200,000 was waiting for him in CR's will; therefore he should make sure she was dead.

"He argued that Clark would insist upon an autopsy, and the drug overdose plus the shot would be detected. It would all fall on him. You simply suggested, in your calm cool way, that CR should be accidentally cremated before an autopsy could be performed.

"You said your husband, with his persuading powers, would make sure Clark would buy the accident bit. Lopez finished off CR, with a shot. You both left; Lopez took the empty wrappers with him. You forgot to get rid of the powder in that blue box; I took a sample to a chemist; it was chloral hydrate. In excess, deadly to a person with heart trouble.

"Around midnight, Kyle came calling on CR, to kill her. He found her already dead. Upon hearing footsteps in the hall, thinking they belonged to Clark, Kyle hid behind the Japanese screen. Those footsteps belonged to you, Judge Edwards. You came to CR's room with malice of forethought and carried out that malice, by placing a pillow over CR's face. You held that pillow over CR's face until you realized she was already dead. Some one had beat you to your malice."

"As you said, she was already dead," muttered the Judge.

"Holding that pillow over her face, dead or not, is still attempted murder, Judge. The tape recorded your saying 'somebody beat me to you, Carol. I wish I knew who. I'd thank he or she for killing you, you dirty bitch. Now the $800,000 you wanted back so badly is all mine. You didn't need it, you bitch.' You laughed as you left the room."

"When you left the room," interjected Icelynn, "and, as soon as the coast was clear, Kyle left. He came back to the ship, and told me you tried to smother, already dead Carol, by holding a pillow over her face."

A loud silence followed, until Kendra began again: "At 6:30, on the morning of April 13, you, Icelynn, and your husband, Kyle, sailed for England. At 8:00, Josie Sato found CR dead in bed. Clark called Lopez, who wrote the death certificate, stating death had occurred sometime around 4-5:00 that morning, and from natural causes. Heart failure.

"You all know the rest. Clark requested an autopsy; Lopez, with the help of his friend, Prestijockeymoe, had CR's body cremated before any autopsy could take place. Then they blamed the accidental cremation on poor Albert Lepardieux, Prestijockeymoe's assistant.

"As I said, this was not a conspiracy of murder. It had not been plotted and planned. It just happened. Everybody who hated CR got the same idea, on the same day. To kill her. And it all worked out until I listened to that tape. I'm sorry now I told Karl Erpelding what was on that tape. I believe, though I can't prove it Karl, knowing the names of the killers, cost him his life. I believe Lopez some how gave Karl one of his killing shots. How he got to Karl I can only guess. I think he came here, cholorfomed him, and then gave him the fatal injection. On your instructions, Judge."

"Imagination, Miss Applegate, pure imagination," replied the Judge.

"I know you control Lopez' needle work, because I overheard a conversation you had with him, as I hid in the closet of Jack Trenchard's hospital room. Lopez said Jack had a good chance of making it; you said that Allison wanted her freedom so she could marry Claremont. You ordered Lopez to finish off Jack. Then you said the Thibodeaux Construction company had just poured the foundation for Lopez' new clinic, and suggested that the both of you go to the site."

"My word against yours, Miss Applegate."

"True. But this other business, with the tape, your wife's voice, your voice, Lopez' voice, that'll stand up fine."

"Miss Applegate, I suppose your next move is to wait for Hippo Delacroix to show up, hand over the tape to him and have him turn it over to a grand jury?"

"No. that's not my plan. I know Clark said Hippo was on his way over, with Lopez in tow, but I want to tie this up before they get here."

"If you don't want Delacroix and a grand jury to listen to that tape, what do you want?" asked the Judge, with an air of indifference.

"I want to make a deal with you, that'll save your neck and the necks of your wife, Lopez, Prestijockeymoe and Icelynn—"

"I'd say you've lost your mind," calmly responded Eleanor, "but you've got to have one to lose it. You're completely crazy."

Despite Eleanor's unruffled tone, Kendra saw her fingers nervously twisting and twining.

Clark jumped up and stalked across the floor and back. He stopped. "Kendra, come out on the balcony with me." —Kendra followed him out.—"Earlier, when you walked in on Hippo and myself, we had decided there was no way in the world we could get justice for either Carol or Jack; however, at the time I had no idea that a conclave of killers caused Carol's death.

"Now with such evidence, do you think I'm going to let you cut a deal with the Judge, knowing what Eleanor and Lopez did to Carol; knowing the Judge tried to smother my already dead wife; knowing what Icelynn and Kyle had cooked up—Icelynn's legacy's cancelled—knowing that Lopez and Prestijockeymoe purposely cremated Carol to prevent an autopsy. —Vince is resigning now. When I went after Icelynn, I called the lab in San Francisco. Lopez, the Judge's man, murdered Kyle Erpelding."

"I knew it." Their eyes met and held. "You told me the Judge was so powerful, that no one could touch him. At the time, I didn't believe you, but I know now that the Judge is that powerful and would never ever spend a minute in jail. And he won't let his wife, either. Some one would take the fall for him and his wife. Lopez would be murdered before he could tell his side.

"Is that what you meant when you said there were things I could never imagine or understand?"—He nodded slowly—"You told me to let it go. Now I'm asking you, begging you, to let me cut this deal with the Judge. This deal won't put him in jail; but it'll cripple his pride and cast dark shadows upon his character."

"This deal you speak of smacks of selfishness."

"I agree. I'm being purely selfish. Let's go back inside, and you'll find out why I'm acting so selfishly."

Still looking deeply into each other's eyes, Clark, frowning slightly, in his eyes pain as of fear for her, agreed. Before we go back in, I love you."—He hugged her, hard."Now let's go back in and get this over with."

Kendra, without preamble, addressed the Judge: "Attorney Maria Galvez Trenchard, has a client by the name of Johnny Placide who, in self-defense, killed your cousin's son, Leon Delachaise. The original charge was manslaughter, with bail; however, when you learned Delachaise was accidentally killed, and the charge was manslaughter, you bribed Judge Bosco to turn the case over to you, so you could avenge Delachaise's death.

"Then when you learned Johnny Placide was Jack's brother"—Kendra cut her eyes toward Clark and wished those navy eyes of his weren't so keen. She wished she couldn't read words in people's eyes, for his clearly said you care only about justice for Johnny, your brother—"you changed the charge to first degree murder, without bail. And the only witness, who could prove Delachaise provoked the fight, was found floating face down in the Mississippi River, shot in the back."

Seeing the Judge and Eleanor, at last, looked shaken, Kendra pressed on: "I want you, Judge Edwards, right now, to pick up the phone on CR's desk, call the Parish Prison and have Johnny Placide released—today. All murder charges dropped.

"After you make your call, I'll erase that incriminating tape, along with all the other tapes. You might want to keep your love-making tape as a memento," added Kendra, rubbing it into the bone.

"And if I say— NO?"

"Attorney Maria Galvez *Trenchard* has a friend at WWL, and I'm sure that friend will let her play the murder tape over the air. Before the tape is played, I'll personally call the blue-blood Claremonts—Cameron Claremont, Jr. is the father of your new grandson, and Allison is planning to marry him—so before the wedding, the whole Claremont family, and all New Orleans, can listen to how CR was murdered, by Allison's mother.

"And for those who miss hearing the tape over the air, Maria Galvez

Trenchard, who has her husband's diary, will turn it over to the *Picayune* to print. In case you don't know, Jack's diary exposes you, along with Claremont, Sr., that *great* banker. Of course, as soon as the *Picayune* prints that diary, Jack Trenchard will be exonerated of embezzlement, of stealing from you, and of being the ungrateful, low-down son-in-law you branded him in this morning's paper.

"If all this happens, you'll have to resign your judgeship and abandon your law practice. In the event of such a calamity, I doubt Allison's last name will ever be changed to Claremont."

Kendra expected an outburst, but nothing came; a palpitating silence followed. No one moved. The Judge's eyes were fixed on Kendra as if his ears had not heard right.

The Edwardses just sat there, cool, calm, confident and sure-footed. To herself: "Those two fear nothing. They have no remorse about killing CR, Jack's accident and ultimate murder. They wanted them both dead, and they got what they wanted." Suddenly Kendra was seized by the worst fear. "If he doesn't make that phone call and allows me to expose him, have I put my aunt's life on the line, my own, Maria's, Johnny Placide's and maybe even his momma, Mary's?"

And just as she was about to pray in a way that would cut a deal with God, Judge Edwards rose, walked to CR's desk, picked up the phone and set Johnny's release in motion. "He'll be free in half an hour.— Miss Applegate, I want you to know I don't like you."

The blood around Kendra's heart froze. "And, Judge, I want you to know, I don't like you." Then with an eager hand she snatched the phone, called Maria and told her to pick up Johnny at Parish Prison. He was free.

In the next few moments and without warning, Hippo, Lopez, and a policeman, came into the sitting room."Judge," immediately began Lopez, "Vince has resigned; Albert Depardieux has been given a hefty raise; and I'm here to listen to a tape recording of Carol's death . "

"There's no tape," quickly spoke up the Judge. "Keep you mouth shut," he ordered. "You have nothing to worry about. Its all been taken care of."

"I'm sick of you, Judge, and your wife, telling me I have nothing to worry about. Vince had nothing to worry about and, now he's—"

All eyes were fixed on Lopez, so no one saw Eleanor take a small revolver from her pocketbook, rise and shoot Dr. Lopez through the heart before he could finish his sentence. In the blinking of an eye, the Judge sprang at his wife, to wrest the gun away from her; at the same time the policeman pulled his pistol and fired. The policeman's bullet struck the

Judge in the head, came out of his head and grazed Kendra's shoulder. Both the Judge and Lopez were sprawled on the blue velour rug, their blood staining it crimson.

The shock of being nicked by a bullet, and seeing the two dead men, sent Kendra reeling. Before she fell forward, striking her forehead on the sharp corner of the coffee table, she screamed: "Clark—"; and for a few seconds she was stunned. Dazedly, she sat on the floor and watched the red mist close in on Eleanor Edwards. She screamed—screamed out to CR to stop. CR ignored her; and Eleanor was elevated a good four feet off the floor, suspended and screaming.

At this point, Kendra's fears had reached a nightmare crest, as the red mist, CR, empowered by a supernatural force, then turned Eleanor horizontal and, CR, like a kid with a paper airplane, sailed Eleanor headlong from the sitting room, through the open doors leading to the balcony, clear across the balcony and over the iron rail. Eleanor's screams trailing behind her until she landed. Silence. A terrible silence followed. The powder-blue sitting room had become a room of horrors.

Kendra couldn't remember how she got out the sitting room and into her own bed. Or who had stitched the gash in her forehead; the stitches had now been removed. She only remembered being sick to her stomach, dizzy and calling out for Clark. Now when she woke she saw him seated in the bedside rocker: "I'm here, Kendra, I'm right here, darling."

Kendra was too ill to speak, and remained in bed for weeks. Nurses came and went; they fed her custard and soup. Cat Sholar Picarara was allowed in the house for bedside visits. Gussie Rae Booker took care of the house, and Xariffa cooked.

Later she was told Clark never left her side until Dr. Herbert said she was out of danger. She was also told that her aunt had had gallbladder surgery, and would be in the hospital for another two weeks.

Still later, Clark holding her hand, told her: "When the ambulance came for Dr. Lopez and the Edwardses, and while the attendants were wheeling the bodies out, I heard snatches of soft music floating through the house. The big Steinway was being played. I went to the music room and saw the ivory keys playing, but no one was at the keyboard. I saw a red mist hovering over the piano bench. The music being played was Debussy; and when Carol was happy, really happy, she played Debussy."

"If she's happy, then I won't be seeing her again. She's on the other side by now. I had wished her to hell, but I don't wish that any more. After all I was CR and CR was me—a couple times."

Kendra had suffered a slight concussion, and had slept a lot. Even when she was awake, she was drowsy; however, every time she woke up, Clark was there, saying: "I love you, Kendra."

After her body had healed, her mind hurt. She had gone through an emotional upheaval, finding out Jack was her brother, and then having him murdered in his hospital bed; finding out she had another brother, and then almost losing Johnny to the electric chair, had caught up with her. Not to mention hiding Jack's $300,000, and shipping it off to Sonny, in Korea; then Sonny getting married, and everybody on Starlight Street saying Kendra Louise had a nervous breakdown cause Sonny Ganucci jilted her for a Jap girl.

"Kendra Lou, don't pay that gossip no never mind. I told you gossip lies nine times out of ten, and on the tenth time tells half a truth."

Kendra knew what her aunt had said was true, but that hateful talk still bothered her. And there was another bother, a big bother, the ghost of CR. More and more she thought of her. "I was a part of CR, CR was a part of me. When inside me, she breathed when I breathed."

Clark, upon Dr. Herbert's advise, got Dr. Charles Arcenaux, a psychiatrist, to see Kendra. For five months, .Kendra poured out and wrote down her story and feelings to a very understanding psychiatrist.

Dr. Arcenaux told her there were so many things that no one could explain. He said there was no answer to be found for what had happened to her; and she had to accept that. Her encounters with the ghost CR could have been an over active imagination, an illusion, a hallucination. Kendra knew better.

At any rate, Dr. Arcenaux had discharged her. Said it was time to get on with her life. Time for her to marry Clark Rogers. Even now it seemed like a dream, that Clark loved her, and she'd say to herself: "Clark, Clark, I'm the luckiest girl in the whole world."

Back in May she and Clark had said they'd marry in October; and then there was the business of Jack coming back to her, asking her to elope to Mexico City. Now she couldn't believe five months had passed, and she would marry Clark in two weeks, on October 14th.

Her brother, Johnny, back at Tulane, studying medicine, would give her away; Maria, whose baby was due around Thanksgiving, would be her bridesmaid. All the folk of Starlight Street were invited. Aunt Molly Primrose, Mary Placide and Stella Dora Wheelerhand would see to the refreshments: finger sandwiches, cake and champagne; a special tray of egg and olive sandwiches for the bride and groom would be served, along with pink and white petit fours and two kinds of coffee: one, monkey pee; the other, Creole.

Archbishop Jean Claude DuPlessix would marry them in the parlor of their new home. Kendra wouldn't be wearing white. She'd wear a simple beige silk suit, with brown accessories and a brown silk broad-brimmed hat. That same outfit would do to fly to Lake Tahoe, where she and Clark would spend their honeymoon in his five-bedroom cabin, in the middle of a hundred acres.

They'd return to Starlight Street before Christmas, stopping in San Francisco, to shop for furniture. They had bought the master bedroom suite, parlor, dining room, breakfast room and kitchen appliances from D.H. Holmes. They'd be looking in San Francisco for four bedroom suites; library, study and sitting room furniture; and oriental rugs.

Afterwards they'd spend some time with Jean and Gen, Carol's two adopted sisters. Gen now owned the Willowwynn in San Francisco. A month after the tragic deaths of Dr. Lopez and the Edwardses, Clark put Willowwynn on the market.

Clark had bought the three lots next to Aunt Molly Primrose's double, the day after he had visited Kendra and her aunt, to inspect their home. He built a very simple, graceful two-story, white wooden house, with a wrap around gallery. A detached double garage, with an apartment on top, for Gussie Rae Booker, the housekeeper, and Xariffa Diamond, the cook, to live in.

Everyone on Starlight Street was buzzing about the new two-story house being built in a neighborhood of doubles; and with an apartment over the garage, for the housekeeper and the cook. No one suspected or dreamed Kendra and her husband would live in the lovely new house. They learned of this astonishing news when they got their wedding invitations. Then they started buzzing all over again.

"Kendra Lou, now that everybody knows you gunna get married and live in that fine big white house, everybody's forgot about poor Antlee Theaud jumpin' off the Huey P. Long bridge; and Poochie Pujowl gettin' killed by a big hawg. I do believe your good fortune will be passed down from one generation of Starlight folk to the next.—

"By the way, I heard that Allison's baby boy has jet black hair and pansy blue eyes. Her husband has blonde hair and brown eyes. That's aud. I don't see how those two could live at Greenwood Manor—"

Molly Primrose, now retired, because of Clark Rogers' insistence and generosity, was busy listenin' to gossip when it pertained to her niece. She was also busy getting things ready for Kendra's wedding, but found time to knit. She was knitting blue and pink baby booties to "put by" in the cedar chest, to be given to her niece when ever the time came.

Kendra was now seated at the gatelegged table with her aunt, having coffee. "Kendra Lou, I can't believe my table is good as new. The chairs look beautiful; and so does the kitchen cabinet. Well, you said Clark said Louie Winner was a magician."

"And he is," smiled Kendra.

"I'm so glad you told Clark about you sending Jack's money to Sonny Ganucci, to invest. That was mighty nice of Clark to let that money there. Well, as soon as I finish my coffee, I'm goin' next door to Stella Dora's. I'm gunna show her how to knit some white booties, to put by for you."

A tiny smile played hide-and-seek around the corners of Kendra's mouth. "Tante, you, Miss Stella Dora and Mrs. Ganucci do have a way of rushing things." — Clark will be here any minute. I'm going to wait for him in the back yard."

The yard was noisy with chirping birds, and the flower beds were full of curly-leafed yellow and bronze chrysanthemums, standing tall on stout stalks. Every where Kendra looked she saw signs of fall.

She sat on the bench beneath the old oak tree, its branches covering her like a big tent. Pale sunshine filtering through the leaves, splashed her honey olive face. Sholar Picarara joined her, curling at her feet.

"Kendra darling," called out Clark, coming toward her. "I'm sorry I'm late." He sat next to her, gathered her in his arms, hugged her hard, and kissed her. "When I handed over the keys to Willowwynn, Mr. and Mrs. Grace wanted me to have a sherry with them. They're going to enjoy Willowwynn." He looked thoughtful. "They're the right people for Willowwynn."

"I know what you mean. I've been feeling sad all day, knowing that Willowwynn would be handed over to new owners. Like you, I know, after what happened, we couldn't ever have lived there. I just hope and pray CR is on the other side, and won't go back to Willowwynn."

"Have you been sitting here waiting for me and thinking of CR?" he asked, looking deeply into her soft amber eyes.

"No. I've been thinking of our children. They'll have two pretty back yards to play in; two lovely flower gardens to see and love; two houses; two parents and an adoring great aunt to love them." She laughed a bubbly laugh.

"That they'll have, along with a lot of booties.—Kiss me, darling, kiss me! Paradise on earth only happens once in a life time."

"Yes, I know. I love you, Mr. C.C. Bennett, *yardman.*"

The End